CAMPUS CRUSH

CFU HOCKEY
BOOK 1

CADENCE KEYS

Playlist

ABBY & FOSTER

Feel Like This – Ingrid Andress
Sparks Fly (Taylor's Version) – Taylor Swift
Champagne Coast – Blood Orange
Linger - SiriusXM Session – Royal Otis
eat me alive – Alessi Rose
See Her Out (That's Just Life) – Francis and the Lights
2 hands – Tate McRae
She Calls Me Back (with Kacey Musgraves) – Noah Kahan,
Kacey Musgraves
I Hear the Bells – Mike Doughty
I'll Be – Edwin McCain
Disco – Surf Curse
Rust. – Mon Rovia
Runnin (with JP Saxe) – Ingrid Andress, JP Saxe
You Are In Love (Taylor's Version) – Taylor Swift
Unholy (feat. Kim Petras) – Sam Smith, Kim Petras

Listen now on Spotify

FOREWORD

This is a work of fiction and as such I've taken some liberties. Not everything in their gaming world is accurate (but I thought it was funny) and please don't look too closely at the timeline of the hockey season and games and the players abilities to be out and about instead of at hockey or classes all the time.

Sit back and enjoy the book for what it is—a product of my imagination.

Happy reading,

Cadence

ONE

Why, in God's name, was there a dildo on my couch?

I froze in the entryway of my apartment and then closed the door behind me with a heavy sigh as I stared at the offending phallic object.

"Please don't be used. Please don't be used," I muttered quietly, taking slow steps forward and approaching the couch.

"Sam," I hollered, my eyes not leaving the large blue dildo. Dicks weren't actually that big, were they? And why the hell was it blue?

"Sam," I called again, a little more urgently.

No response.

"Samantha." My patience was running out faster than the battery on that dildo probably did.

"One sec," I heard her shout from down the hallway of our shared apartment just off campus.

"Do you have a guest?" I called. I was two seconds away from spinning around and walking right out the door. I'm sure I could waste some time around campus if need be. I'd been hoping to get a little time at home to decompress, maybe even play a little *Stardew Valley*, which had become my ultimate stress management tool.

That, and I loved chatting with BigBear88 and seeing what shenanigans he had gotten into. We'd met on a Discord server for fans of the game and talked nearly every day now—although usually only about the game. He couldn't have a more different approach to how he played than I did. Whereas I was more a min-max girly, he was all kinds of chaos.

It was easy talking to him. Comfortable in a way real life never seemed to be. I was the epitome of awkward when it came to the opposite sex. I'd tried to be "cool" once and it had epically backfired. And then life had smacked me in the face, and I felt like I'd been holding on by my fingernails ever since.

Some days, the game—and BigBear88—felt like the only place I could actually breathe.

My gaze caught on the bright blue object again and I fought a shiver of repulsion. I'd seen enough of Sam's "guests" to know I didn't want to see another toned butt of some random dude I would likely never see again.

Her silence made me nervous.

This wouldn't have been the first time I'd walked in on her hooking up with someone. It wasn't even the first time I'd found a sex toy lying around our apartment. Although they weren't usually this large...or blue.

Dicks seriously couldn't be that big, right? That had to be some kind of kink thing.

"Nope, just me," she said, walking down the hallway, her hair up in a towel wrapped like a turban around her head.

She wore her favorite pair of fitted leggings and a tight top. Sam loved to show off her body, as she should since it was "banging"—her word, but I wouldn't argue. She had the kind of curves women around the world would kill to have, and she wasn't afraid to show them off.

Sometimes I was envious of how confident she was in herself—her sexuality, her independence, her free spirit.

What I wouldn't give to have just an ounce of her confidence. Maybe then I wouldn't hide in my textbooks like she constantly accused me of doing.

I pointed to the object. "Uh, is this your dildo?"

She laughed, the sound light and carefree. "Oh, yeah, sorry about that."

I rolled my eyes to the ceiling. "Please tell me that was not used out here on our couch—our *shared* couch."

I loved Samantha Lowe like a sister—that had to be the reason we had been roommates since freshman year even though we couldn't have more different personalities—but sometimes her actions drove me crazy.

She shot me a knowing grin. "Relax, Mom. I did not have sex on our communal couch. You don't need to deep clean it. I was showing one of my sorority sisters how to put on a condom, because she's about to lose her V-card tonight."

"Shouldn't the guy be the one who knows how to put on a condom?"

Despite Sam's best efforts, I was still about as sexually savvy as a Victorian maiden. Hence why I wasn't confident if that dildo was to scale or not.

Once upon a time, I'd thought I would finally lose my virginity freshman year, but instead of losing it to the guy I'd been secretly crushing on since the first day of classes, it turned into the most mortifying night imaginable. I might've been able to move past the humiliation if it hadn't been followed immediately by the worst days and months of my life.

After that, sex had been nowhere on my mind. And whenever I thought about that time of my life, I was unfortunately reminded of the mortification that preceded it. It was a vicious cycle I never seemed to be able to escape.

For a while, Sam had been my rock—I genuinely don't know if I would've survived the rest of freshman year without her—but lately it felt like she was trying to push me out of the comfort zone I'd settled into.

"It's always good for a girl to know how to do it and know what she's doing, so the guy doesn't try to pull some bullshit like, 'Oh, I don't have any condoms. I'm gonna have to go in raw,' or whatever." She rolled her eyes like that was an excuse she'd actually heard. "We gotta look out for ourselves."

I would take her word for it.

Sam picked up the dildo and set it on the coffee table, which wasn't much better than the couch, but at least I knew it was clean. Then she sat down on the couch. "I didn't expect you home so early. I thought you had to work at the tutoring center tonight."

I sat down next to her. "I do, but I've got some time to kill before my shift," I said, kicking off my shoes. Scholarships covered tuition, but rent, books, and groceries still needed paying—and two part-time jobs barely made a dent some months.

One of them was working in the tutoring center of our university, and the other was a low-pay internship with an engineering firm in the nearest city, Missoula. The tutoring center had needed tutors who were available to help with the summer sessions, and I needed the extra cash.

"Cool. Wanna watch an episode of *Real Lives of Mormon Wives?*"

Sam was obsessed with that reality show—probably because she'd grown up in a strict Catholic household and had a thing for religious drama. Or maybe it was just the chaos of reality TV in general. That definitely wasn't the only show she binged like her life depended on it. Since freshman year, she'd exposed me to so much reality TV that now I was a bit of a junkie for it myself. It was the one thing that was completely out of character for me. One of those little tidbits I could use in the game of "Two truths and a lie" and everyone would assume it was the lie.

Despite my logical brain and my love of math and science, she had brought me to the dark side of loving the chaos of reality television.

Before I could answer, she looked at me knowingly. "Or did you really come home to play *Stardew Valley?*"

She said it with a smile, but my cheeks still flushed with a hint of embarrassment. I knew she didn't judge me for playing, but I also knew she thought there was something flirty going on with me and BigBear88. She'd been pushing for me to try to meet him in real life—I knew he went to CFU with us—but I didn't want to lose what he and I had online. I was worried meeting in person would ruin the relationship we'd built, and that wasn't a risk I was willing to take.

I couldn't stomach the thought that he wouldn't like what he saw in real life. I wasn't innately gorgeous like Sam or nearly as confident. I knew from experience that a guy was more likely to look right past me than to notice me. And I was invested in my online relationship with Bear enough to know I'd be totally crushed if we met in real life and he decided I wasn't his type.

"I thought I'd play for a little bit. Clear my head before I go to work."

"Mm-hmm," she said, her lips pursed together but tilted at the corners as if she was fighting back a smile.

I rolled my eyes and grabbed my stuff, taking it into my room, but before I could shut my door, she called out, "Say hi to BigBear for me!"

I shook my head, but couldn't ignore the smile already on my face or the swirl of butterflies that took off in my belly as I dropped my bag by the door and grabbed my laptop.

A minute later, the familiar chime of a new message lit up my screen.

BigBear88:
Emergency.
I accidentally gave Pam a diamond and now she thinks we're dating. Send help. 😭

A laugh slipped out before I could stop it—real, full, and warm. I hadn't even realized how much I needed that until right then.

PeachyKeen:
You reap what you sow, my guy. Good luck explaining that one.

BigBear88:
I panicked! I thought it was wine! Now she's calling me "her shining star."
This is slander. I demand a trial by farming committee.

PeachyKeen:
You're on your own, Bear.

Also, I'm 100% putting this on the bulletin board.

BigBear88:
This betrayal will be remembered. 🤧

I grinned, shaking my head as I settled against my headboard. The tightness in my chest I hadn't even noticed before started to loosen, and all my stress eased.

If only real life was as easy as this game.

Too soon, I had to exit out of the game and head to campus. This was the first summer I'd worked at the tutoring center during a summer session. My boss had told me it wasn't usually as busy this time of year since a lot of summer classes were done online, but they always had a need for math and science tutors, and those were two subjects I excelled at.

It was still hot and the sun was beating down, but there was a cool breeze coming off the Clark Fork River that made the short walk bearable. I knew during the cold winter months, I'd miss being able to take this walk.

Clark Fork University sat on the edge of the river in the small town of Dunridge, right outside of Missoula, Montana. It was a small university with only about 4,500 students.

It was quiet along the riverside trail that led from our apartment to campus. People walking their dogs, couples holding hands, and a group of moms pushing strollers all walked by, but they didn't acknowledge me, too lost in their own conversations.

Most days, I didn't mind being invisible. It was safer than being truly seen.

I mean, what would people see if they really *saw* me?

Would they see the girl who was still living in the shadow of her mother's death?

Would they see the girl who was both so confident in what she wanted to do with her future and so terrified of the unknown that the future held?

Would they see a plain, boring college student with no life outside of work or school?

Would they see a girl who preferred to plant seeds in a pixelated field because it felt safer than trying to build something real that could be ripped away from her without a moment's notice?

If they looked closely enough, would they see the way my heart ached to find someone who got me and could love me the way I'd once wished for before life had made me scared to hope?

It was silly to worry about it when it seemed like no one saw me at all. I was just another face in the passing crowd as I walked on campus and past clusters of people—some students, some locals enjoying the beauty of our small campus since it wasn't overrun with students like it would be when fall semester hit.

A girl who looked about my age lifted her hand in a wave, her face breaking out in a smile as she walked toward me. For a moment, my heart lifted along with my hand. Warmth flowed down my spine, even though I didn't recognize her. And then we got closer and the girl spoke, her eyeline somewhere just over my shoulder, and I realized she hadn't been waving to me at all.

Embarrassment burned my cheeks as I put my hand down, worried she'd see it and pity me. But that worry was all for naught because she didn't acknowledge me at all as she passed on by.

And even though I tried to convince myself that's how I wanted it, it didn't change how painfully alone it made me feel.

I ducked my head and walked faster.

I hadn't always felt this way.

Freshman year had been filled with hope and possibility that I wouldn't have to be that girl who was constantly studying and always had her head in a book like I had in high school. I could be someone new. I could still be that girl, but I could also be a more adventurous version of her.

Someone who flirted with boys and went out on dates and got drunk at a college party.

I'd even tried that once.

In fact, I'd managed to kiss one of the most popular boys on campus, who I'd had a secret crush on since the first day of classes.

But that night didn't go at all the way I'd hoped or planned. It'd left me feeling beyond embarrassed and confused.

And then two nights later, my whole world shifted with one phone call.

If it hadn't been for Sam, I don't know how I would have made it through that semester. I'd considered taking it off to help my younger brother grieve the loss of our mother, but my grandmother, Gram, teamed up with Sam and they refused to let me. Instead, I'd switched most of my classes to online work with the approval of several of my professors, which helped lighten my load while still keeping me on track to graduate on time. It had also allowed me to get out of seeing that guy again—although considering he was one of the most popular jocks on campus, I still saw him from a distance from time to time and heard his name more often than I would've liked.

I was grateful now that they hadn't let me give up my dreams when I was drowning in grief. It had been during those first few months of losing her that I also discovered *Stardew Valley* and became obsessed with the game. Maybe it had started as a way to escape my painful reality, but it had turned into a community for me—a safe haven.

It took time to find my footing after losing my mom, but I'd found small ways to make the real world a little more bearable without her. Holding on to the dreams I had before she passed was one of them.

One dream, especially.

My mom had gone to Clark Fork University, and I had been so excited to follow in her footsteps. I still was, even if I missed her with a fierce longing every single day.

It had been almost two years, and sometimes I couldn't stop myself from wondering what my life, especially my college experience, would have been like if she hadn't gotten in that car accident driving home from work.

Who would I be now?

Would I have pushed aside that awful night with Foster? Would I have dated someone else, fallen in love, made more friends besides Sam?

I guess it didn't matter because I was who I was. I'd done what I had to do to stay on track with getting my degree. Relationships, boys, dating in general were all distractions from my ultimate goal. After my mom's accident, my brain had focused on logic.

Math and science made sense. I knew what to expect from them. Always.

They never surprised me or hurt me or confused me.

There was always an answer that made sense.

And there was comfort in that, I reminded myself. It didn't matter if I was invisible and had zero social life outside of a farming game.

While I may have been invisible on the greater campus, as soon as I walked into the tutoring center, I was greeted with warm smiles and waves from the two other tutors working here this summer.

A sense of pride warmed me before I could remind myself that I'd just told myself I didn't need acknowledgment.

But I couldn't deny that I loved being good at helping others find academic success. I loved that my boss knew I was reliable and that I'd made a name for myself as the best whenever he needed an exceptional math and science tutor.

Here in the tutoring center, I had value and people saw what I brought to the table, so it didn't matter if I was invisible to the rest of the world.

Pushing those lingering thoughts aside, I got to work.

THREE

My stomach sank as I stared at the screen of my laptop.

Fuck.

I'd failed the math test I'd studied so hard for. And not just an "almost" D kind of failed, but in a totally-bombed-it kind of failed.

My entire life it had been beaten into me to not be a failure. But for some reason, math managed to make me feel stupid every time I tried. I could figure out most things if I gave it enough attention, but no matter how much attention I gave to math—regardless of the level—I struggled.

My elementary school teacher had suggested that I might have a learning disability, which sent my dad into an absolute rage. He claimed the teachers were idiots and moved me to a private school where he donated extra money every year to be reassured that I was progressing as normal, even when I wasn't. Not even the expensive tutors he hired seemed to help. My only saving grace was that I was a strong writer and an articulate speaker who worked hard. I was also good with tasks that let me work with my hands, so even when math wasn't going well, I was still regarded as a good student.

If only I didn't constantly feel like a fraud because I struggled with the most basic math skills. Sometimes even time was an issue. I'd found ways to work around it—such as setting alarms on my phone for things so I didn't have to worry about always looking at the time, but that didn't help me with passing this math class that was a prerequisite for my business finance class.

I'd even taken it during summer term so I wouldn't have to talk about it with my friends. They knew me as the confident captain of our hockey team—the go-getter who helped rebuild this team my freshman year. They had no idea the secret shame I carried when it came to my math skills—or lack thereof.

There was a note next to the test results, and I clicked on it, opening it up to see a message from my professor.

Hey, Foster. This test was to determine where everyone was at, and I did not expect to see a student of your caliber score so poorly. I'm worried about how well you'll be able to keep up and I highly recommend you get some assistance from the tutoring center as soon as possible. The tutoring staff is fantastic. I've seen a lot of improvement with several students that have worked with them.

The last thing I wanted was anyone else to know how dumb I was. But failing wasn't an option. Not for my team. Not for my future. And not for the kid who still wanted to prove he was worth something.

I had to pass this class to get my degree, and I'd already talked to my advisor who'd told me I'd put the class off as long as possible. I couldn't put it off anymore without messing up my major courses and my graduation date. And if I didn't graduate on time, I was pretty sure my dad would lose his shit.

My only hope now was that the tutoring center would offer some discretion, because the last thing I needed was to be the laughingstock on campus.

That was the downside of being as popular and well-known as I was—the higher you were on the social hierarchy, the further you had to fall. And if anyone found out, I had no doubt that fall would hurt significantly.

Hockey had always been my go-to when I needed to get out of my head—until a teammate introduced me to *Stardew Valley* last year. It was just supposed to be for shits and giggles, but I'd gotten hooked on the game.

Although chatting with Peach might've also had something to do with my obsession with the game. She didn't know me in real life and there was something freeing about that. I could just be myself with her, without any expectations.

When I was on the ice, it was all instinct—muscle memory and adrenaline and gut decisions. It was the one place in my life where I didn't have to think so damn hard to succeed. *Stardew Valley* gave me a weirdly similar feeling. It wasn't about being perfect; it was about showing up, putting in the work, and watching something grow. And if anything, I'd gotten into the habit of being what Peach called a chaotic gremlin. Sometimes I stirred up chaos just to see her reaction.

Talking to Peach made everything better. She didn't care if I was good at math or good at anything, really. She didn't know how many goals I'd scored last season or how many people expected me to lead our team to the conference championship. With her, I got to be a freer version of myself.

And maybe that was the real reason I couldn't stop playing—or why every time her name popped up in the chat, it felt like I could breathe a little easier.

BigBear88:

Just tried to give Mayor Lewis a void egg. He looked… concerned.

PeachyKeen:

Did you expect him to appreciate cursed produce??

BigBear88:

I thought it was mysterious.

PeachyKeen:

That man's biggest thrill is judging the grange display. He can't handle mystery.

BigBear88:

Tragic.

PeachyKeen:

A true loss for Stardew culture.

BigBear88:

You're the only one who gets me.

PeachyKeen:

That's because I'm a mystery appreciator. 😌

A small smile tugged at my mouth—real and unforced, which felt rare lately. For a minute, it was easy to forget the gnawing pit in my stomach, easy to pretend that failing didn't make me feel like my whole world was tilting sideways.

But it was still there.

Heavy.

Sickening.

The kind of shame that wasn't new but hadn't dulled over the years either. It was the same feeling I used to get as a kid when numbers started swimming on the page and I knew—*knew*—I was going to get them wrong no matter how hard I tried. The same feeling when teachers pulled me aside and talked in quiet voices that made me feel broken.

I hated this.

I hated that I had to ask for help like I was a little kid again, like I hadn't worked my ass off to become someone better. Stronger. Someone people looked up to.

Getting help meant admitting I wasn't enough on my own.

And that terrified me more than anything.

BigBear88:
You ever just… really suck at something and feel like it's never gonna get better?

There was a longer pause this time, long enough that I thought maybe she wasn't going to answer. Then her message popped up.

PeachyKeen:
Yeah. All the time.

But it usually does get better. Eventually. Especially when you let someone help you carry the weight.

I stared at her message until the words blurred.

I didn't know how she always managed to say exactly the thing I needed to hear.

Maybe I didn't deserve it.

Maybe she didn't know what kind of failure she was really talking to.

BigBear88:
Thanks, Peach.

PeachyKeen:
Anytime, Bear. 🐻💛

I lingered there longer than I should have, fingers hovering over the keyboard, wanting to say more but not knowing how.

Finally, I logged off before I could make myself look even more pathetic.

Besides, I had somewhere I needed to be.

Her words had given me the strength and resolve I needed to face my shame.

Which meant I was off to the tutoring center because I was determined to pass this class, no matter what it took.

The tutoring center was quiet as I walked in for my shift. I made my way to my favorite table, tucked in the back corner and partially hidden by a bookshelf. It wasn't much, but the illusion of privacy seemed to help students feel more at ease. They were shielded from the worry of being overheard or judged for the areas they struggled with.

Despite the judgment-free signs posted around the center, it often took students time to relax. But the sooner they did, the quicker the breakthroughs came—which was why I was so attached to this spot. I wanted every student I worked with to leave feeling more confident than when they arrived.

Summer session was *much* slower than fall or spring, which was why there were only three tutors working here now.

I didn't mind.

During the school year, life moved so fast it was hard to catch my breath. Having a little extra downtime—and getting paid for it—felt like a small luxury.

I settled into my seat, pulled out my laptop, and slipped into the familiar comfort of my farm. Planting, harvesting, and tending to the quiet, steady world I'd built.

Bear wasn't online, but I told myself it was fine. This part—the peace, the soft hum of the center around me—was enough. Even if I missed his chaos and commentary.

For ten minutes, I enjoyed my quiet solitude and the familiar comfort of my own little world.

Until movement caught my eye and I glanced up.

With a pop that I felt in my soul, my bubble burst and my calm evaporated.

Foster Kane walked into the tutoring center, and my heart stalled in my chest.

I blinked out of my sudden stupor and jumped out of my seat, scampering behind the nearest bookshelf. I stared at the wall, chest heaving, as I was thrown straight back to a time that felt like it belonged to someone else.

The party at The Den, the notorious football house, was packed wall-to-wall with people as Sam and I looked around the space, our Natty lights in hand. Now that I was on my third one, it was finally bearable to taste.

"Oh, look, there he is."

"Who?" I asked Sam, looking in the general direction she seemed to be focused on.

"Ryan Donovan." Oh, right, the hot quarterback she was obsessed with and likely the whole reason we were at this party to begin with. "Right there talking to the guy that's on the hockey team. Foster. That's his name."

I stilled when she said his name and then my heart started racing as my gaze landed on the only boy who had ever made me catch my breath.

Foster Kane.

He was in my English 101 class, and in just the couple of weeks we'd been in school, he'd shown me that I was not, in fact, immune to the charms of a hot jock.

Foster was insanely attractive with his over-six-foot athletic build, his dark brown hair that curled ever so slightly around his ears when it grew too long, and his bright blue eyes. But even better than that was that Foster was smart.

In our English class he was always well-spoken. He answered the questions thoughtfully. He engaged in discussion. He was a unicorn as far as I was concerned.

A hot jock who was smart and seemed kind.

To say I'd had a crush on him would be an understatement.

For the first time all night, I was excited that Samantha had talked me into coming to this party because now maybe instead of being the girl who always sat back and watched as cool and exciting things happened to other people, I would get to be the girl something cool and exciting happened to.

We made our way over to the guys and I snuck a glance at Foster as Sam chatted with Ryan.

He pointed at me, his eyes narrowed like he was trying to remember how he knew me. "You're in my English 101 class, right?"

My heart felt like it took off in flight. "Uh, yeah, that's right."

The lighting wasn't great in here, but I could have sworn I saw a flush on his face. "Can you remind me of your name again? I'm not the best with names."

"I'm Abby."

"Abby." He said it like I'd just given him the answer to a question on a make-or-break test. "Well, nice to put a name to a face, Abby. I'm Foster."

As if he needed an introduction. "I know," I said, giggling.

And then pure mortification hit me because that totally made me sound like a stalker.

I cleared my throat. "I just mean, I know who you are, as in, I'm good with names, and I was paying attention in class, and so I know who you are." I clamped my lips shut to stop my rambling.

His smile told me that he found it endearing, but my cheeks were hot from embarrassment.

This could not be happening.

Foster Kane couldn't be in the tutoring center right now.

What the hell would he even need a tutor for?

I glanced around the corner at him, my heart now racing like I'd just gone for a mile run while being chased by a bear.

Seriously, why was he here? I mean, okay, of course he was here because he probably needed a tutor, but he was *Foster Kane.* Everyone knew he was smart and funny and hot and perfect.

Maybe he was here to pick up a date with one of the staff. My stomach cramped at the idea, and self-loathing flooded my veins like poison.

It'd been well over a year since I was in the same room

with him, and I hated that my heart still raced at the sight of him. I'd done everything in my power to avoid him since that horrible night freshman year.

If I saw him walking my direction on campus, I went a different route.

If I saw him in the Student Union Building, or SUB as most students referred to it, I'd duck my head and hope he didn't notice me.

He never did.

It should've been a relief, but instead it left me feeling even more humiliated.

Now I knew that I wasn't just a bad kisser, but I was also entirely forgettable.

Just what every girl dreamed to be.

He ran his fingers through his dark brown hair that was long on top but short on the sides. I still remembered how thick and smooth it felt between my fingers. His blue eyes were the color of the recycling bin sitting on the floor by the door—I refused to compare them to anything flattering. He was just as tall as I remembered, although his muscles seemed thicker than they were freshman year. If I had to guess, I'd say he was six three or six four. I remembered how he'd towered over my five six body when we'd first met and he ducked down to whisper in my ear.

I loathed that the sight of him still made my pulse all fluttery and my stomach swirl with *something*. I decided it had to be dread because I refused to believe that I could have any lingering attraction for him after all this time.

No, any attraction I had for Foster Kane died a painful death freshman year.

My boss, Marco, walked over to him with a big smile on his face and an extended hand. I was too far away to hear exactly what they were saying, but they seemed friendly.

"Holy shit, is that Foster Kane?"

I jumped and spun around to see Layla, another tutor, staring between the books at Foster. I could practically see the hearts beating out of her eyes.

"I wouldn't mind tutoring that man," she said. "It's not often I get eye candy while I work."

"You can have him," I muttered.

The last thing I wanted to do was to be stuck tutoring Foster Kane when I could barely stand to look at him without thinking about that night almost two years ago.

But apparently the universe was having a good laugh in my face because not five seconds after I had the thought, all my worst fears came true.

My boss started looking around the room and said loud enough for me to hear, "I know I saw her here. Abby," he called out.

Suck a lemon drop.

I closed my eyes and composed myself. I could do hard things. I'd been doing hard things for years now. This would be no different.

Even if looking at him reminded me of the most humiliated I'd ever been in my entire life. Followed by the worst days and months of my life for a very different reason.

With a neutral expression, I spun around and walked out from behind the bookshelf.

Marco's face lit up. "Ah, there you are."

I glanced nervously at Foster and then back at Marco. "What's up?"

My gaze darted back to Foster, unable to stop myself from seeing his reaction to me. Vaguely, I heard Marco talk about how Foster needed help with math, and since I was the best math tutor here, he wanted me to work with him exclusively.

My boss continued to very enthusiastically talk me up to Foster, and the whole time, my body braced for Foster to recognize me—to say something snarky or witty or whatever.

But nothing came. He smiled at me in that way you smile at a stranger you're meeting for the first time, and my heart fell to the pit of my stomach.

Was it really possible that the night that lived on in my memory as the most humiliating night of my life was a night he seriously didn't even remember?

Foster extended his hand to me. "Hey, Abby. Foster Kane. It's great to meet ya."

I took his hand woodenly, my grip firm, but slightly clammy—or maybe that was him. No. There was no way Foster Kane was nervous enough to have clammy hands.

The second our palms touched, the past slammed into me.

His hand brushing my hair aside, his mouth slanting over mine, the two of us tangled together on his bed.

The heat of his hands on my hips.

The desperate crush of our bodies—until suddenly he wasn't moving anymore.

Until I pulled away and found him slack-mouthed, snoring, passed out cold beneath me.

Mortification roared through me all over again, fresh and searing.

I squeezed his hand once, firmly, professionally, and let go before he could feel the tremble in my fingers. "Abby Walker," I responded, even though it was clear he already knew my name because Marco said it several times already.

Marco clapped Foster on the back. "Great, I'll let you two get acquainted and get a schedule going."

Then he darted off, leaving Foster and me standing

alone in the entryway of the tutoring center. Foster stared at me like he was excited to work together while I was desperately wishing the floor would open up and swallow me whole.

But I wasn't that lucky.

"Um, here, come on. I've got a table set up this way."

"Great," he said, although there was a hint of something in his voice that lacked sincerity. I took a covert glance at him and noticed his smile was still on his face, but there was a stiffness to it I hadn't seen before.

Not that I made a habit of noticing Foster Kane.

I led him to my table and gestured to the seat across from me, tucked safely out of sight from the entrance. Not wanting to extend our time longer, I got right to work and pulled out my notebook. "So, you need help with math? What math class are you taking?"

He glanced over to where the door would be if he had a clear shot of it and grabbed the back of his neck in what was clearly a nervous gesture.

"Uh, do you guys do, like, um, confidentiality agreements here or anything?"

I arched a brow. "Why?"

He leaned forward and I caught a whiff of his clean and woodsy scent. I hated the way it made my stomach tighten.

Maybe I just ate something bad, and my stomach was

cramping. That was preferable to admitting there was anything I still found attractive about Foster.

"I don't really want people to know I'm getting tutoring," he said.

His blue eyes pierced into me with a hint of desperation like he was genuinely concerned about people finding out he was at the tutoring center.

I swallowed thickly, ignoring the way my heart was racing.

Maybe I was coming down with a cold.

"We don't go advertising who we tutor," I told him, keeping my voice even and gentle and not giving away how much his anxiety concerned me.

I'd never seen Foster as anything but completely confident and sure of himself.

This version of him was...disconcerting.

Foster let out a sigh of relief as his shoulders dropped, and he took a breath like he'd been holding it this whole time. "Okay, cool." Then, taking another deep breath, he pierced me with those eyes again, his face pinched like he was embarrassed about what he had to say. "I need help with Mitchell's math class."

My pen had been poised over my paper, expecting him to say one of the notoriously hard math professors like Hopkins or Kenney, but Mitchell was one of the easier math professors at CFU and typically only taught intro math classes.

"Which section?" I asked, wondering if maybe Mitchell had added an upper-level section this semester.

"104," he said.

Only practice kept the surprise from showing on my face. I'd tried to ignore Foster's presence over the last couple of years. But when I had paid attention to him freshman year, it seemed like he excelled at everything he did.

He'd brought the hockey team back to life in a way that most people said was impossible, especially considering hockey wasn't the most popular sport in Montana.

So to find out he was struggling with a math class that was considered easy by most students was shocking.

"What exactly are you struggling with in his class?"

Those vivid blue eyes met mine again, and I fought every urge in my body not to suck in a breath. There must've been some dust or something in the air here that was affecting my allergies. That could be the only explanation for why my body was suddenly going haywire.

He looked reluctant to answer my question, but eventually said, "Here, let me show you."

He removed his laptop from his backpack and pulled up the student portal where we had access to all our courses. He spun it to fully face me, displaying what looked like a test. It only took me a quick glance to realize it was a basic math skills test that I knew Mitchell used to see what his student's baselines were, so he could meet them where they were.

"This is helpful," I told him, as I started looking at the problems and his answers. There were some notes throughout the test from the professor, and I nibbled my lip as I scrolled down. Some of these problems were fourth-grade math basics, but Foster got them wrong.

Some of his answers look flipped—like instead of 35, he put 53.

I'd think some of these errors were careless errors if it wasn't for the anxiety that was rolling off Foster in waves the longer I looked at his screen.

He was really stressed about this.

"We can work with this," I said, even though I was worried it would take a miracle to help him pass a college level math class when he was struggling with basic elementary skills. "Do you mind if I get a copy of this test so we can use this as our baseline?"

His whole body stiffened, and I looked up at him to see pure panic on his face. "You're not going to show anyone, are you?"

Who was this person sitting in front of me? The confident jock I'd crushed on so hard freshman year and saw on campus over the last two years was definitely not the same guy sitting in front of me.

I placed a hand over his and sucked in a sharp breath at the zap of electricity that shot up my arm and felt like it went straight to my heart. Ignoring it, I focused on him, hoping he could see the sincerity in my eyes. "I'm not going to tell anyone, Foster. Your secret is safe with me. I promise."

He stared at me for a moment longer, and something passed through his gaze that made me hold my breath—a look of familiarity that passed so fast, I would've missed it if I'd blinked.

"Thanks," he said, his voice low and hoarse. "I-I'm not a guy who fails, but math seems to be my Achilles' heel."

I squeezed his hand. "We all have one."

The panic that had been on his face receded, replaced with warmth and gratitude.

I broke our gaze and slid my hand back to my lap. I needed to remember that I didn't like Foster Kane. I could be nice and professional, but I couldn't let myself get soft around him again.

I already knew that road only led to disaster and humiliation. Not to mention that Foster was now so far out of my league, it wasn't even funny.

Clearing my throat, I said, "I'll make a game plan for where to start and strategies we can try. We should probably meet at least twice a week." Truthfully, depending on how busy he was, we might need to make it three days a week to get him where he needed to be for Mitchell's class.

We made a plan for the next few weeks with our first official tutoring session happening in a few days. That would give me enough time to go through his skills test and figure out where to start.

He stared at me again with what looked distinctly like gratitude in his eyes, and then said wholeheartedly, "Thank you, Abby."

"Sure," I said lamely.

With a wave, I watched him walk away, angry at myself, but angrier at him.

Of all the guys to walk in looking for a tutor, did it really have to be him?

But the question that ate away at me was the one that whispered through my mind every time I tried to work on a strategy for him and thought about how he looked at me like I was a stranger.

Was I really so forgettable?

I wasn't sure I wanted the answer.

BigBear88:

If anyone needs me, I'll be crying into a bag of frozen peas.🥲

PeachyKeen:

Again??
What did the peas ever do to you??

BigBear88:

They witnessed my downfall.
Can't have loose-lipped veggies out here spreading slander.

PeachyKeen:

LMAO
Peas are snitches confirmed.

BigBear88:

Never trusted them.
It's always the quiet ones.

PeachyKeen:

Okay but seriously
What happened??
Peas therapy session? 

BigBear88:
Just... dumb today.
Like, Olympic-level dumb.
Gold medal in making everything harder than it needs to be.

PeachyKeen:
Gold medalist??
You're out here achieving greatness and you're still complaining?

Smh. Overachiever.

BigBear88:

Put that on my grave:
"Here lies BigBear88. Dumb as hell. Overachieved anyway."

PeachyKeen:
You know I'd bring flowers.
And a trophy.

BigBear88:
I'm keeping this receipt.
When I inevitably crash and burn, you're contractually obligated
to hype me up.

PeachyKeen:
Deal.
Official hype woman status achieved.

BigBear88:

You're a menace.

But also

Thanks, Peach.

Seriously.

You're the best person I've never actually met.

PeachyKeen:

Right back at ya, Bear.

SEVEN

Foster

My new tutor didn't seem too excited to work with me.

It was our first official session, and I had to admit I was a bit thrown by her cold shoulder. I didn't expect everyone to bend over backward for me, but I was used to most people being excited to at least be around me.

She seemed like she'd been sucking on a sour lemon all day at simply being near me, which seemed completely at odds with how kind and understanding she'd been when we first met a few days ago.

I discreetly tucked my nose toward my armpit while she was distracted writing down a math problem for me and took a whiff. I didn't stink.

I rubbed my hand over my chin and then moved it to cover my mouth and nose and let out a silent breath. Nope, my breath was minty fresh.

So why was she acting like I suddenly had the plague and she wanted to be anywhere but sitting next to me?

She'd held her body stiff and her face pinched when we'd first started, but the longer we worked and the more focused she became on the math in front of her, the more her face softened and I couldn't stop staring at her.

She had walnut-brown hair with lighter shades throughout that seemed natural. It fell in soft waves past her shoulders, although she'd had it up in a ponytail when we first met. I liked it better down.

Her face was clear and looked incredibly smooth. Apart from some mascara, I didn't think she was wearing any makeup. If she was, it was definitely a natural look. But what captivated me were her big brown eyes. There was something familiar about them that I couldn't put my finger on.

I was sure I would remember if we'd met, so it couldn't be that, but I wasn't sure what it was about her that made me feel like I'd been lost in her eyes before.

She hadn't been wearing glasses when we first met, but she was today. They were simple, thin, black frames that sat on the bridge of her button nose and made her look nerdy hot.

Like a sexy librarian.

Especially with her curves. She had small breasts, but what she lacked up top, she more than made up for with her round ass. I'd always been a butt guy, and now that I wasn't buried under anxiety like I was the first day we met, I was having a hard time keeping my thoughts focused on math and not how she looked in her black shorts that stopped mid-thigh but showed off the curve of her behind followed by smooth, lightly tanned legs.

She didn't seem comfortable with me, but there was something about her that made me feel safe. Something familiar and warm, like a memory that flickered just out of reach.

But it wasn't really a memory—more like a dream. Because there was no way I'd forget this girl.

Regardless, the last thing I needed was a crush on my tutor. I needed her help with math, and I needed her discretion which meant I couldn't piss her off.

More importantly, I didn't have time to date.

But despite telling myself that I couldn't be attracted to my tutor, I also couldn't help but try to get to know her. Unfortunately, she seemed determined to stonewall me at every turn.

If I asked her a question about her favorite color or what she did on her days off, I got nothing but a redirection to a math problem.

If I asked her how her day was, I got a "fine."

She either took her job extremely seriously or she genuinely didn't like me for reasons I didn't know or understand. I decided to ease up on my attempts, considering we'd be working together for the next seven weeks.

I'd have plenty of time to get to know her, especially since she'd recommended we meet three times a week instead of just two.

When she looked at me again, the cool detachment was back in her eyes. "Okay, let's try this one."

She pointed down to the paper, and it took more effort than it should have to pull my attention away from her and to the paper on the table in front of us.

I tried to focus, but the numbers jumbled and didn't make sense.

Picking up on my unease, she walked me through the steps we'd already gone over several times.

I swallowed thickly, stress sweat starting to bead at my temples as I looked down at the page. Under the table, I tried to use my fingers to count.

It was supposed to be a simple sequencing problem—or at least that's what she said when she put it in front of me—but there was nothing simple about it.

My cheeks heated as embarrassment flowed like hot lava through my body, and I wished with desperation it would burn me up.

There was no point in finding Abby attractive because I had no doubt after today's session, she'd realize how dumb I really was and never give me the time of day.

Popularity and athleticism probably didn't matter to a woman as smart as she was.

I was the top hockey player in the state—although a player from Montana State's team was hot on my heels—and yet simple math made me feel like a complete idiot.

But worst of all, it made me feel like an idiot in front of *her*.

I'd never wanted to disappear more than I did right that moment.

If I thought she was cold before, I had no doubt she'd get even worse now that she knew my secret shame.

Instead, she surprised me. Her voice softened and she leaned a little closer, close enough for me to catch a whiff of her fresh, citrus scent. "It's okay, Foster. Walk me through what's going on in your head."

I swallowed past the lump in my throat, keeping my eyes locked on the numbers on the page. The last thing I wanted was to meet her gaze and see the same frustration and disappointment I'd seen a hundred times before from teachers and even my own parents.

But Abby's voice stayed gentle. "What do you see when you look at the problem?"

I exhaled slowly. "A bunch of numbers that don't make any sense." I forced a laugh, trying to downplay the shame pressing in on me, but she didn't laugh with me. She didn't even look annoyed.

She just nodded like that was a perfectly reasonable answer. She looked down at the problem, her brow furrowed, and I could practically see the wheels in her head turning.

"I wonder…" she murmured, more to herself than me.

She opened her laptop and started typing something, leaning toward the screen like she was searching for something in particular. Her eyes lit up a little and I guessed she'd found what she was after.

She glanced at me. "Do the numbers move? Flip around?"

I frowned, my heart starting to race with nerves. "What?"

"Do you ever look at a number and it switches places on you? Or maybe you think it's one number, but it turns out to be another?"

I blinked at her, caught off guard that she'd actually pegged what happened in my head so quickly. "Uh, yeah… sometimes eights and threes get mixed up. And sixes and nines." I felt stupid admitting it, but she didn't react like it was weird.

She nodded and then looked back at her computer screen, asking me another question, like what I'd just told her was completely normal. "What about sequencing? Like, if I gave you a list of numbers to put in order, would that be difficult?"

My gut twisted, and reluctantly I admitted, "Yeah."

She nodded again, completely unfazed. "What about word problems? Do they make more sense than just numbers on a page, or are they just as confusing?"

I hesitated. No one had ever asked me this many questions about how I struggled before. They'd just told me to try harder. Study longer. "Word problems are a little easier. At least then I can try to picture what's happening."

"That tracks," she murmured, tapping her pencil against the paper, her focus still locked on her screen.

I didn't even know what she meant.

All I knew was she wasn't looking at me like I was dumb.

She wasn't frustrated or impatient. She was...thinking. Like she actually cared about what I said and was trying to figure out how to help.

For the first time since I sat down, my chest didn't feel so tight.

Abby adjusted her glasses and gave me a small smile, the first one she'd sent my way all session. "Okay, I've got an idea. We'll take a different approach next time. Something that might work better for you."

I stared at her, waiting for the frustration to set in, for her to roll her eyes and tell me I was just making excuses, but she didn't.

She just looked at me like I wasn't broken.

Like I wasn't stupid.

Something in my chest eased, and for the first time in my life, I left a tutoring session without feeling like a total idiot.

BigBear88:

Just died on level 93 of the mines. Again.

PeachyKeen:

BRING FOOD. You can't just raw dog the mines like that.

BigBear88:

I had algae and a dream.

PeachyKeen:

That is not a survival strategy.

BigBear88:

It was a vibe though.

"Gram? Mason?" I called out as I entered Gram's house. Her car was in the driveway, so I knew she was home.

I'd already been living on campus when my mom passed away in the car accident, but my brother was still a minor, so Gram became his legal guardian and we sold my childhood home when he moved in with her. Gram put the funds from the sale in a trust for Mase and me to be disbursed in increments. I started getting small amounts monthly and used the money to help pay some of my rent.

As much as I loved Gram, it was hard to come home sometimes. It was weird for a house to be both a sanctuary and a hard memory to face.

This wasn't the house I was raised in, and it was difficult to see memories of my mom and her childhood when I missed her so desperately.

My mom had been my first best friend. She'd been my cheerleader, always on the sidelines rooting for me. When I felt awkward and clumsy, she made me feel strong and brave. She made me believe that it didn't matter how mean kids were at school because I was the nerdy girl who preferred math and science over doing girly things. She always taught me to embrace what made me unique. She used to tell me that the most important thing we could do as human beings was to embrace our brand of special—the thing that made us different from everyone else—and that society focused so much on "sameness" because people were afraid of standing out.

I'd felt lost without her.

Gram did her best, but it wasn't the same.

Nothing felt the same without Mom here.

But as hard as it was to come here and see memories of Mom, I couldn't avoid it because I loved Gram and my brother needed me. Mason had become a shell of himself since our mom died. I hadn't seen him smile since before her accident, which was crushing because he had one of the best smiles of anyone I'd ever met.

We were a close-knit family, and we felt her loss with every aching breath, no matter how much time passed.

I'd thrown myself into my studies and work and trying to leave a legacy at CFU that I knew my mom would be proud of, whereas my brother had stopped all of his activities, except for one. Football.

I was pretty sure he still played because the coach refused to accept him quitting. When Mason had tried to turn his pads back in, Coach Clyde told him that he could turn them in at the end of the season with everyone else, but he expected him to show up to practice. For nearly two years, he'd kept Mason engaged with football. He'd even gone so far as to pick him up for practice until he was sure Mason would show up on his own.

I owed Coach a huge thank you.

Mason was still quieter and more withdrawn than he'd ever been. He still refused to get his license—something I suspected was in part because our mom was killed in a car accident—and had only started hanging out with his friends more often in the last few months. But at least I knew he had some kind of outlet, especially since Coach Clyde did summer football sessions to keep the players engaged. It gave me a bit of comfort to know he had a community around him and wasn't here drowning in his grief.

Mason had left a voicemail for me that he was worried about Gram, and so instead of coming home for a visit tomorrow like I had originally planned, I decided to come a day early.

Gram didn't live far from the university—only about a thirty-minute drive if traffic was good. Campus was quieter in the summer, which sometimes made it easier to slip away for a visit. But with my work schedule and internship, it still felt like there were never enough hours in the day.

"Mase," I called again.

Instead of calling back, he walked around the corner. He'd grown taller since the last time I was home. He'd already been taller than my five feet six before our mom passed away, but he'd shot up in the last year and a half and was apparently still growing. His dark brown hair that was the same shade as our dad's was shaggy, and I had to fight back the revulsion at the mullet cut.

How the hell had that trend made a comeback? I didn't understand it. His dark brown eyes met mine, and my heart ached at the way they didn't light up like they used to. He'd been such a happy, carefree little kid. Part of me felt like I'd lost the brother I'd known my whole life when our mom died.

"Hey, what's going on?" I asked.

"Something is up with Gram, but she won't tell me." His voice was deep and scratchier than I remembered.

I placed the back of my hand on his forehead to check if he was getting sick, and he instantly pushed it away.

I furrowed my brow but let it slide. I knew from experience that pestering him with questions about his well-being would get me nowhere.

"What do you mean something's up with her?" I asked.

He shrugged, and God did I hate that teenage boy shrug he'd adopted. It never told me a damn thing even though he always acted like it should explain everything. I arched a brow, and he rolled his eyes before continuing. "She's been weird lately—quiet—and she started going through her stuff in the attic."

That *was* concerning.

For one thing, Gram had the biggest personality of anyone I'd ever met. She could walk into a room with complete strangers and walk out with dozens of new friends.

But even more concerning was that she was hanging out in the attic. Gram had once told me she stored all the memories that were too hard to see up there so that she still had them, but didn't have to look at them every day. I knew all of Grandpa's stuff was stored up there, and most of the things from my mom that we'd kept. I hadn't seen her go up there in years.

"Is she up there now?"

It was the only logical reason why she hadn't greeted me at the door like she always did.

He nodded, and then started to turn around like that was the end of our conversation.

"Hey, how are you doing?" I asked before he could escape to his room.

He shrugged his shoulders again in that way that seventeen-year-old boys do. "Fine."

I knew that wasn't true. I wasn't sure anyone in this house had been fine since my mom's accident, least of all my brother.

I grabbed his hand before he could walk away. "Hey, I love you," I told him.

My mom had said "I love you" to us every day. She had said it was important that we always felt her words and knew how proud of us she was. I knew she would never want a day to go by where her baby boy didn't know that he was loved. And so I tried to carry on the tradition, even if it was via text message.

It wasn't lost on me that the little boy who had once giggled "I love you" every time she said it hadn't uttered those three words since the day of her accident.

He didn't utter them now, either. He simply gave me another nod and then disappeared down the hall to his room.

With a heavy sigh, I went up to the attic.

Gram lived in an old farmhouse on twenty acres of land that had been passed down from her mother and her parents before them.

"Gram, you up here?"

There was a narrow staircase that led up to the attic, and I climbed it until I could peek up into the large open space. The attic wasn't cramped like most attics I was aware of and instead could have been its own room. It had six-foot ceilings and spanned the entire top of the nearly two-thousand-square-foot house. It was mostly cluttered with boxes that had black scrawl on them to give an idea of what was stored in each box. Along the right wall was an old wooden rocking chair that I knew from stories and pictures had been used when my mom was a baby and Gram would rock her to sleep.

That was where I found Gram rocking gently as she looked at a photo album on her lap.

I quietly made my way up the rest of the stairs until I was in the room with her and approached her slowly.

"Gram, are you okay?" My breath caught when I looked down at the photo album on her lap. It was the last photo that had ever been taken of us as a full family before we'd lost my grandpa, then my dad, and then my mom.

Dad had a heart attack in his sleep and was gone before any of us could have ever done anything. I'd been seven and Mason had been only three years old. It was the first horrible memory I had, and sometimes I wondered if I only remembered it so vividly because Mom had been devastated. She'd tried her best to hold it together for us, but he'd been her soulmate, and his loss carved a hole in her heart that left a permanent mark.

Gram looked up, tears glistening in her eyes. She reached for me, and without hesitation, I slipped my hand into hers. Her frail hands were cold, and I held them just a little tighter as anxious worry knotted in my stomach.

"What's going on?"

"Just missing everyone today," she said.

"Are you sure that's all?"

Her smile was soft and sad, and the burn of tears threatened behind my eyes.

"Gram," I repeated, my voice choked. "Are you sure you're okay?"

She squeezed my hand and stood up. "I'm just fine."

Her voice was steady, but I was sure it was a lie because

there was something in her eyes, a sadness that I hadn't seen there before that made me think fine was the opposite of what she was feeling right now.

But my grandmother was a stubborn woman, and if she didn't want to tell me what was going on, I knew she wouldn't.

She set the album down on the rocking chair and said, "Are you staying for dinner?" Her voice was light again as if she didn't have a care in the world.

"Yeah, I can," I said. Staying for dinner sounded like a good idea given how out of character she was acting.

She smiled fondly at me. "I think Mason would appreciate that."

"Is something else going on with him?" He was the hardest to read of my family members.

Her brows furrowed. "It's hard to tell these days if it's new or old pain that he's carrying. I can't seem to break through to him, and I only hope his coach is having better luck than I am."

"I'll stay and hang out, see if he'll talk to me."

We'd been close our whole life. Mason was the baby brother I'd always wanted, and I looked out for him with the fierceness of a lioness protecting her cub. But even I struggled to get through the walls he'd put up since Mom died. I was scared what would happen to him if he held all his pain inside without letting it out.

I couldn't lose another family member.

As we sat around the dining room table later that evening, I couldn't help but notice that each of us seemed somewhat lost in our own heads. Gram didn't ask as many questions as she usually did. Mason was as silent and stoic as a guard at Buckingham Palace.

And while I had plenty to worry about between the two

of them, my thoughts kept veering to a too-handsome-for-his-own-good hockey player with a charismatic smile that reminded me why I'd had such a crush on him freshman year.

The same hockey player that I suspected had a learning disorder he didn't seem to be fully aware of.

PeachyKeen:

I messed up my crop layout and now my iridium sprinklers aren't aligned. I hate it here.

BigBear88:

Chaos is part of the charm.

PeachyKeen:

I live in organized harmony. This is personal.

BigBear88:

Want me to come move them for you and ruin everything evenly?

BigBear88:

Be honest. You romance Sebastian, don't you?

PeachyKeen:

Excuse me, what makes you think I go for broody emo boys in the basement?

BigBear88:

The spreadsheet you sent me about optimal gift-giving.

PeachyKeen:

That was for science.

BigBear88:

Science. Sure.

PeachyKeen:

Did you just pass out in the greenhouse?

BigBear88:

I got distracted trying to pet the cows.

PeachyKeen:

Bear.

BigBear88:

It was worth it. They looked happy.

PeachyKeen:

I'm docking your allowance.

Foster stared at the math problem like it was written in ancient hieroglyphics, his pencil gripped so tightly I was amazed it hadn't snapped.

Math wasn't always the easiest subject for some people, but his struggles weren't from a lack of intelligence. He was sharp in conversation, quick-witted, and had a great memory when it came to real-world examples. But the moment numbers came into play, it was like his brain short-circuited.

His jaw clenched, and then he set the pencil down and dropped his face in his hands, his elbows resting on the table. "I don't know. I don't know," he said again louder, defeat suffusing every ounce of his voice and body.

We'd been stuck in the same frustrating loop for two sessions now, and neither of us knew how to break it.

I was honestly astounded by how much he was struggling and how he'd even made it to the college level without understanding some of the basics.

"How have you gotten past math before?" I asked him.

He grabbed the back of his neck, and I tried to ignore the way his biceps bulged.

"Honestly, I've kind of avoided it as much as possible. As far as college level classes, I pushed them off as long as I could. In high school, I had...friends who helped me out."

The way he hesitated on friends made me think maybe they were more.

"Girls," I clarified.

He smiled sheepishly, but there was still a hint of shame in his eyes. "Sometimes, yeah. Not that I'm proud of that. They would offer and I would accept their help."

His smile fell. "My dad...he's kind of a prominent figure in our community where I grew up in Bozeman."

"Hold up. You grew up in Bozeman and you didn't go to MSU?" I was shocked. There was a lot of pride in our state schools. Since Montana State University was in Bozeman, it surprised me that he'd come to Clark Fork University instead.

He chuckled. "Everyone in my family has gone to CFU. So that's why I came here. Plus, a friend of mine was part of the group that restarted the hockey team here, and I really wanted to be a part of that—help it grow and get established."

He had done just that. I might have tried to avoid him as much as possible because of what happened freshman year, but it was impossible to deny the impact he'd had on the sports community here at CFU.

He leaned forward, and I pretended like my breath didn't catch at the close proximity and the way his subtle cologne wafted into the air. "Why don't you like me?" he asked.

"I like you just fine," I said, brushing off his question as much as I could and focusing back on the task at hand.

But his hand covered the sheet we'd been working on, and when I looked up, his blue eyes caught my gaze. Once again, my breath caught and it was infuriating that my body still responded to him, despite the humiliation he'd once made me feel.

Maybe I should go to campus health and see if I was developing asthma or something.

"Abby, did I do or say something that offended you?"

Now I was struggling to breathe for a whole different reason. I couldn't possibly tell him the truth. It was embarrassing enough that I had to remember it, but to say it out loud... absolutely not.

"No, of course not."

"When I walked in here you were talking to that other tutor girl and you had this big, gorgeous smile on your face. How come you don't smile like that with me?"

I knew we were at a higher elevation here in the mountains, but it felt like the air thinned instantly at his question. Did he just call my smile gorgeous?

"Maybe I don't smile like that because we're not friends. I'm working. Just because I don't fall all over myself around you—"

He held up his hands. "Woah, I didn't mean I expected that. Maybe I'm not as articulate as I thought I was. All I'm saying is I feel like we've gotten off on the wrong foot. I'm not sure why, but I'd really like to correct it. And maybe we can become friends."

"I think right now we should focus on this math," I said, tapping my pencil against the sheet between us. "Talk me through your thought process on this one."

Foster let out a long sigh and ran a hand through his dark brown hair. He was distracting when he did that.

Distracting in general, really. But now was not the time to let my brain wander.

He talked me through where he was getting stuck and just continued to confirm what I already suspected based on research I'd done.

Because I was a thorough tutor—not because I cared about him.

"Okay, let's try something different."

I grabbed a blank sheet of paper and slid it toward him. "Rewrite the problem, but say it out loud as you do."

His eyes flicked up to mine, wary. "Rewrite it?"

"Yeah. Just copy it exactly. And say each number and symbol as you write it."

He sighed again but picked up his pencil and complied. "Okay...um. Three point five, divided by...wait, no, times—" He stopped, frowning at what he'd just written.

I gently nudged the textbook toward him. "Check it against the original."

His frown deepened as he compared the two. "Shit," he muttered. "I flipped the division sign and multiplication sign."

I nodded again. "Do you mix up symbols a lot?"

"I...I guess?" He rubbed the back of his neck. "I mean, numbers always look jumbled to me. Sometimes I think I read them right, but then when I go back, I realize I swapped them around."

"Foster," I said carefully. "Have you ever heard of dyscalculia?"

His brows pulled together. "Is that like dyslexia?"

"Sort of. But with numbers. It's a learning difference that affects how people process numerical information. A lot of people who have it struggle with recognizing patterns in numbers, mixing up digits, or having trouble holding numbers in their short-term memory for calculations. Does any of that sound familiar?"

He blinked at me, silent for a long moment. I watched as something flickered across his face—reluctance, maybe. Or maybe something deeper.

He exhaled, leaning back in his chair. "Are you suggesting that's the reason I've always struggled with math?"

I nodded.

He swallowed hard, his Adam's apple bobbing with the motion and vulnerability shining in his eyes.

The urge to reassure him kept me talking. "Your brain just processes numbers differently. We can work around it—with smaller steps, visual tools, things like that. And if you want, you could even get tested for accommodations."

He stared at me, his expression shifting again to something between relief and something else. The usually confident, easygoing facade was gone, and my chest tightened at the sight of this version of Foster Kane.

"You're saying...this isn't just me being stupid?" he asked quietly.

I reached across the table and couldn't stop myself from covering his hand with mine. "You're not stupid, Foster. Far from it. I promise."

He held my stare, and the weight of understanding that passed between us had me holding my breath, afraid to break the moment.

"Okay," he said finally. "Let's try again."

And for the first time since we started tutoring, I saw something new in his eyes.

Hope.

If I could've faked a head injury to get out of going home for the weekend, I would've. But the drive from Dunridge to Bozeman was only four hours, and my mom had already ferreted the truth out of me that I was completely free this weekend.

I was dreading going back.

Avoiding my home over the summers had become a skill of mine. In high school, I filled the time working construction jobs whenever I could. Going off to college had been easier because I could always find excuses to stay in Dunridge and work in nearby Missoula instead of going home.

But as much as I loathed being under the oppressive weight of my father's attention, I still hadn't managed to find the courage to stand up to him. And saying no to my mom wasn't an option.

I'd always thought math was my only weak point, but I had to admit my father was my other.

He never failed to remind me that everything he did

was for me—so I could have the best possible future. But did he have to be such a dick about it? The future he was building wasn't a future I wanted, but my opinion had never mattered.

Over the last two weeks working with Abby, I'd felt my confidence lift back up, but the closer I got to my parents' house, the more that confidence was replaced with dread.

Keep the peace.

That had become my mantra for any interaction with my father. I never knew what would tip him over the edge, and while he wasn't physically abusive, his mood swings were something I wanted to avoid at all costs—for my mother's sake as much as mine.

The door had barely shut behind me when my father walked out of his office. He looked down at his watch and then back at me. "Was traffic bad?"

Irritation fluttered along my spine, but I kept my face neutral. "Not too bad."

"Hmm. Thought you'd be here sooner."

Before I could say anything, my mom popped around the corner, drying her hands on a dish towel. "Foster, honey, come have a seat. You're just in time for lunch."

Her smile stretched too wide to be real, her eyes a silent warning that I was all too familiar with—just play along.

I dropped my bag by the stairs and followed them into the kitchen, instinctively taking the stool farthest from my dad. His laptop sat open at the counter, filled with spreadsheets and blueprints, as if he couldn't bear to spend five minutes unplugged from his job as a real estate developer—even on a Saturday.

"I have some good news," he said, tapping the counter with the edge of his phone. He loved delivering announcements like they were blessings I should be grateful for.

"You know that Missoula project I've been handling?" he went on.

I nodded cautiously.

"Well, it's going so well we were able to get another contract there. So, I bought an office space downtown—right in the heart of Missoula. I'll be closing on it in a few weeks. Pretty soon The Kane Group will be a household name."

The Kane Group was the real estate development firm my dad had founded in Bozeman before I was born. Most days I was pretty confident he loved his business more than he loved me or my mom.

His grin was self-satisfied, like he was waiting for applause.

"But you live here... Who's going to run the Missoula office?" I asked, even though I already suspected I wouldn't like the answer.

"Me, of course. Like I'd leave the setup of a new branch of my business to anyone else. I also bought a condo near the office building. I'll be splitting time between here and Missoula until you graduate and can take over operations." His tone shifted subtly—less suggestion, more command. "It'll give you a head start."

A head start on a life I didn't want.

My fingers curled tightly around the glass of water my mom had set in front of me when I sat down, but the chill of the glass did nothing to cool the fire of frustration growing inside me.

Across the kitchen, she kept her back to us, wiping down the already clean counters. She hated these conversations as much as I did. She just wasn't allowed to say so.

Neither could I because it would just start an argument that I would lose and that I didn't have the energy for.

"That's...great," I said, voice even. Flat.

His jaw clenched and his eyes flashed. "You know, most kids would be grateful that their parents are setting up a legacy for them. I expect a little more enthusiasm when we start working on the builds together."

He nodded like it was settled. Like it always was.

I tuned out after that, letting his words blur into meaningless noise—percentages, contracts, profit margins.

I stared at the sandwich my mom placed in front of me and thought about how college had been my one escape.

And now even that was slipping away.

The longer I sat there, the tighter the walls closed in.

By the time I made it back to my old room that hadn't changed since high school, I felt hollowed out.

I sank onto the bed and pulled out my phone, needing *something* to tether me back to myself.

A notification blinked across the screen.

PeachyKeen:
You alive over there, BigBear?

A shaky breath escaped me, and I didn't realize how tightly I was wound until that tiny message unraveled the helplessness in my chest.

I thumbed out a reply, fast.

BigBear88:
Barely. Visiting family. Send help.

She sent back a crying-laugh emoji, then a GIF of a little bear waving a white flag.

I smiled in spite of myself.

My thumb hovered over the keyboard. I wanted to tell her everything.

About how fake everything felt here.

About how trapped I was.

About how it was easier to be someone else when I was with her—even if it was just behind a screen.

Instead, I typed something simpler.

BigBear88:

You busy?

PeachyKeen:

Nah. Just messing around on my farm. Wanna hang out?

God, yes.

Gaming suddenly seemed like the best way to escape reality right now.

But playing with Peach wasn't enough anymore. Not when the real world kept closing in tighter.

My fingers hesitated.

I knew she went to CFU, but we hadn't shared more specifics about our lives besides that. We'd both seemed content to keep our game personas separate from real life, but what if our connection in the game could be real?

Heart pounding, I typed:

BigBear88:

Crazy idea… what if we met up sometime?
No pressure or anything. Just…thought it could be cool to actually hang out. In person.

I stared at the message for a full minute before hitting send.

Immediately, nerves twisted in my gut.

What if this changed everything?

BigBear88:

Crazy idea… what if we met up sometime?
No pressure or anything. Just…thought it could be cool to actu-
ally hang out. In person.

I stared at the screen, my mouth opening and closing as my brain raced with how to respond.

The idea of meeting BigBear in real life was both terrifying and thrilling in equal measure.

What if he didn't like me when he saw me?

What if I wasn't who he expected?

What if this ruined everything?

I was still frozen, phone clutched in my hand, when the front door opened and Samantha breezed into our apartment.

"You're tutoring Foster Kane?" Samantha squealed as she closed the door behind her.

I blinked, completely caught off guard. "How'd you know?"

Samantha dropped her bag on the floor and kicked off her sandals before joining me on the couch. "Celeste saw you guys walking out of the tutoring center and overheard him say he'd see you next week. I can't believe I had to find out through the grapevine that my best friend is tutoring one of the hottest guys on campus. And of all the hockey hotties, it's Foster. Does this mean we can finally go to some of the hockey house parties this fall? Next to the football house, they're some of the best, I've heard."

I felt like I was experiencing déjà vu because going to a party was exactly how the most humiliating night of my life happened.

"Sam, I'm not asking him to invite us to a party."

"Why not?"

I gave her a look because she of all people should know exactly why not.

Her face fell. "Wait, are you serious, Abby? Are you still upset about what happened freshman year?"

"Are you kidding?" I asked her. "It was humiliating."

She sighed and looked at me with sympathy. "Abs. You know I love you but what happened that night was—"

I cut her off. "Embarrassing. Humiliating. Mortifying. Pick a synonym." She gave me a look, so I continued. "Sam, he fell asleep *while* we were making out. I was in the middle of kissing him and he just conked out. Who even does that?"

She opened up her mouth to speak, but I held my hand up.

"And worse, he doesn't remember me." I hated how my voice broke on that sentence. Nearly two years later, that memory still haunted me, but it wasn't the memory that hurt as much as it was learning I was forgettable.

Her eyes widened as she stared at me, clearly at a loss for what to say.

"He doesn't remember you from freshman year?"

"Nope."

"Are you sure?" she asked. "I mean, he seemed totally into you that night. You two couldn't stop staring and smiling at each other like lovesick fools. Even with all we'd had to drink, I can remember that much."

"Yeah, and I'm sure he seemed totally into a dozen other girls since then," I said.

Except the words felt like a lie even as I said them.

I'd never really known Foster to be a womanizer. Not that I knew him much at all, but when I'd seen him on campus, he didn't seem like a guy who played women, or even dated all that often.

Sam reached for my hand. "Abby, he deserves to know that you guys have a little bit of a history if he doesn't remember for himself."

I pulled my hand away and covered my face. "I can't. It's just so pathetic, no matter how wasted we were. I can't tell him about that."

She brushed a strand of hair from my face, and I reluctantly dropped my hands. "Abby, you are my best friend and you are the most intelligent person I know. But in this, I think you're letting the events that followed that night make it seem worse than it really was."

"You weren't there," I told her.

"I was there up until you guys left, and he was definitely into you. I don't care how much we had to drink."

"Well, he couldn't have been into me that much because he fell asleep mid-kiss."

For months after, I questioned if I was that bad of a kisser—that boring—that he could just fall asleep mid-makeout.

Sam gave me her no-nonsense look. "Babes." Oh no, I

knew that tone. "While I've never had a guy fall asleep in the middle of making out, I have had other poor experiences, and guys can't always perform when they drink too much. Honestly, there are any number of things that can impact performance, if you know what I'm saying. But you've held on to that night like Rose on the door in *Titanic*. And you've let it hold you back like there was something wrong with you when there's not. Foster got drunk and passed out. It happens to the best and the worst of us. That's not a reflection on you or how good a kisser you are."

She squeezed my hands. "Don't hate me, but I think you've been holding on to this like a shield."

"What's that supposed to mean?"

"You crushed on Foster hard before that night. Then you finally got the chance to hook up with him and it went poorly. I remember how upset you were when you came home and then, before you had a chance to see him again and maybe clear the air, your mom died."

The familiar burn of tears stung behind my eyes, but I gritted my teeth and swallowed down the emotion bubbling up.

She continued. "I think the grief of losing her combined with...I don't know, feelings of failure or embarrassment, just turned that night into this giant thing for you. When to anyone else it would have been something that a few weeks later you could laugh at. I've watched you practically bury yourself under work, classes, and your internship—all of it to avoid *feeling*. And Abby, that's no way to live. Your mom wouldn't want that for you. She would want you to *feel*. She would want you to embrace life and dating, to have a crush, to maybe fall in love."

I swallowed thickly because she *would* want that. I

knew it was true, but that didn't make it any easier to acknowledge out loud.

And if she was right about my mom, was Sam also right about that night? Had I let my mind twist that night with Foster into something worse than it actually was? Had I gotten in my own way because of everything that happened after?

What would have happened if I had seen Foster again before my mom's accident? Would he have remembered me? Would we have cleared the air?

Sam squeezed my hand. "Please don't let that night hold you back, and don't hold it over Foster."

"It doesn't matter," I said. "He doesn't remember me, and I doubt he would be interested in me in that way. I'm just his tutor."

"He liked you once," she said with a beguiling smile. "I'm pretty sure he could fall for you again."

Maybe the more important question was, did I want him to?

Or was there someone else I'd also avoided taking a chance with because of fear?

With a pat on my knee, she headed down the hall to her room. I picked up my phone again and saw that Bear had left another message.

BigBear88:

If you don't want to, it's totally cool. No pressure at all.

A smile tugged at the corner of my mouth.

Maybe it was time to take a risk.

My fingers hovered over the keyboard for a second longer. Then, heart pounding, I typed back:

PeachyKeen:
I'd love to meet.

Sam was right about one thing. It was time I put myself out there again, and hopefully this time things would turn out better than before.

The café Peach and I had agreed to meet at was packed when I arrived. My nerves were a mess and I was too jittery for caffeine, but I felt like I should get something while I waited for her. I glanced around the space, looking for a woman sitting by herself with a small plush peach on the table—that was what Peach had said she'd bring to identify herself, and I'd had a good chuckle at that.

The only woman alone at her table was working on a laptop and didn't seem like she was waiting for anyone. I checked my phone for the time. Maybe I'd beaten her here.

I didn't want to think about the possibility that she changed her mind and wasn't coming.

I got in line behind a few other people and then caught sight of familiar brown hair. Abby was standing behind the woman currently ordering at the counter. There was one person between us, but Abby didn't seem to notice me behind her.

She wore a simple fitted green tank top that hugged her curves in a way that made my mouth water.

Abby was the kind of beautiful that was understated but completely disarming.

She shifted her weight from one foot to the other, and I was drawn to the way her jean shorts fit her ass, which was...well, distracting in the best possible way. When she reached up to tuck a strand of hair behind her ear, I caught a glimpse of her profile—the gentle slope of her nose, her full lips pressed together in concentration as she studied the menu board.

There was something captivating about the way she carried herself—confident but not showy, like she had nothing to prove to anyone. It was refreshing compared to the girls who usually threw themselves at me just because I played hockey.

I shifted my weight, suddenly aware that I'd been staring for too long. The last thing I needed was for her to turn around and catch me ogling her like some creep, or worse, for Peach to see me.

Guilt heated my cheeks. I shouldn't be checking out Abby when I was here to meet Peach. What the hell was I doing?

"Do you have another card?" the cashier asked the girl who was standing in front of Abby at the register.

The girl shook her head. Her voice caught as she asked, "Can you try it again, please? I just... It's been a really bad day, and I just really need this coffee."

The cashier held the card out to her. "I've already tried three times. It didn't go through. Sorry, hon."

The girl's shoulders dropped, and when she glanced behind her at the rest of us in line, her cheeks flushed bright pink in embarrassment.

Abby immediately stepped up and told the cashier to put it on hers, holding out her card, and then placed her order for a vanilla latte. The girl seemed profusely grateful, but I couldn't catch the rest of what she said to Abby once she lowered her voice.

But I could see Abby's face as they turned. Her expression was full of kindness and understanding, and I didn't miss her melodic voice saying, "Pay it forward someday."

Something deeper than attraction or lust tightened in my gut the longer I watched her.

She fascinated me and drew me in like no one else ever had, although there was also still this niggling feeling in the back of my mind that I'd felt this before, but I couldn't quite place it.

I was desperate to know more about her, to figure out what made her tick and what she was passionate about.

And for the first time, I admitted—at least to myself—that I had feelings for two women at the same time. I could only hope that meeting Peach today would help me figure out which one I felt stronger for.

I stepped up to place my order when the barista working behind the bar called out, "Peach."

I snapped my head and struggled to breathe as Abby walked up to the counter and grabbed her drink with a smile. My gaze was glued to her as she walked back to her table and sat down, setting the drink down carefully before she dug in her bag and pulled out a plush peach the size of a baseball.

No fucking way.

Abby was Peach.

Peach was Abby.

And in the same second that my heart soared because I wouldn't have to pick between them, my stomach plummeted because I knew with a certainty that made me want to puke that Abby didn't like me. She'd been professional during our tutoring sessions, but kept a clear line between us.

I wasn't sure why she didn't like me, and without that knowledge, I wasn't sure she'd accept that I was Bear.

If I walked up to her now and told her who I was, would I lose my only connection to her?

"Sir?"

I pulled my gaze away from Abby and faced the cashier.

"What can I get you?" she asked, her brow arched.

"Uh..."

Fuck. What did I do?

I made my decision in a split second and hoped it was the right one. "A drip coffee with a little room for cream and sugar. To go, please."

I paid and grabbed my coffee before making my way over to Abby's table, my nerves a hot mess as I questioned if my gut instinct was right or if I was making a colossal mistake.

She glanced up with a nervous smile on her face that drooped when she met my gaze.

Yeah, that wasn't how I wanted her to look at me—not as Abby *or* Peach.

"Hey, how's it going?"

Her gaze darted around the room like she didn't want to be seen with me. "Fine. Just waiting for a friend. You?"

Her words couldn't have been more clear—she didn't want me to join her, which meant I was right that she'd never accept the truth that I was BigBear88. Not unless I got her to like me—as Foster, not Bear.

"Just grabbing a coffee before I go meet some friends."

"Cool."

Awkward silence ensued, and it only made me more

confident in my decision, even if I knew I'd need to smooth things over with Peach later.

"Well, I guess I'll see you at tutoring tomorrow," she said with another glance toward the door as it opened and a guy in his thirties walked in.

She sagged in her seat when he joined another guy across from us.

"See you tomorrow, Abby."

"See ya." She gave me a smile that looked forced, and my gut twisted again.

How the hell was I supposed to win this girl over so she'd accept me as Foster and Bear?

I stepped outside and opened up Discord.

BigBear88:
Hey Peach, sorry to do this to you last minute, but I can't make it today.
Rain check?

BigBear88:

Hey, sorry again about today.

PeachyKeen:

Is everything okay?

BigBear88:

Sorta. I chickened out.

PeachyKeen:

…

BigBear88:

I saw you

PeachyKeen:

What?
You were there…?

BigBear88:

Yeah…

PeachyKeen:
I'm trying really hard not to take offense to the fact that you saw me and left.

BigBear88:
No! It wasn't like that.
I saw you and didn't think you'd like me
Honestly, you're way outta my league
Like rocket launch into space out of my league.

PeachyKeen:
Bear.
Are you being serious?
Because even if you were my sworn enemy, I would've wanted to know.
It's not fair that you know who I am and I don't know who you are.

BigBear88:
I know.
I'm sorry.😢
I promise I do want you to know who I am…
But not yet, okay?
I can't lose you, Peach. 🧡

The next day, I walked into the tutoring center and found Abby at our usual table. Despite the term being halfway done, there was hardly anyone here. It should've made things feel more relaxed, but the tension in Abby's body said otherwise.

Her shoulders were hunched, and the usual confident demeanor I'd grown accustomed to with her was nowhere to be found.

Guilt ate away at me.

Was this because of yesterday?

Had I screwed up and made a mistake by not telling her I was Bear?

No. I'd made the right decision.

And now I needed to activate part two of my plan, which was figuring out why she didn't like me so I could come up with a way to change her mind.

She glanced up at me and gave me a soft smile. "Hey."

"Hey."

"How'd your quiz go?"

I smiled wide and pulled my laptop out of my bag. "You're gonna need to see it to believe it."

Her lips curled up more as I opened the student portal and found my math quiz results. I spun my laptop to face her so she could see. The bold B- wasn't exactly honor roll material, but compared to my previous F, it might as well have been an A+. "I passed the midterm, and if I can keep this up, I'll definitely pass the class."

"Foster!" Abby's face lit up, and she squeezed my arm. "That's amazing!"

Her touch sent a jolt through me, and when she quickly pulled her hand away, I wondered if she'd felt it too. There was a moment of awkward silence before she cleared her throat and returned to teacher mode.

"The number tracking app I recommended—have you been using it?"

I nodded. "Every day. Ten minutes of practice, just like you said." The app was designed for people with dyscalculia, giving exercises that strengthened number recognition and sequencing. "I'm up to level four now."

"Already? That's really impressive progress."

I shrugged, trying not to look too pleased with myself. "Turns out I'm competitive even with math apps."

She laughed, and the sound made warmth fill my chest. "Who would've thought, a hockey player being competitive?"

This was new territory—Abby making jokes, being comfortable enough to tease me.

I liked it.

I wanted more of it.

"So," she said, getting back to business, "where are you still struggling?"

For the next hour we worked on my math skills.

As we were packing up, I mentioned something I'd been thinking about since yesterday. "That was a nice thing you did for that girl at the café yesterday."

Abby's cheeks flushed, and my mind veered in a dangerously dirty direction, imagining making her flush like that for a very different reason.

"Oh, well, she was just down on her luck and having a really bad day. A lot had gone wrong, and everyone experiences that at one point or another. I believe in karma and putting good juju out in the universe."

She hesitated and then added quietly and almost reluctantly. "My mom taught me that."

There was a slight catch in her voice, and it made me ache to reach out and touch her, but I didn't know if she'd appreciate that, so I kept my hands to myself.

"Are you close to your mom?" I asked.

She looked up at me and I didn't miss the shine in her eyes, although no tears fell.

"My mom died freshman year. It wasn't a good year."

"I'm so sorry," I said. It felt weak, but I didn't know what else to say. I'd never lost anyone close to me before.

"I think she'd be really proud of you," I added, dipping my head so I could make eye contact with her.

She returned it with a soft smile. "I hope so." She nibbled her lip and then admitted, "Sometimes I worry she'd be disappointed that I haven't taken more risks. I attempted to go outside my comfort zone freshman year and go to parties, but then..." Her voice faded and she shrugged.

Then her mom died.

"College parties aren't really that great. You haven't been missing much. I partied *way* too hard freshman year and I'm not proud of that. It's easy to go overboard and make choices you wouldn't otherwise. I think the freedom kind of got to me and I went a little wild." I grabbed the back of my neck. "I don't even remember most of it, which is a little embarrassing."

I don't know why I just admitted all that. If I was trying to convince her to give me a chance, sharing my mistakes was not the way to do it.

Or maybe it was because when I looked up at her, the stiffness that always seemed to be in her shoulders when I was around dissipated a little, and when she looked at me, it felt like she was seeing me for the first time.

"Foster, I have a confession to make."

Panic gripped me. Did she know I was BigBear88? "Okay," I said slowly.

"Um..." She covered her face with her hands. "We made out."

There was no way I heard her right.

"We what?"

She pulled her hands away from her face and looked completely miserable. "We made out. Freshman year, after we met at a party at the football house."

I'd partied a lot at The Den—the name given to the football house—especially freshman year when I'd gone a little too wild with my newfound independence.

I stared at her, racking my brain for any memory of kissing Abby. I'd had a few dreams about kissing her since we started tutoring, but was it possible those were rooted in memories that I couldn't recall unless I was unconscious?

How the fuck could I forget kissing this girl?

"I don't...I don't remember that," I admitted, even as my gut tightened.

As soon as the words left my mouth, I knew they were the wrong thing to say. Abby's expression shuttered, and she turned away, focusing on packing up her bag.

"Abby, I'm sorry," I said, floundering for how to fix this. "Like I told you before, freshman year is kind of a blur for me. I was drinking way too much, doing a lot of stupid things I'm not proud of."

"It's fine," she said, but her tone made it clear it was anything but fine. "It was a long time ago. It doesn't matter."

"It *does* matter," I said, reaching for her hand. She let me take it, but her fingers remained limp in mine. "Please, tell me what happened. I want to understand."

Was this the reason she had her guard up around me?

She sighed, finally meeting my eyes again. "It was the first big party of the year. Sam, my roommate, dragged me there. I'd had a crush on you since the first week of classes, and I'd had just enough to drink that I actually had the courage to talk to you. One thing led to another, and we ended up making out in your room."

I closed my eyes, trying to recall that night. There had been so many parties that year, so many faceless girls. The fact that one of them had been Abby—smart, beautiful, kind Abby—and I couldn't remember it made me feel sick.

"What happened?" I asked, dreading the answer.

Abby gave a humorless laugh. "Nothing, really. We were kissing, and then...you fell asleep."

"I *what*?" My eyes flew open in horror.

"You fell asleep," she repeated. "Mid-kiss. I thought at first you were just taking a breath, but then you started snoring."

"Fucking hell." I dropped my head into my hands, mortification washing over me. No wonder she'd been so cold to me when we first started tutoring. No wonder she'd looked at me like I was the last person she wanted to see. "Abby, I am *so* sorry."

"It's not your fault," she said, though her voice was still

tight. "You were drunk. I was drunk. It was a stupid freshman mistake."

"No, it's definitely my fault," I insisted, looking up at her. "I was an idiot freshman year. I drank too much, partied too hard, and apparently missed out on getting to know an amazing girl because I passed out like an asshole." I took her hand again, squeezing it gently. "But I'm not that guy anymore, Abby. And I promise you, if I had been sober enough to remember kissing you, I never would have forgotten it."

She looked up at me, the vulnerability in her eyes betraying the courage it took for her to confess all of this to me. It was clear by the hesitant smile she gave me that she wasn't sure she believed me.

I'd work on that.

This girl was burned onto my soul and she had no idea.

As Peach, she'd become a lifeline, but as Abby, she was someone real.

I would do whatever it took to make this right, to make her see that I was so far from that guy freshman year, it wasn't even funny.

I would prove I was worthy of her attention.

Abby Walker didn't know it yet, but I was about to woo the shit out of her.

I wasn't dumb enough to let a woman like her go again.

Bear went radio silent on me.

At first, I was relieved. It saved me from having to figure out what to say after he bailed on our in-person meetup. I was struggling with how to get back to our easy exchanges while dealing with the hurt after learning he'd seen me and still chosen not to come up and introduce himself. It had been my worst fear—the worst-case scenario about finally meeting up with him that I'd convinced myself wouldn't happen. But it had.

He said it was because I was out of his league, but was it really? Or was he just trying to make it seem that way so he wouldn't hurt my feelings more? I couldn't help but wonder if there was something else going on.

But as the hours and days ticked by with no new messages from him on our Discord chat, relief turned into something heavier.

The truth was, I missed him.

I missed our late-night messages, the dumb jokes about mayonnaise machines, the way he always knew how to make me laugh on the worst days. He'd become a constant in my life—someone I relied on and got to be goofy and ridiculous with. Losing him, even temporarily, felt like losing a part of myself that he'd helped me rediscover.

But while Bear was MIA, Foster was...not.

He showed up to every tutoring session early. He smiled when he saw me. He listened in a way that made me feel like my voice had weight and like the things I said mattered.

And slowly, subtly, he started closing the space between us. Both literally and figuratively.

At first, it was just a glance that lingered a second too long. Then, he started sitting closer—just enough that I could feel the warmth of his body radiating beside me, and occasionally feel the brush of his knee against mine.

It wasn't overt. Nothing he did crossed a line. But it felt deliberate, especially when he'd glance at me at the smallest touch and his blue eyes seemed to darken with a look I was terrified to identify.

The lingering looks, the accidental-on-purpose touches, the way his subtle, manly cologne seemed to permeate the breathing space while we worked and made me lightheaded—it was wreaking havoc on my body and mind.

Because for every flutter he caused in my stomach, or catch of my breath, there was a swell of guilt right behind it.

I wasn't supposed to like him.

Not when I had feelings for Bear.

Not when Bear and I had shared real conversations and quiet confessions and a bond that felt like more than just shared pixels and game mechanics.

I'd put Foster Kane in a box after our night together freshman year, and he was supposed to stay there as a bad decision I'd made once upon a time, but now I was starting to question if that was fair.

He clearly wasn't the party guy he'd been freshman year.

And spending three days a week with him made it impossible not to get to know him more with each tutoring session. That crush I'd had freshman year wasn't buried as deep as I thought it had been.

My nerves were a jumbled mess when I showed up to our latest tutoring session. My heart felt like it dipped in my chest when I saw he wasn't at our usual table.

I checked my phone to see if he'd texted me. He'd convinced me to exchange numbers so he could reach out if he was ever running late or needed to change our schedule. A part of me was still expecting him to use it for something else, but so far he hadn't texted me at all.

When he walked in the door with two coffee cups in hand, those butterflies once again took off in my stomach.

Coffee wasn't that big a deal. It didn't warrant the swarm that took flight or the weird giddiness that filled my chest.

I couldn't explain the emotions and feelings Foster brought out in me, and maybe that's what scared me the most.

He placed one of the cups on the table beside my laptop like it was no big deal. Like he hadn't just set off a full-on emotional crisis in my chest.

"What's this?" I asked, my voice even and not conveying in the slightest the chaos going on inside of me.

"Vanilla latte," he said casually, sliding into the seat beside me. His knee brushed against mine as he got settled, and it took everything to ignore the warmth that bloomed from that spot.

I blinked at the cup, then at him. "How'd you know?"

He shrugged like it was no big deal, but I didn't miss the subtle pink on the tops of his cheeks. "It's what you ordered at the café when I ran into you."

I hadn't even realized he'd been paying that close of attention.

His gaze caught mine and the air thickened between us. I wasn't sure either of us took a breath as we held a silent conversation with our eyes. The way he looked at me now—it wasn't how he looked at everyone else. There was a gentleness to it, almost reverent. Like he was trying to memorize my every reaction.

The words might've been unsaid, but I couldn't deny the feeling—it was one I'd felt before.

I *liked* him.

That nearly all-consuming crush I'd had before was back with a vengeance.

And I hated how much that scared me.

Because I wasn't supposed to fall for him again. Not after everything. Not when he'd once made me feel so small, even if he hadn't intended to. And definitely not when Bear existed—although hadn't he also hurt me?

I didn't know what scared me more—the possibility that Foster could hurt me again...or the possibility that he wouldn't.

Was the way I'd felt hurt with him really all that different from how Bear had made me feel?

And I couldn't deny that I knew I'd forgive Bear and move forward, so why was I holding on so tightly to the idea that I couldn't forgive Foster?

I broke our gaze and focused on the reason we were meeting.

Math was logical. It made sense.

It didn't make me feel like I was on a stormy sea on a flimsy raft.

It didn't have me questioning if someday I was going to be forced to pick between two guys who couldn't be more different, but both stirred up a confusing mix of emotions inside me.

EIGHTEEN

(UNSENT)

PeachyKeen:
Are you okay?

PeachyKeen:
I wish you had just come up to me at the coffee shop instead of making me feel unwanted.

PeachyKeen:
I miss you.

"So walk us through this? You're trying to woo this girl by bringing her coffee? No offense, man, but that's kinda weak. I thought you had more game than that."

"Monty, leave the guy alone. We all know he hasn't gotten laid in ages. I'm pretty sure lack of sex causes deterioration of the brain which would explain his weak attempts at wooing," Liam said to Drew as he passed me the puck. Born and raised in Montana, Liam still carried a trace of his mother's thick Donegal accent.

I fought against an eye roll as I flicked the puck toward Gordy in the net.

Drew Dumontier, Liam Farrell, and Harrison "Gordy" Gordon were my housemates and best friends. While Drew and Liam were only sophomores this year, Gordy was a junior with me. Drew and Liam had spent most of the summer in their hometown just a little bit south of here in Meadowbrook, Montana, while Gordy had spent the summer at his grandfather's ranch in Big Sky. But he'd come back a month before school started and Drew and Liam had driven up so we could play some pickup hockey at the local rink.

"I'm not wooing her with coffee, you jackass. It's a multi-phase process, okay? Bringing her coffee shows that I pay attention to what she likes. I have to play this carefully or I'll lose my shot."

Because if she figured out I was Bear before she was ready... I didn't even want to think about how bad that would be for my chances at winning her over.

"Multi-phase?" Liam skated past me with a laugh. "Dude, are you trying to date her or launching a rocket to Mars?"

"It's not like you couldn't get any girl you wanted on campus though," Drew said as he skated around the back of the net and passed the puck to Liam.

"I don't want anyone else. I want Abby. And once...she wanted me. I just need to remind her of that without reminding her of what an epic fuckup I was back then."

I hadn't told them about our Discord chats. That felt too private.

Liam took a shot at the net, but Gordy blocked it and then passed the puck back to me.

"So, what's phase two?" Gordy asked.

I hesitated, stick tapping the ice, then said, "Get her to actually enjoy being around me."

"Yeah, that's usually a good starting point," Liam deadpanned.

"I'm not joking. This isn't just some girl. She's"—I paused—"different. She doesn't fall for charm or flash. She's guarded. Smart as hell. Way out of my league."

I hadn't been kidding when I'd told her that as Bear. Whether she believed it or not was another issue, but as far as I was concerned, Abby was so far out of my league I might as well have been trying to plan a rocket launch to Mars like Liam had teased me about.

That earned a round of groans and dramatic eye rolls.

"Jesus," Gordy muttered. "You're one sad playlist away from becoming the plot of a CW drama."

"She's not out of your league," Liam said. "You're Foster Kane."

"That's exactly the problem," I muttered.

They didn't know the full story—just enough to give me shit when I needed it. But the truth was, Abby Walker didn't give a damn about my reputation on campus. In fact, I was pretty sure it was one of the things she held against me.

Which meant I needed something more than coffee and proximity.

I needed a way in.

"You said she's guarded," Drew said thoughtfully. "What's she into? Like...besides math and giving you disapproving looks?"

Before I could answer, Liam snapped his fingers and his eyes lit up. "You should make her something."

I blinked. "What?"

"You know—something custom. Thoughtful. Girls eat that shit up."

"Make her something?" I stared at him. I wasn't exactly an arts and crafts kind of guy, but if it would sway Abby my way, I'd try anything.

"Better than your coffee stunt," Drew said with a shrug.

"He's not wrong," Gordy added.

I didn't say anything for a minute, letting the idea sink in.

It was ridiculous.

But it was also...good.

Abby definitely seemed like the type of girl who preferred handmade gifts to something flashy and expensive.

Plus, it was exactly the kind of gesture she'd never see coming. Quiet. Personal. Maybe I could even make it *Stardew Valley* themed and broach the topic of telling her I'm Bear.

"You're serious? You think she'd like that?" I asked finally.

"Dead," Liam said. "You want to win her over? Speak her language."

"And stop being a chicken about it," Drew added. "Give her something that says, 'I see you,' not just 'I think you're hot.'"

I grinned.

For once, their trash talk was useful. Who knew these two playboys could actually come up with something genuine and heartfelt.

"I'm gonna need art supplies," I muttered.

"And a crafting playlist," Gordy said solemnly, but there was a slight twinkle in his eye.

I laughed—the first real one all day.

Maybe they were onto something.

Maybe this was how I showed Abby that Foster Kane wasn't just a walking regret from freshman year.

I could be the guy who deserved her.

BigBear88:

You know what happens to your crops when you don't water them for a week?
Nothing good.

PeachyKeen:

I get hives just thinking about it.
I hope everything was okay with you this week. You disappeared on me.

BigBear88:

I know. I'm sorry.
I needed some time away.

PeachyKeen:

From me?

BigBear88:

No. Just time to wrap my head around some things.

I didn't mean to hurt you—I just got overwhelmed and did the stupid thing where I vanish instead of talking it out.

PeachyKeen:
I'd gotten used to you being around.
It sucked when you weren't.

BigBear88:
Trust me, it sucked for me too.
I've missed you.
I thought stepping away would give me clarity and in a way, it did.
I've never connected with someone the way I connect with you. I don't want to lose you.
I can't.

PeachyKeen:
Then don't disappear on me again.
It's not cool to just pop back in and pretend everything's fine.

BigBear88:
I know.
I'm not expecting everything to go back to how it was.
But I'm hoping I can start watering the soil again.

PeachyKeen:
🙄 *That was so corny.*
But also appropriate.
No more disappearing acts.

BigBear88:
You'll see me every day.
In the mines. In the field. In the co-op barn.

PeachyKeen:

Don't forget the greenhouse. I've got ancient fruit to harvest.

BigBear88:

Ancient fruit? Damn. You really are wife material.

PeachyKeen:

Don't push your luck, Bear.

BigBear88:

Don't worry, Peach. I've got a plan.
I'll win your heart eventually. 😉❤️

PeachyKeen:

Well, looks like someone's been eating Spicy Eel.

Sam claimed this indie music festival was a personality test. So far, mine was "socially anxious with a popcorn addiction."

She had begged me for weeks, claiming I was wasting my summer working instead of experiencing the few months a year Montana was hot enough to justify shorts and sunburns. I'd resisted at first—because of crowds, noise, and the fact I preferred A/C over the eighty- to ninety-degree dry heat we had this time of year—but I caved when she bribed me with kettle corn, root beer floats, and the promise of uninterrupted indie music under the stars.

I was a sucker for good food and music.

"I can't believe you're actually here," Sam said, slipping her arm around mine as we wove through the food truck area. "Abby Walker, willingly at a festival. This is character growth."

"Let's not get carried away," I said, putting on my sunglasses. "I came for the music and snacks. Not the socializing."

"Uh-huh. Sure." Her grin grew as she focused on something to my side. "Tell that to the guy checking you out by the kettle corn stand."

I frowned and followed her gaze.

My heart felt like it slammed against my chest as my eyes landed on the guy in question.

Foster.

He was wearing a fitted navy blue T-shirt that clung in all the right places and a backward baseball hat that I knew had the Clark Fork Hockey logo on it because he'd worn it to tutoring a few times. I'd nearly gone into cardiac arrest the first time he lifted it, ran his fingers through his hair, and then twisted it around so he was wearing it backward. I don't know why the move was so hot, but I was sure I was going to melt into a puddle when he did it.

The reaction my body had to him now wasn't far off from that first response.

His aviators were hanging from his shirt collar since he was standing in the shadow of the food stand, and he had a long bag of popcorn in hand.

He was staring straight at me, and the corners of his lips lifted up as we made eye contact.

I froze. Sam squeezed my arm reassuringly as she whispered, "Stay cool."

Foster walked toward us, a guy with pitch-black hair walking next to him.

His eyes were bright and his smile wide when he reached us. "Hey."

"Hey," I echoed, trying to sound breezy, like my stomach hadn't just done a somersault at that smile.

"I'm Sam," my best friend said beside me when Foster and I had been staring at each other just a beat too long.

He extended his hand. "Nice to meet you."

Before I could worry that he might find Sam attractive—

because who wouldn't?—he focused back on me. He gestured to the guy next to him. "This is Gordy."

"Gordy? Is that your real name?" Sam asked.

"Harrison Gordon. Gordy is a nickname."

Sam hummed softly beside me. "I think I'll call you Harry."

Gordy arched a brow and looked like he was preparing to be offended. "Like Harry Potter?"

Sam's smile grew. "No, like Prince Harry. You've got that regal air about you."

Gordy tilted his head, clearly weighing whether to be flattered or offended. "As long as it's not Harry Potter, I'll allow it."

Sam grinned. "I mean, you do have the dark hair and tragic backstory look about you, but Prince Harry is hotter than Harry Potter."

Foster chuckled, and I couldn't help but smile as their banter eased the tension slightly.

"Are you guys headed anywhere specific?" Foster asked.

"Just wandering," Sam replied. "We caught some of the earlier sets, but now we're mostly hunting shade and snacks."

"Same," Gordy said.

"You want to walk together for a bit?" I wasn't sure if I was imagining it or not, but Foster asked the question as if my answer would determine whether or not he enjoyed the rest of the festival.

The question itself was casual, but the way he asked it—like it genuinely mattered to him what I said—made my heart stutter.

"Sure," I said, looping my thumb through the strap of my crossbody purse because I needed something to do with my hands.

We fell into step, the four of us drifting toward the tree-lined edge of the field where a local band was setting up. The music had quieted during the changeover, and the air was full of low conversation and the occasional burst of laughter from larger groups.

Sam and Gordy walked ahead, and based on the snippets of their conversation, Sam was doing her best to make Gordy blush. But then she glanced back and gave me a subtle wink, and I caught on to exactly what she was doing—trying to give Foster and me a little space.

"This is a good look for you," Foster said after a moment, pulling my attention away from Sam and Gordy.

I arched a brow. "Sweaty and borderline sunburnt?"

He smiled. "No. Relaxed." He gripped the back of his neck, and the move showed off his biceps in a way that had my mouth watering. "I didn't expect to see you here," he said. "You strike me as the type who'd rather spend a Saturday mining for gold than sweating through a music festival."

I stared at him for a beat. "Did you just make a gaming reference?"

Normally, that's exactly what I'd be doing in *Stardew Valley* along with teasing Bear about his failing crops. But there was no way Foster could know that unless he'd figured out how little of a social life I really had.

He laughed. "Maybe. You just strike me as the type. But I gotta admit, I like this version of you. The one that comes out in the sun and listens to sad indie ballads."

"Only because Sam dragged me here."

"I owe her a thank you then."

That caught me off guard. "You owe her?"

"For convincing you to show up. Otherwise, I'd be stuck

debating Gordy on whether or not banjos have a place in modern music instead of getting to know you better."

I smiled despite myself. "And what's the verdict on banjos?"

"He says no. Passionately. Like, full TED Talk-level opposition."

I laughed—it was surprisingly easy to be around Foster like this.

It was the first time we'd really hung out—sober and without math tutoring as an excuse—and it was nice to feel so relaxed in his presence.

But it didn't make my confusion about him and Bear any easier. If anything, seeing Foster like this was making me even more confused.

We kept walking without speaking, our feet crunching softly on the gravel path that curved through the booths and shaded tents. The band on stage started playing something soft with slow beats and smooth vocals that had me relaxing even more.

Maybe coming to this festival hadn't been such a bad idea after all.

TWENTY-TWO

Foster

I'd been looking forward to this festival for weeks, but now all I could focus on was Abby. Even when I was looking at the stage, I was hyperaware of her presence beside me—the way the wind sometimes blew her silky light brown hair against my arm, the way she'd hum in the back of her throat and close her eyes when she took a bite of kettle corn.

I'd already made a mental note to always have kettle corn on hand if this was her reaction.

If she moaned one more time, there would be no way to hide how hard her sounds made me.

"So," I said, trying to sound casual. "Be honest—how close were you to faking a stomachache to get out of coming today?"

She smiled, a little crooked and a little shy. "Closer than I'd like to admit."

"I figured since you said you don't really do stuff like this." I nudged her lightly with my shoulder. "But you're glad you came, right?"

Her eyes flicked toward mine, and something shifted in the air between us. "Yeah," she said quietly. "I think I am."

When the set was over, we decided to walk around and explore some of the booths. None of us were in a rush, and I was grateful that Sam and Gordy seemed to get along, so I could have some time with Abby. I hadn't expected to run into her here, but I couldn't deny it was helping move my plans along faster than I could've ever hoped for.

She was different today—far less guarded than she used to be with me.

"That's a good color on you," she said casually before stuffing some popcorn in her mouth.

I looked down at my blue shirt. "Yeah?"

"It brings out the blue in your eyes." Her cheeks flushed pink and I knew it wasn't from the heat. I don't think she'd meant to say that, but I'd already tucked it away in my memory. If she liked me in this color, I'd fill my closet full of it.

We stopped by one of the booths that Sam wanted to look at. While we were standing there, Abby tipped her popcorn bag toward me. "Want some?"

Just then, the breeze picked up and a strand of her hair flew across her cheek. Without thinking, I reached up and brushed it away from her face, tucking it behind her ear.

Her breath caught and my gut clenched with so much need, my knees almost shook.

Fuck, I wanted to kiss her, to touch her, to make her fall apart beneath me.

My fingers hovered for a second too long, but she didn't pull back. Her eyes were locked on mine, wide and uncertain, but also filled with what looked undeniably like the desire I was sure was reflected in my gaze.

If I leaned in, even a little, I knew what would happen.

And I wanted it more than my next breath.

But I wasn't sure if she was ready for everything I wanted.

So I didn't close the distance and kiss her like I was dying to.

Instead, I let my hand fall away, slowly, like I was trying not to spook her.

Her throat bobbed, and she looked away first, breaking the spell. "You're different outside of tutoring," she said after a moment, like she needed to fill the quiet.

"Yeah? Better or worse?"

Her lips twitched and her eyes filled with a playfulness that I was quickly growing addicted to. "Still deciding."

I chuckled. "Fair. Let me know what I need to do to earn brownie points and I'll do it."

Her cheeks flushed the prettiest shade of pink. "I'll keep that in mind."

Sam was still looking at the art prints and Gordy was watching her attentively.

"Wanna take a seat while they shop?"

"Sure."

We ended up at the edge of the field again, near a half-shaded spot under a tree. It wasn't exactly private, but it felt removed enough.

She sat first and tucked her legs underneath her while I dropped down beside her, resting my arms on my knees and pretending like I wasn't still buzzing from our almost kiss.

"I wish I remembered," I said before I could think the words through.

"Remembered what?"

"Freshman year."

"The night we kissed?" she asked, her voice quiet.

I nodded. "I haven't been able to stop thinking about it since you told me. I remember...flashes. I remember being in my room, the party, someone laughing in my ear. I remember music. But not the kiss, and I hate that I don't. Especially now."

She looked over at me, her expression unreadable. "Why now?"

I held her gaze. "Because if I could go back, I wouldn't waste it. I wouldn't drink myself stupid. I'd remember every second."

Her eyes widened, and for a breathless moment, she didn't speak. Her lips parted slightly, like she was going to say something—but then she looked away again.

"I should probably find Sam," she said, pushing herself to her feet.

I stood with her, not wanting the moment to end but knowing it had to.

She looked up at me. "Thanks for hanging out. This was nice."

"Anytime, Abby."

I meant it.

Something had shifted between us today and it gave me hope.

Later that night...

PeachyKeen:

Bear, I need a distraction.

Know any good Stardew mods that keep you from making stupid romantic choices?

BigBear88:

None that I've found.

If you download one, send it my way.

PeachyKeen:

I might be in trouble.

I think I've got a thing for someone. And not in a "hot farmhand"
kind of way.

BigBear88:

Is it serious?

PeachyKeen:

Feels like a soft panic attack. But with butterflies.

BigBear88:

Sounds like a crush to me.

Want my advice?

PeachyKeen:

Always.

BigBear88:

If he's got half a brain, he's already falling back.

It was time for Phase Three.

"What the fuck happened here?"

I looked up from where I was gluing the final piece of the diorama I made for Abby. I'd spent more time scouring Pinterest than I ever thought was possible before I stumbled on the idea of a homemade diorama that looks like her farm —or at least it was supposed to.

"This wasn't as easy as it looks."

"It doesn't look like it was easy at all." Gordy scanned the mess that covered our kitchen table, half the counter, and had somehow managed to get on the floor.

"Is that glitter?"

"Uh, yeah. The woman at the craft store talked me into it."

He shook his head. "We're never getting rid of that now. They'll be finding glitter in here for years to come. Forget rebuilding the hockey team as our legacy. It'll be that this house was glitter bombed."

I sat back in my chair with a heavy sigh. "This shit was hard, okay?! Haven't you ever had to make one of these?"

"Not since the second grade." Gordy leaned in to inspect the diorama. "Is that...a chicken coop?"

"It's a barn," I muttered. "But I messed up the proportions."

He blinked. "*That's* a barn?"

"Look, I didn't go to art school, okay? The important part is the idea behind it."

Gordy scratched the back of his neck. "Which is?"

I stood and paced a few steps, dragging a glitter-covered hand through my hair and immediately regretting it. "It's a *Stardew Valley* diorama. You know, that farming game."

"I know *of* it, but I've never played it."

"Well, Abby does." Time for brutal honesty. "And so do I. In fact, I've been playing *with* her for months. Online."

Gordy's brow furrowed. "Weird that you didn't mention that when we ran into her at the festival."

"Yeah, well...she doesn't exactly know that I'm her online friend," I exhaled.

His eyes widened. "Are you catfishing her?"

"No!" I sat back down. "No. I didn't know it was her at first, and by the time I did, I knew she'd never accept me as Bear."

"Bear?"

"BigBear88."

He laughed. "You used the name of your childhood dog and your hockey jersey number for your handle?"

I gave him a look. "Not the time, man."

He sobered. "Okay, so let me get this straight. You've been secretly playing a farming game online with a girl who turned out to be the tutor you're crushing on?"

"Yeah."

"And now you need to find a way to tell her the truth without her losing her shit on you."

"Pretty much."

"Shit."

"I know."

He took a seat across from my chair. "When are you planning to tell her?"

"This week. It's our last week of tutoring, so I was planning to use that as an excuse to maybe go somewhere else, do something fun to celebrate, and then I would give her this and tell her the truth."

I hadn't been sure about the timing, but her reaction to me at the festival gave me hope that this wouldn't blow up spectacularly in my face.

He let out a slow breath, then nudged the glittery base of the diorama with one finger. "Well... for what it's worth, this is actually kinda sweet. Messier than I thought it would be. But sweet."

"I'm banking on the effort winning me points."

"She's into you, man," he said quietly. "Why do you think I spent so much time with her roommate at the festival? It was clear you two were feeling each other."

I sat back down and stared at the tiny barn, the mini crops I'd glued in with tweezers, and the hand-lettered sign I'd made that said, "To Peach, from Bear."

"I hope you're right."

Because this was either going to be the moment that changed everything...or the last time I ever got to be part of her story.

So far my plan was off to a great start.

When I'd showed up for my final tutoring session, I

convinced Abby to let me take her somewhere. It wasn't all that hard to convince her, especially after I reassured her that I felt confident about using the skills she'd taught me on my final.

She'd given me the tools and confidence to pass math—now I just needed to use that confidence to win her heart.

Instead, I was nervous as hell.

I kept sneaking glances at Abby as I drove, trying not to be too obvious about it. She looked stunning tonight. Not that she didn't always look pretty, but there was something different about her now—maybe it was the way her hair fell in shiny waves around her face, or the way that red sweater brought out flecks of gold in her brown eyes. Or maybe it was just seeing her outside the tutoring center, knowing she was here because she wanted to be. Not for class. Not out of obligation. Just...for me.

"Are we going to the movies?" she asked, peering out the window as we passed the downtown theater.

I grinned. "Nope."

"Dinner?"

"Not exactly, though I did bring snacks." I nodded toward the back seat where I'd stashed a thermos of hot chocolate and a cooler with cookies, some fruit, and other treats I thought she might like.

Her brow furrowed adorably. "The bowling alley?"

"Wrong again." I turned onto the road that led to the rink where our team practiced. "One more guess."

She looked around, recognition dawning as the familiar building came into view. "The ice rink?"

"Yep," I said, pulling into the empty parking lot. "I called in a favor. We've got the place to ourselves for two hours."

Her eyes widened, a mix of excitement and apprehension crossing her face. "I told you I don't know how to skate."

We'd talked about it at one of our tutoring sessions.

"I know. But you also said you've always wanted to learn. So...I was thinking I could teach you."

I parked and turned to face her fully. "Is that okay? We can do something else if you'd rather."

She bit her lip, considering, then a small smile spread across her face. "No, this is...it's perfect, actually. I can't believe you remembered I said that."

"I remember everything you say," I admitted, my chest tight. I'd been thinking about getting her on the ice since she first mentioned it. And there was something about teaching her how to do something that was such an integral part of my identity that made me feel like if she liked it, then maybe she'd like me.

I got out and circled around to open her door, then reached into the trunk to pull out a gift bag. "Here. These are for you."

Abby took the bag with a curious expression, then gasped as she pulled out a pair of white figure skates. "Foster, you didn't have to—"

"I wanted to," I said, a little nervous now. "The rentals are pretty terrible, and I thought...well, if you liked skating, you should have your own pair. If they don't fit, we can exchange them."

She ran her fingers over the white skates, her smile soft and genuine. "They're beautiful. Thank you."

"You're welcome." I grabbed my hockey bag and the cooler, ignoring the diorama tucked behind her seat—I was saving that for later. "Ready to hit the ice?"

The rink was eerily quiet as we walked in, our footsteps

echoing in the empty space. I flipped on the lights and led Abby to a bench near the rink entrance.

"I've never been here when it's so empty," she said, looking around. "It's kind of magical."

I smiled, pleased by her reaction. "Have you secretly been coming to my games all this time?" I teased her.

Her cheeks flushed. "I came to your first game freshman year."

Her admission filled my chest with warmth, but I didn't want to bring too much attention to our past by commenting on it. The only thing that mattered was our future.

I set down my bag and pulled out my skates, then gestured to hers. "Let's see if those fit you."

Abby sat beside me and pulled off her boots, then slipped her feet into the figure skates. "They're perfect," she said, sounding surprised. "How did you know my size?"

"I may have asked Sam," I admitted. It hadn't been hard to get her number and ask her a few questions. If anything, I'd been surprised that she'd been so eager to give me the details I needed without giving me the third degree.

Abby's eyes seemed brighter than normal when she looked at me, and her smile made my heart do a weird little flip in my chest. I'd been on plenty of dates before, but none had ever made me feel like this.

This wasn't even officially a date, but fuck did I want it to be.

"Here, let me help you with those," I offered, kneeling in front of her. I showed her how to properly lace the skates, making sure they were tight enough to support her ankles but not so tight they'd cut off circulation. My fingers brushed against her calves, and I tried to ignore the electric feeling that shot through me at the contact.

"Thanks," she said softly when I finished, her eyes

meeting mine. For a moment, I forgot what we were doing, lost in the warmth of her gaze.

Did she have any idea how badly I wanted her? The lengths I was willing to go to win her heart?

"Um, right," I said, clearing my throat and standing up. "Let's get you on the ice."

I put on my own skates quickly, then stood and offered her my hands. "First rule of skating—it's all about balance."

Abby took my hands, her grip firm as she stood shakily. "I feel like I'm on stilts."

I laughed. "You'll get used to it. Walk with me to the entrance. Keep your knees slightly bent and your weight centered."

She took a few tentative steps, wobbling but managing to stay upright. "This is harder than it looks."

"You're doing great," I assured her as we reached the rink entrance. I stepped onto the ice first, then turned to face her, still holding her hands. "Okay, now step onto the ice. I've got you."

Abby took a deep breath and placed one skate on the ice, then the other. Her fingers tightened around mine as she tried to find her balance. "Oh my God," she breathed, looking down at her feet. "How do you make this look so easy?!"

"A lot of practice," I said with a grin. "You're doing great. Better than most beginners. You haven't even fallen."

"Don't jinx me," she warned, but she was smiling too.

I kept hold of her hands and started skating backward slowly, pulling her gently along with me. "The key is to keep your weight forward. If you lean back, you'll fall on your butt."

She nodded, concentrating hard on her feet. "Forward. Got it."

"And relax your ankles a bit. You're too stiff."

"Easy for you to say," she muttered. "You've been doing this since you were what, five?"

"Four, actually," I said. "But everyone starts somewhere. Don't be afraid to fall. It's part of learning."

She took a shaky breath. "I'll try to remember that when I'm flat on my back."

"If you fall, I'll help you up," I promised. "But let's try to keep you vertical for now. Ready to try moving on your own?"

Abby nodded, determination setting her jaw. I slowly released one of her hands, keeping a firm grip on the other. "Push off with the side of your blade, like this,"—I demonstrated with my foot—"then glide and repeat with the other foot."

She mimicked my movement, wobbling a bit but managing to propel herself forward. "I'm doing it!" she exclaimed, her face lighting up with pure joy.

My chest tightened at her expression. She looked so beautiful like this—cheeks flushed, eyes bright, her usual reserve forgotten in the excitement of learning something new. I wanted to see her look like that all the time.

"You're a natural," I said, and I meant it. For someone who'd never skated before, she was picking it up quickly. But I shouldn't have been surprised. I suspected that Abby excelled at anything she set her mind to.

We made a slow circuit around the rink, Abby gaining confidence with each stride. She was still wobbly and relied heavily on my support, but she hadn't fallen, and her smile hadn't dimmed.

"This is amazing," she said, looking around at the empty rink. "I can't believe I waited this long to try it."

"Better late than never," I replied, enjoying the warmth

of her hand in mine. "Want to try a full lap without stopping?"

She bit her lip, then nodded. "Let's do it."

We picked up the pace slightly, and I watched as Abby concentrated on her movements, her tongue peeking out between her lips in focus. It was adorable, but I bit back my smile because I didn't want her to be self-conscious, especially not when she was doing so well. We were about halfway around when her skate caught on something, and she lurched forward with a startled cry.

I reacted instinctively, catching her around the waist and pulling her against me to keep her upright. She crashed into my chest, her hands grabbing my shoulders for balance. For a moment, we just stood there, breathing hard, our faces inches apart.

"You okay?" I asked, my voice coming out rougher than I intended.

She nodded, her eyes wide. "Thanks to you."

I should have let her go then, made sure she was steady on her skates before continuing our lesson. But I couldn't bring myself to release her. She felt too perfect in my arms with her warm body pressed against mine.

"Foster," she said quietly, and something in her voice made my heart race.

"Yeah?"

"I think... I think I'd like to try again."

For a second, I thought she meant skating, but then she reached up and wrapped her hand around the back of my head, pulling me closer to her, until our lips were almost brushing and my brain short-circuited. I swallowed hard, my gaze dropping to her lips.

"Are you sure?" I asked, giving her a chance to back away if I'd misread the situation.

Instead of answering, she rose up on her toe picks and pressed her lips to mine.

The kiss was gentle at first, tentative, as if she was testing the waters. But then I responded, letting out a deep groan as I slid one hand up to cup the back of her neck. She melted against me and her mouth softened under mine. I kissed her slowly, savoring the moment I'd been thinking about for weeks.

She tasted like mint and something sweet, and when her fingers threaded through my hair, I pulled her closer, deepening the kiss. She made a small sound in the back of her throat that nearly undid me.

If I thought I'd been enamored with her before, it was nothing to how I felt now with her lips on mine. It felt like I'd spent my whole life lost at sea and she was my lighthouse guiding me home. We were a perfect fit and I never wanted it to end.

When we finally broke apart, we were both breathing hard. I rested my forehead against hers, unwilling to put any more distance between us than necessary.

"Wow," I breathed, a smile tugging at my lips.

The moment the word left my mouth, Abby stiffened in my arms. Her hands dropped from my neck, and she took a step back, nearly losing her balance on the ice.

"Abby?" I reached for her, confused by the sudden change. "What's wrong?"

"Nothing," she said, but her voice was tight, and she wouldn't meet my eyes. "I just... I think I need a break."

"Sure. We can take a break, maybe have some hot chocolate, if you want."

She let me help her off the ice, but as soon as we reached the bench, she dropped my hand and busied herself with unlacing her skates. The easy warmth between us had vanished, replaced by a tension I didn't understand.

"Did I do something wrong?" I asked, sitting beside her. "If I misread the situation—"

"No, it's not that," she said quickly, still not looking at me. "The kiss was... it was nice."

Nice? Nice was not what a guy wanted to hear when the kiss for him had been earth-shatteringly good.

But it felt like something else had happened after that kiss—something I was missing. Everything had been going so well, and then suddenly it wasn't. "Please, Abby. Talk to me."

She finally looked up, and the vulnerability in her eyes felt like a punch to the gut. "I-I don't know if I should've done that. This wasn't supposed to happen. You weren't supposed to be so...fun and wonderful and attractive. You weren't supposed to make me feel like this."

"Like what?"

"Like butterflies have taken permanent residence in my stomach, and my heart is constantly racing, and...honestly, just confused."

"Confused about what?"

She hesitated and then the words came out in a rush. "I haven't been completely honest with you. There's...there's someone else. Another guy I've been talking to for a while... someone I thought maybe I had feelings for."

Bear. She was talking about Bear.

It was time to tell her the full truth.

"I had something I needed to tell you tonight too, but I think it might be easier if I show you."

She gave me a quizzical look and then followed my lead in taking off her skates. When we had our street shoes back on, I stretched out my hand. "Come with me."

TWENTY-FOUR

I followed Foster out of the rink in silence, my pulse thudding in my ears while I tried to wrap my head around what I'd just done.

I'd kissed him.

With his arms wrapped around me and our breath mingling, the only thing I'd been able to think about was if his lips felt as good as I remembered.

My memory wasn't even close.

Because his kiss felt better than any memory I could've scrounged up.

But then when I'd pulled back, it was like a record scratch went off in my head.

What about Bear?

I tried to tell myself I didn't owe Bear anything. He's the one who'd bailed on meeting me.

But I still felt guilty—because I liked him.

And I liked Foster.

God, how had this gotten so complicated?

Never in a million years did I think I'd ever find myself in this type of situation.

I wrapped my arms around myself as we stepped into the cold night air. The warmth from the kiss—his hands, his mouth, his steady voice—had faded into this trembling uncertainty. I felt like I'd just split myself in two.

He walked next to me, just as silent and seemingly lost in his own thoughts. What was he thinking?

When we got to his truck, he opened the back passenger door and grabbed something off the floor behind my seat.

I thought I was confused before, but now I was super confused.

What the hell was that?

It looked like a box, but it was clunky, uneven, and covered in glitter.

And then he spun it around and I realized it wasn't just a box.

It was a diorama like something elementary school kids make.

Inside were mini crops, a little wooden house, and tiny pathways lined with trees. It took a second too long to register the significance.

It was *my farm*. The one I'd built in *Stardew Valley*. The one Bear had complimented—and teased me about— night after night.

"Foster?" I whispered, the words barely audible because this couldn't be happening.

He held the diorama between us and stepped closer. His eyes searched mine, and I didn't miss the hint of fear, like he was bracing for a storm.

"I made this for you," he said, voice low. "Every piece of it. Took me forever and I still managed to mess up the barn."

My throat felt tight. "Why?"

"Because there's something I need you to know. Something I should've told you weeks ago, but I didn't know how." He glanced down, then back at me. "I'm Bear."

For a second, I couldn't breathe. The world went still. There was no wind, no traffic, no sound except my heart throwing itself against my ribs like it wanted out.

"No," I said automatically, shaking my head. "No, you're not. Bear is... he's—"

"Me," he repeated, stepping closer. "I'm BigBear88. You're PeachyKeen. We met on that server in January, remember? You posted a screenshot of your farm and I asked if Lewis ever paid you back."

My knees nearly buckled. Because I remembered that.

I remembered everything.

The way Bear listened. The way he noticed the smallest things. The way he never pushed, but always seemed to know what I needed before I said it.

And now Foster was standing in front of me telling me he was the online friend that had become a lifeline for me.

"I don't understand," I whispered.

Logically, I did, but I couldn't wrap my head around who I'd known as Bear and what I'd known about Foster. Maybe there were some similarities, but if someone had told me they were the same person, I would've sworn up and down it was impossible.

But apparently I would've been wrong.

"I didn't know it was you at first," he rushed out. "When we started tutoring, I had no idea. But then when we were supposed to meet at the café—"

"You were there. You talked to me."

"I did."

He'd talked to me and then he'd left and Bear had messaged me, bailing. The betrayal that he had seen me and walked away cut deep, and it took everything in me to swallow down the painful emotions bubbling up into my throat. Tears burned behind my eyes, but I blinked them away.

"Why didn't you tell me then?" My voice was choked, but I needed to know the truth.

"I should've. I almost did. But I was scared you'd think it was all some trick or that I was messing with you."

I crossed my arms, a fresh wave of emotion crashing into me before I could brace for it. "You mean like a guy who made me feel safe just so he could pull the rug out from under me?"

His jaw tensed. "Yeah. Like that. But that's not what this is. I swear."

I stared at the diorama, my vision swimming. I could see the details in every part of it. The orchard I built in spring. The coop where I said I wanted to name all my chickens after historical women. The pond I told him I wished I had in real life, just so I could sit beside it and think.

It might've been messy, but I couldn't deny that he'd captured it well.

He took a step toward me, and I hated that I was torn between wanting him even closer and pushing him away. "I didn't mean to lie, and I swear to you, I didn't keep it from you to mess with your head. I kept it because...I didn't want to lose you. Not as Bear. Not as me. Abby, you have no idea how much you mean to me. Sometimes you're the only bright spot in my day. But I knew how you felt about me, especially after you told me about what happened freshman year. I was sure that if you knew who Bear was before you'd gotten to know the real me, that I'd lose you. I couldn't risk that."

Tears threatened, but I blinked them back again. I

wasn't ready to give in to the part of me that wanted to believe him.

This was too much to grasp.

"I need some time," I whispered, my voice hoarse.

Foster's shoulders hunched, even as he nodded. "I'll drive you home."

TWENTY-FIVE

Coach Maxwell blew the whistle, and we all skated to center ice, our breath fogging in the crisp air of the rink. The guy wasn't much older than we were—late twenties— but he had an air about him that demanded respect. He crossed his arms over his chest, watching us with a keen eye, then his stern expression broke into a grin.

"Alright, guys," he called out. "Time to see if you actually belong on this team or if I've inherited a bunch of—"

"Hold up, Coach," Liam interrupted, twirling his stick in his gloved hand with a flourish. "Before you go insulting Gordy's summer training regimen, I think we should have a moment of silence for his dreams of interpretive dance on ice."

Gordy sighed dramatically and shook his head, but he was too reserved to take Liam's bait.

Drew snickered. "Yeah, well, at least Gordy's 'dreams' stay in the rink. Unlike some people," he said pointedly to Liam, "who dream of being the campus welcome wagon, one horizontal hula at a time."

"Funny, Monty," Liam deadpanned, "coming from a

guy who got undressed so many times last season, people thought he was moonlighting as a streaker."

We all burst out laughing, even Drew, who took off his glove long enough to flip Liam off before putting it back on and settling into his stance. "Alright, alright, touché. Let's just get this over with. Who's taking first shots?"

I grinned, tapping my stick against the ice. "I got this."

Coach clapped his hands. "Alright, Kane. Show me what you got."

I scooped up a puck and took off toward Gordy, my skates cutting sharp lines across the ice. He squared up, locked in, but I'd played against him long enough to know his tells. His left pad always dropped a fraction too early when he anticipated a shot. Exploiting it was like breathing at this point.

As I closed in, I faked a wrist shot and waited. Sure enough, his pad twitched just enough for me to see the opening. At the last second, I pulled the puck across my body and flicked it high, right over his blocker and into the net.

"Boom!" I crowed, pumping a fist as pride filled me.

Liam quickly deflated it with a shout. "Candy Kane delivers."

I groaned. "Can we *please* retire that nickname?"

It wasn't even original. With a last name like Kane, I'd heard it far too often.

"Not a chance, sweetheart," Drew said, slapping my helmet. "Textbook Kane. You practically patented that move," he said with a head nod toward our goalie.

Gordy scowled as he fished the puck out of the net. "It's the *only* move you've got, Kane."

"Hey, if it works, it works. Maybe if you finally stopped

telegraphing your every move like a damn carrier pigeon, I wouldn't take advantage."

Coach chuckled and gestured for Liam and Drew to take their turns. "Alright, Farrell, Dumontier—let's see if you can do better than the hotshot."

Liam went first, his movements deceptively smooth for such a big guy. He was a defenseman with Drew, but he moved with a fluid grace that made me suspect he could easily play any position we put him in. He came in from the side, deking left and right so fast that even I could barely track the puck. Gordy tried to follow, but Liam waited until the last possible second to lift the puck, roofing it just under the crossbar.

Drew whistled. "Damn, Li."

Liam smirked. "Hey, maybe if *some* people spent less time practicing their 'naked and afraid' routine, they'd have time to improve their game."

Drew groaned. "One time. It happened *one* time." And Liam was one to talk considering he was caught with his pants down far more often than Drew. But Drew had a propensity for having sex in public and trying not to get caught. Unfortunately, one of those public places had been our rival's locker room—where he got caught mid-thrust with the rival captain's ex.

Coach shook his head, amused. "I don't care what you do off the ice, Dumontier. Just put the puck in the back of the net."

"Yes, sir," Drew said before speeding in on Gordy. He faked Gordy out completely, dragging the puck out wide and flipping it in on his backhand.

I grinned. "Oof, Gordy, you might want to check your pulse. That's three for three."

Gordy threw his glove down. "I hate all of you."

Coach laughed and blew the whistle again. "Alright, enough chirping. Let's run it again. Faster this time. Gordy, work on your tells. If Kane can figure them out, then so can our opponents."

We all got back in line, the teasing still flying between us, but our focus sharpened. The season was coming, and we were going to be ready.

After practice, we walked into the locker room, sweaty and desperately in need of showers. It was still the butt crack of dawn, but we all had classes that we needed to get to. The teasing from the ice carried over as we got cleaned up and ready for the rest of our day. My mood was light as I bent over to lace up my boot.

Every day that started with hockey was a good day.

But then I checked my phone and my high from practice faded.

For two weeks, I hadn't heard a word from Abby—or Peach.

The silence was slowly killing me.

I tucked my phone back in my bag and sat on the bench, running a towel over my face to hide the frown I couldn't quite suppress.

"You good, Kane?" Liam asked.

"Yeah," I lied. "Just tired."

"You know they'll figure it out, eventually. They're too nosey, so you might as well just tell them," Gordy said.

"Tell us what?" Drew asked like an eager puppy with the nose for gossip.

But Gordy was right. We all lived together, so they'd find out eventually.

"I messed up with Abby."

I gave them the *SparkNotes* version.

Enough to get the gist, but without going into the nitty-gritty details that felt far too personal to share.

I didn't say anything about how I still opened our Discord chat sometimes just to stare at the last message she'd sent me before everything got fucked up.

Drew whistled. "Dude. That's rough."

"Yeah," I said, running my hand through my hair. "Kind of feels like I broke something I don't know how to fix."

Liam slumped onto the bench across from me. "You told her the truth, though, yeah?"

"Yeah."

"Then you did what you were supposed to do. Doesn't make it easier, but it means the ball's in her court now."

"You regret telling her?" Gordy asked quietly.

"No," I said immediately. "I just... I hate that it hurt her. That I couldn't find the right way to do it."

"Sometimes there's no right way," he said. "Just the honest one."

I nodded, but the weight in my chest didn't budge. It had been sitting there since the moment I'd dropped her off at home after the skating rink. I'd watched her until the building door had closed behind her.

She hadn't looked back once.

I kept waiting for the guilt to get lighter. For the ache to dull.

It hadn't.

Drew slapped my shoulder. "For what it's worth, I don't think it's over."

I looked up.

"Yeah, she ghosted you. But if she really didn't care, you'd be blocked, not benched."

"Or it means she doesn't know how to say goodbye," I said, voice low.

"Yeah, well...you won't know unless she says it." Liam stood and grabbed his hoodie from his locker. "Until then, show up. That's what Coach says, right? Keep showing up."

"Even if I'm benched?"

"Especially then."

They filtered out one by one, joking and arguing about breakfast burritos versus breakfast sandwiches like we hadn't just had an entire emotional intervention in the locker room.

I stayed back for a minute, sitting in the quiet.

I didn't know what Abby was thinking.

But I knew exactly how I felt.

And I wasn't ready to let her go.

TWENTY-SIX

If there was one thing I didn't like about being the captain of CFU's hockey team, it was coming up with fundraising ideas.

As a club team, we weren't given athletic funds like recognized sports, and instead had to put on fundraisers or pay for everything ourselves. Our campus government had a certain allotment for clubs, but hockey was a fucking expensive sport, and it barely made a dent. We basically used it to pay for our coach.

On top of the cost of uniforms and equipment, we also had to pay for travel and the use of the local rink, although the owner had given us a deal because he was an alumnus and a huge Lumberjacks hockey fan.

For once, I was grateful for all the admin tasks my dad had made me do—organizing, reaching out to businesses, negotiating—because they helped me land better contracts and cut down our travel costs.

But we still had to come up with the funds to do it, which was why we were trying to figure out a new fundraising venture that would last a while.

So after our hockey practice on Wednesday, Drew, Liam, Gordy, and I went back to our house, which had been given the unoriginal name of "the hockey house."

It was in between the Den—best known for the killer parties the football guys hosted—and the music house, which never seemed to party at all.

"Okay, okay, I've got it," Liam said, standing up with his hands spread out like he was trying to captivate the whole room.

"Spit it out already," Gordy said.

Liam had spent the last five minutes saying he had a genius idea, and our patience was all running thin.

We'd already tried the usual fundraiser avenues—restaurant takeovers, car washes, etc.

"We should have a hockey player auction or dance revue like that one Christmas movie that came out on Netflix."

Drew turned to him. "*Merry Gentleman*? You actually watched that?"

Liam shrugged off his best friend's disbelief. "The girl I wanted to hook up with wanted to watch it, okay?"

Why was I not surprised that this idea stemmed from an experience with a girl? Every time Liam had a story or idea, it had something to do with a girl. Liam was the biggest playboy of anyone I'd ever met, and had a new girl practically every week.

Our campus was big, but not *that* big.

I didn't know how any girl still put up with his antics.

"Okay, movie aside, a guy auction probably isn't a bad idea," Drew said.

I shook my head. "No way. We won't be able to get approval for that."

Not to mention I couldn't stand the thought of spending

time with any woman besides Abby—even if she was currently freezing me out.

"I'm not taking my shirt off in front of an audience," Gordy added. He was more reserved and upper-crust than the rest of us. His family was very well-off and had a summer home in Big Sky, while they spent the rest of the year either in New York or Connecticut or wherever rich folks lived on the East Coast. Gordy had been kind of stingy on the details.

He'd come to CFU because his grandpa had grown up in Montana, and he loved it here and wanted to get as far away from his parents and city life as he could.

I rubbed my forehead. "Okay, we need serious ideas that we can run through the club board."

All club activities had to be pre-approved by the university's club board. A couple of years ago, one club threw a kegger and called it "Kegs for a Cure" claiming all the money went to cancer research. The money had in fact gone to support breast cancer research, but the university had fielded tons of calls from locals who'd been pissed when word got out. So the student government had created the club board to oversee club fundraisers. Any club who ran a fundraiser without pre-approval faced getting shut down.

We couldn't afford that risk when we were still a relatively new club after a fifteen-year hiatus that ended my freshman year. Maybe that was why I felt so much pressure to see our team find roots on campus. I'd been integral in building this program into what it was, and I didn't want to see it fail.

"What about a Las Vegas night where we create a casino vibe?" Liam threw out.

We all looked at him.

"Gambling? For a fundraiser?" Gordy asked, his brows raised.

"Hey, I heard about a house that did it not that long ago. They did it to raise money for replanting trees or something."

"Yeah, no," we all said at the same time.

He threw his hands in the air. "Fine, I give up. I'm not coming up with any more ideas because you guys keep shooting me down."

Drew laughed at him. "Because your ideas will get us kicked off campus."

He huffed. "I already talked to the club board, and they seemed open to a bachelor auction as long as we kept it classy. We can't take anything off below the belt."

"Oh, that's reassuring," I murmured.

Liam winked. "It leaves a little something to the imagination—unless you wear really tight pants."

"You're insane, you know that, right?" Gordy asked him, stoic as ever.

"This form has to be turned in this week in order to get everything rolling and moving so we can get the fundraiser done before we need the money. Last year's funds should get us through this season, but we'll need some massive fundraising to get next season started off on the right foot," I said.

"I'm going to get a beer," Liam said. "I think better with alcohol in my system."

I didn't think that had ever been true for anyone, but I let him go.

Drew pulled his phone out of his pocket and started texting.

"Are you seriously texting right now when we're trying to come up with some ideas?"

"Relax," he said, not even bothering to look at me. "I'm texting my sister. She might have some suggestions."

Drew's twin sister, Ava, was a marketing major, so it wasn't a bad idea to see if she could come up with something. Clearly putting our four heads together wasn't getting us anywhere.

I stared at the blank paper in front of me, feeling frustrated that we couldn't come up with any original ideas that could give us a good boost in funding.

The frats did car washes and shit like that, but we wanted to stand out.

Unfortunately, with every second that passed, Liam's idea of a bachelor auction looked better and better.

Apparently, I wasn't the only one who thought so.

Gordy sat forward, resting his elbows on his knees. "You know, Liam might be onto something as loath as I am to admit it."

"With the bachelor auction?" I confirmed.

He nodded. "It's not something the frats have done, surprisingly. We could probably get it approved quickly. We don't need a lot of extras. It doesn't take a ton of time or effort. We just need a space, the time, and an emcee, which we could easily recruit somebody else to do, maybe even Drew's sister, or one of the football guys next door. It's doable. We can do a quick turnaround, depending on what spaces are available on campus."

"Fuck, his ego is gonna fucking blow up if we agree to do this."

Gordy chuckled. "Yep, probably. But it's not a bad idea and we need something quick."

I turned to Drew. "Hey, Ava come up with anything?"

He shook his head. "No, but she does have an in with

the sororities and frats. She said they've got a couple of fundraisers already lined up. All the usual stuff."

Which meant if we wanted to get a lot of attention on our event, we needed to do something different. Something flashy.

"I told her about Liam's idea," Drew interrupted my thoughts, "and she agreed it's not a bad one, especially because hockey is so hot right now."

Gordy and I both looked at him. "What do you mean hockey's hot right now?"

His smile grew like a Cheshire cat grin. "You know, there's all these girls reading, like, hockey romances. Getting hot over the exercises we do and shit like that. How do you think Liam and I get as many chicks lately as we do? We tell them we play hockey, and their panties practically fall to the floor. They want to live one of their book romances, and we give them a night they'll never forget."

Gordy and I glanced at each other.

"Hockey *romance?*" he asked, the disbelief clear in his voice.

Liam walked back into the room and handed each of us a beer. "What did I miss?" he asked as he sat down heavily.

I shook my head, silently telling him it didn't matter. I could not believe I was about to say what I was about to say. "Looks like your idea isn't so stupid after all. How do you feel about being bachelor number one?"

TWENTY-SEVEN

"Tell me again why we're hiding in the bushes at eleven o'clock at night?" I whispered, crouching lower as a pair of students walked by on the sidewalk. The branches scratched at my arms, and I was pretty sure I'd just gotten a spider web in my hair.

Drew was beside me, his eyes gleaming with mischievous intensity in the darkness. "Because Harper Tinsley is a demon spawn who needs to be taught a lesson."

I sighed, glancing at Gordy and Liam, who were similarly hunched in the shrubbery that separated the hockey house from the music house next door. We'd been out here for twenty minutes already, waiting for Drew's signal to execute what he called "Operation Tinsley Takedown."

"Aren't we a little old for pranks?" I asked, shifting my weight to relieve the cramp forming in my calf. "I mean, we're in college, not high school freshmen."

Drew's head whipped around, his expression deadly serious. "There is no age limit on justice, Kane."

Gordy cleared his throat. "Didn't Harper organize that collection and meal train for those three local families that lost their homes in the fire last month? The ones over on Seventh Street?"

I raised an eyebrow. Gordy had a point. I remembered seeing flyers around campus about the fundraiser. It had been pretty successful too—raised something like ten thousand dollars plus clothing, furniture, and other essentials.

"Don't get him started—" Liam warned, but it was too late.

Drew's face flushed even in the dim light from the streetlamps. "That's exactly what I'm talking about! It's all a front. A carefully crafted public image to hide her true nature. You think she actually cares about those families? Please. The Tinsleys have been pulling this kind of PR stunt for decades."

"Don't argue," Liam said, resigned. "The Tinsley/Dumontier feud goes back like three generations," he explained. "There's no reasoning with him on this topic."

Drew was still going. "And now she's here, at our university, living next door, playing her violin at six in the morning like some kind of psychopath."

I had to admit, the early morning violin wasn't my favorite thing either, but it wasn't exactly a capital offense.

"So what exactly is the plan here?" I asked, trying to redirect Drew's increasingly passionate rant. "Because I've got an eight a.m. class tomorrow, and I'd rather not spend the whole night in these bushes."

Drew's focus returned to the mission at hand. He reached into his backpack and pulled out what looked like several packages of plastic wrap.

"When she comes home and goes to sleep, we're going to plastic wrap her car."

Gordy arched a brow. "That's your master plan?"

I frowned. "Drew, man, I don't think—"

"Relax," he cut me off. "It won't cause any permanent damage, but it will mess with her perfectly composed schedule that she never deviates from."

Liam sighed. "This seems childish, even for you."

"You don't understand," Drew insisted. "Last week, she reported our house to campus security for noise violations. Three times. We got a formal warning from housing and we didn't even have any parties! I can't let that go without retaliating."

I was starting to wonder if Drew had built this rivalry up in his head a bit too much. I'd seen Harper Tinsley around campus a few times—a slender, curly-haired redhead who was a music major and mostly kept to herself from what I could tell. She didn't exactly scream "evil nemesis."

"There she is," Drew hissed suddenly, ducking lower into the bushes.

I peered through the branches and saw Harper get out of her car and walk toward the music house, violin case in one hand, a stack of sheet music in the other. She was wearing jeans and an oversized sweater, her hair pulled back in a messy bun. She looked tired, probably coming back from a late practice session.

"Perfect," Drew whispered. "She's going inside. Once the lights go out in her room, we'll make our move."

Gordy shifted uncomfortably beside me. "Drew, I'm not sure this is a good idea. What if someone sees us?"

"That's why we're doing it at night, genius," Drew replied. "Besides, it's harmless."

I wouldn't exactly call making someone late because they couldn't get into their car in the morning "harmless," but arguing with Drew when he was in this mood was pointless.

We watched as Harper entered the house, and a few minutes later, a light came on in a second-floor window.

"That's her room," Drew informed us. "Now we wait."

Forty-five minutes later, I was seriously reconsidering my life choices. My legs had gone numb, I was pretty sure I'd been bitten by at least three different insects, and Drew was still glaring at Harper's window with the intensity of a sniper waiting for his target.

"Why couldn't we wait in our house instead of the bushes?"

"Because then you guys would find excuses not to help me."

He was right about that.

"Maybe she's not going to sleep," I suggested. "Maybe she's one of those people who studies until three in the morning."

"She'll sleep," Drew said confidently. "She always turns her light off by midnight."

I exchanged glances with Liam. "You've been tracking her sleep schedule?"

"Know thy enemy," Drew replied without a hint of irony and keeping his gaze fixed on her window.

"Someone doth protest too much," Gordy mumbled.

Drew whipped his gaze to Gordy. "What did you just say?"

"Hey! Her light went out," Liam interrupted, saving Gordy from having to face off with Drew. Although I was in agreement with Gordy.

"It's go time."

Before any of us could protest further, Drew ran across the lawn toward the driveway where Harper's small blue Honda was parked.

Like idiots, we followed him.

"I'm going to regret this," I said.

"Get in line," Gordy added.

Drew handed each of us a box of plastic wrap and then got started wrapping her car. We stared, watching him with dread.

"Hurry up," he whispered, not really paying any attention to the fact that none of us had moved to help him yet.

"Drew—" I started.

"What are you doing to my car?"

We all froze. The voice had come from behind us, female and distinctly unamused. Slowly, we turned around.

Harper Tinsley stood there in sweatpants and a CFU Music Department hoodie, her hand on her hip, her brows arched in judgment, looking significantly less demonic than Drew had described. Mostly, she just looked tired and annoyed.

"Uh..." Drew eloquently responded.

Her eyes narrowed on the plastic wrap in Drew's hand. "Are you serious right now, Dumontier?"

Drew quickly stood up, attempting to hide the evidence behind his back. "What are you doing out here? You're supposed to be asleep."

"I was going to my car to get my other rosin that I left in there," she replied, then shook her head in disbelief. "You are un-fucking-believable."

"You started it," Drew said, his voice cold and lacking any of the usual playfulness.

"We'll agree to disagree because I'm too tired to list all the ways *you* started it."

She shook her head and took a deep breath. "You know what," she continued, "I'm not even that surprised. This is exactly the kind of childish stunt I'd expect from you."

Drew bristled. "Oh, like you're so perfect?"

"Look, this got out of hand," I said, stepping forward. "We'll just go back to our house and forget this happened. We're sorry."

Drew looked at me like I'd just announced I was quitting hockey to join a boy band. "Dude, what are you doing?"

"Being an adult," I replied. Then I turned back to Harper. "Seriously, we apologize. It won't happen again."

Gordy and Liam quickly nodded in agreement.

"Speak for yourselves," Drew muttered.

Harper sighed, looking weary. "Just...go home. And take your stupid plastic wrap with you. My car better be in pristine condition when I wake up in the morning."

Drew glared at her. "This isn't over, Tinsley."

"It is for tonight," she replied firmly.

As we trudged back toward the hockey house, Drew was seething. "I can't believe you guys caved like that."

"What were we supposed to do?" Liam asked. "She caught us red-handed."

"We could have denied it! Said we were looking for a lost...I don't know, Frisbee or something."

"At midnight?" Gordy questioned skeptically. "With plastic wrap?"

"You guys don't understand," Drew insisted. "The Tinsleys have been getting away with stuff like this for generations. They act all innocent and make us look like the bad guys."

I clapped a hand on his shoulder. "Look, man, I get that there's history there, but maybe it's time to let it go. We're in college now. We've got bigger things to worry about than some old family feud."

"Like not getting suspended from the team," Gordy added.

Drew shrugged my hand off. "Whatever."

"I'm going to bed," I announced. "And Drew, I'm serious—no more pranks. If Coach finds out we were messing around like this, he'll have our asses."

"Fine," Drew grumbled before heading upstairs without another word.

Gordy followed, yawning widely.

Liam lingered in the living room with me.

"You think he's really going to let this go?" I asked.

He snorted. "Not a chance. These two have literally been trying to one-up each other since grade school. I doubt a little lecture from you will change that. It'd take a miracle for those two to get along."

TWENTY-EIGHT

The purple Discord icon was taunting me, but I fought the urge to open it. Instead I closed my laptop and stared unseeingly at the TV in front of me.

For nearly two years, I'd made Foster the villain in my mind for what happened that night freshman year. And then I'd gotten to know him this summer, and my whole view had shifted.

But then he'd dropped the truth bomb on me that he was Bear, and now I was more confused than ever. More than that, I couldn't let go of the hurt and betrayal I felt knowing that he'd known it was me for weeks before he told me.

I avoided Discord and *Stardew Valley* like the plague.

I focused on the start of fall semester.

I dove headfirst into volunteering for any extra work Holt & Associates wanted to give me as an intern.

But nothing cleared my head. Nothing helped me make sense of the conflicting emotions swirling inside me. I felt like I should be furious at Foster for the secret he'd kept, especially once he found out the truth.

Except...

The longer I thought about it, the more I realized he was probably right. I would've pushed him—and subsequently Bear—away. I'd still kept Foster at arm's length at that point.

I remembered quite vividly running into him at the coffee shop and the panic that ensued when he walked up to my table. There was no way I would've embraced the idea that he was Bear.

I could admit my flaws, but figuring out how to bridge the gap that I'd put between us was a lot harder. The more time that passed, the harder it was to figure out what to say to finally break the ice.

"You seem lost in your thoughts," Sam said from her spot on the couch beside me where she'd been scrolling on her phone while some new reality show played on our TV.

I picked at my thumbnail. "I think you were right."

She cupped her hand around her ear and leaned toward me, her brow arched. "I'm sorry, say that again."

I whacked her with the throw pillow before bringing it back and hugging it to my chest. "I think you were right about that night with Foster. I blew it out of proportion—made it a bigger deal than it was."

She placed her hand on my knee. "Abby, you went through a lot in a very short amount of time. Frankly, I don't blame you for feeling how you felt. It was the first time you really put yourself out there for a guy, and it ended up being a big letdown. Anyone in your shoes would have been disappointed."

I swallowed hard but nodded.

"But also," she added, giving my knee a squeeze, "can I just say for the record—falling asleep while making out doesn't make *you* a bad kisser. It makes *him* bad at pacing his drinks."

A reluctant laugh escaped.

Her expression turned thoughtful. "What brought on this change in thought?"

I hugged the pillow tighter and finally confessed the truth about Bear being Foster. By the time I was done, Sam's jaw was on the floor.

"You're shitting me?"

"I wish I weren't."

"Are you being serious right now? This is amazing news!"

I frowned in confusion. "How do you figure?"

She set her phone aside and twisted her body to face me. "Because now you don't have to choose between two guys. You get the best of both because they're one and the same."

I'd been so focused on the betrayal, I hadn't even thought of it like that.

"Come on, it's clear you need to get out of your head. Let's take a break. I hear they're having a poetry jam at The Grindhouse. Let's go check it out."

Normally, I would've said no or made some lame excuse, but she was right. I needed to clear my head, and maybe doing something different for a change would give me the clarity I was searching for.

We were almost to the SUB when Sam grabbed my arm and gave it a small squeeze.

"Don't look now," she whispered, eyes wide. "Actually, do look. Hockey boys at three o'clock."

I turned my head just in time to see him—Foster—walking alongside two other guys in Clark Fork hockey T-shirts.

My stomach flipped.

Nearly three weeks. No texts. No *Stardew*. No Bear.

But now here he was. Heading right toward me and already looking at me.

He stared at me like I was water in the desert—a mirage that he couldn't believe was real. His jaw was scruffy in a way it hadn't been before, and somehow it made him even more stupidly attractive.

As they got closer, I noticed the apprehension in his gaze and my chest ached. I didn't want him to look at me like that. I wanted him to look at me the way he had on the ice when he'd caught me before I could fall.

The two guys next to him were watching us with twin expressions of interest by the time we crossed paths.

"Hey, Abby."

"Hey, Foster."

The guy beside him with sandy-brown hair grinned. "Ah, so you're the girl that's got our boy here all broody."

My already small smile faltered. "What?"

Foster groaned and slapped the guy in the stomach, causing him to bend over with an "oof." "Ignore Drew. He's an idiot."

The one next to Drew nodded solemnly. "Confirmed."

Foster glanced back at me. "This is Drew and Liam— my roommates and teammates. Guys, this is Abby."

I waved to both. "This is Sam, my roommate and best friend," I said, gesturing to her beside me.

She was already giving her flirty smile to Liam. "Were you guys heading into the poetry jam?" she asked them.

"Oh no, just carb loading. Then we gotta study before getting up at the butt crack of dawn for practice again," Drew said.

Sam tilted her head. "Why is it always so early?"

"Because the rink's open to the public during normal hours," Foster explained. "We get whatever slots are left—early mornings, late nights. That's the life."

Liam added, "It's not as intense as NCAA schedules, though. Those guys are in full-on grind mode for a whole two months longer than we are."

I glanced at Sam and saw her looking between me and Foster. Panic started to hit me. I knew that look—those diabolical best friend eyes that screamed *brace yourself, this is for your own good.*

And sure enough, the next words out of her mouth confirmed my fears.

"You know, if you guys aren't busy this weekend, Abby and I were thinking of going to karaoke at a local bar—The Old Pine. They're having an inaugural karaoke night Saturday at seven, and we thought it would be loads of fun. You should totally join us."

My stomach dropped. "I'm sure they're busy—"

Foster was still looking right at me, but this time he was smiling. Those damn butterflies that had been still for the last three weeks took flight in my stomach. "Actually, that sounds fun and we don't have any games this weekend, so we're free."

Sam beamed. "Great! We'll see you guys there."

I glared at her. She ignored me.

As we walked away, I whispered, "Are you insane?"

"What? You like him. He likes you. Let's quit pretending otherwise. And as much as I love you, sometimes you need a little push to go after what you want. This is your chance."

I bit my lip. She was right. Again.

Maybe it was time to stop looking for reasons to keep Foster Kane out of my heart.

Because the truth was, he was already there, and seeing him for the first time in three weeks only confirmed what I'd already felt.

I missed him, and it was time to take a leap.

I wasn't typically a nervous person.

I was usually confident and sure when it came to my academics and my job.

Socially, I was maybe a little awkward, but the only times I could recall being truly, gut-wrenchingly nervous both involved Foster.

And tonight was one of them.

When Foster walked into The Old Pine, I swore every head in the building turned his way.

He wasn't alone. Liam and Drew flanked him on either side with Gordy trailing behind them, looking less than thrilled to be there. They all seemed to command attention without even trying. Foster wore dark jeans and a sapphire blue button-up that made his blue eyes pop even from across the bar. His sleeves were rolled up to his elbows, showcasing his muscular forearms, and those now-familiar butterflies took off in my stomach at the sight.

"Holy crap. Talk about fucking eye candy," Sam whispered beside me. "Is there some kind of rule that you have to be hot to play hockey? Because damn, those boys are fine."

I couldn't disagree with that assessment, but I only had eyes for Foster. When his gaze swept the room and landed on me, his face broke into a smile that made my stomach flip.

"Act cool," I muttered to myself.

"What?" Sam asked.

"Nothing."

Foster and his friends made their way over to our table, and I tried to look casual, like my heart wasn't threatening to beat out of my chest.

"Hey," Foster said, his eyes roaming over me appreciatively. "You look amazing."

I smoothed my hand over the deep purple fabric of my top and tried to remember how to breathe. The V-neck wasn't even that low, but under Foster's gaze, it felt borderline scandalous.

"Thanks," I managed, feeling heat rise to my cheeks. "You too."

Drew slid into the large U-shaped corner booth beside Sam. "Hey, Abby. Foster hasn't shut up about you all day."

Foster shot him a death glare. "Dude."

"What? It's true." Drew turned to me with a grin. "It was all 'Abby this' and 'Abby that.'"

My eyes widened, and I glanced at Foster, who looked like he wanted the floor to open up and swallow him whole.

"Ignore him," Foster said, sliding in next to me. "He was dropped on his head as a child. Multiple times."

"It's true," Liam added, squeezing in beside Drew. "I was there for at least three of those times. But it's also true that our captain here is a smitten kitten."

"You're both assholes," Foster muttered, but there was no heat behind it.

Gordy, who seemed to be the quietest of the group, took the remaining seat beside Liam. "I apologize in advance for anything these three might say or do tonight," he said to me with a small smile.

I laughed, feeling some of my tension ease. "Noted."

Sam, ever the social butterfly, kept the conversation flowing. She asked the guys about their hockey season, which led to animated stories about their games and practices. Drew and Liam were natural storytellers, acting out plays and mimicking their coach's expressions. Even Gordy joined in, his quiet demeanor giving way to dry humor that had me laughing more than once.

Throughout it all, I was hyperaware of Foster beside me. Our arms would occasionally brush, or our knees would touch under the table, and each time it happened, my heart would skip a beat. It reminded me of the times during tutoring when he'd moved closer to me.

It had wreaked havoc on my emotions then just like it did now.

And as the night stretched on, I just wanted to be alone with him—to have the talk I knew we needed to have so we could clear the air and move forward.

Hopefully together if I wasn't too late.

"So, Abby," Drew said, pulling me from my thoughts, "are you going to grace us with a song tonight? It is karaoke night, after all."

I shook my head quickly. "Oh, no. I'm just here to watch. I don't sing."

"Everyone sings," Liam argued. "Some just better than others."

"Trust me, you don't want to hear me sing," I insisted. "I'm tone-deaf. Like, clinically."

"I'll go up if Sam goes with me," Drew offered, turning to my roommate with a charming smile.

Sam, never one to back down from a challenge, grinned. "You're on. But I get to pick the song."

"Deal," Drew said, extending his hand for her to shake.

As they debated song choices, Foster leaned in close to me, his breath warm against my ear.

"For what it's worth, I bet you'd be great up there."

I turned my head slightly to look at him, suddenly aware of how close our faces were. "Trust me, I wouldn't be. But thanks for the vote of confidence."

He smiled, and my eyes dropped to his lips for just a moment before I caught myself and looked away. From the corner of my eye, I saw his smile widen, and I knew he'd caught me looking.

Sam and Drew eventually decided on "Unholy" by Sam Smith and Kim Petras and put their names in with the emcee. When their turn came, they took to the small stage with surprising confidence. Sam had a great voice, and Drew wasn't half bad either. The crowd went wild when he rolled his hips while he pulled his shirt off, showing off his abs.

Gordy shook his head. "He will use literally any excuse to take his clothes off."

"They're good together," I remarked to Foster as we watched.

"Yeah," he agreed. "I haven't seen Drew have this much fun in a while."

When they finished their performance to enthusiastic applause, they returned to our table, flushed and laughing.

"Your turn, Foster," Drew said, clapping him on the back.

"Not a chance," Foster replied, shaking his head. "I've heard dying cats that sound better than me."

"Aw, come on," Liam goaded. "Show your girl what you've got."

"What I've got is a healthy respect for everyone's eardrums," Foster shot back.

Liam raised his hands like he was backing off, but after a few minutes, both he and Drew stood up.

"We'll be right back," Drew said, a mischievous glint in his eye.

"Where are you going?" Foster asked suspiciously.

"Bathroom," Liam replied innocently—too innocently.

"Together?" Foster raised an eyebrow.

"What? You've never heard of the buddy system?" Drew quipped before they both headed off.

"That can't be good," Gordy muttered, watching them go.

"What do you think they're up to?" I asked Foster.

He sighed. "With those two? Who knows. They could be going to flirt with girls they saw or planning something diabolical."

I looked over my shoulder. They hadn't even gone near the bathrooms—they were lingering by the karaoke table, laughing like they'd just pulled off a heist.

When Liam and Drew returned a few minutes later, they were both wearing identical shit-eating grins.

Foster narrowed his eyes at them. "Why do you two look like that?"

"Like what?" Drew asked, the picture of innocence.

"Like you just—"

Before Foster could finish his sentence, the emcee's voice boomed through the speakers.

"Alright, folks! We've got a special request tonight. Can I get Foster Kane up here to sing for us, please?"

Foster's face went pale, then red. "You didn't."

Liam and Drew burst into laughter.

"Oh, we absolutely did," Liam said, looking far too pleased with himself.

"Come on up, Foster Kane!" the emcee called again. "Don't be shy! Your friends tell me you've got a special song to sing for a special someone."

All eyes in the bar turned to our table, and I felt my own face heating up as Foster slowly stood, looking like a man headed to his execution.

"I'm going to kill you both," he muttered to his friends before making his way to the stage.

THIRTY

I could not believe they did this.

The emcee grinned at me as I approached the stage, his eyes twinkling with mischief that matched the expressions on my so-called friends' faces.

"What am I singing?" I asked through gritted teeth, already dreading the answer.

The emcee leaned in and whispered, "Your boys picked 'Sparks Fly' by Taylor Swift. Said it was perfect for your situation."

My eyes widened. "You've got to be kidding me."

"Nope." He handed me the microphone. "Good luck, buddy."

I turned to glare at Drew and Liam, who both shot me enthusiastic thumbs-up, their shit-eating grins wide enough to split their faces. Even Gordy was smiling, and that guy was normally as stoic as they came.

Traitor.

But it was Abby's expression that caught and held my attention. She looked mortified on my behalf, her cheeks flushed pink, but there was something else there too—

curiosity, maybe even anticipation. Our eyes locked for a brief moment before the opening notes of the song started to play.

Well, I was already up here. I could either half-ass it and be embarrassed, or I could own it and maybe use this ridiculous situation to my advantage.

I took a deep breath and made my decision.

If I was going to sing a Taylor Swift song in front of a bar full of people, I was going to sing it to Abby. Because honestly, she was the only girl I could ever imagine singing a romance song to.

The lyrics appeared on the screen, and I started singing. I wasn't great—I definitely wasn't going to win any singing competitions—but I wasn't terrible either. And what I lacked in vocal talent, I made up for in enthusiasm.

As I sang about dangerous smiles and getting swept away, I kept my eyes on Abby. The crowd seemed to realize who I was singing to pretty quickly, and a path cleared between us, giving me a direct line of sight to her. Her hands were covering her mouth, her eyes wide, but there were crinkles beside her eyes and it was clear she was smiling.

I moved through the crowd as I sang, making my way back toward our table. Drew and Liam were practically falling over themselves laughing, but I ignored them.

This was for Abby.

By the time I reached the chorus again, I was standing right in front of her. I extended my hand out to her and waited with bated breath.

For a moment, I thought she might refuse, but then she took my hand and stood up to join me.

I sang directly to her now, not caring how cheesy it was

or who was watching. As far as I was concerned, there was no one else in the room but us.

Her face was flushed, but she was smiling as she looked up into my eyes, and it was easily the most beautiful sight I'd ever seen.

My heart took flight in my chest because a part of me had been certain I'd never see her smile at me like that again.

The fact that she was gave me a stupid amount of hope.

When the song ended, the bar erupted in cheers and whistles. I handed the microphone back to the emcee, who clapped me on the shoulder.

"That was something else, man," he said, laughing.

"Yeah, well, don't expect an encore," I replied, but I was smiling too.

I led Abby back to our table, where our friends were waiting with varying expressions of amusement and approval.

"I can't believe you actually did that," Abby said, her voice somewhere between impressed and mortified.

"Neither can I," I admitted. "But if they thought they were embarrassing me, they failed. I regret nothing."

Drew slow-clapped. "I have to say, Kane, I didn't think you had it in you. That was...spectacular."

"Truly a masterpiece," Liam agreed, wiping away a fake tear. "I'm moved."

"You're both dead men," I informed them cheerfully. "You just don't know it yet. Get used to sleeping with one eye open."

Gordy raised his beer in a toast. "Worth it."

"Et tu, Gordy?" I shook my head in mock betrayal.

Abby laughed, the sound light and genuine, and

suddenly the embarrassment seemed like a small price to pay to hear that sound.

We settled back into our seats, and the conversation flowed easily. Abby seemed more relaxed now, leaning slightly into my side when she laughed at something Drew said. Every now and then, someone from another table would walk by and compliment my "performance," which would set everyone off again.

After about an hour, Sam checked her phone and frowned. "Oh, shoot. I forgot I have to head over to my sorority house to help with our social event we're hosting tomorrow."

Abby's shoulders fell a little. "It's almost eleven. You have to go help now?"

"Yep," Sam said, with a look that was far too innocent to be genuine. "The social committee just texted me."

"Oh," Abby said, looking uncertain. "Um...I guess I can wait in the car. Do you think it'll take long?"

I saw my opportunity and took it. "I can give you a ride home. It's no problem."

Now I was glad I'd only had the one beer when we first got here.

Abby looked between Sam and me, clearly catching on to what was happening. "Are you sure? I don't want to put you out."

"It would be my pleasure," I said, meaning every word.

Sam beamed. "Perfect! It's settled then." She stood up and grabbed her purse. "Tonight was fun. We should do this again sometime."

"Definitely," Drew agreed, a little too quickly. I narrowed my eyes at him, but he just smiled innocently.

I noticed Gordy was also glaring at him and that gave me pause. Why did Gordy care? I knew why I didn't want

Drew to make a move on her—because the last thing I needed was for one of my best friends to break Abby's best friend's heart—but why would he?

After Sam left, we stayed for another half hour or so before deciding to call it a night. As we walked out to the parking lot, Drew pulled me aside.

"You're welcome, by the way," he said smugly.

"For what, exactly? Publicly humiliating me?"

"For giving you the perfect opportunity to show her how you feel." He grinned. "And don't pretend you're mad. I saw your face when she took your hand."

I couldn't help but smile. "Yeah, well, next time maybe just give me a heads-up?"

"Where's the fun in that?" He clapped me on the shoulder. "Go get her, Candy Kane."

I rolled my eyes at the nickname but headed toward Abby, who was waiting by my truck. The guys had all conveniently decided to take an Uber so they could check out another party on campus.

"Ready?" I asked, unlocking the doors.

She nodded, sliding into the passenger seat. "That was... unexpected."

I laughed as I started the engine. "Which part? The Taylor Swift serenade or the obvious setup by our friends?"

"Both," she admitted with a small smile. "But it was fun. I'm glad you guys were able to come tonight."

"Me too," I said softly.

The ride back to her place was quiet at first, the kind of silence that hummed with unspoken things. I didn't want to ruin it by rushing, but I also couldn't take another night of wondering where we stood.

She'd smiled at me and leaned into me, and it had made me feel like maybe I hadn't broken things beyond repair.

And now that we were almost to her apartment, I was worried about when I'd get to see her again.

"I've missed you," she said quietly, before I could speak. When I glanced over at her, her hands were folded in her lap, but her eyes were on me. "Not just Bear. Or Foster. Both. *You.*"

My chest tightened. A part of me had feared she'd miss who I represented as Bear more than *me.* "I missed you too. Every damn day."

I wished we were already at her apartment so I could look at her more instead of having to watch the road. But maybe it was the darkness in the cab of my truck and knowing that I couldn't see her that allowed her to open up to me.

"I was hurt at first." Her voice trembled, and she stared down at her hands. "It felt like you didn't trust me. Like I'd been made a fool of."

I started to speak, but she cut me off gently. "The more I thought about it...the more I realized you were right."

My grip tightened on the wheel. "What do you mean?"

"If you'd told me who you were back when you first figured it out, I would've pushed you away," she said quietly. "I would've panicked. Convinced myself it was all some cruel joke or twisted plan. I would've cut you off. I would've hurt us both. Hell, I've kind of done that anyway." Her voice cracked a little, and I reached for her hand without thinking.

It felt like another victory when she didn't pull away.

"You gave me space to figure it out," she said. "You let me get to know you—not just as Bear—but *you.* And now that I have..."

I pulled into a parking space in front of her building and she turned fully toward me, her hand curling around mine and her thumb brushing over my knuckles in a way that had pleasure shooting through my nerve endings.

"I want you. Both versions. All of it. The guy who makes dad jokes in Discord and the one who sings Taylor Swift in front of a bar full of people just to make me smile."

My breath left me in a rush, like she'd reached into my chest and knocked all the air out.

"I want you too," I said, because I had to. Because it was the truest thing I'd ever said. "More than I've ever wanted anything."

Her lips curved, soft and hopeful. "So, I'm not too late?"

"Hell, no." I cupped the side of her neck. "Abby, I would've waited for however long it took. You are worth it."

Her eyes shimmered. "I've missed you so much," she whispered, and then her gaze dropped to my lips.

That was all the permission I needed. I leaned across the console and kissed her.

It wasn't rushed or desperate.

It was quiet, certain, filled with all the words we didn't need to say.

Her fingers gripped the front of my shirt like she was afraid I'd disappear, and I kissed her like she was the only thing tethering me to the ground.

Fuck, it was the best kiss of my life.

Because this time I wasn't drunk or keeping a secret. This time she knew everything and she still wanted me.

When we finally pulled apart, she was smiling and breathless. She'd never looked more beautiful.

"So we're really doing this?" she whispered.

"Yeah." I ran a hand down her cheek, memorizing everything about this moment. "We are."

The seatbelt felt like a noose as I clicked it into place while my dad sat in the driver's seat. I had barely buckled in when he started driving.

"Now that your business classes are underway, I really want you to see one of our real estate development projects from start to finish," he said.

It was only the third week of classes, but my dad had officially opened his Missoula office and wasn't wasting any time.

"This new venture is going to bring in millions of dollars, and we get to boost housing for the community. Although the most important piece is that it's going to be our name, The Kane Group, that will be everywhere."

"Here's a quick lesson in business advertisement," my dad continued. "Get your name on as many properties as possible because people trust name recognition and value that. If we're the ones getting all these big contracts, that proves we are the best. Right, Foster?"

There was only one answer he wanted.

"Yep."

I'd seen bits and pieces behind the scenes of my dad's real estate development business, but this was the first project he was bringing me in on from start to finish.

"Do you always work with the same engineering firm?" I asked him.

"Not always. It depends on the project—commercial, residential, or mixed use. For this one, we're using Holt & Associates. They're known for their due diligence, and that reputation helps boost ours. It gives The Kane Group credibility as we try to establish a foothold in the area. They'll handle land development, infrastructure design, permits—everything to make sure the project works with the environment. There's already some pushback from the community about water rights, so Holt will also help with public engagement. They'll oversee parts of the construction too, and help us decide on a contractor."

We pulled up to Holt & Associates which had an office between Dunridge, where CFU was located, and Missoula. When we walked in, the petite blonde receptionist gave my dad a bright white smile.

He leaned on the desk and said, "We're here to see Parker Holt. I'm Dennis Kane and this is my son, Foster. Parker should be expecting us."

Her eyelashes fluttered in a way that made me want to vomit. She couldn't have been much older than me, twenty-five at most. Yet, she looked positively breathless at my dad's attention. I always hated that he had a charismatic personality when he was such a dick underneath.

"Of course, Mr. Kane," she said. "I'll call him right now and let him know you're here."

She picked up the phone beside her, pressed a button, and waited, her flirty gaze never once straying from my father's.

Suddenly, that gag reflex wasn't just for her behavior, but his.

I couldn't remember the last time I'd thought highly of my dad, but to watch him shamelessly flirt with another woman, knowing my mom was waiting at home, made my stomach churn.

But what was worse was the feeling of helplessness.

I couldn't even call him out on his inappropriate behavior because I knew that would just result in me embarrassing him, and then him taking it out on me later.

And knowing my dad well, he wasn't one to use his fists.

No, he preferred manipulation and having power over people to physical violence.

He was one to always manipulate a situation in his favor. I didn't like constantly feeling beholden to him, but I didn't know how to escape from under his thumb.

The door down the hall opened, and Parker Holt—whose picture I'd seen on the website—walked out with a friendly smile on his face.

But it wasn't Parker that made my breath catch. It was the woman next to him.

Abby.

I blinked, thrown for a second. She'd mentioned an internship, but she'd never said it was here.

"Mr. Kane, pleasure to have you here," Parker said. "I hope you don't mind that our fabulous intern, Abby Walker, will be joining us today."

My dad extended his hand with that same charming smirk he'd offered the receptionist. "Nice to meet you."

I had to bite back a smile when Abby's expression didn't even flicker. She stayed cool and professional, not giving him an ounce more than necessary. She was good at that—holding her ground without breaking a sweat.

A flurry of pride, lust, and satisfaction swirled in my gut. It only intensified when she gave me a gentle smile as Parker led us down the hall.

In the conference room, neatly prepared folders waited at each seat. Parker gestured to the materials.

"In front of you, you'll find an overview of the proposed mixed-use development—about fifty acres with roughly 150 residential units, some retail, and a community park. The terrain's level, but there's a small creek along the southern boundary."

He turned toward Abby. "So what does that tell us, Miss Walker?"

If she was startled by the spotlight, she didn't show it.

"It means we'll need to assess stormwater management and any floodplain risks. We'll also have to evaluate access to utilities and the cost of connecting to municipal lines. Those could become major factors."

Parker beamed like a proud older brother.

And if I was honest, I was impressed too. I'd seen Abby confident before—mostly when she had been tutoring me— but this was different. Here she was sharp and self-assured. If Parker hadn't said something, I would have thought she was an employee and not an intern.

I'd never been turned on in a meeting before, but once again, Abby was stirring up something new in me.

Something I wanted a whole lot more of.

Parker continued, "Given the site's history, we'll need a Phase I environmental site assessment. You'll see it listed in your packet as ESA. That'll tell us if there are any potential liabilities—soil issues, contamination, that kind of thing."

"What's involved in a Phase I ESA?" I asked.

My dad clapped me on the back like he was proud I

remembered how to form a question. "First time through this process for my son. He'll be asking plenty of questions."

Parker just smiled. "We love learners here. Abby, want to walk him through it?"

She nodded smoothly. "It's a historical and regulatory review—researching past land use, checking public records, and inspecting the site to flag anything that could suggest contamination. If we find issues, then we'd need to do a Phase II—sampling, testing, deeper evaluations."

"Any known concerns in this region?" my dad asked.

"Unfortunately, yes," Parker replied. "There's some history of mining operations nearby—arsenic, heavy metals, that kind of thing. That's why Abby's also starting to work on the environmental review so we're in compliance with the Montana Environmental Policy Act."

My dad's shoulders stiffened. Subtle. But I knew that tic. He was pissed.

"Parker," he said slowly, "I respect your commitment to mentoring, but I'd prefer if your intern didn't learn hands-on with *my* project."

The whole room went silent.

I hated the way Abby's face blanched. Even Parker looked slightly taken aback, although he recovered much faster than she did. Which I only knew because he was the one who spoke first.

But my gaze was still stuck on Abby.

Sometimes she was hard to read, but right now a range of emotions flitted across her eyes—shame, anger, embarrassment, and then the one I hated the most, doubt.

I knew too well what it was like to be on the other side of my father's heartlessness.

I didn't want that for her.

How dare he put that look on her face. How dare he make her doubt how fucking amazing she was.

"I assure you, Miss Walker is quite adept at her job," Parker said. "And although she's an intern, she's the best intern we've ever had. She even outpaces some of our associates with her work ethic. I'd hire her on the spot if she wasn't in school full-time. But if you would prefer an associate to oversee this, then I will respect your wishes."

"I'm sure Annie is fine, but—"

"Her name is Abby," I said, my anger coming through loud and clear. When I looked at my dad, it was with daggers in my eyes. "Her name is *Abby*," I said again. "And she's the smartest person at CFU. By insulting her, you're insulting your alma mater."

I knew the only thing that would get through my dad's misogyny was his own love of his alma mater.

Parker's eyes lit up like he was biting back a smile, while my dad turned to face me, fire in his gaze and his cheeks slightly flushed. But he didn't say anything to me, just like I knew he wouldn't.

He'd never let the rest of the world see the devil he hid inside.

"Well. This has been...informative. We'll review the folder with our people and circle back. Sound good?"

"Sounds good," Parker said. "I'll show you out."

They stood and headed for the door, but I stayed behind.

Abby was already gathering the packets, her movements efficient but quiet. I reached out, placing my hand gently over hers.

"Hey, you okay?"

She didn't look up right away. "I'm fine."

Then she did—and the second our eyes met, my chest loosened just a little.

"Thank you," she said softly. "For defending me. You didn't have to do that."

"I did," I said. "He was being a dick."

A ghost of a smile curved her lips. Not the full one I loved, but it was still beautiful. I was starting to think that there wasn't a single thing I didn't find attractive about this girl.

"I should get back to work," she said. "But I'll see you tonight?"

"Wouldn't miss it."

She gave me one last look before slipping out of the conference room, her fingers brushing mine for half a second on the way out. Just long enough to short-circuit my entire brain.

I let out a breath and raked a hand through my hair, trying to get my heartbeat back under control.

Somehow I'd walked into this meeting thinking I'd be bored out of my mind and walked out even more obsessed with my girlfriend.

I was so far gone for that girl, and I didn't think she had a fucking clue.

I was about to pull out my sociology assignment when there was a knock on the door.

Those butterflies that had made a home in my stomach over the last several weeks fluttered happily as I opened it to find Foster on the other side, his backpack slung over his shoulder.

"Hey," I said, leaning against the door.

His smile grew. "Hey, yourself, Gorgeous."

He stepped forward, closing the distance between us, and wrapped his hand around my neck, pulling me closer as he dipped down. The moment our lips touched, I melted against his body. I didn't have a lot of experience, but I'd had several kisses in my past and not a single one held a candle to how Foster kissed me—like I was something worth treasuring while at the same time he couldn't get enough.

He pulled back but kept his forehead against mine, both of us taking a moment to catch our breath.

"You're dangerously addicting," he said.

"Don't distract me or you won't be allowed to study here," I teased him.

He put up three fingers. "Scout's honor. I'll do my best to behave. Just try not to be so tempting, okay?"

We moved to the couch and pulled out our study materials while he told me a story about Liam and Drew's latest antics at practice. Apparently Drew tried to fake a pulled hamstring to skip sprints, and Gordy nearly launched a puck at his head.

"How's the semester going so far?" I asked, nudging his leg gently with mine.

He let out a breath and leaned back, running a hand through his hair. "It's fine. I mean, the classes are manageable. Just more of the same—business this, management that. All stuff I'm supposed to care about."

The way he said it made my chest pinch.

"But you don't?" I asked carefully.

His mouth lifted in a crooked half-smile. "Let's just say I'm not exactly as passionate about my major as you are. But it keeps my dad happy, and passing keeps him off my back." He looked at me then, softer. "And having you around makes it suck a whole lot less."

"What major would *you* choose?"

His smile seemed a little wilted at the edges. "Never really thought about it because it's never been my choice. My dad has planned for me to take over his business since I was born—actually probably since the pregnancy test came back positive. I'm just lucky he let me do hockey."

That took me by surprise. "He didn't want you to play?"

"He'd rather I spent that time doing something 'productive' that could help his business. To him, hockey is frivolous."

"Isn't it also really expensive?"

"Yeah, but he had a client who was big into hockey when I was a kid—hence why I started so young—and then let me keep playing because that client led to more clients and he could still brag about me being good. But my success on the ice isn't necessarily something he's proud of—more something he uses to his advantage when he can. And now hockey is in my blood. For a long time, it was the only thing that got me excited to get up in the morning. Until I met you."

My cheeks flushed and I shook my head as I bit back a smile. "Flattery will not distract me from the fact you came here to study and that's what we need to do. I will not be held responsible for the star hockey player failing his classes."

"Yes, ma'am," he said with a mock salute, but instead of opening his book, he leaned closer to me, his blue eyes darkening slightly. "But first..."

His mouth found mine again, and despite my half-hearted protests about studying, I found myself responding eagerly. His hand slid to my waist, warm and secure, and I let my fingers thread through his soft hair.

"Foster," I mumbled against his lips. "We're supposed to be studying."

"I am studying," he murmured, trailing kisses along my jaw. "I'm studying how your breathing changes when I kiss you here." His lips brushed the sensitive spot below my ear, and I couldn't suppress a small gasp. "And here." He moved to the curve where my neck met my shoulder.

"That's not going to help you pass your classes," I said, though my voice lacked conviction.

He pulled back just enough to look at me, his expression surprisingly serious. "You know what? I think it actually might. Whenever things feel like too much—when the pressure hits, or my brain won't shut up—I'll think about you. About this. The way you make everything feel a little less heavy. You made me feel that way even before I knew who you were."

As Peach.

His thumb brushed my cheek. "You're the calm in my chaos, Abby."

My heart raced at his words. It was these moments—these glimpses of sincerity beneath his confident exterior—that had gradually broken down my defenses over the past few weeks.

"That's...actually really sweet," I admitted.

"Don't sound so surprised," he said with a laugh. "I can be sweet."

"I know." And I did know. Despite my initial reservations, Foster had proven himself to be thoughtful, determined, and genuinely kind. "But we still need to study."

He sighed dramatically. "Fine. But I'm going to need brain breaks. Regular ones—that include kissing."

"Deal," I said, trying to sound stern but failing miserably when he grinned at me.

Only half an hour later, he closed his textbook and stretched. "Brain break time?"

I rolled my eyes but couldn't help smiling. "You just want to make out again."

"Can you blame me?" He leaned back against the couch cushions, his arm stretching along the back. "But actually, I was thinking we could talk about something."

"Oh?" I set my notes aside, curious about his suddenly serious tone.

"Yeah. The hockey house always throws a big party early this time of year, and it's happening next weekend. Will you come with me?"

I bit my lip. We'd only been dating for a couple of

weeks, but a party at the hockey house felt significant somehow—like a public declaration.

And I guess in college, showing up to one of the biggest parties of the year on the arm of the guy who hadn't had an official girlfriend his entire college career was definitely a declaration.

"It's okay if you don't want to," he added quickly, misinterpreting my hesitation. "I know parties aren't really your thing."

"I'd love to," I told him sincerely. He was right that parties weren't my thing usually, but I felt like this was the year I would finally break out of my comfort zone. And I wanted to be at Foster's side.

This time when he kissed me, there was something different about it—a certainty, a promise. His hand cupped my face, his thumb tracing my cheekbone with such tenderness that my heart ached. I leaned into him and my hands rested on his chest, feeling the steady thump of his heart beneath my palm.

The kiss deepened, and he gently guided me back until I was lying on the couch with his body hovering above me, his weight supported on his forearms. His body was warm against mine, and when he shifted, a rush of heat spread through me like a wildfire.

"Is this okay?" he whispered, his eyes searching mine.

I nodded, unable to find my voice for a moment. "Yeah," I finally managed.

His lips returned to mine, more insistent now. One of his hands slid down my side to my hip, his touch leaving a trail of fire even through my clothes. I let my hands explore the broad expanse of his back, marveling at the firm muscles beneath his shirt.

When his mouth moved to my neck, I couldn't hold

back a soft moan. He groaned as his hips pressed against mine in a way that made my breath catch. The evidence of his desire was impossible to miss, and while it sent a thrill through me, it also triggered a flutter of nervousness, and I stiffened beneath him.

Foster must have felt it because he immediately pulled back. "Too much?" he asked, his voice husky.

"No, I..." I took a breath, trying to organize my thoughts through the haze of lust. "I just... I don't have a lot of experience with *this*."

His expression softened. "We don't have to do anything you're not ready for, Abby. I'm perfectly happy just kissing you."

"I want to kiss you," I assured him. "And...more. Just maybe not everything. Not yet."

He smiled, brushing a strand of hair from my face. "We've got all the time in the world. No rush."

The tenderness in his voice made my chest tighten. How had I ever convinced myself that this man was just a shallow jock? The Foster I'd come to know was patient, considerate, and surprisingly vulnerable at times.

"Thank you," I whispered.

"For what?"

"For being you."

He laughed softly. "That's the easiest thing I've ever done."

I pulled him down for another kiss, feeling a new confidence. His hand remained at my waist, respectful of my boundaries, but when I arched against him, he groaned into my mouth.

"Abby," he murmured, his voice strained. "You're killing me here."

"Sorry," I said, though I wasn't really sorry at all.

"No, you're not," he said with a knowing look.

I bit my lip, trying to suppress a smile. "Maybe not."

His eyes darkened as he watched me, and then he was kissing me again, more intensely this time. I felt his hand slide tentatively under the hem of my shirt, his fingers warm against my bare skin.

"Is this okay?" he asked again.

"Yes," I breathed.

His hand moved slowly up my side, his touch gentle but confident. When his thumb brushed the underside of my breast, I gasped, and he froze.

"Still okay?"

I nodded, unable to form words because it felt so good. He continued his exploration, his hand cupping my breast through my bra. The sensation was overwhelming in the best possible way, and I found myself pressing into his touch, wanting more.

We were so lost in each other that we didn't hear the key in the lock. It wasn't until the door opened and Sam's voice called out, "Honey, I'm home!" that we sprang apart like guilty teenagers.

Foster sat up quickly, running a hand through his disheveled hair while I adjusted my shirt, my face burning with embarrassment.

Sam stood in the doorway, a knowing grin spreading across her face. "Well, well, well. What do we have here?"

"We were studying," I said lamely.

"Mm-hmm. Anatomy, was it?" She winked at Foster, who had the good grace to look slightly abashed despite the smile tugging at his lips.

"We may have gotten a bit...distracted," he replied.

Sam laughed. "No judgment here. I'm just going to grab

something from my room and then head back out. Don't mind me."

As she disappeared down the hallway, I buried my face in my hands. "Oh my God."

Foster chuckled, gently pulling my hands away. "Hey, it's okay. We weren't doing anything wrong."

"I know, but..." I gestured vaguely. "It's embarrassing."

"Why? Because your roommate knows you're attracted to your boyfriend?" He raised an eyebrow. "I hate to break it to you, but I think she already suspected that."

I couldn't help but laugh at his teasing tone. "You're impossible."

"And yet, you like me anyway."

"I do," I admitted, the words coming easier than I expected.

His expression softened, and he leaned in to press a gentle kiss to my forehead. "For what it's worth, I like you too. A lot. More than I knew was possible to like someone."

Our gazes locked and the air seemed to thin between us under the weight of his words.

Sam broke our trance when she reappeared, a jacket slung over her arm. "Alright, lovebirds, I'm out. Don't do anything I wouldn't do!"

She blew us a kiss and left, the door closing behind her with a click.

Foster and I looked at each other for a moment before bursting into laughter.

"Well, that was..." I began.

"Perfect timing?" he suggested.

"Not the words I was going to use."

He smiled, reaching out to tuck a strand of hair behind my ear. "Maybe it's for the best. I was getting a little carried away." He glanced at his watch and sighed. "I should probably actually study a bit more before I head out. As much as I'd rather keep doing...other things."

"Responsible of you," I teased.

"I have my moments." He picked up his textbook again.

We settled back into studying, though there was a new awareness between us, a current of electricity that hadn't been there before. Every now and then, our eyes would meet over our books, and I'd feel that now-familiar flutter in my stomach.

After another hour, Foster reluctantly packed up his things. "I gotta go. Early practice tomorrow."

I walked him to the door, suddenly shy again despite everything we'd shared. "Talk tomorrow?"

"Definitely." He kissed me once more. "Goodnight, girlfriend."

"Goodnight, boyfriend," I replied, the word still new and thrilling on my tongue.

I'd never had a boyfriend before.

I closed the door behind him and then leaned against it, a smile spreading across my face. If someone had told me six months ago that I'd be dating Foster Kane—that I'd be falling for him—I would have laughed in their face.

Yet here I was, my lips still tingling from his kisses, my heart full in a way it hadn't been in years—maybe ever.

For the first time since my mom died, I felt like I was truly living again, not just going through the motions.

And it felt amazing.

It was stupid to be nervous at my own house party, but as I waited for Abby to arrive, I was. I wasn't worried about what other people would think, or about finally letting her stake her claim on me. I wanted everyone to know I was taken.

But I was nervous that this party might bring up bad memories for her. While I couldn't remember our night together freshman year, it was clear she did, and I did not want that negative memory to pop up tonight when it was supposed to be about us moving forward.

I checked my hair in the hall mirror one last time and readjusted my shirt when Liam walked around the corner. "Dude, what is your deal? I don't think I've ever seen you this nervous before."

Liam was right. I was fidgeting like I was about to take the ice for a championship game, not host a party I'd been to a hundred times before. My hands kept smoothing down my dark blue shirt that I'd chosen specifically because Abby had once mentioned she liked that color on me.

"I just want tonight to go well."

"Relax," Liam said, slapping me on the back. "We won't let anything happen with your girl. We'll make sure she's protected from any of the vultures."

What he meant was puck bunnies.

It didn't matter the popularity of the sport—athletes were never short on their choice of girls. Girls who'd throw themselves at any guy wearing our team's logo, looking for a hookup and the status that came with bedding one of us.

Before Abby, I might have indulged occasionally. But now the thought of anyone but her made me feel hollow.

Liam's hand gripped my shoulder as he guided me down the hall and into our living room, which was already teeming with people. The bass from Drew's carefully curated playlist thumped through the floorboards, and the scent of beer and perfume mingled in the air. Red plastic cups already littered every flat surface despite the trash cans we'd strategically placed around the room. With one last slap on the back, Liam made his way over to a group of girls, his arms extended.

I scanned the crowd for Abby even though I knew she likely wasn't here yet. She said she was going to text me when they were close. I checked my phone again but still no text. The screen remained stubbornly blank, making my stomach twist with anticipation.

"Hey, Foster," a sultry voice said from my side. I glanced over and found Brittany Armstrong standing much closer than I was comfortable with. Her blonde hair was perfectly styled, her makeup flawless, and her top cut low enough to leave little to the imagination.

We'd never hooked up but it wasn't for her lack of trying. I had a strict rule about not dating or hooking up with girls that my teammates had hooked up with, and Brittany had gotten around. Last I heard, she'd been with both

Drew and Liam at different points, though neither of them talked about it.

"Brittany," I said, acknowledging her while still scanning the space for Abby's arrival. I didn't want to be rude, but I also didn't want to encourage her.

Brittany placed her hand on my chest and started sliding it up before I grabbed her wrist and removed her hand. Her touch felt wrong, invasive even.

"Don't touch me," I told her, my voice firm but not cruel.

She batted her eyelashes, unperturbed by my rejection. "I bet I could make it good for you."

Her breath smelled like rum and Coke, and I took a small step back.

"I'm not interested," I told her, still trying to remain polite. I wasn't going to slut shame her, especially considering the guys that I lived with and their body count, but I also had firm boundaries and wanted her to respect them.

She gave me a faux pout, her glossy lips forming an exaggerated frown. "Foster, you know we'd be great together."

"I'm in a relationship," I told her, and heat infused my body as the words came out of my mouth. It felt good to be claimed. To belong to someone. To have someone who belonged to me in a way that meant something beyond physical attraction.

Brittany's jaw dropped. "What?"

Maybe I should have accounted for how surprising this news might be considering I hadn't had a relationship the whole time I'd gone to CFU. I'd been too focused on helping the hockey team get reinstated and find success to make time for a girlfriend. Between practices, games, and the pressure from my father about the business, relationships had always seemed like an unnecessary complication.

Until Abby.

"You heard me," I told her because it was clear she had. "I'm in a relationship, so please keep your hands to yourself. I'm sure there are other guys here who'd be happy to give you attention."

She frowned for a moment and then shrugged, her eyes gleaming with something that made me uncomfortable. "Your girlfriend doesn't have to know."

So, clearly Brittany wasn't a girl's girl. The casual way she suggested betraying Abby made my skin crawl. As if my relationship was just an inconvenient obstacle to be worked around rather than something I valued.

"*I* would know, Brittany, and I'm not gonna mess up what I have."

Abby was one of the first people in my life to make me feel things I hadn't known were possible. I wouldn't do anything to risk my relationship with her.

"Oh, come on, Foster," Brittany said and I opened my mouth to respond, but before the words on the tip of my tongue could come out, another familiar voice interrupted.

"I think he made himself pretty clear."

I looked away from Brittany and found Abby standing in front of us, Sam by her side staring daggers at Brittany, even though Abby had been the one to speak.

My heart did a somersault in my chest. Abby looked stunning in a simple green sweater that complemented her brown eyes and jeans that hugged her curves in all the right places. She wore her hair the way I loved it best— falling loosely around her shoulders. She looked fucking beautiful.

"You're the girlfriend?" Brittany asked, looking Abby up

and down with an expression that made me want to step between them.

I hated the judgment in her gaze, and before Abby could answer, I said, "Yeah, she is. Now you can either go enjoy the party around other people or you can get out of my house."

She huffed, spun on her heel, and then stormed away, her blonde hair whipping behind her as she disappeared into the crowd.

I turned to Abby, hoping this hadn't already ruined the party for her. "I'm so sorry."

The last thing I wanted was for her to feel uncomfortable or unwelcome at my house.

She moved closer until our bodies were nearly touching, and I gave in to the impulse to wrap my arms around her waist. Relief infused my body as she leaned against me and her hands rested on my chest. The warmth of her body eased the tension Brittany had caused.

These were the only hands I wanted on my body.

She smiled up at me, no trace of discomfort in her expression. "It's okay. You don't have anything to apologize for. Sorry we were a little late."

I smiled down at her and slid my hand through her hair then cupped the back of her neck. Her hair was like silk between my fingers. I used my thumb to tilt her chin up as I angled my face down and kissed her gently. Her lips were warm and yielding under mine, tasting faintly of cherry lip balm.

"I'm glad you're here," I said as I pulled away, though I kept her close, unwilling to break contact completely.

"Me too," she whispered against my lips, her breath mingling with mine.

"Alright, you two are adorably sickening so I'm gonna go

make the rounds," Sam said, rolling her eyes but smiling as she did.

We both grinned at her as she walked away, disappearing into the crowd with a confidence I'd come to associate with her. Then I took Abby's hand in mine and our fingers interlaced perfectly, like they were made to fit together. "You want a drink?" I asked her.

She nibbled that bottom lip of hers, and a bolt of lust struck me. My gaze darkened as it narrowed on her plump pink lip, and the ache to replace her teeth with mine was almost too strong to ignore. Heat pooled low in my stomach as I imagined all the ways I wanted to taste her.

"Or we could skip the party and go up to my room."

Red stained her cheeks, spreading across her face in a blush that I found endearing. For all her intelligence and confidence in some areas, she still had this adorable shyness that made me want to both protect her and corrupt her in equal measure.

"I think we should stay. You wanted this to be our big coming out. We can't really announce to the world that we're together as a couple if we hide away in your room."

She had a point. Plus, I didn't really want to rush this.

Don't get me wrong. I was desperate to be inside her, but I also wanted to savor every touch and every moment we had.

I wanted to take my time with her.

The guys would probably have called me a pussy for that, but Abby made me want to be tender. I wanted to make it special for her in a way it had never been for me. I'd always seen it as scratching an itch and a brief moment of connection. But I felt more connection with Abby just holding her hand, looking into her brown eyes than I ever had when I'd been having sex with someone else. And I knew being with her like that would ruin me for anyone else.

We walked around the party and I got us some drinks. I introduced her to people, my arm around her waist, my thumb occasionally brushing the strip of skin exposed when her sweater rode up. Each touch sent electricity through my fingertips.

We joined in a game of beer pong and it was fun to teach Abby how to play. Her aim was surprisingly accurate, and the concentration on her face as she lined up her shots was adorable. She was pretty good although she claimed it was beginner's luck.

I wasn't so sure about that. She seemed to be good at anything she put her mind to. I'd seen how she approached her studies, how she'd figured out methods to help me with math when no one else had ever been able to. She had a way of breaking problems down and finding solutions that was nothing short of impressive.

It only took a few introductions of her as my girlfriend before word spread through the party. It was almost amusing watching the looks and the whispers, the awe in some of the faces, the smiles and the claps on the back from other guys.

A few of the hockey guys who didn't live with us came over to meet her, and I could tell they were impressed by how easily she kept up with their banter. Seeing her fit in so seamlessly with my friends just drove home the fact that she was perfect for me.

As I looked around the room, very few of these people actually knew me, and none of them knew me as well as Abby except for maybe Gordy, Drew, and Liam. So why did it even matter what they thought?

Why did it even matter that we made this official in this way?

Abby was mine and I was hers. No one else got a say in that.

As if sensing my thoughts, she squeezed my hand and leaned up to whisper in my ear, "I'm having a really good time."

I pulled her closer, wrapping both arms around her waist and resting my forehead against hers. In a room full of people, it felt like we were the only two that existed. "Me too," I murmured. "But mostly because you're here."

Her smile in response was worth every moment of nervousness I'd felt earlier. This wasn't just another party. This was the start of something that felt bigger than anything I'd experienced before. And for once in my life, I wasn't thinking about hockey or my father or what anyone else expected of me.

I was just thinking about her.

I was just finishing my makeup when my phone started to buzz on the bathroom counter. I figured it was Sam, or maybe Foster letting me know he was on his way, but when I saw Mason's name, my heart dropped.

My brother didn't call.

Ever.

Not unless something was wrong.

I swiped to answer, nerves already tingling beneath my skin. "Hey, Mase. Everything okay?"

There was a pause, and then his voice came through, quieter than usual. "I don't know. Gram has gotten worse." His voice dipped lower like voicing the words would make his fears come true.

I sank onto the edge of my bed. "What's going on?"

"It's a bunch of little things—not being as active, losing weight, dark circles under her eyes... She looks like she's in pain, but she tries to hide it. She's not eating much and sleeping a lot. She hasn't even gone to the community center at all this week."

That *was* a big deal. Gram had been volunteering at the

community center for as long as I could remember. She was always going there to help with one thing or another.

"Have you asked her about it?"

With all the craziness of school starting and dating Foster, I hadn't made it home in a few weeks. Now, I felt guilty for not making it a priority. I'd texted Mason nightly to check in, but clearly he'd been holding back on me and this wasn't something he should have to deal with on his own.

"I told you she hasn't been herself in months," he said quietly. "Do you think she's...dying?" He choked out the last word like even speaking it would make it true.

The threat of tears burned behind my eyes, but I refused to give in. My brother and I had suffered enough loss for a lifetime, but I had to be strong for him. I was the big sister. The responsible one. The one who was supposed to have answers.

But the truth was I was afraid to answer his question because I didn't know how he'd handle it if she was.

I didn't know how *I'd* survive it if she was dying.

Gram had been our rock through the loss of both of our parents, and losing her would shake our foundation in a way that terrified me. She was all we had left. The only adult who'd been a constant in our lives. The only person who remembered all the little details about our childhood that our parents had taken with them.

"I don't know," I told him honestly. I wished I had a better answer. I wished I could tell him everything would be fine, that Gram was just having a bad week, that she'd bounce back like she always did. But I couldn't ignore what he was telling me.

We were both silent before he made an excuse to cut the call short. That didn't ease my worry any.

I sat on my bed, a familiar numbness starting from my toes and moving up my body. It seemed my response to grief was to shut down and lock all emotion away.

What were we going to do if Gram was dying?

My phone started vibrating in my hand, and Foster's name flashed on the screen. Just seeing his name brought a small measure of comfort.

"Hey," I said, answering the phone.

"Hey yourself, Gorgeous. I just got done with practice. Still on for dinner?"

For a second, I debated canceling. I knew I wasn't in the best mindset, but Foster had been my comfort for far longer than he'd been my boyfriend, and I needed someone to lean on right now.

"Yeah, we're still on. But how about I meet you there."

"You sure?"

"Yeah. See you in a few."

I got to the restaurant a few minutes earlier than I'd expected and sat in my car, staring out the window as emotion hit me unexpectedly.

Maybe I wasn't as good about keeping everything in a box as I used to be.

Before I could spiral into a full-blown meltdown, there was a knock on my window. Foster was standing there with a warm smile on his face. I quickly got out of the car, and immediately his strong arms wrapped around me, giving me the exact comfort I needed.

It was hard to hold back the tears this time. The solid warmth of him, the familiar scent of his cologne, the gentle way his hand cradled the back of my head—it all threatened to break the dam I'd carefully constructed.

He pulled back just enough to cup my cheeks, his blue

eyes searching mine with genuine concern. "Hey, what's going on?"

"I think my grandma's sick. My brother called me before you did and he thinks she might be—"

I choked on the final word, and the tears I'd been holding back spilled out like someone had flipped on the switch to a water fountain. Foster brushed them aside with his thumbs and held me tight as I finally let out the fear I'd held close to my heart. I pressed my face against his chest, my shoulders shaking as silent sobs worked their way through my body.

He didn't judge me.

He didn't try to shush me or tell me it would be okay.

He simply held me and offered comfort, one hand rubbing slow circles on my back while the other remained steady against my head, anchoring me to him as the storm passed through me.

It was the exact thing I needed from him.

When I pulled away again, there was a damp spot on his blue shirt where my tears had soaked through the fabric.

"I'm sorry for getting your shirt all wet," I said, embarrassed by my outburst.

I was not a girl who fell apart in public—or in front of people at all.

"It's just a little water. I'll survive," he said with a gentle smile, tucking a strand of hair behind my ear. His expression grew serious again. "What do you need? How can I help?"

I looked up into his clear blue eyes, taking in the genuine concern written across his features, the way his brow furrowed slightly as he waited for my answer, the steadiness in his gaze that promised he wouldn't look away from my pain. And I was pretty sure in that moment my heart would beat for only him for the rest of my life.

"You're already doing it," I told him, reaching up to place my palm against his cheek. "Thank you."

"You don't need to thank me, Abby. I want to be here for you with whatever you need."

And that was the very reason I was already falling so hard for him.

THIRTY-FIVE

For the last week, Abby had been distant. She'd gone to visit her Gram after Mason's worrying call, but she'd confessed that seeing her grandma hadn't eased any of her worries, and when she'd tried to talk to her about it, her concerns had been brushed aside. Since then, she'd been lost in her own head, clearly still worried. I knew my plan for tonight wouldn't fix what was going on with her grandma or ease her worry over her brother, but I hoped it would give her a much-needed chance to just disconnect and relax.

When she showed up to my place, I had a handful of options ready to go—a large bowl of popcorn, a variety of candy choices, and an assortment of drinks. I wanted this night to be relaxing and low-key for her. I'd even cleaned our living room, which was saying something considering I lived with three other guys who weren't exactly known for their tidiness.

"You've thought of everything," she said, a genuine smile spreading across her face as she surveyed the coffee table laden with snacks.

"I just want you to be able to relax tonight," I told her,

pulling her into my arms and pressing a gentle kiss to her forehead. "No worrying allowed."

We got snuggled on the couch with a Marvel movie—*Thor: Ragnarok*, because she wanted action and a laugh. I draped my favorite blanket over our laps, and Abby nestled perfectly into the crook of my arm, her head resting against my chest. The weight of her against me felt right in a way I was getting dangerously addicted to.

The longer we were together, the greater my sense of peace when she was around.

The movie had just started when the door opened and Drew and Liam walked in.

"What are you guys doing here? I thought you had dates tonight." My tone made it clear I wasn't thrilled with the interruption.

"Nah," Liam said, shrugging off his jacket and tossing it over the back of a chair. "The girls found out we'd hooked up with their other roommates and got pissed, so the dates ended early and we decided just to cut our losses and come back home."

"Hey, is that *Thor*?" Drew asked, his eyes lighting up as he recognized the movie playing on the screen.

Drew and Liam started to take seats on the other couch and I sat forward. "Whoa, whoa, whoa, what are you guys doing?"

"We're joining you," Liam said, like it should be obvious. He flopped down on the couch to our left, immediately reaching for the bowl of popcorn. "This is one of our favorite movies."

"I'm on a *date*," I told them, gesturing to Abby who was sitting there, biting back a grin. Her eyes danced with amusement as she watched the exchange.

Liam arched a brow, his expression completely unapologetic. "Dude, you take your girl *out* to a movie when you're on a date. You're just hanging out at home, so you get what you get. We're here now and we want to watch the movie."

"Yeah, if you wanted privacy, you would have watched the movie in your room," Drew added, already making himself comfortable next to Liam and grabbing a handful of my carefully prepared snacks.

"I thought you guys were going to be out for the night," I said, not bothering to hide my frustration.

"Well, now we're not." Drew's smirk was infuriating.

Before I could fight with them anymore, the front door opened again and Gordy walked in.

"What are *you* doing here?" I asked, completely exasperated with my housemates now. I wasn't sure where he'd been, but he told me he had plans tonight.

He shrugged. "My plans fell through. What are you guys watching?"

"*Abby and I*," I enunciated, emphasizing each word, "are on a date watching *Thor: Ragnarok*."

He stared at me and Abby and then his gaze moved to Drew and Liam before they bounced back to me. "Well, if you wanted privacy, you should have watched it in your own room."

Abby let out a choked snort beside me that quickly turned into a full belly laugh, and I couldn't fight the grin that spread across my face. "This is amusing to you, huh?"

The smile that lit up her face made my heart race as her beautiful brown eyes connected with mine. "I mean, I've got to be the luckiest girl on campus to be on a date with four of the best players on the hockey team."

Liam sat forward and opened his mouth, but I held up my finger. "Don't even say it. I don't share," I said.

Abby's cheeks blushed my favorite shade of pink and I

wrapped my arm around her, holding her close. Then I let out a heavy sigh, giving in to the losing battle. "Fine, I guess we're all watching the movie."

It was well past midnight by the time the movie ended. The guys had been decent company, keeping their commentary mostly funny rather than obnoxious. Abby had laughed at their jokes, once again proving how seamlessly she fit in with my friends and making my chest tight with an emotion I wasn't quite ready to name.

Now we stood in the entryway as she gathered her things, and I was worried about her driving home this late at night.

"What if you stayed here?" I said, the words coming out before I could overthink them.

"With you?" Her eyes widened slightly, a mix of surprise and something else—anticipation, maybe—flickering across her face.

"Yeah, my bed's big enough. And I'd feel better knowing you're not driving this time of night."

She nibbled her lip and I used my thumb to pull it away from her teeth. The soft fullness of her bottom lip beneath my touch sent a jolt of desire through me. "You know, every time you do that, you make me want to bite this lip. You have no idea what you do to me, do you?"

"No," she said, her voice barely above a whisper.

I bent my head down, close enough that our foreheads nearly touched. "You make me feel things I've never felt before." The admission felt raw and honest in a way I'd only ever allowed myself to be with her.

She swallowed thickly and looked up at me, her eyes filled with vulnerability. "I'm a virgin," she said quickly like she was confessing a crime.

I suspected as much, based on things she'd said and how she'd acted before, but hearing it, feeling the weight of those words, knowing eventually I would be her first—and if I was lucky, her only—hit me hard. The responsibility of that trust settled over me, and I knew in that moment I would do anything to be worthy of it.

"We're not having sex tonight," I told her, my voice gentle but firm.

The spot between her eyebrows furrowed. "We aren't?" A hint of confusion—maybe even disappointment—crossed her face.

I shook my head, brushing a strand of hair behind her ear. "No, because I want it to be special for you, and losing your virginity after the guys just crashed our date is really not romantic in the slightest."

She giggled and the sound warmed me to my core. "No, I suppose it's not," she said, her shoulders relaxing. "So then what would we do?"

I kissed her nose, loving the way it scrunched up in response. "Well, first I'll get you into one of my T-shirts." I kissed her cheek, feeling the silkiness of her skin against my lips. "And then I'll pull you close." I kissed her other cheek, breathing in the light vanilla-citrus scent of her body lotion. "And then we might make out a little bit, if you want." I kissed her lips, gently at first, then with more pressure as she responded before I reluctantly pulled away. Fuck, I loved kissing her. "And then we'll go to sleep."

Her pout was adorable, her bottom lip jutting out just enough to make me want to capture it between my teeth. "That's it?"

I laughed, pressing my forehead against hers. "That's it for tonight. I want to take my time with you, Abby. I want it to be perfect."

She nodded, her features relaxing into an achingly tender expression. "Okay."

I took her hand and led her to my bedroom, closing the door behind us. My room was probably the cleanest in the house, mainly because I'd cleaned it before she came over. My queen-sized bed was pushed to the right against the wall, covered in a dark blue comforter I'd purchased a few weeks ago. My dresser, closet, and desk were on the other side.

I pulled out a clean T-shirt from my drawer and handed it to her. "Bathroom's through there if you want to change," I said, nodding toward the en suite and suddenly grateful that I paid more to have the primary bedroom. The other guys had to share a bathroom, and I didn't like the idea of them seeing her in this state of undress.

When she emerged a few minutes later wearing nothing but my shirt, which fell to mid-thigh on her shorter frame, I nearly forgot how to breathe. Her hair was down, cascading over her shoulders. She looked impossibly beautiful.

I'd told her once she was way out of my league, and I still thought that was true.

"Is this okay?" she asked, tugging at the hem of the shirt.

"More than okay," I managed, my voice rougher than I intended. I'd changed into a pair of sweatpants and a fresh T-shirt while she was in the bathroom. I normally slept in my boxer briefs, but more clothes seemed like a good idea if I was going to keep from going too far.

I pulled back the covers and gestured for her to get in. She slid between the sheets, and I followed, immediately drawing her into my arms. She fit against me perfectly, her back to my chest, her curves molding against my body like she was made for me.

"This is nice," she murmured, her voice already heavy with sleep.

I pressed a kiss to the back of her head. "Yeah, it is."

"Foster?"

"Hmm?"

"Thank you for tonight. For trying to give me a break from everything."

I tightened my arms around her. "Anytime, Babe. I mean it."

She turned in my arms to face me, her eyes searching mine in the dim light filtering through the curtains. "I know you do," she whispered, leaning forward to press her lips to mine.

What started as a gentle kiss quickly deepened as she parted her lips, inviting me in. I groaned softly against her mouth, my hand sliding up her back, feeling the warmth of her skin through the thin fabric of my shirt. Her fingers tangled in my hair, pulling me closer as our tongues met in a slow, sensual dance.

We kissed until we were both breathless, until my control started slipping. I was sure she could feel what she did to me since my cock was hard as a rock and pressing against her. Reluctantly, I pulled back, pressing one last chaste kiss to her swollen lips.

"We should probably stop," I whispered, my voice strained.

She nodded, though her eyes were still dark with desire. "Probably, but I don't want to."

She pulled my head back down and I went willingly, kissing her with everything I had.

Her body arched against mine, our legs intertwining

until her soaked panties ground against my thigh and it nearly broke me. The heat of her against my leg had me harder than steel.

She whimpered as she found a rhythm, grinding against me. I moved my mouth, kissing down her neck, as I slipped my hands into her underwear, gripping her luscious ass that I'd had too many dreams about to count.

"Foster," she moaned. "Please," she begged, her voice taking on a needy edge.

"Please what, Baby? Tell me what you want."

"Touch me," she whispered.

"I am touching you."

"Make me come...please."

Fuck. I couldn't deny her when she begged me like that.

I slid my hand around to the front of her body and then pressed two fingers against her swollen clit. Her whole body shuddered against mine as she let out another breathy moan that had me dangerously close to the edge of coming.

"Oh, God. That feels so good," she sighed.

I was desperate to taste her—to feel her come on my tongue—but I wouldn't push her that far tonight.

"Fuck, Baby. You're so wet for me."

She whimpered, nuzzling her face against my neck. Fuck, she was going to make me come. It had been too long, and touching her like this already had me so fucking close.

"You gonna come for me?"

"Y-yes," she stuttered, her body tensing against me as I continued to rub circles over her needy little clit.

She cried out as she came, and the way her wetness coated my fingers had me so hard, it was a miracle I didn't come in my pants.

She sagged against me, while both of us tried to catch our breath.

I tucked her head under my chin, holding her close as our breathing gradually slowed. The feel of her in my arms, the scent of her hair, the steady rhythm of her heart against mine—it all felt right in a way nothing ever had before.

It felt even better knowing I'd given her pleasure no one else ever had.

As she drifted off to sleep, her breathing becoming deep and even, I realized something that should have terrified me but somehow didn't. I was falling in love with Abby Walker. And for the first time in my life, I wasn't afraid of what that meant.

"Sweet dreams, Baby," I whispered into the darkness, knowing that mine would be filled with her.

I stepped onto the ice for warm-ups, my skates cutting clean lines across the freshly smoothed surface from the Zamboni. The rink smelled like home—that distinct mix of cold air, sweat, and rubber that had been part of my life since I was four years old. Our first official game of the season always carried a special energy. The stands were packed with students and alumni, and I could feel the buzz even during warm-ups.

Thursday night games were always a rush because we weren't competing with the football crowd. Football reigned supreme at CFU, but hockey was a close second.

"Heads up, Captain!" Drew called before firing a puck my way.

I caught it on my stick, transitioning smoothly into a dangle before sending it back his way. We'd been doing this pre-game ritual since his freshman year, and it still settled my nerves every time.

"Looks like a good crowd tonight," Liam commented as he skated past, nodding toward the bleachers that were filling up fast.

I scanned the crowd, my eyes automatically searching for one person in particular. Abby had texted that she and Sam were running late but would make it before puck drop. I tried not to feel disappointed when I didn't spot her familiar face.

"Your girl's not here yet?" Gordy asked, coming to a stop beside me and spraying ice across my skates.

"She's on her way."

"Good, because you play like shit when you're distracted," he said with a smirk.

"Fuck off," I laughed, shoving his padded shoulder.

Coach Maxwell called us over, and we gathered around him for final instructions. Tonight we were playing against Bozeman Tech, a team we'd narrowly defeated last season. They had a solid defensive core and a goalie who seemed to have magnets in his gloves.

"Alright, gentlemen, time to focus," Coach said. "Kane, start the pressure early. Farrell, be ready to pinch hard if they try to chip it out. Let's start this season with a win."

We tapped our sticks on the ice in agreement before dispersing for the final minutes of warm-up. As I skated toward our bench, I glanced at the stands again, and a sense of giddiness unfurled in my gut when I spotted Abby and Sam making their way to seats in the second row. Abby caught my eye and waved, her smile so beautiful it nearly took my breath away. I raised my stick in acknowledgment, suddenly feeling like I could take on the entire opposing team single-handedly.

"There's your girl," Drew said, nudging me. "Try not to show off too much."

"Says the guy who does a spin-o-rama every time he's trying to impress a girl at the game," I retorted.

"Hey, I'm a defenseman with many talents, including

pulling the offensive, so sue me for wanting to show off my skills."

The buzzer sounded, signaling the end of warm-ups, and we headed to the locker room for final preparations. As we filed in, I couldn't help but look back one more time at Abby. She was wearing my away jersey—the black one with my number 88 on the back. Our jerseys didn't have our names on them because that would be too expensive to replace every year, but knowing she was wearing my number was enough. Seeing her now, I had no doubt she would've looked incredible in our maroon home jerseys too. Something primal and possessive flared in my chest at the sight.

I'd never let a girl wear my jersey, and now I couldn't picture anyone but her in it.

In the locker room, I focused on getting my head in the game. As captain, the guys looked to me to set the tone. Coach gave his final pep talk, and then it was time.

"Alright boys," I said as we huddled up. "Let's fucking go!"

We lined up out of the tunnel and skated onto the ice to the cheers of the crowd, the adrenaline surging through my veins. I took my position for the opening face-off, grasping my stick above the ice as I squared off against Bozeman's center. The referee dropped the puck, and the game was on.

I won the draw cleanly back to Drew, who quickly moved it up to Liam streaking along the boards. The first few minutes were fast-paced, both teams testing each other's defenses without any clear chances.

Midway through the first period, Bozeman caught us on a bad line change. Their winger broke free and fired a shot that Gordy managed to deflect with his pad, but the rebound went straight to their trailing center who buried it before any of us could get back.

"Fuck," I muttered as the red light flashed behind our net. 1-0 Bozeman.

"Shake it off," Coach called from the bench. "Plenty of game left."

We reset for the center ice face-off, and I could feel my competitive instinct kicking into overdrive. I hated being behind, especially at home.

The rest of the period was a battle, with neither team giving an inch. When the buzzer sounded, we headed to the locker room still down by one.

"We're playing well," Coach said, adjusting the whiteboard to show a new forecheck pattern. "But we need to create more traffic in front of their goalie. Kane, I want you to park yourself in the crease more. Make it impossible for him to see the puck."

The second period started with renewed energy. True to Coach's instructions, I positioned myself directly in front of Bozeman's goalie every chance I got, using my size to screen him while our defensemen fired shots from the point. Five minutes in, our strategy paid off. Drew fired a shot from the blue line that the goalie never saw thanks to my screen. The puck sailed past his blocker and into the net, tying the game at 1-1.

The crowd erupted, and I pumped my fist, feeling that rush of adrenaline I'd only ever felt on the ice. As we skated back to the bench for a line change, I looked for Abby and found her jumping up and down, high-fiving Sam. Seeing her excitement had me grinning like an idiot.

"Nice screen," Coach said as I took my seat on the bench. "Keep it up."

The momentum had shifted in our favor, and we

pressed our advantage. Liam nearly scored on a breakaway but was denied by a spectacular glove save. The pace was frantic, both teams trading chances. Gordy stood tall in our net, making several key saves to keep the game tied.

With two minutes left in the period, I got on the ice for my shift and immediately found myself in the middle of a scramble along the boards. I dug the puck out and fed it to Drew at the point. He fired a shot that was blocked, but I managed to corral the rebound. Out of the corner of my eye, I saw Liam—normally holding the blue line—slip behind their coverage at the far post.

Without hesitation, I threaded a pass through two defensemen, and Liam one-timed it into the open net. 2-1 our lead.

The crowd went wild.

"Fucking beautiful pass, Kane!" Liam shouted over the noise.

The period ended with us clinging to that one-goal lead, though Bozeman had pushed hard in the final minute. As we headed to the locker room, I felt confident but knew we couldn't let up.

"Twenty more minutes, boys," Coach said. "They're going to throw everything at us. Stay disciplined, block shots, and take care of the puck."

The third period was a battle from the opening face-off. Bozeman came out desperate, forechecking aggressively and hemming us in our own zone for long stretches. Gordy made save after save, some of them bordering on miraculous. We blocked shots with every part of our bodies, throwing ourselves in front of pucks without hesitation.

Midway through the period, I took a slap shot to the inside of my knee where there was a gap in my pads. The pain was immediate and blinding, but I gritted my teeth and finished my shift before limping to the bench.

"You good?" Coach asked, his eyes assessing me critically.

"I'm fine," I said. There was no way I was missing the end of this game.

With five minutes left, disaster struck. Drew got called for a borderline tripping penalty, sending us into a penalty kill at the worst possible time. As one of our primary penalty killers, I took the opening face-off in our defensive zone, winning it cleanly and clearing the puck down the ice.

For the next two minutes, we defended like our lives depended on it. Gordy made three spectacular saves in succession, and I blocked a shot with my shoulder that would definitely leave a mark. When Drew finally stepped out of the box, the crowd gave us a standing ovation for surviving the penalty kill with our lead intact.

"Three minutes left," Coach called as I gulped water on the bench. "Smart hockey now. No turnovers at the blue lines."

The tension in the arena was palpable as they pressed for the tying goal. I won a crucial face-off in our zone, and we managed to clear the puck, but they quickly regrouped and came back on the attack.

With thirty seconds left, their defenseman fired a shot from the point that Gordy stopped, but the rebound bounced right to their winger. He had a wide-open net, but somehow—I still don't know how—Drew dove across the crease and blocked the shot with his stick. The puck skittered to the corner where I battled for it, eventually chipping it out of the zone and down the ice.

The final buzzer sounded. We'd held on for a 2-1 victory.

"Fuck, yeah!" I shouted, skating over to Gordy and tackling him in celebration. The rest of the team piled on, a mass of sweaty, exhausted, and elated hockey players.

After shaking hands with the Bozeman players—a few of whom I knew from playing against them over the years—we started heading for the locker room. I sought out Abby in the crowd and found her beaming with pride, my jersey loose on her smaller frame. Her smile made our victory all the sweeter.

In the locker room, all the guys were amped up from our win. Someone had connected a speaker, and music blasted as we changed out of our gear.

"Party at the house!" Drew announced to nobody's surprise. Our post-win celebrations were legendary on campus.

I peeled off my sweaty equipment, wincing at the already-purpling bruise on my knee. Our trainer came by to check it, confirming it was just a bruise and nothing structural.

"You'll live," he said dryly. "Ice it tonight and try not to do anything stupid at your party."

"No promises," I replied with a grin.

After a quick shower, I checked my phone to find a text from Abby.

ABBY

You were amazing out there! We'll wait for you by the main entrance.

I smiled, typing back:

Be there in 5. btw my jersey looks good on you.

As I finished getting dressed, Coach came by to give me

a fist bump. "Good leadership tonight, Kane. Way to battle through that shot block."

"Thanks, Coach. Gordy's the real hero tonight."

"True," he laughed. "But that pass to Farrell on the second goal was a thing of beauty. Keep that up and maybe we'll make it to the conference playoffs."

I gathered my gear bag and headed out to meet Abby, my body sore but my spirits high. The main entrance was crowded with friends and family waiting for players, but I spotted Abby and Sam immediately. Abby's face lit up when she saw me, and she rushed over, throwing her arms around my neck.

"That was incredible!" she exclaimed, her eyes bright with excitement.

I laughed, wrapping my arms around her waist. "So I take it you enjoyed your first official game as the captain's girlfriend?"

"I definitely did. You were amazing out there," she said earnestly. "And that save Gordy made in the third period? I thought Sam was going to fall off her seat."

"It's true," Sam confirmed, joining us. "I've never screamed so much at a sporting event in my life. Also, I'm pretty sure I'm in love with your goalie now."

"I'll be sure to tell him," I teased.

Drew and Liam emerged from the locker room, immediately drawing a small crowd of admirers. Gordy followed a minute later, looking stoic as usual, despite the attention he was receiving for his stellar performance.

"Party at our place," Drew announced to the group at large. "Starting as soon as we get there."

As we all headed to the parking lot, I kept my arm around Abby's shoulders, enjoying the way she fit perfectly against my side. My knee throbbed and my shoulder ached from the blocked shot, but I couldn't remember the last time I felt this content.

"You're limping," Abby observed as we neared my truck. "Are you okay?"

"Just a bruise," I assured her, touched by her concern. "Occupational hazard."

She frowned slightly. "Maybe we should skip the party so you can rest?"

"Not a chance," I said, kissing her forehead. "Captain can't miss the victory celebration. Besides, I want to show off my beautiful girlfriend."

Her cheeks flushed at the compliment, and she ducked her head in that shy way that never failed to charm me. "Fine, but you have to promise to ice that knee later."

"Yes, ma'am," I agreed solemnly, then I lowered my voice and whispered in her ear. "If you really want to make me feel better, you could always sit on my face while I'm icing my knee." If I thought her cheeks were pink before, it was nothing compared to now as she playfully swatted me on my stomach with the back of her hand.

"Behave."

THIRTY-SEVEN

The hockey house was already buzzing with energy when we arrived. Music thumped through the walls, and the living room was already packed with people celebrating the win against Bozeman Tech. I'd never been much of a party person before Foster, but being with him made me feel more comfortable in these situations.

"Want a drink?" Foster asked, his arm around my waist as we navigated through the crowd.

"Just water for now," I replied, noticing how he was favoring his right leg. "You sure you should be standing?" I asked him as he handed me a water bottle.

He grinned, pulling me closer. "I'm fine. Hockey players are tough. I've played through worse injuries than this. A little ibuprofen and ice and I'll be good as new."

"Mm-hmm," I hummed skeptically, watching him wince slightly when someone bumped into him.

We spent the next hour mingling with his teammates and their friends. I was still getting used to being "Foster Kane's girlfriend" and the attention that came with it. But tonight, I found myself caring less about what others thought and more about the way Foster's hand never left mine, how his eyes kept finding me even in mid-conversation with someone else.

When someone started recounting Foster's game-winning assist for what must have been the fifth time, I leaned in closer to Foster. "How about we get some ice for that knee?"

He turned his head, brushing his lips against my ear, his voice low so only I could hear. "How about we skip the ice and just go straight to my room?"

I wrapped my hand around the back of his neck, holding his gaze. "But I was promised something contingent on you icing that knee...and I really want to try it."

He groaned and pulled me tight against his body where I could feel his hard length against my stomach. "Fuck, Abby."

Without another word, he grabbed my hand and headed straight for the stairs. I pulled back and let out a laugh at the disgruntled look he gave me for slowing him down.

"You're forgetting something."

He stepped forward, trapping me between the wall by the stairs and his big, hard body. "All I can think about is getting a taste of your pussy. You have no idea how long I've been thinking about it. About how sweet you probably taste or how it'll feel to have your thighs hug my cheeks as you come."

A shiver of need slid through my body.

"But if you insist on the ice—"

"I do," I said with a wicked smile. I kind of loved seeing him all worked up like this knowing it was because of me.

He let out a heavy sigh. "Stay right here." He kissed me hard and then before I could catch my breath, he hustled off to the kitchen. He returned to my side in record time with an ice pack in one hand. Then he took my hand again and led me upstairs to his room.

It was so much quieter up here than it was downstairs, especially with his door closed and locked. Yet we could still hear the heavy bass pumping through the house from Drew's playlist and feel the subtle vibrations through the floor.

But I couldn't think about all the people downstairs when Foster was looking at me like a lion who finally found his prey.

"Before you go getting any ideas, you need to lie down and put that ice pack on your knee."

His grin was playful compared to the lust shining in his eyes which I swore had turned a darker blue than normal. Without a word, he grabbed the back of his shirt and pulled it over his head. It ruffled his hair, and my breath caught at the sight of him so sexy and disheveled, especially when I looked down to his six-pack abs that looked way too perfect to be real.

"What are you doing?" I asked, my voice hoarse as he unbuttoned his pants and pushed them off.

"I'm just getting comfortable before I ice up."

I swallowed thickly. "You're telling me whenever you need to ice after a game, you strip down to your boxer briefs?"

He nodded, his gaze filled with hunger. "You should join me."

Not one to step back from a challenge—especially after the orgasm he'd brought me to with just his fingers the other night—I kept my gaze locked on his as I pulled off my shirt and then kicked off my shoes and pushed down my pants until I was standing before him in just my bra and underwear.

He rubbed a hand over his mouth and jaw as his hungry gaze slid down my body before coming back up to meet mine. "You're the most beautiful woman I've ever seen. Inside and out."

Heat flooded my cheeks, but I couldn't look away from him. I was growing addicted to the way he looked at me— the way he made me feel.

He closed the distance between us and wrapped his hand around the back of my neck, pulling me close as he dropped his head down and kissed me. This kiss was filled with longing, and it felt like a possession—like he owned me as much as I owned him.

He rotated us and only broke the kiss to lie down on the bed. He took the ice pack that was already wrapped in a dish towel and placed it over his knee. Then he lay completely flat and reached out to tap my thigh.

"Take off your underwear and come sit on my face."

If I thought my cheeks were hot before, they were nothing compared to how they felt at those words leaving his lips.

Nerves threatened to overwhelm me, but I trusted Foster and wanted to experience this—everything—with him. Before I could change my mind, I unhooked my bra and pushed my panties down my legs. A low rumble came from his throat as he watched my every move.

The way he couldn't take his eyes off me made me feel more powerful than I'd ever felt before. With a newfound confidence, I crawled over his body until I was straddling his face and my nerves flared back to life.

What if there was something wrong with me down there?

Sam had talked me into getting regular waxes with her, so I knew things were tidy, but what if my vagina didn't look normal? Was there such a thing? What if it smelled or didn't taste good? I didn't buy for a second that it tasted like honey and roses or whatever BS people spouted.

What if he didn't actually like it?

"Baby, I don't know what you're thinking, but if you're worried about how you appear right now, I can assure you, I've never seen anything sexier in my whole life."

"Have you done this before?"

The words were out before I could stop them, and I immediately regretted the question. Of course he'd done this before. I knew Foster wasn't a virgin. Not even close, although I didn't know his exact number.

He squeezed my thigh where it rested next to his cheek and I sat back. God, this was so awkward. I couldn't have a serious conversation with him when my pussy was right in front of his face like this. "Never mind. Forget I asked that."

His smile was the same one that always disarmed me. "I've never done this position before, but I've seen it in porn and thought about it a lot—specifically trying it with you. There's a lot of things I'd like to try with you."

"Really?"

He placed a sweet kiss on my thigh, easing some of my sudden insecurities. "Really. Now, can I enjoy my treat? Because I haven't stopped thinking about this pussy since I felt you come on my fingers, and I'm getting desperate for a taste."

"Okay," I whispered, my voice suddenly dry as I stared down at him.

And then he licked up the seam of my pussy and all my thoughts fled from my mind like water down a drain.

I grabbed the headboard as a flash of pleasure hit me. "Oh, God."

He groaned and wrapped his arms around my thighs, pulling me tight so I was *literally* sitting on his face—no hovering, no trying to maintain some semblance of control. I tried to pull back, but he shook his head no and sucked on my clit.

"What if I suffocate you?" I cried out as another bolt of pleasure went off inside me.

He pulled back just enough for his hot breath to cause a different kind of pleasure to tighten inside me. "Then I'll die the luckiest man alive."

Then he was back to licking and sucking me like I was the most delicious dessert he'd ever tasted.

My thighs shook around his cheeks while I held on to the headboard for dear life. I was already so close. I never knew oral could feel like this. No wonder so many people loved it.

"F-Foster," I whimpered as my core tightened, my pleasure ramping up to a tipping point. "I'm so close."

He groaned against my sex and then his tongue swirled around my clit before he sucked on it hard.

I detonated, my body tensing as my climax barreled through me unlike anything I'd ever experienced before.

He slowed his ministrations as my body shook with aftershocks and then, with one final lick, pulled away. His eyes were glazed with lust, and satisfaction filled his face.

"You taste even better than I imagined. I think I might be addicted."

I think I was a little addicted myself.

I slid back on his chest and leaned down to kiss him, surprised by the taste of myself on his tongue—not surprised that it was there, but surprised that I enjoyed tasting myself in his kiss.

"Your turn?"

His cheeks flushed bright red. "Uh...I, uh..." His sheepish look was so out of character, I was worried for a second, until he finally finished what he was going to say. "I kinda came already."

I reached behind me, and sure enough, there was a wet spot on his underwear. A smile pulled at my cheeks.

He frowned. "Don't let this mislead you into thinking I don't have stamina because I definitely do and someday I'll prove it to you." He wrapped his arms around me, his own lips curling in a small smile. "But you are so sexy when you come, I was already coming before I even realized it."

"That's kinda hot," I admitted.

His eyes lit up. "Yeah?"

"Yeah," I said, leaning down to kiss him again. "You know, we could do more tonight, if you want to."

He slid a piece of hair behind my ear. "I believe I promised you romance for your first time, and romance you'll get."

"I don't need romance. It's not like I held on to my virginity as some kind of romantic gesture. I just never found the time or person I wanted to lose it to."

He wrapped his strong arms around me. "I want sex to be special with us. We don't have to wait long if you don't want to, but at least let me make it a little romantic for you."

I snuggled into his arms, resting my head on his chest. "If you insist."

I just hoped he wouldn't make us wait too long because I already knew I was ready for that next step.

He didn't make me wait long at all. After a few more nights of hot hookups that had both of us pushing the line closer and closer, I wasn't surprised that he was ready to give in. But I *was* surprised when I showed up to the hockey house to find it empty. Usually there was at least one of his roommates home when I'd come over.

Foster was quiet as he walked me up to his room, and when he opened the door, my breath caught.

There were rose petals scattered on the bed and string lights set up on the walls, creating a romantic ambiance that hadn't been here yesterday. There was even soft music playing from the laptop on his desk.

"Foster..." I whispered, my voice hoarse with emotion.

I never thought I wanted hearts and flowers. I wasn't holding on to my virginity as if it was some gift or anything. But I'd never expected this.

"I know it's not much—"

"Are you kidding? Foster, this is...it's a lot more than I ever thought I'd have."

He frowned. "You deserve the world." He gripped the

back of his neck. "I thought about booking a nice hotel room and making it romantic, but that felt a little too cliché, and I don't want you to feel pressured—"

"I don't," I assured him. If anything, I was the one who'd been pushing for us to take this next step. It was Foster who kept slowing us down because he wanted me to be sure.

I was sure.

A moment passed between us, the air heavy with what was coming. Foster's eyes never left mine as he closed the distance until I could feel the warmth radiating from his body. His fingers found the hem of my shirt, and with deliberate slowness, he lifted it over my head.

The cool air kissed my skin, but it was his gaze that sent goosebumps racing across my body. His finger traced my collarbone, feather-light, before dipping down between my breasts. My lungs struggled to find a rhythm as each shallow breath came faster than the last. The intensity in his eyes made me feel like he was seeing parts of me no one else ever had—not just my body, but something deeper.

"Do you have any idea how beautiful you are?" His voice was rough, like sandpaper wrapped in velvet.

"I do now," I whispered, the words catching on my breath. Every day, Foster made sure I knew—with his words, his eyes, his touch.

"You should be worshipped every day" —a sly grin lifted the corner of his lips—"and I volunteer as tribute."

I huffed out a laugh before all the breath was sucked from my lungs when he replaced his finger with his lips.

My hands were shaking—partly because I didn't know what to do with them and partly because his slow teasing touch was wreaking havoc on my body. He kissed down to my stomach and then got down on his knees.

He looked up at me, and in that moment I understood what it meant to feel powerful.

Here was this sexy as hell man on his knees *for me*.

"You good?" he asked, his voice low and a little ragged.

It was reassuring to know I wasn't the only one affected.

"Don't stop," I whisper-begged.

He kissed my skin right above the button of my jeans. "I've dreamed of this."

"I hope it doesn't disappoint."

He paused and looked up at me, his gaze fierce. "Abby, you could never disappoint me. Not in a million lifetimes."

My insecurities got the better of me. "What if I'm not as good as other—"

He stood up so fast, his lips on mine cutting off my sentence before I could even finish it. "Don't. Don't bring anyone else in here with us. You are the only one I see. *You* are the only one I want. Don't compare yourself to anyone else because I won't be. No one would even come close."

I swallowed thickly. "Okay."

What else could I say to that?

When he looked at me like he was right now, I believed him—I was the only one he saw.

"Now, where was I?" he asked with that sexy little grin before he dropped back down to his knees and unbuttoned my jeans. He slowly pulled them down my legs and then tossed them to the side. His hungry gaze ate up every inch of my bare skin.

He was still fully clothed while I stood in my bra and underwear.

His fingertips grazed a gentle trail from my ankles up to my knees and then my thighs. Just like before, his lips followed. This time, I gave in to what my body wanted. My head dropped back as a ragged breath escaped my mouth.

My hands found the thick tendrils of his hair as I desperately grabbed his head, needing an anchor to keep me tethered as all my nerve endings fired with pleasure.

"So soft," he whispered. "So sexy."

He made me feel sexy.

He kissed his way back up my body, then slid his hand to my back and unhooked my bra. The straps fell to my elbows, and I watched in fascination as I let the bra fall to the ground and his eyes seemed to darken to a deep, ocean blue.

"Fuck, Abby."

I'd always been self-conscious about my small breasts. I was more pear-shaped—with round hips, thighs, and butt.

But the way Foster was looking at me right now made me feel like a Victoria's Secret model.

He slid his hand around my waist, and then his mouth was on mine and I was melting against his body. He walked us backward as he plundered my mouth and I was lost to him—to the way he made me feel, the way his hands roamed my body like I was a treasure.

He was going to ruin me for anyone else, but truthfully, I couldn't imagine wanting anyone but him.

Once on the bed, he laid me down and then moved to take off my underwear. He pulled the fabric down my legs and then threw it behind him while he gazed hungrily at the space between my thighs.

"You're already so wet for me."

"I'm always wet for you," I admitted.

He hummed deep in his throat like he was pleased to hear that. "Tonight is all about you. If I do anything you don't like, tell me, okay?"

I nodded.

He shook his head. "I need your words. Let me hear that sexy voice, Abby. Tell me."

"Okay," I whispered, my voice already ragged and he'd barely gotten started.

"That's my girl," he said before dipping his head down and kissing right above where I was already soaked for him.

He teased me, kissing the inside of my thighs and moving closer to where I was becoming desperate for him.

"Foster, please," I begged, the need inside my body spiraling out of control. I needed release.

"Tell me what you want, Baby."

"Kiss me."

"Where?"

"You know where."

"That's not how this works. Use those words, my smart girl. Tell me exactly where you want me to kiss you."

My heart was racing in my chest, but my inhibitions had left the room. I met his gaze. "I want you to kiss and suck on my clit."

His smile was wicked. "There's my dirty girl."

And then his mouth was right where I wanted it, and he was licking and sucking like I was the most succulent meal of his life. My back arched off the bed as pleasure exploded through me.

I gripped his head as my hips bucked against his mouth, desperate to be pushed off the ledge. He hummed in his throat and then sucked hard and I was lost.

The pleasure was so intense, I wasn't sure if I blacked out or if the world just went completely still and silent as my body shook with the aftershocks of my orgasm.

By the time I became aware of my surroundings again, Foster was naked and sliding a condom over his hard cock. I sat up on my elbows and took in his insanely sexy body.

He seriously looked too fit to be real. His six-pack abs gleamed with a light sheen, and his hand was wrapped around his cock which seemed slightly larger than average—although I really had no frame of reference apart from what I'd seen in movies.

"You ready for more?" he asked, his voice husky.

"Yes."

His smile was sweet as he crawled over my body until his cock was hovering over my entrance. He looked down at my face, his expression suddenly serious. "Tell me if you need me to stop, okay?"

"Okay," I whispered, but I had no intention of stopping this.

"I want this to be good for you," he confessed, and my heart felt like it swelled in my chest.

I cupped his cheeks and brought his face to mine, kissing him with all the emotion I had inside me. He had no idea what he was doing to me—what he made me feel for him. All the feelings I'd been so afraid of for so long.

When we broke the kiss, he gripped his cock and rubbed the tip slowly up and down, coating it with my slick juices. My stomach tensed as he pushed it gently inside me just an inch. I sucked in a sharp breath at the stretch as he pushed in a little deeper, and he stilled.

"Is this okay?"

"Yeah, don't stop. Please." I gripped his arms, my legs instantly wrapping around his hips, afraid he'd pull out and say we should try another time. But the movement caused him to move a little farther inside, and both of us shuddered at the exquisite feel.

"Please, Foster," I whimpered. "Keep going."

"I don't want to hurt you."

"You won't." And I meant it. I knew he would never

hurt me. As sure as I knew my name, I was confident in him —in us.

He canted his hips and slid the rest of the way in, causing me to moan from the intensity of the pressure. It was such a bizarre feeling at first, but quickly, the full feeling turned to pleasure. When he started moving, the pleasure intensified.

We found our rhythm as we rocked our hips, until he was hitting a spot so deep inside of me that a new kind of pleasure started coiling in my gut.

"Fuck, you feel unbelievable."

"Foster," I choked out as he slid his hand between us and started rubbing tantalizing circles on my clit. That, combined with the spot he kept hitting deep inside me with every thrust, had my toes curling. I screamed as my orgasm hit me, this one so much stronger and deeper than I'd ever thought was possible. It was a full body release that seemed to go on and on and on.

With a grunt, Foster increased his thrusts and then stilled completely, his body stiff as he shuddered out his release.

He collapsed next to me, keeping our bodies so close I wasn't sure where he ended and I began.

My voice was quiet, but sated, when I broke the silence. "Was that good for you?"

"Are you serious? Fuck, Abby. That was incredible." He turned onto his side. "It's never been like that for me." He rested his forehead against mine. "You make me feel things I've never felt before."

"Foster," I whispered, those three little words on the tip of my tongue.

He kissed me, his tongue slipping through my lips and

sliding against mine. When he pulled back, I was once again breathless.

"Don't say it yet. What we just experienced was intense, and when we say those words to each other, I don't want it to be after your mind is flooded with serotonin and endorphins from mind-blowing sex, okay?"

"Okay."

I wouldn't say the words yet, but that didn't change that I felt them to my very core.

THIRTY-NINE

The next morning, I woke up to a text from Gram asking if I was coming to Sunday dinner. I glanced over at a sleeping Foster. He looked younger, more carefree in his sleep. But he was still disheveled from last night, and the sight of him made heat curl low in my belly.

I considered waking him up for round two, except there was something more important than sex that I wanted from him.

I pressed a kiss to his shoulder.

"Mmm." His arm wrapped around me and pulled me flush against his body. "I could get used to waking up like this," he mumbled, his voice thick with sleep.

I closed my eyes and snuggled deeper against him, soaking in his warmth for a second before I worked up the courage to speak. "Foster, can I ask you something?"

He opened one eye and then the other when he must've seen the serious expression on my face. "What's up?"

"I was wondering if maybe you'd come to Sunday dinner with me tonight at my grandma's house?"

The smile that spread across his face was so bright it

could light up the entire hockey house. "Are you asking me to meet your family?"

I nibbled my lip. "Yeah." Why was I so nervous about this?

Maybe because I'd never brought a guy home to meet Gram before, or even talked about liking guys before.

This was a big step for me.

Seemed to be the theme of the weekend.

He hugged me tighter and dropped a tender kiss to my forehead. "I'd be honored. What time should I pick you up?"

And just like that, all my worry about seeing Gram and facing the reality that she might be seriously sick dissipated because no matter what, I wouldn't be alone.

My nerves ramped up as Foster pulled into my grandmother's driveway that evening. The familiar farmhouse looked exactly as it always did—weathered white paint, wraparound porch with the swing my grandfather had built decades ago—but everything felt different with Foster beside me.

I knew he came from a rich family, and while I didn't think he'd judge me for coming from more humble beginnings, it felt like bringing him really put a microscope on our different upbringings.

"You okay?" Foster asked, turning off the engine. "Your leg hasn't stopped bouncing since we left campus."

I glanced down and then put a hand over my knee to stop from jittering. I gave him a sheepish smile. "I didn't realize I was doing that."

Foster reached across the console and took my hand, his thumb brushing over my knuckles. "Hey, look at me." When I did, his eyes were warm and steady. "Everything's going to be fine."

I squeezed his hand. "Thank you again for coming."

"There's nowhere else I'd want to be."

We got out of the car, and he grabbed something from the backseat before he came around to my side.

"You brought a bouquet of flowers?"

He shrugged. "My mom always taught me to never show up empty-handed. I thought your grandma would appreciate flowers since you told me she likes gardening."

"These are beautiful, Foster," I said, surprised by his thoughtfulness.

We walked up the porch steps and before I could even reach for the doorknob, the door swung open. I froze mid-step, stomach dropping. Mason stood in the doorway, arms crossed like a sentry, his expression unreadable as he sized Foster up.

"Hey, Mase," I said, but he didn't even look my way, his focus still on Foster.

"Who are you?" he asked, his voice deeper than I remembered.

Had Gram not told him I was bringing someone? I'd told her over the phone when I confirmed I was coming so she'd know to set an extra place at the table.

Foster extended his hand. "Foster Kane. Nice to meet you."

Instead of taking it, Mason narrowed his eyes. "And who are you to my sister?"

"Mason!" I hissed, mortified. What on earth had gotten into him?

To my surprise, Foster didn't laugh or brush it off. He

kept his hand extended, meeting my brother's gaze directly. "I'm her boyfriend, and I hope we can be friends too. It's nice to see she's got other people looking out for her."

Mason studied him for another long moment before finally shaking his hand. "If you hurt her, I swear I'll find a way to ruin your life."

"Mason James Walker," I scolded.

"I'd expect nothing less," Foster replied as if I hadn't said anything.

I stared at my brother in disbelief. This was the most focused and direct I'd seen him in years—since before we lost Mom.

Mason caught my stare, and the corner of his mouth twitched upward—not quite a smile, but the closest thing to it I'd seen in forever. "Gram is in the kitchen."

He spun around, but before he could go back in the house I grabbed his arm. "How is she?" I said, keeping my voice low because I didn't want Gram to hear.

And just like that, all his confidence faded. "I think it— whatever it is—is getting worse."

That's what I was afraid of.

When we entered the kitchen, the rich aroma of Gram's lasagna filled the air. She stood at the counter with her back to us as she arranged garlic bread on a baking sheet.

"Gram, they're here," Mason announced.

She turned, and my heart squeezed painfully. Her presence filled the room like it always had, but now, it felt like she was holding herself together through sheer force of will. Mason hadn't exaggerated—if anything, he'd underplayed how bad she looked compared to the Gram we were used to. Her clothes hung loose where they once fit perfectly, and dark circles shadowed her eyes next to sunken cheeks. Her smile was still filled with warmth, but it looked like it took effort when it had always come easy before.

I couldn't ignore what I was seeing with my own eyes. Gram was sick.

"There you are!" she exclaimed, wiping her hands on her apron before approaching us.

Foster stepped forward with an easy smile. "Mrs. Thomas, thank you for having me. I brought these for you." He handed her the bouquet of flowers he'd brought.

"Oh my, how lovely," she said, accepting them with a beaming smile directed at Foster. "And please, call me Gram, or Daniella if you insist on being formal, but as you'll see, we're all pretty casual around here, and Mrs. Thomas makes me feel ancient."

She glanced at me with approval before turning back to Foster. "Would you help me reach the vase on that top shelf? My old bones don't stretch like they used to."

As Foster helped her, I caught Mason watching me with an odd expression.

"What?" I whispered.

"He seems decent," he muttered back.

I had to bite back a laugh. What a ringing endorsement. Seemed Gram would be easier to win over than my brother. Although I suspected that once they got talking about sports, Mason would love Foster.

Dinner was surprisingly comfortable. Gram asked Foster about hockey, his family, and his studies. I watched in amazement as he charmed her completely, helping serve the food and complimenting her cooking with genuine enthusiasm. As dinner progressed, my nerves about bringing a boy home had dissipated while my fears about Gram's health had only increased.

"This lasagna is incredible, Daniella," Foster said after his first bite. "I think it might be the best I've ever had."

Gram waved him off, but her pleased smile was unmistakable. "Oh, it's just a family recipe. Nothing special."

"It is special," I insisted. "Mom always said your lasagna could end wars."

The mention of Mom brought a momentary silence to the table, but instead of the usual heaviness, it felt almost reverent. Foster's hand found mine under the table and squeezed gently.

"So, Foster," Mason said, breaking the silence, "you're the captain of the hockey team? That's a big responsibility."

Foster nodded. "It is. But we've got a great team this year."

"Do you plan to play professionally after college?" Gram asked.

Something flickered across Foster's face—the same expression I'd seen when we discussed his future before. "No. It's rare for a club hockey player to go pro. I just play because I love it. I'll actually be taking over my father's business when I graduate." His expression soured—just for a second, like he'd swallowed lemon juice and was trying to hide his reaction.

"Is that what you want to do?"

"It's what my dad wants."

"And what do *you* want?" Gram asked, her gaze sharp despite her frail appearance.

Foster hesitated. "I'm not really sure. That option was never on the table."

"That's what your twenties are for," she said with a smile. "To figure out who you are. Not just who you're expected to be."

After we finished eating, Gram shooed the boys out of

the kitchen. "Mason, why don't you and Foster go in the living room and get to know each other a little better? Abby can help me with the dishes."

My grandma wasn't old-fashioned and normally had Mason do dishes. So if she was keeping me behind instead, it meant she wanted to talk in private.

My nerves rose. This was the moment I'd been waiting for and dreading in equal measure.

Once the guys left, I started clearing the table. "Dinner was really nice, Gram."

"He's a good one," she said, running water in the sink. "I can tell by the way he looks at you."

"How does he look at me?" I asked, curious.

"Like you hung the moon and stars." She smiled at me. "And you look happier than I've ever seen you."

I felt my cheeks warm. "I am happy."

It had been a long time since I'd been so genuinely happy, which only made the ominous dark cloud of whatever was going on with Gram even more noticeable.

We worked in companionable silence for a few minutes before I gathered my courage. "Gram, are you sure you're feeling okay? You seem...different."

Her hands stilled for a moment before she resumed scrubbing a dish. "I'm just getting older, sweetie. It happens to the best of us."

"Mason's worried about you. I am too."

She kept her gaze fixed on the sink as she handed me a plate to dry. "Like I told you before, there's nothing to worry about."

"Gram," I pressed, setting down the dish towel. "Please look at me."

When she finally turned, her eyes were guarded in a way I'd never seen before. She wouldn't meet my gaze directly, and in that moment, I knew with absolute certainty that something was very wrong.

"It's nothing for you to worry about right now," she said softly. "You have your studies, your new relationship. I don't want to burden you."

"You could never be a burden," I whispered, my throat tight. "Please tell me what's going on."

She patted my hand. "Soon, sweetie. But not tonight. Tonight is for celebrating you and that wonderful young man." She nodded toward the living room, where Foster's laugh mingled with what sounded like Mason's voice, more animated than I'd heard in ages.

I wanted to push, to demand answers, but the fragile happiness of the evening held me back. Not to mention that Gram's stubbornness was legendary.

The truth would have to wait, but my fear wasn't going anywhere. Something was wrong with Gram, and I didn't know if I was strong enough to face losing another person I loved.

FORTY

Foster

The next week went by in a blur of sex, hockey, and playing *Stardew Valley* next to my girl.

And it was perfect.

Every moment with Abby felt like discovering something new. The way she'd arch her back when I kissed that spot just below her ear. How she'd bite her lip to keep from making too much noise when my roommates were home. The soft, breathy way she'd say my name when she was close.

When we weren't having sex, I'd find myself captivated, watching her build her farm like her life depended on it—naming cows after classic authors and planting neat rows of strawberries. It was even more endearing to see the fierce concentration on her face or the way she tilted her head when she was meticulously organizing her farm. These were all things I hadn't been able to witness before, and too often I'd find myself mesmerized by her.

On the ice, things were just as good. Our team was on a winning streak—three games in seven days, and we'd taken all of them. Coach Maxwell had even pulled me aside after

Thursday's game against Helena College to tell me he'd never seen me play better.

"Whatever's got you so focused, Kane, keep doing it," he'd said with a knowing smirk.

I was walking on cloud nine until a single text message threatened my bliss.

DAD

> Great game last night. Let me take you out to dinner Sunday night to celebrate how great your season is going.

> You should bring your girlfriend too.

The messages had come in Friday morning as I was getting dressed for class, and my stomach had immediately knotted. I stared at my phone for a full minute, reading and rereading the texts.

The whole pretense of celebrating had me on edge. My father didn't "celebrate" my hockey accomplishments—he tolerated them at best. And he certainly didn't take interest in my dating life unless he thought he could use it somehow.

But when I brought it up to Abby, she thought it might be a good idea—that maybe it was an olive branch. She was more optimistic than I was about my relationship with my father.

So on Sunday, Abby and I joined my dad at one of his favorite restaurants in town. It was one of those upscale places with white tablecloths and waiters who looked down their noses at college students. The kind of place where the menu didn't list prices because if you had to ask, you couldn't afford it.

Abby squeezed my hand as we walked inside. "Relax. I'm sure it's going to be fine."

"You don't know my dad," I said. I couldn't help but be wary. "He never does anything without an ulterior motive."

But it made me especially nervous that he had specifically asked for Abby to come. I didn't know what his play was, but it made me tense, nonetheless.

I wanted to protect her from my dad's vitriol.

The hostess showed us to my dad's table and he stood, his eyes brightening as he saw me. He was wearing one of his expensive suits—tailor-made and probably costing more than my entire semester's tuition. His silver-streaked dark hair was perfectly styled, and his smile was practiced and polished like everything else about him.

"My boy," he said, clapping me on the back and pulling me in for a hug. I returned it stiffly, the familiar cologne he wore bringing back a flood of memories—most of them involving disappointment and criticism.

Then his gaze landed on Abby. "Abby, so nice to see you again. You've done well, son," he said, giving me a wink that made me feel gross. Like Abby was some trophy I'd won rather than an amazing person in her own right. "Aren't you just a cutie? I didn't notice the last time we met," he said to Abby.

Abby stiffened beside me. She was wearing a simple blue dress, and her hair down. She looked beautiful, but I knew she hated being reduced to her appearance, especially by men like my father.

Her smile was fixed on her face, but didn't reach her eyes. "Thanks," she said.

He laughed, but only he was in on the joke. "Oh, no need to be so short. We can forget that little thing with Holt."

My hackles raised. That "little thing" was him refusing to learn her name and then insulting her intelligence. My jaw tightened as I remembered how dismissive he'd been of her at Parker's office.

"It's no wonder my boy stood up for you. I should have known things were getting serious."

I frowned. "I didn't defend her because she's my girlfriend. I defended her because you couldn't even get her name right."

He brushed his hand across the space between us like he was sweeping the past under the rug. "Oh, that's old news. Let's move forward now. Take a seat."

"Where's Mom?"

"She had a headache, so she decided to stay in tonight," he shared, not an ounce of concern for his wife's well-being in his tone. His behavior wasn't necessarily better with her present, but it made me even more nervous that he'd say something out of line with just the three of us here.

The restaurant buzzed with quiet conversation around us, the clink of silverware against fine china creating a background melody to my growing anxiety. I glanced at Abby, hoping maybe she'd indicate that she wanted to bail as badly as I did, but she just moved toward her chair. I held it out for her as she sat down and then, with a sigh, I took my own seat next to her, already regretting this dinner.

A waiter immediately appeared with water and wine menus. My dad ordered a bottle of red without consulting either of us, something pretentious and expensive that he probably knew the vintage of.

He made polite conversation and actually deigned to take interest in Abby, asking her about her major and her plans for the future. He nodded appreciatively when she spoke about her internship at Holt & Associates, and even seemed genuinely impressed when she mentioned her academic scholarships.

It wasn't an interrogation like I expected. In fact, the dinner was almost pleasant. My father even asked about our classes, and showed genuine interest in my hockey season.

By the time dessert arrived—a chocolate soufflé that my father insisted we try—I had almost relaxed. Maybe I'd misjudged him. Maybe he really was just trying to get to know the woman I was dating.

I should have known it was all a ploy so I would let my guard down.

FORTY-ONE
Abby

After our not-so-stellar first meeting at Holt & Associates, I'd been nervous that Foster's dad wouldn't be supportive seeing as he hadn't seemed to like me much at that meeting. But throughout dinner at Missoula's most expensive restaurant—Summit Hills—Mr. Kane had been surprisingly pleasant, asking questions about my engineering studies and even complimenting my academic achievements.

Foster had seemed tense at first, his hand repeatedly finding mine under the table as if seeking reassurance. But as dinner progressed and his father continued to be cordial, he'd relaxed, even laughing at one point when his dad recounted an embarrassing childhood story.

"Remember when you tried to make pancakes for Mother's Day and nearly burned down the kitchen?" Dennis chuckled.

Foster rolled his eyes good-naturedly. "I was eight, Dad."

It was the most normal interaction I'd witnessed from them, given what Foster had shared about their strained relationship.

That was, until the evening came to an end.

As we were walking out, Dennis patted his pockets. "Oh, shoot! Foster, I forgot my valet ticket on the table. Would you run in and grab it for me?"

Foster hesitated and looked down at me, checking to make sure I'd be okay. His protective instinct made warmth spread through my chest.

I nodded at the silent question in his gaze. "Go."

I watched him walk away, his pace quick, and I fought back a smile. Even in dress pants and a button-down shirt, his athletic grace was evident. The way he'd held my hand throughout dinner, thumb occasionally stroking my skin, had left me feeling cherished in a way I'd never experienced before.

But when I turned around, his father had stepped closer to me. The pleasant mask he'd worn all evening had vanished, replaced by cold calculation that made my skin prickle with unease.

"Listen, we don't have a lot of time, so I'm just going to cut to the chase. You're not good enough for my son."

The words hit like a blow to my stomach, and I could barely breathe as he continued.

"I have plans for him, and he needs to marry into a certain caliber of family of which you do not have." His voice was calm, matter-of-fact, as if discussing a business transaction rather than his son's happiness. "I'll tell you what. I will pay off your tuition and pay for your future grad school expenses if you agree to break up with Foster. Immediately," he added.

My ears were ringing, and for a moment I wondered if I'd misheard him.

But no, I hadn't.

He'd just offered me money to break up with his son.

The frigid Montana air suddenly felt even colder. I stared at him in stunned silence, insulted by his offer, while simultaneously heartbroken that Foster's dad would do something like this, even knowing it could hurt him. The string lights illuminating the restaurant's entrance cast harsh shadows across Dennis Kane's face, highlighting the ruthless businessman Foster had described.

I thought of Foster's smile when he looked at me, the way he'd struggled to learn math concepts that didn't come naturally to him, how he'd defended me at Holt & Associates without hesitation. How could this man not see the wonderful person his son was? How could he do this behind his back and try to hurt him this way?

I finally found my voice. "Absolutely not. I cannot be bought and your son, he—"

Before I could finish my statement, Mr. Kane rolled his eyes. "He's young and stupid and following his dick."

I blinked at him unfathomably. The crudeness of his statement made my cheeks burn with both embarrassment and anger. He didn't know his son at all if he actually believed the garbage he'd just said to me.

This guy could not be real. I couldn't believe that someone would actually do this. Maybe it was naïve to think that. My fingers tightened around my purse strap, knuckles white with tension.

"It's a lot of money you're turning down, Abby." His voice softened to something almost sympathetic, which somehow made it worse. "I've done a little digging into your finances. I know your situation. I'm offering you life-changing money."

He'd looked into me? The invasion of privacy felt violating. I swallowed hard against the lump forming in my throat.

I didn't need his "life-changing money."

Foster had already changed my life. He'd made it better in ways I hadn't even imagined possible. He was someone I'd come to rely on, and I knew without a shadow of a doubt that I was in love with him.

I straightened my spine and met Mr. Kane's calculating gaze. "I already told you no."

My voice was steadier than I felt, fueled by indignation on Foster's behalf. There was no amount of money in the world that would make me give up what Foster and I had. Not when I'd finally found someone who made me feel both safe and excited about the future.

We had a silent stare off that was thankfully cut short by Foster's return. I could see the moment Dennis rearranged his features into the pleasant mask he'd worn all evening. Now I fully understood why Foster had been so worried about tonight.

"Here it is, Dad," Foster said, handing his dad the valet ticket.

Mr. Kane's demeanor changed so fast, I wondered if I'd just hallucinated the last few minutes alone with him. "Thank you, son. Well, it was a pleasure visiting with you both. Have a wonderful evening."

His lip curled with slight disdain when his gaze met mine, confirming I hadn't misunderstood anything. He was pissed I hadn't taken his offer.

"Everything okay?" Foster asked as he placed his hand on my lower back. His brow furrowed with concern as he studied my face. "You look pale."

I couldn't bear to tell him the truth. I hated the thought of what it would do to him to know that his dad was willing to pay off his girlfriend. There was no coming back from that kind of betrayal, and Foster still had to work with his dad. I didn't want to be responsible for causing that kind of damage between them, especially since I knew their relationship was already rocky.

Foster had shared how much pressure his father put on him, how nothing he did was ever good enough. I'd seen firsthand how Foster tensed whenever his phone displayed "Dad" on the caller ID. The last thing he needed was to know his father had tried to buy me off.

So instead, I just smiled up at him, relieved that he'd returned when he had. I leaned into his warmth, drawing strength from his solid presence.

"Everything's fine," I said.

Even if it wasn't fully the truth.

It was official—Abby was stronger than I was.

Our study sessions had become a regular thing—a way to see her, even when our schedules were insane. Two birds, one stone.

Except...

I couldn't study when Abby smelled like fucking heaven and my dick grew harder by the second just from her proximity to me.

She, on the other hand, seemed completely unaffected by my presence. I wasn't sure if that was a total blow to my ego or if I should be proud of her for being so focused.

I was trying not to distract her, but it was getting harder to ignore her beside me. Every so often, she'd shift on my bed, her leg sliding against mine, and my cock would strain against the seam of my zipper.

I discreetly glanced over and caught her nibbling on her lip.

Biting back a groan, I tipped my head back and stared at my ceiling, begging for strength I wasn't sure any man could possess.

What made Abby so attractive was that she had no fucking idea what she did to me. How men glanced at her whenever we went out together. How her smile had people stopping in their tracks.

She thought she was plain, but in the dictionary of Abby, plain didn't exist.

She was vibrant, smart, sexy, and so completely unaware of her own power that it wrecked me.

She didn't try to be anything other than exactly who she was—no filters, no pretending.

I was so sunk for her, it wasn't even funny.

"Foster?"

"Hmm?"

Her brown eyes were mesmerizing until I recognized the vulnerability shining in them.

"What is it?"

"Could you...um...could you teach me something?"

I frowned, confused. "Maybe. Depends what it is?"

What on earth could I possibly teach the smartest girl on campus?

A blush creeped up her neck that had heat zinging down my spine. "Could you teach me how to give head?"

I cough-choked as I sat up, sure I'd misheard her. My dick, on the other hand, was already harder than stone and eagerly anticipating her mouth.

"You want me to teach you how to give a blow job?"

She nodded.

I scrubbed a hand over my face, trying to pull myself together enough to go slow with this. Not that I was complaining that she wanted to learn. I was more than eager to feel her mouth on me, but I wanted her to be sure.

"You know you don't have to, right? I'm more than happy with our sex life."

She placed a hand on my arm, her eyes sincere. "I know I don't have to. I *want* to. I want to make you feel good like you make me. I've been thinking about it for a while. But I have no idea what I'm doing and I don't want to do it wrong."

Her words sent a rush of heat through me. I loved that she wanted to please me, but I also wanted her to enjoy the process. The best oral came when the other person was into it.

I took her hand in mine, tracing circles on her palm with my thumb. "Okay, but we go at your pace. If you want to stop at any point, just say the word," I assured her.

She nodded, a determined look in her eyes. I leaned in and kissed her, slow and deep. My tongue licked across the seam of her lips, and she parted them on a gasp. I slipped inside, massaging her tongue with mine until she was melting against me and whimpering into my mouth.

"Fuck, Baby," I murmured as I broke our kiss.

Before I could get anymore carried away kissing her, I stood up from the bed and stripped off my shirt, then pushed down my sweats and boxers and kicked them aside. Abby's heated gaze slid down my naked body before meeting mine.

"First things first," I said, my voice already a little hoarse from desire. "You don't have to take all of it. The tip is the most sensitive, so don't feel like you have to deepthroat or anything. Just do what feels comfortable for you."

Her gaze was locked on my cock, and she licked her lips before nodding absentmindedly like she was listening, but already thinking ten steps ahead. Knowing Abby, she probably was.

I took her hand and wrapped it around the base, guiding

her to stroke me gently. Her touch was tentative but eager, and I couldn't help but groan at the sensation.

Her hands were so much softer than mine when I jacked off.

"You can squeeze harder," I told her, my voice hoarse.

She tightened her grip and I shuddered. "Fuck. That's it."

Before my brain could even come up with the words, her mouth was lowering, her lush lips placing a delicate kiss on the head. I watched her, my breath held in my chest as she looked up at me with hungry eyes. She squeezed my shaft again and precum beaded on the tip.

"Taste me." The words were a plea.

Without breaking eye contact, she lapped up my precum with her tongue before swirling it around the head, and it took all my restraint not to come right then.

"Fuck, Baby. You're such a good girl when you lick me like that."

Her eyes flared, and I made a mental note that she liked praise.

"Do it again," I begged, my voice ragged. No one had ever made me feel so close to the edge so quickly. I wasn't sure if it was her eagerness, or knowing I got to teach her how to do it, but I couldn't get enough of watching her explore how to pleasure me with her wicked mouth.

She licked around the head again before the warmth and wetness of her mouth enveloped me. I held myself painfully still, letting her explore as her tongue swirled around the tip before her lips tightened around me.

"Goddamn, that feels so good," I murmured, my hand gently cupping the back of her head. "Now, take a little more."

Without hesitation, she took more of my length into her

mouth. I sucked in a breath and jolted when her teeth slid across my shaft, and she immediately pulled back, her cheeks flushing with embarrassment.

"I'm sorry," she said, looking up at me with worried eyes.

I smiled reassuringly, brushing a strand of hair behind her ear. "It's okay. I should've thought of that. You've got my head a goddamn mess right now. But I promise, you're doing amazing. Just try to sheath your teeth with your lips."

She tried again, this time taking me deeper without her teeth touching me.

"Fucking perfect," I whispered, my hips involuntarily lifting slightly. Pleasure rippled up my spine. She was going to fucking wreck me. "Now, use your hand and mouth together. Whatever you can't take in your mouth, stroke with your hand." My voice grew more ragged with each word as she followed my instructions with such blatant enthusiasm, my barely restrained control slipped even more.

"That's it, Baby. Just like that. Fuck, that feels so good. You don't even know..."

But I should've known I wouldn't need to direct her too much. Abby was an eager learner. Her tongue traced the length of my cock before she took me back into her mouth, her tongue sliding along the underside of my cock until I hit the back of her throat.

"F-fuckk." My voice shook as the word escaped and I had to close my eyes, the pleasure too much. If I watched her, I'd come right this second and this felt too good to stop now.

So good, I wished I was strong enough to let her suck my cock for hours, but there was no way in hell I'd last that long.

Then she moaned as she squeezed my shaft and sucked, and I only had seconds to warn her. "Abby, Baby, I'm so fucking close."

She pulled away and ripped her shirt over her head. Before I could even process the view, her mouth was back on me.

Holy hell, she was going to kill me.

"Fuck, I'm going to come," I groaned, giving her one last chance to pull back.

She did, her mouth leaving me just as I reached the point of no return. I came hard, my release spilling over her chest and bra as a guttural groan ripped from my throat. My whole body shook from the force of my orgasm.

She looked down at the mess and then back up at me, a mix of pleasure and vulnerability in her eyes.

"Sorry," she said softly. "I should have just swallowed. That's probably what you're used to—"

I cut her off, cupping her face in my hands and forcing her to look at me. "Abby, you have nothing to be sorry for. Not a damn thing. That was fucking perfect. I loved every second of it."

And I meant it. Seeing her marked with my release was strangely satisfying, a primal claim that she was mine. I leaned down and kissed her hard, pouring all my emotion into it.

"Thank you," I whispered against her lips. "You continue to make me feel like the luckiest guy in the whole damn world."

She smiled, her eyes shining with happiness. "I'm glad you think so. I was nervous I wouldn't do it right."

I shook my head, brushing my thumb over her cheek. "There's no universe where you could've done it wrong." I slid my hand through my release on her chest and then down her stomach and to the edge of her leggings. She sucked in a breath as I reached between her legs where she was soaking wet. "I need a taste, Baby."

She laughed softly, her cheeks flushing pink. I loved seeing her like this, open and vulnerable, trusting me with her desires.

I reached behind her and unhooked her bra, pulling it away to reveal her small, beautiful breasts. Leaning down, I kissed her again, my tongue exploring her mouth as my hands roamed over her body. Her nipples hardened beneath my touch, and she moved easily when I pulled her against me and guided her to the bed.

"Foster," she whispered against my lips, her voice breathy with need.

"What do you want, Baby? Tell me what you need."

She hesitated for a moment, her cheeks flushing pink. "I want you to touch me," she admitted softly.

I smiled, my hand sliding down her stomach to the waistband of her leggings. "Like this?" I asked, my fingers tracing the edge of her pants.

She nodded, her breath hitching as I slid them down her legs, bringing her panties with them.

I took a moment to admire her naked body on my bed, my gaze roaming over her, taking in every curve and line. She was so beautiful it made me ache. I wanted to worship her, to make her feel as incredible as she made me feel.

I leaned down and kissed her stomach, my lips trailing a path down to her hips. She trembled beneath me, her body already responding to my touch. I looked up at her, my gaze meeting hers.

"I want to feel you come undone beneath me."

Her eyes were filled with trust and desire that I would never take for granted. I kissed her stomach as my hands slid up her thighs and spread her legs wide. Her pussy was glistening with arousal, and it made my mouth water.

Leaning in, I took a deep breath, inhaling her intoxicating scent—a mix of sweet and musky that was uniquely Abby.

My tongue traced a leisurely path up her inner thigh that made her shiver beneath me. Her breath hitched as I got closer to her center.

"Tell me what you want, Baby," I murmured, my breath hot against her skin. "Tell me where you want me to kiss you."

I wanted her confident enough to always ask—or demand—what she wanted.

She hesitated for a moment, her cheeks flushing pink. "Kiss me...there," she whispered, her voice barely audible.

"Where? Be specific."

"My pussy," she said, a bit of challenge in her voice that had me getting hard again.

I smiled and then flicked out my tongue to taste her. She gasped, and her hips lifted slightly as I circled her clit with my tongue. I wrapped my arms around her thighs, holding her still so I could give her all the pleasure I knew she wanted. Her body tensed as a moan escaped her throat, and she tossed her head back, her fingers gripping the sheets with a death grip.

"Is that what you want?" I asked, my voice low and husky. "Do you want me to kiss your clit?"

"Yes," she choked out. "Yes, please, Foster. Don't stop."

Fuck, she made me want to live between her legs.

I grinned, my tongue flicking out to taste her again. Her body responded to me instantly as her hips lifted to meet my mouth. I took my time, exploring her with my tongue and learning new things that made her gasp and moan.

I slid a finger inside her, feeling her tighten around me. Her body was already on the edge, her breath coming in short gasps as I continued to tease her.

"Foster," she moaned, her hands gripping the sheets beneath her. "Please, d-don't stop."

I had no intention of stopping. I wanted to make her come undone, to feel her shatter beneath me. I increased the pressure as my tongue continued to circle her clit while I slid another finger inside her.

She cried out, and her body tensed as her orgasm hit her. Her pussy pulsed around my fingers as her she shook with the force of her release. I continued to lick and suck her, drawing out her pleasure until she was a trembling mess beneath me.

She was beautifully flushed, her breath coming in short gasps and her body still shaking with the aftershocks of her orgasm. I had never seen anything more beautiful in my life.

I kissed my way up her body until my lips found hers. My kiss was filled with the three words I hadn't said yet. I wouldn't say them now either. I refused to say them right after sex. I wanted her to believe them with every bone of her body and not think it was just some crazy hormonal response to earth-shattering sex.

But I'd say them soon.

Because she deserved to know that I was hers—one thousand percent.

She owned me—mind, body, and soul.

FORTY-THREE

I had just walked into The Grindhouse—the coffee shop on campus—to grab an afternoon pick-me-up when my phone started vibrating in my hand. The familiar scent of coffee beans and pastries that normally brought me comfort did nothing to ease the sudden dread that washed over me when I saw the name of a local hospital on my caller ID.

"Hello?" My voice was steady despite the rapid beating of my heart.

"Hi, is this Abby Walker? This is Melody Tynes. I'm a nurse at Mountain View Medical Center." The woman's professional tone did little to mask the seriousness behind her words.

"Yes, this is Abby. Is everything okay?" That felt like the dumbest question to ask because of course if the hospital was calling me, everything wasn't okay. I gripped my phone tighter, bracing myself for whatever news was coming.

"Your grandmother was brought to us by a neighbor after she collapsed in her garden."

I didn't need to hear any more—not over the phone at least. "I'll be right there." I was already rushing out of the café and toward my car, nearly colliding with a student entering as I pushed through the door, the coffee I'd been craving completely forgotten.

With trembling fingers, I texted Foster and Sam since I had plans with both of them today and didn't think those plans would be happening now. I kept the message brief, unable to type more as I fumbled with my keys.

> emergency with Gram, heading to Mountain View now, will update when I can

The hospital wasn't far from campus, so it only took me about fifteen minutes to get there, though every red light felt like an eternity. I circled the parking lot twice before finding a spot, then practically ran to the entrance. When I walked in, I rushed straight to the receptionist counter, my breath coming in short bursts.

"I'm here to see my grandmother, Daniella Thomas." My voice cracked slightly on her name.

The receptionist—a middle-aged woman with kind eyes behind tortoiseshell glasses—looked at her computer, fingers clicking efficiently on the keyboard. "Room 406," she told me and then gave me directions for how to get to the nearest elevator, pointing down a corridor to my right.

I thanked her and hurried through the antiseptic-scented hallway, past rooms with partially closed doors where I caught glimpses of other patients and their worried families. The elevator seemed to move in slow motion, and I found myself counting each second that passed, acutely aware that time might be precious now.

A nurse with auburn hair pulled back into a neat pony-tail was just walking out of my grandmother's room, clip-board in hand, when I made it there.

"Are you Abby?" she asked, her voice gentle.

"I am." I tried to peek around her into the room, desperate for a glimpse of Gram.

Her smile was kind, but it didn't ease any of my worry. It was that practiced hospital smile that medical professionals perfect—sympathetic but carefully neutral. "I'm glad you could make it. Dr. Spencer is just checking in on another patient, but I'll have him come talk to you once he's done there. You can go on in and see her."

"Is she going to be okay?" I asked, unable to keep the desperation from my voice.

Her expression remained frustratingly neutral. "I'm afraid I can't answer any questions. You'll have to wait for Dr. Spencer."

"Thanks," I said, even though gratitude was the last thing I was feeling at that moment.

I didn't want to wait to hear what was going on, and I hated the stupid policy that only doctors could answer questions. I knew she knew just as much as the doctor—probably more since she'd likely been caring for Gram directly.

I walked into Gram's hospital room and found her asleep on her bed, the steady beep of monitors creating an ominous soundtrack. They said that a neighbor brought her in, but no one was in the room now. She looked so fragile and frail against the stark white sheets. Her skin seemed sallower than it had been before—her cheeks sunken in, the wrinkles around her eyes deeper than I remembered.

She looked like a shell of the Gram I'd grown up with, and the way she'd declined in such a short amount of time had terror creeping up my spine.

I knew she was sick, but why hadn't she told us what was going on before it got this bad?

I sunk down into the chair next to her bed, the vinyl squeaking under my weight, and reached for her hand. Her fingers were cold, and the bones felt fragile and breakable, like bird bones. I covered her hand with mine, wanting to give her my warmth. I'd give her all the strength I had if it would make her better.

The IV in her arm and the monitor on her finger made her look weaker than I could ever remember, and the hospital bed itself made her look smaller somehow. This was the woman who'd held us all together when Mom passed away. She'd always been a force of nature—strong, resilient, unbreakable. Seeing her like this, diminished and vulnerable, made my chest ache with a pain I couldn't articulate.

A few minutes passed before a tall blond man in a white doctor's coat walked in. His name badge read "Dr. Spencer" and he carried a tablet, his expression professionally somber.

"Are you Abby Walker?" he asked, his voice calm and measured.

"Yeah." I straightened in my chair but didn't let go of Gram's hand.

"I'm glad you could make it."

"What's wrong with her? Is she gonna be okay?" The questions tumbled out, my voice catching on the last word.

He hesitated. "You're listed as her emergency contact, and her primary care physician has her advanced care directive on file, which gives us permission to share what's going on."

"Okay," I said, nervous at his formal tone. The knot in my stomach tightened.

"Just to confirm—she hasn't talked to you about her condition?" he asked, watching me carefully.

I shook my head, a lump forming in my throat. "My brother and I have been concerned for months, but whenever we asked her, she just brushed it off. Said she was just getting older and slowing down." I remembered the way she'd wave away our concerns, changing the subject to Mason's football games or my studies.

Dr. Spencer frowned, his forehead creasing. "Seems commonplace for many in her generation, unfortunately, especially when they've already made the decision."

"Decision about what?" My voice was barely more than a whisper now, dread pooling in my stomach.

"Your grandmother has advanced pancreatic cancer."

The floor might as well have dropped out from under me as he continued on. The room seemed to tilt slightly, and I held Gram's hand tighter, needing an anchor.

"She was diagnosed several months ago based on information in her chart and the notes from her oncologist. She declined treatment. She was seeing her doctor for some pain management, but didn't want anything else. Her collapse today isn't a surprise, since she's likely in quite a bit of pain and probably has been for a while. We've stabilized her, but given the progression of her cancer, she likely doesn't have much time left."

I couldn't breathe, and suddenly I couldn't see because my eyes were blurring from the tears filling them. The words "advanced" and "declined treatment" and "doesn't have much time" echoed in my head, each one a hammer blow against my heart.

"She's dying?" I asked, surprised my voice came out as clear as it did when I felt like I was going to choke on the grief already rising in my throat.

"I'm afraid so," he confirmed, his voice filled with genuine compassion.

My lower lip wobbled as I tried to hold it together. I could feel my face contorting with the effort not to break down completely. "There's nothing that can be done to save her?" I heard the desperate hope in my question, already knowing the answer.

"She didn't want anything. The cancer was too far along when she was diagnosed. Treatment might have delayed things, but it wouldn't have put her in remission." His words were gentle but unflinching.

"How much time do you think she has?" I forced myself to ask the question I didn't want answered.

He looked at my grandmother lying in the hospital bed, her chest rising and falling with each shallow breath, and then back at me. "It could be days or weeks, but I wouldn't give her much more than that."

Weeks?

I only had weeks with her? And that was only if she lasted that long.

I sat frozen in the chair, tears silently slipping down my cheeks, creating dark spots on my jeans where they fell. This couldn't be happening.

Why was this happening? Hadn't we lost enough? First Dad, then Mom, and now Gram? It was too much. Too cruel. Mason would be devastated.

Oh God, Mason.

He was already struggling so much with Mom's death. How would he handle losing Gram too?

"Is there someone we can call for you to come here?" Dr. Spencer asked, his voice breaking through the fog of my thoughts. He was looking at me with concern, probably worried I was going into shock.

Before I could answer the doctor's question, the door opened and Foster walked in. I'd never been so happy to see him because right now I didn't think I even had the strength to stand. It felt like my whole world was crumbling around me.

His hair was slightly disheveled, like he'd been running his hands through it—something he did when he was worried. His blue eyes immediately locked with mine, taking in my tear-stained face and broken expression.

He rushed to my side, picking me up and holding me as I fell apart. His strong arms wrapped around me, one hand cradling the back of my head as I buried my face in his chest. The dam broke, and I sobbed against him, my body shaking with the force of my grief.

"I've got you," he whispered into my hair, his voice a lifeline in the storm of my emotions. "I'm here, Abby. I've got you."

And for just a moment, in the circle of his arms, I let myself believe that maybe I wouldn't drown in this new wave of loss threatening to pull me under.

FORTY-FOUR

Sam showed up a little after I did and offered to go pick up Mason and bring him to the hospital.

We stayed there until visiting hours were over. The doctors came and went, nurses checked vitals, and we sat in uncomfortable chairs watching Abby's grandmother sleep, her breathing shallow and labored.

The whole time, Abby had a hollow look on her face like she was stuck in a nightmare she couldn't get out of. Her normally bright eyes were dull and distant, her shoulders hunched forward as if carrying a physical weight. She kept rubbing her grandmother's hand, occasionally whispering something I couldn't hear. I didn't know what to say, but I hoped my presence provided some comfort, so she knew she wasn't alone.

"I need to go home with Mason," she said when the nurse finally came to tell us visiting hours were ending. Her grandma had woken up briefly toward the end, but hadn't had much strength to talk before she fell asleep again from the painkillers they had her on.

"I'll drive you guys," I told her. I had no intention of

leaving her side. Even if it meant I had to get up extra early for practice tomorrow. The thought of her facing this alone made my chest ache. Not to mention, I didn't think she was any state to drive right now.

I was considering calling Coach and telling him I couldn't make practice due to a family emergency. I didn't like the thought of Abby being at Gram's or at the hospital to deal with everything by herself. I knew she wouldn't lean on Mason because she was already worried about him, but she deserved to have someone there so she wasn't carrying all the weight of this situation on her shoulders.

It was bad form for the captain to be MIA.

But I'd finally found something—*someone*—that was more important to me than hockey.

And I wouldn't let her face this alone.

I drove Abby and Mason back to Gram's house, the headlights cutting through the darkness as we navigated the quiet country road. Mason had been in a daze since we'd left the hospital. He was beating himself up for not realizing the severity of the situation, even though I'd heard Abby tell him multiple times that it wasn't his fault their Gram was in this condition.

He'd shoved his earbuds in once we got in the car, his face turned toward the window. As soon as we walked into the house, he went straight to his room and closed the door with a quiet click that somehow seemed more concerning than if he'd slammed it.

I was worried about him, but I was most worried about Abby.

"Why don't you head upstairs and I'll find us something to eat?" I suggested, squeezing her hand gently.

She nodded but didn't speak as she walked woodenly

up the stairs, her hand gripping the banister like she needed the support to keep from collapsing.

After searching the fridge and cupboards, I found some bottles of water, bananas, and crackers. It wasn't a gourmet meal, but I didn't think Abby or Mason had much of an appetite. Still, they needed to eat something, even if just to keep their strength up for the difficult days ahead.

I stopped at Mason's room first—which was easy enough to find because it had a football and some band stickers on the door. I knocked softly.

"Mason? I brought you some water and food."

When he didn't respond, I knocked harder, until finally he opened the door, one of his ear buds in his hand.

"I thought you might want some snacks."

"Thanks," he mumbled before taking them and closing the door again.

When I got to Abby's room, I found her standing in the center, arms wrapped around herself. The space was dimly lit by a small bedside lamp, casting long shadows across the walls. It wasn't as decorated as I expected, which I supposed made sense—this hadn't been her childhood bedroom. She'd told me she lived in a different house until her mom died.

As I walked closer, I realized she was shaking. It was probably the shock and drop of adrenaline from the day.

I'd never lost a loved one, and now Abby was about to lose the third parent figure she'd had. I felt helpless to ease her pain. All I could do was be here and yet that didn't feel like enough.

I set down the water and snacks on her desk and then wrapped my arms around her. Her body was cold despite the warmth of the room, and she felt fragile in a way I'd never seen her before. She hugged me back and pressed her cheek against my chest.

"What do you need?" I asked, my voice barely above a whisper as I rubbed her back.

"You," she whispered, her voice breaking on that single word. She looked up at me, her brown eyes begging me. "I need you to make me forget—even if just for a little while."

"Abby—" I started, uncertain.

Her arms tightened around my waist, her fingers gripping the fabric of my shirt. "Please, Foster." The desperation in her voice made my heart clench.

I knew sex wouldn't take away her pain, but I couldn't bear the thought of her feeling rejected when I knew how scared and lost she felt.

Leaning down, I placed a gentle kiss against her lips. She responded immediately, pressing herself closer, her mouth seeking mine with an urgency that spoke of her need to feel something—anything—other than the pain that threatened to consume her.

I kissed her deeply, trying to pour all the love I felt for her into that connection. My hands moved to frame her face, thumbs brushing away the tears that had begun to fall silently down her cheeks.

"I'm here," I whispered against her lips. "I've got you."

She clung to me, her fingers digging into my back as if she were afraid I'd disappear.

I wasn't going anywhere.

I deepened the kiss, my tongue tracing the seam of her lips, asking for entrance. She opened for me, her own tongue meeting mine in a dance that was both desperate and tender.

I pulled back slightly, needing to see her face. Her eyes were closed, lashes wet with tears, but a faint flush colored her cheeks. "Are you sure?" I asked, my voice rough with a combination of desire and concern.

She nodded, her eyes opening, a raw vulnerability in their depths that tore at me. "I need this, Foster. I need *you*."

I kissed her again, a promise in that kiss, a vow to be whatever she needed me to be in this moment. I lifted her into my arms and carried her to the bed, laying her down gently before following her, my body hovering over hers.

The bedside lamp cast a soft glow over her skin, highlighting the curve of her neck and the delicate line of her collarbone. Her pulse fluttered beneath my lips as I pressed a kiss to the hollow of her throat.

"You're so beautiful," I murmured, my voice thick with emotion.

She reached up, her fingers threading through my hair, pulling me back to her mouth. We kissed again, deep and unrelenting, like we were trying to memorize the feel of each other.

I reached for the hem of her shirt, pulling it over her head, revealing the lacy bra beneath. My gaze lingered there, admiring the small swell of her breasts, before moving back to her face. Her cheeks were flushed, her eyes dark with something that looked like the way I felt—raw, reverent, and completely undone.

I unclasped her bra, letting it slip away as I kissed my way down. When I took one of her nipples into my mouth, her back arched off the bed and a soft moan escaped. Her hands gripped my shoulders and her nails dug into my skin when I moved to the other breast, lavishing the same attention on it, until a soft cry came from her lips.

Fuck, I loved the sounds she made.

My hand moved lower until I reached the waistband of her jeans. I quickly unbuttoned them and slid them over her butt and down her legs. By the time I'd stripped her bare, my hard cock was pushing painfully against my own jeans and desperate to be let out.

I grabbed a condom and shed the last of my clothes, too desperate to care where they landed. Once the condom was on, I crawled onto the bed, positioning myself between Abby's gorgeous legs. Her arousal glistened in the light and I couldn't stop myself from tasting her. My mouth covered her clit, sucking teasingly as her flavor burst on my tongue. I loved the breathy moan that escaped her throat at my ministrations.

If she wanted out of her head, I knew what would work the fastest. I repositioned myself so I could lie flat and wrapped my arms around her thighs, hugging her tight as I licked and sucked her clit until she was a panting mess on the bed. Her thighs shook around my ears, and her hands gripped the sheet as an orgasm racked her body.

I lapped at her clit once more before I kissed my way up her body and positioned my cock at her entrance. "You still want this?"

Her eyes met mine and she nodded. "More than anything."

Without another word, I slid inside her, stretching her as I went. Dropping my head to her shoulder, I let out a groan. "Fuck, you're still so tight."

She felt so good—so perfect—pulsing around me with the aftershocks of her last orgasm.

We began to move together, finding a rhythm that spoke of comfort as much as passion. It wasn't frantic or desperate, but slow and deep, each thrust a reminder that she wasn't alone in her pain. My hands never stopped touching her—caressing her face, tangling in her hair, tracing the curve of her breast, the dip of her waist.

As our movements grew more urgent, I slipped a hand between us, finding her clit.

"Let go," I whispered in her ear. "I've got you. Let go."

She came with a soft cry, her body tensing beneath mine. The sight of her, lost in pleasure rather than pain, was enough to push me over the edge. I buried my face in her neck as I found my own release, her name a prayer on my lips.

Afterward, I held her close, her head on my chest, my fingers tracing idle patterns on her back. We didn't speak—there were no words that could make the situation better. But in the quiet aftermath, she seemed more relaxed and less burdened than she had been all day.

She pressed a kiss to my chest, right over my heart. "Thank you," she murmured, her voice thick with emotion. "For being here. For not letting me be alone."

I tightened my arms around her, pressing a kiss to the top of her head. "I'm not going anywhere," I promised. "Get some sleep. I'll be here when you wake up."

As her breathing deepened into sleep, I stared at the ceiling, thinking about the woman in my arms and the pain she was facing. I couldn't fix this for her. I couldn't make her grandma healthy or erase the grief that was coming. But I could be here—by her side—making sure she knew she wasn't alone.

I could be the safe harbor she needed in the darkness. More importantly, I *wanted* to be that for her.

My body ached like I had been run over by a semi—or like I'd run a marathon without any prep. I opened my eyes but didn't get out of bed.

I didn't move at all.

I simply stared at the ceiling, wondering if yesterday had all been just a really bad dream—except for the end.

The memory of Foster's touch, his gentle hands and reassuring whispers, was the only bright spot in what had otherwise been the worst day I'd had since my mom died.

Sometimes physical connection was the only thing that could break through overwhelming grief, providing a temporary escape from the crushing weight of reality.

But the pain always had a tendency of coming back, and now in the light of day, it was coming back in a rush.

And my reality was that I was going to lose another person I loved and there was nothing I could do to stop it.

The only positive was that at least this time I'd get to say goodbye.

I'd heard people debate about whether it was easier to lose someone knowing it was coming or to have someone taken from you quickly. Now that I was living through this experience with Gram, I could say with one hundred percent certainty that they both sucked.

Nothing about loss or death was easy or better than another alternative. No matter how you lost someone, it felt terrible.

But I couldn't fall apart again because Mason was counting on me and I had to be strong for him.

I got up and went to the bathroom to wash my face with cold water, pressing it against my eyelids in a weak attempt to get the swelling down from all the crying I'd done yesterday. It didn't help much. I would need to put some ice packs on them for a few minutes before I went to the hospital because I didn't want Gram to see me with red and swollen eyes.

When I walked into the kitchen, I froze. Sitting at the kitchen table, talking, were Mason and Foster. I watched them for a second in awe. My brother was more animated than I'd expected him to be as he told a story to Foster that seemed to be about something that happened with his football team.

Foster caught sight of me first, and heat curled like smoke in my stomach at the way his face lit up with a smile.

"Morning, Gorgeous," he said, already getting up and walking over to me.

"Morning," I said, as he wrapped his arms around me in his signature hug that I was officially addicted to. His warmth enveloped me, and for a moment, I let myself lean into him completely, drawing strength from his solid presence.

He dropped a kiss on the top of my head. "Want some coffee?" he asked.

"Coffee would be great." I padded over to the table

where my brother still sat. "How are you holding up?" I asked Mason as I joined him.

He shrugged. "As well as can be expected, I guess." He hesitated, and when he looked up at me, it was with that same innocent yet scared look he'd sometimes get when he was little. The look that always made my heart ache with the need to protect him from whatever was troubling him.

"Did you know?" he asked.

Of all the things for him to ask me, I hadn't expected that one. I'd thought my shock and devastation yesterday had been an obvious sign that I had been as out of the loop as he was, but clearly not.

"I had no idea until the doctor told me, I swear."

He nodded, but I didn't miss the way his shoulders almost seemed to sag in relief.

I reached out and squeezed his hand. "Mase, I would have told you if I knew. I wouldn't keep that secret from you."

"*She* did," he said, and I hated the slightly bitter note in his tone. His fingers tightened around mine, betraying the hurt he was trying to hide.

"Yeah, she did, and maybe we can learn from her mistake because I don't think it was right that she didn't tell us."

It honestly felt like a betrayal that she would keep this from us—especially after everything we'd already been through as a family—but it explained so much of her behavior over the past several months.

Her trips down memory lane in the attic.

The way she'd watch us like she was trying to memorize it all.

A thought suddenly hit me and I turned to Foster. "Didn't you have practice this morning? And classes?" I added as I checked the clock. It was almost nine, and I knew the hockey team usually had early morning practices.

"I called Coach this morning to get out of practice, and I'm skipping my classes today. I thought I'd help you guys out here and then we can drive into town together. I can do food runs or whatever while you stay at the hospital and visit with Gram. That way you don't have to worry about anything but spending time with her."

He was too good to be true. Emotion bubbled in my throat as I got up and wrapped my arms around his neck. He held me close like he needed that hug as much as I did. His hands rubbed gentle circles on my back, and I fought back a fresh wave of tears at his soothing touch.

"Thank you."

His eyes warmed with an emotion I was afraid to name as he looked down at me. "You don't have to thank me, Abby. I want to be here for you."

"Okay, that's my cue to go. You guys look like you're about to make out," Mason said as he pushed back his chair and left the kitchen. There was a hint of teasing in his voice that I hadn't heard in ages.

"What were you guys talking about earlier?" I asked Foster after Mason had disappeared down the hallway.

We sat down at the kitchen table, but he kept his hand on my leg, the contact warming me from the inside out. His thumb traced small circles on my knee, and the gentle touch grounded me.

"Not much," he said. "Sports mostly, football specifically."

"You know football?"

He gave me a look, and a smile pulled at the corners of his mouth. "I live in Montana. Of course I know football. Just because I play hockey doesn't mean I don't also enjoy football." He nodded his head in the direction my brother had disappeared to. "You know, he's a pretty cool kid. It was nice getting to know him a little better."

"I appreciate everything you've done, and I know you told me I don't need to say thank you," I said hurriedly as he opened his mouth. "But I want to tell you that it means a lot to me to have you here. But you don't have to come to the hospital if you have other things to do. I know you've got a big series of games coming up this week."

Now that the season was well underway, they were trying to maintain their lead in the conference so they could go to the state playoffs in February.

He squeezed my hand. "Missing a day won't ruin anything. I'm right where I need to be."

The sincerity in his voice made my throat tight. I took a sip of the coffee he'd placed in front of me, buying time to compose myself. It was perfectly prepared—just the right amount of cream and sugar. Another small detail that showed how much attention he paid to the little things about me.

Foster's hand was warm in mine, his presence a silent support as we approached Gram's hospital room. Mason walked slightly behind us. He'd been tense since we parked the car.

The nurse at the station recognized us from yesterday and gave us a sympathetic smile. "She's awake and had a decent night," she said quietly. "The doctor will be by again in about an hour."

I nodded my thanks, steeling myself before entering the

room. The whole way here, I'd hoped she would be awake and alert today, but now I was scared to face her. To have the conversation I knew we needed to have.

Foster squeezed my hand, and his touch gave me the last little bit of strength I needed.

The first thing I noticed when I pushed open her door was that Gram looked even smaller than she had yesterday, her skin nearly as pale as the white hospital sheets. The machines around her beeped steadily, monitoring her vital signs. But unlike yesterday, her eyes were open, and when she saw us, her face lit up with a smile that still held traces of the vibrant woman she'd always been, although I didn't miss the guilt in her eyes.

"Hey there," she said, her voice weaker than I'd ever heard it.

Mason approached first, awkwardly leaning over to kiss her cheek. "Hey, Gram."

I followed, gently taking her hand, mindful of the IV line. "How are you feeling?"

"Oh, about as well as can be expected," she said, her attempt at humor breaking my heart. Her gaze shifted to Foster, who stood respectfully near the door. "It's nice to see you again, Foster."

"You too. Wish it were under better circumstances."

Gram looked down and cleared her throat before pasting a smile on her face. "Yes, well, any young man who shows up at the hospital during a family crisis is worth keeping, I'd say."

"I agree," I said, glancing at Foster with a small smile.

After a few minutes of gentle conversation, Foster excused himself to get us coffees, tactfully giving us time alone with Gram.

As soon as the door closed behind him, the facade crumbled. Tears filled Gram's eyes as she looked between Mason and me.

"I'm so sorry," she whispered. "I should have told you."

The question that had been burning inside me finally spilled out. "Why didn't you?"

She sighed, the sound rattling slightly in her chest. "It was already too far advanced. After everything you two had been through...losing your father, then your mother... I couldn't bear to put that burden on you."

I felt the tears I'd been trying to hold back begin to fall. "How long have you known?"

"Since early summer," she admitted. "The doctors gave me options, but at my age, the treatments would have just made what time I had left miserable. I wanted quality over quantity."

"But—" I started to protest.

She squeezed my hand with surprising strength. "Abigail Jane Walker, don't you dare second-guess my decision. I've lived a full life, and I made my choice with a clear head and a full heart. I wanted to enjoy the rest of my life with you kids instead of being pumped full of poison and watching you two worry yourselves sick."

I nodded, unable to speak. I still wasn't happy with her decision—I wasn't sure I'd ever be okay with it—but I understood it. If I only had a limited time with her, I wasn't going to spend it arguing.

"Now," she continued, her tone softening, "I need you both to listen to me. I've made all the arrangements. The house has been paid off for years, and it'll go to both of you. You can keep it or sell it to use the money for your education or whatever else you choose. I wish I had more to leave you—"

"Gram, we don't need to talk about this now," I said.

"Yes, we do," she insisted. "Because I feel weaker every hour, and I need to know you'll be okay. I need to know you'll take care of each other."

"We will," Mason promised, his voice steady despite the tears streaming down his face.

We spent the next half hour talking—about memories, regrets, and hopes for the future. But it was obvious Gram's energy was fading fast.

Foster returned with not only coffee, but food for us, and we spent the day in Gram's hospital room. Foster's steady presence beside me was the anchor I needed to keep from feeling like my grief would suck me under as we faced head-on the reality that Gram would very likely never leave this room before she succumbed to her cancer.

I wasn't ready to lose her, but once again, life hadn't given me a choice.

I stayed at the hospital most of the day with Abby and Mason, but had to get back to my normal schedule for the rest of the week. Whenever I wasn't in class or practice, I was with Abby at the hospital, and would stay with her at her Gram's house each night.

The rhythmic beeping of Gram's monitors had become a constant soundtrack to our vigil. Sometimes I'd catch Abby staring at those monitors, her eyes following each peak and valley as if they contained some secret code that might tell her how much time remained. In those moments, I'd silently take her hand, and she'd squeeze mine gratefully without looking away.

I'd explained the situation to the guys, and they'd immediately stepped up in a way that made my chest tighten with pride. They organized a rotation, taking turns bringing actual edible food to Abby and Mason so they wouldn't be stuck with the bland, rubbery hospital cafeteria offerings.

But they did more than just drop off food. They stayed, sometimes for an hour or more, filling the small hospital room with stories and laughter that seemed to momentarily lift the heavy cloud of grief that hung over Abby and Mason.

I could tell they made quite the impression on Mason. The way his eyes lit up when one of them walked through the door spoke volumes. According to Abby, he didn't have many male role models in his life beyond his football coach. She'd mentioned several times how he'd become increasingly withdrawn since their mom died, and I could see the worry etched in her face about what losing Gram would do to him.

"He used to be so outgoing," she'd whispered to me as we lay in her bed late one night. "He was always the first to raise his hand in class, the first to make friends with new kids. After Mom died... it was like something inside him just shut down."

I wanted desperately to ease that fear for her, to give Mason another shoulder to lean on that wasn't just his sister. Abby had been carrying the weight of responsibility for him for too long already.

What I wasn't prepared for was for Mason to turn the tables on me a few days after Gram had been admitted to the hospital. Abby had stepped out to take an important call with Parker Holt about her internship, leaving Mason and me alone with a sleeping Gram. The room was quiet except for the steady beeping of monitors and the occasional squeak of rubber-soled shoes passing in the hallway.

"What are your intentions with my sister?" Mason asked suddenly, his voice deeper than usual, clearly trying to sound authoritative.

I glanced at the bed, but Gram was still asleep—she'd been sleeping more and more with every day that passed, the medication and disease progression pulling her under for longer stretches.

"Are you guys just like casual or is this serious?" he added, his eyes narrowing as he studied my face.

I set down the sports magazine I'd been flipping through and gave him my full attention.

"It's very serious," I told him, maintaining eye contact so he could see the truth in my expression.

"Do you love her?" he asked bluntly.

The question caught me off guard, not because I didn't know the answer—God, yes, I loved her more than I thought possible—but because that wasn't something Mason should hear before Abby did. I wanted the first time those words were spoken to be special, between just the two of us.

"I haven't had that conversation with your sister yet," I replied carefully, "and I think that should be one I have with her first."

He seemed to accept that answer, nodding slightly. "You won't break her heart?"

This kid impressed the hell out of me. Given the devastating situation his family was facing, I wouldn't have expected him to be focusing on his sister's emotional well-being right now. But here he was, seventeen and stepping into the role of protective brother despite his own grief. It was nice to know Abby had another person who had her back—first with Sam, who'd also made frequent visits to the hospital to check on her, and now her little brother.

"I have no intention of breaking your sister's heart," I said, my voice dropping to match the seriousness of the moment. "She's the most amazing person I've ever met. She's changed my life in ways I didn't see coming."

It was true. I had never expected to meet the person I wanted to be with for the rest of my life when I was twenty-one. I hadn't really thought much about it at all except that it would happen someday in the distant future. But every day I spent with Abby, I became more certain. She was the one I wanted standing next to me for the rest of my life. I wanted to wake up with her every morning and go to sleep with her every night. I wanted to live life with her. Through the good times and the bad, I would prove that she was my person and I would always choose her. I'd prove it to her over and over for as long as it took until she believed me with absolute certainty.

"I'm not going anywhere," I told him, the promise feeling weighty and significant. "She's safe with me."

"Good, because I really like you, Foster," he said, his serious expression relaxing slightly. "I like your friends too. But if you hurt my sister, I'll kick your ass."

I let out a chuckle, but his straight expression told me he was dead serious. Despite the fact that I had at least fifty pounds of muscle on him and years of hockey conditioning, I didn't doubt for a second that he'd try if I ever gave him reason to.

"I like you too, Mase," I said sincerely.

At the use of his nickname, he seemed to light up more than I'd ever seen, a genuine smile breaking across his face. It was small, but it was there—a crack in the armor of grief he'd been wearing.

It felt like progress.

The sound of the door opening drew our attention as Abby returned, slipping her phone into her pocket. Her eyes darted between Mason and me, clearly sensing something had shifted in her absence.

"Everything okay?" she asked, her voice tired but curious.

Mason and I exchanged a look, a silent agreement passing between us.

"Yeah," he said, reaching for the bag of chips I'd brought earlier. "Everything's good."

FORTY-SEVEN

I'd ignored my dad's calls as long as I could, but I knew if I didn't answer now he'd likely just show up at my house, and I didn't need the guys dealing with that mess. When my phone buzzed for the fifth time in an hour with "Dad" flashing across the screen, I reluctantly stepped out of the hospital room, giving Abby's shoulder a gentle squeeze before slipping into the hallway.

"Hey, Dad, I can't really talk," I answered, keeping my voice low. This unit was quiet except for the occasional squeak of nurses' shoes on the linoleum and the distant beeping of medical equipment.

"What the hell is going on with you? I've been trying to reach you for days," he said, his voice sharp with impatience. I could picture him sitting at his massive mahogany desk, expensive pen tapping against the polished surface like he did whenever he was irritated.

"I'm at the hospital. My girlfriend's grandma has cancer. She's dying, so I've been here supporting Abby and her brother."

He let out a sigh—one I knew too well because it was

the typical disappointed sigh he always gave me. "Son, Abby's a nice girl and all, but I think it's safe to say she's a distraction to you. I need you at the meeting we're having tomorrow afternoon at Holt to go over the next stage for the development. You need to be part of this process if you're going to take over the business."

I closed my eyes, leaning my head against the cool wall of the hospital corridor. I thought about Abby inside that room, holding her grandmother's hand as if she could keep her tethered to this world through sheer force of will.

"Dad, I just told you I can't. I'm not going to leave her to deal with this shit on her own. It's only one meeting that I'm going to miss. Being here for her is more important." My voice came out stronger than I thought it could when talking to my dad.

The silence on the other end of the phone was deafening. I could imagine him straightening in his chair, his jaw tightening the way it did when he was about to lay down the law. I'd never pushed back like this before.

When he finally spoke, it was with a tone of such authority combined with malice that it made bitterness roil in my gut.

"This girl is a burden and I'm telling you right now, Foster, I will not let her destroy the future I have built for you. The same one that I am wrapping in a perfect bow for you to take over, and now you're acting like an ungrateful little shit. First you ignore my calls, and now you're suggesting you skip a meeting? Absolutely not."

"Dad—" I tried to interject, but he cut me off, his tone cold as ice.

"I will destroy her if you don't break up with her. Fall back in line, and get your shit together. You *will* come to this meeting tomorrow, and she will no longer be a part of your life. Your focus needs to be on what's best for The Kane Group, which means being at this meeting tomorrow. And let's not forget, son, I'm friends with powerful people and I can destroy her before she even gets a career going. I could have her fired as an intern from Holt. I could blacklist her in this community faster than she can blink. Do not push me. I expect you to end it and to end it immediately. I will see you tomorrow at four."

He hung up, but I was frozen, still holding my phone to my ear as I stared unseeingly at the wall in front of me. My heart hammered against my ribs, and I felt a cold sweat break out across my skin. A nurse asked if I was okay as she passed, but I barely managed a nod.

Goddamn, I hated my dad.

But what was worse was that I knew it wasn't an empty threat. He *did* have friends in high places and could easily sideline Abby's career before it ever got a chance to start. The Kane name carried weight in Montana and the surrounding areas—my father had made sure of that with his ruthless business tactics and strategic "friendships" with the right people.

She'd already lost so much, and she was about to lose more.

I slumped into one of the uncomfortable plastic chairs lining the hallway, my head in my hands. I couldn't stomach the idea of bringing more pain to her life by breaking her heart when she was already being faced with a mountain of grief. The thought of walking back into that room and going back on my promise to be there for her made me physically ill.

But as I walked back into the hospital room and saw her with one hand holding Gram's while the other arm was wrapped around her brother's shoulders, all I could think about was how much I fucking loved her.

I loved her quiet strength, her brilliance, the way she bit her lower lip when she concentrated, how she brought out the best in me.

My life would be a black void without her. Maybe it made me weak, or maybe loving her was finally making me strong, but I couldn't risk losing her.

She looked up as I entered, her eyes red-rimmed but dry for the moment. She gave me a small, tired smile that broke my heart and pieced it back together all at once. Mason nodded at me, the small gesture of acknowledgment significant from the typically withdrawn teenager.

I couldn't give her up, but I couldn't be the reason she never got the career she'd worked so hard for.

I had no idea what I was going to do.

Foster drove us back to Gram's house at the end of visiting hours, the silence in the car heavy with unspoken tension. I'd noticed the change in him after he'd stepped out to take a phone call earlier—his shoulders had stiffened, his easy smile replaced with a tightness around his eyes that he tried to hide whenever I looked at him directly.

Something was wrong, and after watching my grandmother's health deteriorate while she pretended everything was fine until it was too late to do anything about it, I was sick of people not telling me what the hell was going on.

As soon as we got home from the hospital, Mason grabbed a duffle bag I hadn't noticed he'd left on the stairs earlier. "Where are you going?"

"Colt offered to let me stay at his house. He's already on his way here."

He hit me with those deep brown eyes that were far too weary for someone his age. "Please, Abby. I-I can't stay here tonight. It's hard to be here without Gram."

I swallowed thickly because I knew what he meant. I nodded, even if I was still worried about him.

A few seconds later, headlights swept across the front windows, and with a thank you and a quick wave, he was out the door.

I stood there for a moment, staring after him, then turned to find Foster standing in the kitchen with a distant look in his eyes. Maybe it was for the best that Mase wasn't here because clearly something was going on with Foster and I wanted to get to the bottom of it.

"What's going on?" I asked, my voice coming out more demanding than I'd intended, but I couldn't handle any more secrets.

Foster leaned against the counter, arms crossed defensively over his chest, his gaze locked on the floor as though the answers to whatever was troubling him might be found in the pattern of the linoleum.

"I'm a selfish dick," he finally said, the words falling between us like stones.

I frowned, confusion washing over me. After the last few days, "selfish" was absolutely not a word I would use to describe Foster. He'd stepped up and taken care of me and Mason in ways I had never expected of him—bringing us food when we forgot to eat, holding me through tearful nights, making Mason crack the first genuine smile I'd seen from him in days. He'd been my rock when everything else was crumbling around me.

I closed the gap between us and placed my hands on his chest, feeling the steady thump of his heart beneath my fingertips. He grabbed my waist, his large hands spanning my sides as he pulled me against him, almost desperately.

"Why would you say that?" I asked, keeping my voice soft.

He looked so defeated it made my chest ache. "I was

given an ultimatum today," he said, his voice low and strained, "and I'm a selfish dick because I can't let you go."

"What?" The word came out barely above a whisper, confusion and fear swirling inside me.

Foster took a deep breath, his chest expanding under my hands. "That call I got earlier was my dad and he...he threatened to destroy your future in the industry if I don't break up with you."

I felt like I'd been doused with ice water. "He *what?*"

His jaw clenched like he was barely holding it together, the muscle ticking visibly. "He said he'd make sure you lost your internship at Holt, that you'd never work in any engineering firm in Montana. He has the connections to do it too." His voice cracked slightly. "Abby..."

My throat felt pinched as I waited to hear the words I was dreading. I knew his relationship with his dad was complicated, but that he'd also nearly always put his dad's wishes first. So I braced myself to hear him say the words I was sure would break my heart—that we were over.

Instead, he cupped my face in his hands, his eyes intense and vulnerable in a way I'd never seen before.

"I love you," he said, his voice rough but sure. "I'm not strong enough to let you go. I would take a bullet for you, but I can't live without you and I'm so sorry. I should be strong enough to walk away to protect your future, but I'm not."

Relief and love flooded through me so powerfully my knees almost buckled. I wrapped my arms around his neck and kissed him with every ounce of love and longing I had inside me. His arms tightened around me as he kissed me back just as fiercely.

"I love you too," I whispered against his lips when we finally broke apart, both of us breathing heavily. "And you're not selfish for wanting to be with me. That's not how this works."

I think I'd been falling in love with him since long before we even got together—back when I only knew him as Bear.

"I need to tell you something," I said, pulling away slightly because if we were being honest then we were going to be all the way honest. "Your dad tried to pay me to break up with you when we had dinner with him."

For a second he looked shocked, his eyes widening and lips parting, and then his expression transformed into pure fury. "Are you fucking kidding me?"

"I wish I was," I said, my hands moving to his shoulders, feeling the tension that had instantly gathered there. "When you ran in to get the valet ticket, he told me he'd pay off all my tuition and all my future grad school fees if I broke up with you. Said I wasn't good enough for you, that you were just..." I hesitated, not wanting to repeat the crude way his father had dismissed our relationship.

"That fucking bastard," Foster growled, his hands tightening on my waist. "I can't believe he would...actually, no, I can absolutely believe he would do that. He's always seen people as pawns he can move around to get what he wants." He shook his head, his expression shifting to curiosity. "Why didn't you tell me?"

"You already have such a difficult relationship with him," I said. "I didn't want to make it worse, especially when I had absolutely no intention of taking his offer. It wasn't worth hurting you over."

Foster shook his head in disbelief. "I should've seen this coming."

I cupped his face, wanting him to see in my eyes the sincerity behind my words. "Foster, I love you so much, and

I don't want to lose you. I *can't* lose you. Not now, not with everything else..." My voice broke as I thought about Gram lying in that hospital bed, about how many people I'd already lost.

"You're never gonna lose me," he said with fierce conviction, his forehead pressing against mine. "We'll figure this out. My dad doesn't get to dictate who I love or what I do with my life anymore. I'm done letting him control me."

The weight of his words, of his love, wrapped around me like a protective blanket. In the midst of so much uncertainty and grief, he was my one constant, the solid ground beneath my feet when everything else felt like shifting sand.

I kissed him again, slowly this time, pouring all my emotions into it—my love, my fear, my desperate need for him. His hands slid under my shirt, warm against my skin, and I melted into him, needing the connection that I'd only ever had with him.

He lifted me onto the counter, my legs wrapping around his waist, the cool surface a sharp contrast to the heat building between us. I tugged at his shirt, needing to feel his skin against mine and the solid muscle beneath. He pulled it over his head by the back of his neck—a move that felt like it set my panties on fire because it was so sexy—then tossed it carelessly onto the floor. I ran my hands over his chest, tracing the lines of his toned physique and the evidence of years spent honing his body on the ice.

My own shirt followed, and then his hands were on the clasp of my bra, unhooking it and letting it fall away. He looked at me with such reverence, such open admiration, that it chased away any lingering insecurities I'd ever had about my small breasts.

"You're so fucking beautiful, Abby," he whispered, his voice thick with desire. "I don't know how I got so lucky."

He kissed me again, his tongue tracing the line of my lips, asking for entrance so he could kiss me deeper. I opened for him, our mouths melding together in a dance of need and longing. His hands cupped my breasts and then his thumbs teased my nipples into hard peaks.

A needy moan escaped my lips as I reached for the button of his jeans, my fingers fumbling slightly in my eagerness. He helped me, his hands covering mine as we worked together to undo the denim. He grabbed a condom out of his pocket, then kicked off his shoes and shucked his jeans and boxers in one swift motion. He sheathed his hard cock with the condom and then pressed his hot body against mine, his erection positioned at my core.

He entered me slowly, carefully, his eyes locked on mine as he watched for any sign of discomfort. But I was used to the feel of him now—the way he stretched me and made me feel fuller than I ever knew possible. Pleasure lit up my nerve endings as he rocked forward, hitting me deep.

"Okay?" he asked, his voice strained.

"Yes," I breathed. It was perfect.

And then he began to really move, slowly at first, establishing a rhythm that built a fire within me.

Everything else faded away. There was only Foster, only the feel of him inside me, the way he looked at me, the sounds we made together. Each thrust was a spark, igniting a pleasure so intense it felt like I would never be the same when I tipped over the edge. I wrapped my legs tighter around him, anchoring myself to him. My fingers dug into his shoulders and left marks as my body pulsed with my release.

His name became a mantra—a prayer—whispered and gasped as the pleasure intensified, spiraling higher and higher. I was at the precipice of something incredible, and I clung to him, trusting him to take me there because he always did.

"Foster," I cried out, my body arching, as the world dissolved into a kaleidoscope of sensation. He followed me over the edge, dropping his forehead to my shoulder as his own release racked his body.

We clung to each other, breathless and trembling, our bodies slick with sweat and our hearts pounding in unison. He kissed my forehead, my temple, my cheek, murmuring my name like a prayer. The world slowly came back into focus—the kitchen, the quiet hum of the refrigerator, the ticking of the clock on the wall. But everything felt different, transformed by the intensity of what we'd just shared.

We would get through whatever his father threw our way.

Because there was no future where we weren't together.

Finding out my dad had gone behind my back and tried to pay off my girlfriend to break up with me was the final straw. My body was tight as rage fueled me on the drive over to my parents' condo in Missoula the next morning. Each mile I drove, my knuckles whitened on the steering wheel, my jaw clenched so hard I could feel the tension radiating through my skull.

I'd spent the entire night holding Abby while she slept fitfully, her grandmother's condition weighing heavily on her even in sleep. The revelation of what my father had done to her—trying to buy her off like she was some kind of inconvenience to be removed from my life—kept replaying in my mind until I couldn't take it anymore.

I didn't bother knocking when I arrived at his place. I just used the key he'd given me and barged in, finding him sitting at the kitchen island while my mom served him breakfast. The smell of bacon and coffee filled the air, such a normal, domestic scene that it made my anger burn even hotter. How dare he sit here enjoying his morning like he hadn't tried to destroy the best thing in my life?

My mom looked at me like a deer in the headlights, confusion written across her face. I'd never stormed in like this before. I was always the good son who did everything they asked of me. I had sacrificed my own identity for as long as I could remember, swallowing my dreams and desires to fit the mold my father had created for me. The only thing I'd ever done for myself was hockey until Abby.

She was mine, and I was not going to let him take her away from me.

I stared daggers at my father, wondering where the hell he got off thinking he could control every aspect of my life. We may have looked similar—the same strong jaw, the same blue eyes—but we couldn't be further apart in personality. Where he was cold calculation, I at least tried to have some heart.

"Foster, do you want to join us for breakfast?" Mom asked, her voice small and uncertain. She was already reaching for another plate, trying to normalize the tension that had entered the room with me.

I didn't even answer. I just stared at my dad, my breathing heavy. "You tried to buy my girlfriend off so that she'd break up with me." It wasn't a question because I already knew the answer. I trusted Abby more than I trusted him. The words came out low and dangerous, a tone I'd never used with my father before.

He set down his fork deliberately and wiped the edges of his mouth with his napkin, then looked at me like he didn't have a care in the world—like he hadn't done something awful. His casual demeanor made my blood boil even hotter.

"Yes, I did," he admitted without a hint of remorse.

He had zero shame. The bastard actually looked proud

of himself, like he'd made some brilliant business move instead of attempting to destroy my relationship.

"The stupid little bitch didn't take the offer," he continued, his voice dripping with disdain. "She's probably regretting that now that you've dumped her anyway," he said with an arrogant grin.

I saw red. The world around me blurred at the edges, and all I could see was my father's smug face. I liked to believe that I wasn't a hothead unless I was on the ice, and even then it was only with a purpose—to defend a teammate or respond to a dirty hit.

But right then, faced with a new level of my dad's arrogance—hearing him call Abby that term—I felt so much rage and hatred bubbling underneath my skin, I thought I was going to explode. My heart hammered against my ribs as I stormed up to him, grabbed the lapel of his expensive shirt and yanked him up until he was standing face to face with me.

I had one inch on him but easily twenty pounds more of muscle from years of hockey training, and I used all of that to my advantage as I held him there, close enough that I could smell his cologne and see the flecks of gray in his stubble.

"I have done everything you've ever asked of me," I growled, my voice shaking with fury. "How dare you try to interfere in my relationship and manipulate her?"

My mother gasped somewhere behind us, but I couldn't focus on her right now. All I could see was the contempt in my father's eyes.

He sneered, not intimidated in the slightest despite my physical advantage. "Please tell me you aren't that stupid. You didn't break up with her?" His lip curled in disgust. "You think she's good enough for this family? She has nothing to offer you, Foster. So, she's smart. So what? Connections are more important than intelligence."

Each word felt like a slap, not because they hurt me, but because I knew how they would hurt Abby if she heard them. This brilliant, beautiful woman who had helped me overcome my learning difficulties, who had shown me more kindness and genuine care than my own father ever had—and he was reducing her to nothing more than a social disadvantage.

I wanted to punch him so badly. The only thing that kept me from doing it was the fact that I'd have to tell Abby how this encounter went, and I didn't want her to be ashamed of me and my actions. I didn't want to be the kind of man who solved problems with his fists, no matter how satisfying it might feel in the moment.

My father held a finger up to my face, his expression hardening into the business mask I knew so well. "You will back off right now," he commanded, as if I were still a child to be ordered around. "Then, you're going to break up with that girl like I told you to do last night, or I will cut you off at the knees. No tuition, no hockey, no financial assistance, whatsoever." His eyes narrowed. "You really think you'll be able to survive that? You need me, so you will do as I tell you to do."

For a moment, fear flickered through me. He was right —I had been dependent on him for everything. My education, my housing, even my ability to play hockey depended on his financial support. The thought of losing it all was terrifying.

But then I thought of Abby, of how brave she'd been through everything—losing both parents, now watching her grandmother slip away, and still standing strong, still pursuing her dreams with determination and grace. If she could face all that, I could face this.

"Fuck you."

I didn't shout the words—I didn't have to. Every ounce of disdain I felt for my father could be felt in those two words. They hung in the air between us, a declaration of independence more powerful than any I'd ever made before.

He'd gone too far.

It was one thing to manipulate me and treat me like a puppet on some strings, but for him to try to do the same to Abby, to manipulate her, to force her into a corner was crossing the line.

I was done sitting back and letting him walk all over my life. "You're gonna cut me off? Then *do it*," I said, releasing his shirt with a small shove. "As far as I'm concerned, you're dead to me."

A muscle popped in his jaw as he clenched his teeth, the first sign that my words had gotten through his armor of arrogance. "You'll regret this," he threatened, straightening his shirt with an angry tug.

"Not as much as you will," I replied, my voice steadier now that I'd made my decision. "You just lost your only son."

I heard my mother make a small, wounded sound. She stood frozen by the stove, tears in her eyes, but she made no move to intervene or support me. She never did. Part of me wanted to be angry at her too—for never standing up to him, for letting him treat me like a pawn all these years—but mostly I just felt pity. She was as trapped as I had been, maybe more so.

With one final look at my mom, I spun around and

walked out the door, not bothering to look back. I would never live under my father's control again.

As I walked to my car, the weight of what I'd just done settled over me. I had no idea what came next, how I'd pay for school or hockey or even basic necessities. But for the first time in my life, I felt free. Whatever challenges came, I'd face them on my own terms.

And I wouldn't be facing them alone. I had Abby. I had my teammates. And for now, that was enough.

FIFTY

Foster showed up at Gram's house with his jaw set tight and his eyes still burning with anger. The fury was evident in every line of his body, but beneath it, I could see a slight tremor in his hands, a certain vulnerability in the set of his shoulders—like someone who had just jumped off a cliff and wasn't entirely sure there was water below.

Yet despite that uncertainty, there was an unmistakable resoluteness in his stance. The way he held himself taller, as if a weight had been lifted.

I opened the door wider to let him in, scanning his face for any sign of regret. "How did it go?"

When Foster left this morning to confront his dad, I'd been sick with worry about my role in the destruction of their relationship. That worry hadn't dissipated, even as Foster stepped into the house with what appeared to be newfound conviction growing stronger with each passing second.

He didn't answer my question immediately. Instead, he cupped my face in his large, warm hands and bent down to kiss me before pulling me against his chest. He drew in a deep breath as if the scent and feel of me was enough to ground him.

"God, I needed this," he murmured into my hair. "*You.*"

When he finally pulled away, his gaze swept over my face, his expression shifting to concern. He must have seen the worry I couldn't hide because he frowned, his thumb gently tracing the crease between my brows.

"What's going on?" he asked, his voice gentle.

I bit my lip, the guilt I'd been harboring spilling out before I could stop it. "I'm worried I've ruined your relationship with your parents and someday you're going to resent me for this."

He was already shaking his head before I'd even finished speaking. "No, Babe. No." His voice was firm, leaving no room for doubt. "My relationship with my parents has been at a tipping point for a long time. It shouldn't have taken me this long to cut them off—to say enough was enough." His expression softened, tinged with embarrassment. "I'm just sorry that you even had to see or experience that. You deserve better than being caught in the crossfire of my family's dysfunction."

I searched his eyes, looking for any hint of uncertainty, but found none. Still, I needed to know. "So, what did he say?" I asked hesitantly.

Foster let out a heavy sigh before grabbing my hand and leading me over to the couch. When he sat down, he pulled me into his lap and his arms encircled me as if I might disappear. I nestled against him, offering whatever comfort I could through my presence.

"He cut me off," Foster finally said, his voice surprisingly steady. "No money, apart from what I've already got in savings." He ran a hand through his hair, a nervous habit I'd come to recognize. "Fortunately, I've saved up most of my money from construction jobs during summers, although a lot of it has gone toward hockey equipment and travel expenses. Tuition for this year has already been paid, but I don't know how I'll afford next year."

My heart ached for him. I knew how much hockey meant to Foster—it was his escape, his passion. And college wasn't cheap, especially not for someone who suddenly found themselves without financial support.

"We'll figure it out," I told him, with more confidence than I actually felt. I turned in his lap to face him, taking his face in my hands the way he'd held mine moments before. "There are tons of scholarships and different ways to get tuition assistance. Maybe we can even look at talking to your coach to see if he knows of anything or if there might be athletic assistance or club assistance. No matter what, we'll figure it out."

Even as I said the words, I had a nagging worry that this wouldn't be the last time Dennis Kane tried to interfere in our relationship.

FIFTY-ONE

This wasn't how tonight was supposed to go. We'd won our first game yesterday against MSU, but lost tonight—and even though we had one more game against them tomorrow, I was epically pissed off about the loss. The locker room had already cleared out, but I couldn't stop replaying all my mistakes. We were all a little off, but I was the captain. I was supposed to lead but I hadn't been much of a leader during tonight's game.

The door opened and Abby's voice broke the silence.

"Foster? You still in here?"

Her hand was over her eyes and some of my frustrations evaporated at the sight of her.

"You don't have to cover your eyes. I'm the only one in here. Coach asked me to lock up."

She dropped her hand and walked toward me, her gaze sympathetic. I didn't want her to look at me like that. I wanted her to be proud of me.

Not only did I feel like I let my team down, Now I felt like I'd let her down.

She closed the gap between us, her fingers sliding into

my hair as she pressed herself against my half naked body. I only wore a towel wrapped around my waist from the showers since I'd been too pissed and lost in my head to get dressed yet.

"You beat yourself up a lot when your team doesn't do well." It wasn't a question.

"I'm the captain."

"You're also human. You're allowed to have an off day."

I shook my head and moved away from her, even though it physically pained me to do so. Her warmth soothed my soul, but I felt like I deserved to beat myself up over the stupid mistakes I made tonight.

"Foster."

There was a sureness in her voice that got my attention. I looked up and a heavy moment passed between us, the air suddenly thickening.

I wasn't sure who moved first but the next thing I knew, she was in my arms, her fingers back in my hair and her thighs snug against my hips as she locked her ankles at my lower back. Our kiss was filled with savage need as my towel fell and I gripped her ass, grinding her against me.

Fuck, she had me so worked up already.

I reluctantly set her down on the bench, her chest heaving and her eyes filled with hunger.

We didn't speak as I stripped off her shirt and bra.

"Be a good girl and lie back for me, Baby." With a shaky inhale, she did as I asked. "Now put your hands over your head and keep them there." I'd never been bossy when it came to sex, but there was a clawing need to be fully in control right now. Her submission as she once again quickly did what I asked settled the animal inside, even as it made my cock harder than steel.

"You're such a good girl," I murmured, leaning over her

until my lips brushed hers faintly. "I bet that sweet pussy is already soaked for me, isn't it?"

A soft whimper escaped as she nodded.

I kissed her lips, sliding my tongue across the seam until she parted them before slanting my mouth more firmly on hers and plunging my tongue inside to tangle with her own.

I let out a groan when her body arched up to touch me while her mouth met mine stroke for stroke. Fuck, she could kiss. But I needed more.

"You gonna make me feel better?" I murmured as I made my way down her neck to her collarbone. I waited for her shaky "yes" before I sucked one of her pert, pink nipples into my mouth. The moan she made as I teased her with my teeth nearly brought me to my knees. But I wanted her as bare as I was. Thankfully, she was wearing yoga pants that slid off easily, along with her thong.

And then she was laid out gloriously naked on the bench like a feast for my eyes.

"Fuck, you have no idea how sexy you look right now."

Her mouth was parted and her eyes hooded, but it was her hard nipples pointing straight up at the ceiling that snagged my attention. Leaning down, I sucked on a stiff tip, eliciting a moan from her. Moving to her other breast, I repeated the teasing suck while my hand slid up her leg and then over the arousal dripping from her soaked pussy. She sighed as my finger circled her swollen clit.

"That feels so g-good," she stuttered as her pelvis thrust up, seeking more friction.

"Have I told you," I murmured against her skin while I once again worked my way down her body, "that I love how responsive you are?"

Her cheeks flushed pink, and fuck if I didn't love that too.

I spread her thighs wide, my mouth watering at the sight of her exposed pink pussy that practically glittered in the light from her arousal. Dipping my head down, I took a long lick from her pussy lips to her clit. Her thighs clenched, her legs trying to close in on my head, but I was prepared for her body's response and held her legs open with my hands.

Another lick and I had to close my eyes as my cock pulsed with need, precum beading at the tip. Her taste exploded on my tongue—musky and tangy and delicious. I could eat this woman all day every day. But I wanted to see her body explode from pleasure. I wanted to pump every ounce of pleasure out of her until she was limp and content.

Most importantly, I wanted her most recent memory of me to be *this* guy—the one who could make her body feel more than she'd ever known before—not the guy who'd failed on the ice tonight.

Holding her thighs firm, I teased her with my tongue, dipping it into her pussy and pulling it out, mimicking what I planned to do with my finger. Then I moved my mouth to her clit, forming a suction around it and then flicking it with my tongue. She moaned as her back arched on the bench and my gut tightened with want. I needed to make her come soon, or I would lose my resolve to give her two orgasms before I buried my cock inside her.

I alternated sucking and flicking her clit until her cries of pleasure were so loud, they echoed around the room. Then she sucked in a sharp breath, and her whole body tensed before shuddering as her hips rocked against my mouth and her release flooded my taste buds.

"Oh my God," she panted as she started to come down, but I wasn't done yet.

I hadn't been able to master the ice tonight, but I knew without a doubt, I could master Abby's body.

I slid one finger inside her, taking her by surprise but watching her face for any signs of distress or discomfort. Instead that hooded gaze locked on mine and she nodded.

"Make me come again."

Fuck, I loved it when she told me what she wanted.

I pulled my finger out and pushed two in on the next thrust. "Oh fuck," she moaned, her arms tensing as she gripped the top of the bench.

"Oh God, oh God," she started murmuring, her breaths coming faster and her legs tensing up.

"Call me whatever you want, but I'm the only man who will ever make you fall apart like this." And then I picked up my pace and within three thrusts, she went off like a bomb, screaming as her release tore through her and her pussy tightened around my fingers.

"Fuck, you're so goddamn beautiful," I whispered as I leaned over her nearly spent body and kissed her hard. Her arms wrapped around my neck, and I allowed it because I needed her touch.

"Think you can come for me one more time?"

She blinked up at me and then that luminescent smile broke out over her face and sucked all the air from my lungs.

Never in my life would I take the gift of her love and attention for granted.

"I think you'll help me get there," she said as she lifted her lips to mine for another kiss.

"You're fucking right I will."

I snagged a condom out of my locker and rolled it on and then in one smooth motion, I was back between her gorgeous thighs, rubbing the head of my dick over her clit.

Her hips tilted up, and I accepted the invitation, pushing my thick cock into her, relishing in the snug fit.

I tried to hold myself back from the desire pounding in my skull to thrust all the way into her. I didn't want to hurt her, especially as tight she was.

"Goddamn it, Abby," I choked, my body fighting against my mental restraints, desperate to be buried inside her. "You feel so fucking good."

My pelvis rubbed against her clit and she let out a shuddery breath.

"So good," she panted in agreement.

I needed her lips again before I made her shatter underneath me, so I leaned over and took her mouth in a fierce kiss. Her tongue slid against mine, meeting my eagerness and then some. My hips rocked out slightly and then back in, and we both groaned at the heavenly sensation.

There was no better feeling in the world than being balls deep inside her. Not a single fucking one.

My restraint was running thin, and my thrusts started coming faster and harder, her moans only spurring me on until any control I had completely snapped and I was pounding into her like our lives depended on it. Her hands gripped my biceps as her legs locked around my waist. I gripped her hips and canted them ever so slightly to hit her at a better angle, and she let out a scream as her pussy convulsed around me.

"Fuck," I growled, trying to hold off just a little longer, but it was no use. She felt too good and I was too needy for her. With one more thrust, I let out my own shout as my release ripped through me.

When I'd caught my breath, I pulled Abby into my arms and sat on the bench, her chest against mine and her legs still wrapped around my hips.

"Feel better?" she asked, running her fingers through my hair again in a way that eased the last of the frustration I'd carried since getting off the ice at the end of our game.

"Yeah, I do." I leaned my forehead against hers, breathing her in.

I didn't know how she'd figured out what I needed, but I was once again grateful for her. With Abby in my arms, things didn't seem so bad.

FIFTY-TWO

The next day, I got to the rink two hours before game time, my hockey bag slung over my shoulder. The place was nearly empty, just a few staff members setting up for tonight's final game against Montana State. Today's game would determine which team led the Mountain West conference and I desperately wanted to make up for our loss last night. We still had plenty of season left, but winning against one of the best teams in the state would go a long way in making sure we made it to the playoffs a few months from now.

I'd texted Coach Maxwell earlier, asking if we could talk before everyone else arrived. I hadn't had much time to process my fight with my dad and come to terms with my new financial situation, but I knew there was a strong chance I might not be able to play hockey next year. Coach deserved to know what was going on, especially if I ended up needing to get a job before our season was over.

He was already in his office. "Kane," he said when he spotted me.

I dropped my bag by the door and took a seat across from him. "Thanks for meeting me, Coach."

He sat forward, leaning his elbows on his desk. "Everything alright? You seemed distracted during yesterday's game."

"That's actually what I wanted to talk to you about," I said, leaning back in my chair. "I'm dealing with some... family issues."

Coach's expression tightened. "Your father?"

I shouldn't have been surprised he'd picked up on the tension. Coach Maxwell might be young, but he was perceptive as hell.

"Yeah. We had a falling out. It was a long time coming, but he cut me off financially." I took a deep breath. "Which means I might not be able to play hockey next year, depending on what job I can find to finish school."

Coach studied me. "Have you talked to the financial aid office?"

"Yeah, they gave me information on getting loans and applying for scholarships, but said I didn't qualify for any athletic scholarships since our team is only a club team."

He sat back in his chair. "Hmm. Let me do a little digging to see what options I can find for you. I'll do what I can to keep you on this team. You're an incredible leader, Kane."

"Thanks, Coach. I really appreciate that."

Then he asked me something I hadn't really expected from him. "How are you really doing with all this, Foster?"

The use of my first name caught me off guard since he usually only called us by our last names.

"I'm..." I started to say "fine" automatically, then stopped myself. "Actually, I'm pissed. And worried. But also...relieved? Is that weird?"

He shook his head. "Not at all. Toxic relationships drain you, especially when they're with family. Sometimes cutting ties is the healthiest thing you can do."

"A part of me wishes I'd been strong enough to cut ties sooner," I said.

He cleared his throat. "Listen, Kane. You're one of the strongest players I've ever coached. Not just in skill, but in character. The way you lead this team, the way you've stepped up for your friends—that shows me exactly what kind of man you are."

I swallowed hard, unexpectedly moved by his words.

"Whatever your father thinks, he's wrong," Coach continued. "And I'm not just saying that because I need my captain focused for tonight's game, though I do." He cracked a smile. "I'm saying it because it's true."

"Thanks," I said, my voice rougher than I intended. "That means a lot. More than you know."

He nodded once, then his demeanor shifted back to all business. "Now, about tonight's game. MSU's defense adjusted to our offensive strategy yesterday. We need to mix things up."

I straightened, grateful for the change in topic. "I was thinking the same thing. Their defensemen were anticipating our passes across the neutral zone."

For the next thirty minutes, we talked strategy, the weight on my shoulders lightening with each passing minute. By the time the rest of the team started trickling in, I felt centered again, focused on what I could control—my performance on the ice.

Drew was the first to arrive, eyeing me curiously as he dropped his bag next to mine.

"All good?" he asked.

"Yep, just came in early to talk strategy with Coach."

"Good," Drew said, pulling out his skates. "Because we need your head in the game tonight. Yesterday was a shit show."

I couldn't argue with that. We'd been sloppy and unfocused. It had been an off night for all of us, but if we wanted to keep our position in the league, then we couldn't afford any more off nights.

"Don't worry about me," I told Drew. "I'm locked in."

As the rest of the team arrived, I fell into my role as captain, leading warm-ups and keeping everyone's energy up. The locker room buzzed with pregame excitement.

Coach Maxwell entered the locker room as we were suiting up, his game face on.

"Alright, gentlemen. You know what's on the line tonight. MSU is a strong team, and we're pretty evenly matched, which means we need to give it our all to take the edge. Yesterday, we beat ourselves with sloppy passes and missed opportunities." He looked around the room, his gaze landing on each player. "Tonight, we play our game. We control the pace. We finish our checks. And we don't let them get close to Gordy."

He turned to me. "Kane, anything to add?"

I stood, looking at the faces of my teammates—my chosen family. "Whatever happens out there tonight, we stick together. We cover each other. We've worked our asses off all season for this opportunity. Let's make it count."

A chorus of "Hell, yeah" and stick taps filled the room.

As we filed out toward the ice, Liam nudged my shoulder. "You good, Captain?"

I nodded. "Never better."

The arena erupted as we hit the ice for warm-ups. The stands were packed, more people than I'd ever seen at one of our games. My eyes automatically scanned the crowd, finding Abby in her usual spot near the glass. She smiled when she caught my eye, and I tapped my palm against the glass as I skated by.

Warm-ups flew by, and before I knew it, we were lined up for the opening face-off. The MSU center across from me smirked.

"Ready to lose that top spot, Kane?"

I just smiled. "Not a chance, Dwyer."

The puck dropped, and I won it cleanly back to Liam, who immediately fired it up the boards to Drew.

Game on.

The first period was a chess match, both teams feeling each other out, neither willing to make the first mistake. Their goalie made a spectacular save on my breakaway attempt midway through the period. I slammed my stick against the boards in frustration as I returned to the bench.

"You'll get him next time," Coach said. "He's cheating to his glove side. Go blocker."

I nodded, filing away the information.

The period ended scoreless, both teams heading to their locker rooms to regroup.

"We're playing well," Coach said. "But we need to capitalize on our chances. Kane, press hard on the forecheck. Dumontier and Farrell—if the puck gets chipped high, I want aggressive pinches at the blue line. Keep the puck in their zone."

We nodded, determination setting in.

The second period started with a flurry of action. MSU came out flying, hemming us in our zone for the first two minutes. Gordy made save after save, keeping us in the game. Finally, Drew managed to clear the puck, and we changed lines on the fly.

I jumped over the boards just as Liam intercepted a pass at our blue line. He spotted me streaking through the neutral zone and hit me with a perfect pass.

Remembering Coach's advice, I faked to my forehand, then quickly pulled the puck to my backhand and lifted it over Reeves's outstretched blocker. The puck hit the back of the net with a satisfying thud.

The crowd exploded as I raised my arms in celebration. My teammates mobbed me, a tangle of limbs and excited shouts.

"Fucking beautiful, Candy Kane!" Drew yelled, thumping my helmet.

I was too happy to even be annoyed at the nickname.

Our lead didn't last long. MSU tied it up five minutes later on a power play after Liam took a questionable tripping penalty. The momentum shifted, and they scored again with thirty seconds left in the period. We headed to the locker room down 2-1, the energy noticeably deflated.

"We're still in this," I said, looking around at my teammates. "Twenty minutes left. This is where we show what we're made of."

They nodded, but I could see the doubt creeping in. Yesterday's loss was still fresh in their minds.

Coach entered, his expression stern but not defeated. "They're outworking us right now," he said bluntly. "But that ends now. I want every single one of you to win your individual battles. Every face-off, every puck along the boards, every race to a loose puck—win it. That's how we turn this around."

We took the ice for the third period with renewed determination. The first few minutes were back and forth, neither team gaining an advantage. Then, disaster struck.

MSU's top line caught us on a bad change. Their winger, a speedy guy named Ramsey, blew past our defense and tucked the puck around Gordy. 3-1 MSU with fifteen minutes left.

The air seemed to go out of our bench. I looked around at my teammates, seeing shoulders slump and heads hang low.

"Hey!" I shouted, standing up. "We're not done. Not even close."

Drew nodded, his jaw set. "Let's go, boys. One shift at a time."

We pushed hard, throwing everything we had at them. With eight minutes left, Drew scored on a beautiful end-to-end rush, cutting the deficit to one. The crowd came alive again, belief flowing back into the arena.

But time was our enemy now. Every minute that ticked by without the tying goal seemed to drain the energy out of the rink. With two minutes left, Coach pulled Gordy for an extra man on the ice.

We jumped over the boards, six desperate men against five. The puck pinballed around the MSU zone as we fired shot after shot. Reeves stopped everything, some saves more luck than skill.

With thirty seconds left, I won the face-off back to Drew, who fired a hard pass to Liam at the point. Liam wound up for a slap shot, but instead of shooting, he sent a pass right onto my tape at the side of the net. I had a wide-open net, Reeves out of position—and I missed. The puck slid harmlessly through the crease and out the other side.

"Fuck!" I yelled, slamming my stick against the ice.

Before we could reset, MSU cleared the puck down the ice. Drew raced after it, but the clock hit zero before he could retrieve it. Game over.

The final horn sounded like a death knell. I stood motionless, hands on my knees, disbelief washing over me. How had I missed that chance? It was the easiest goal I'd ever have, and I'd blown it.

MSU celebrated at center ice while we filed off in silence, the weight of disappointment crushing us. In the locker room, no one spoke. Some guys stared blankly at the floor; others angrily stripped off their gear. I sat frozen in defeat, still fully dressed, replaying that final missed opportunity over and over in my mind.

How could I miss when it was wide fucking open?

I knew it wasn't the end of the world. We could still make it to playoffs later this season, but now the top spot was going to MSU.

Coach entered, his face somber but not angry. "I know this isn't how any of you wanted tonight to go," he said quietly. "But I want you to know how proud I am of this team. We had a bad week. It happens. Next week, we have three more games to win, so we aren't going to let this week's losses keep us down. Got it?"

We all nodded, but we were still disappointed.

After Coach left, I finally stood, addressing my teammates. "This one's on me," I said, my voice thick. "I had the chance to tie it, and I didn't come through."

"Bullshit," Drew said immediately. "We win as a team, we lose as a team. One play doesn't define a game or a season."

Gordy nodded. "Monty's right, Foster. We all had chances we didn't capitalize on."

Their support meant everything, but it didn't erase the sting of that missed opportunity.

I wasn't going to let this game break me.

We still had more season left.

And I was still their captain—for the rest of this year, at least.

The day after the Lumberjacks' loss to MSU, Gram lost her battle with cancer.

The funeral was held at the small chapel where Gram had attended services every Sunday for as long as I could remember. The wooden pews were filled with neighbors, friends from her quilting circle, and people from the community center where she'd volunteered for years. Outside, the mid-November sky was a clear, brilliant blue—the kind of fall day Gram would have loved.

I sat in the front pew, sandwiched between Foster on one side and Mason on the other. My brother had barely spoken since Gram passed, his grief manifesting in a silence so profound it scared me. He stared straight ahead throughout the service, his face a carefully constructed mask that reminded me too much of how he'd looked after Mom died.

Pastor Mike spoke about Gram's life—her devotion to family, her tireless community service, her famous huckleberry pies that always won ribbons at the county fair. I tried to focus on his words, but they seemed to float around me, never quite landing. Instead, I found myself fixating on small details—the white lilies on her casket, the slight hum of the old heaters, and the steady pressure of Foster's hand holding mine. His touch was grounding and I needed it more than I was proud of, but I was thankful I had him.

"Daniella Thomas lived a life of service," Pastor Mike was saying. "She poured love into this community the same way she poured love into her family. When her daughter passed, she stepped up to raise her grandchildren with the same fierce dedication she brought to everything in her life."

A sob caught in my throat, and Foster's hand tightened around mine. I squeezed back, grateful beyond words for his presence. He'd been my rock through all of this, never wavering, never complaining about how little time I'd had for him over the last two weeks as we'd watched Gram wither away.

After the service, we followed the hearse to the cemetery where Gram would be laid to rest beside her husband. The graveside service was mercifully brief—just a few prayers and the somber lowering of the casket. I placed a single white rose on top, whispering a final goodbye that felt wholly inadequate for the woman who had been my safety net, my champion, and my home.

As we turned to leave, I noticed the row of hockey players standing at a respectful distance, all in suits, their faces solemn. Coach Maxwell stood with them, a beautiful brunette woman beside him. The sight of them—these young men who didn't even know my grandmother—showing up to support my brother and me, brought fresh tears to my eyes.

Sam appeared at my side, linking her arm through mine.

"Let's get you to the reception," she said gently. "You need to eat something."

The local community center had been transformed for the occasion. Tables covered in white cloths held framed photos of Gram throughout her life. One showed her as a young woman, radiant in her wedding dress beside my grandfather. Another captured her holding baby Mason, with me—gap-toothed and pigtailed—grinning beside them.

"Your grandmother was a remarkable woman," said a voice behind me. I turned to find Mrs. Henderson, Gram's next-door neighbor, holding a casserole dish. "She talked about you and Mason constantly. So proud of you both."

"Thank you," I said automatically, the words feeling worn from repetition. I'd been saying them all day as people shared their condolences and memories.

"She made this community better," Mrs. Henderson continued, her eyes misty. "We'll all miss her terribly."

I nodded, unable to form more words. Foster appeared at my elbow, as if sensing my distress, and smoothly took over the conversation. I watched him charm Mrs. Henderson, thanking her for coming and for the casserole she'd brought, which he promised we'd enjoy later.

"You're good at that," I murmured when she moved on.

He shrugged. "Years of practice at my parents' business functions. How are you holding up?"

"I'm..." I searched for the right word. "I'm here. That's about all I can manage."

His eyes, full of understanding, held mine. "That's more than enough for now."

The afternoon wore on, a blur of faces and voices and memories of Gram. I accepted hugs from people I barely recognized, nodded as they told stories about how she had helped them through difficult times or brightened their days with her sharp wit and kind heart. Each story was a gift, a new piece of her to hold on to, but also a reminder of the enormity of what I'd lost.

I kept one eye on Mason, who had stationed himself in a corner, accepting condolences with nods and minimal words. Drew and Liam had taken up positions nearby, occasionally drawing him into conversation. I was grateful for their efforts, even if Mason seemed resistant.

Foster's hockey coach approached me with the brunette woman from the funeral at his side. "I'm so sorry for your loss," he said.

"Thank you for coming," I said, the words automatic by now.

"Abby, I don't know if you've met my wife, Maggie."

"I haven't. Nice to meet you," I said, shaking her hand.

"You too," Maggie said. "I've seen you at some of the games. If you need anything—meals, someone to talk to, whatever—please don't hesitate to reach out."

The genuine kindness in her voice nearly broke me. "That's really thoughtful."

"I mean it," she insisted. "It's hard enough dealing with grief without having to worry about practical matters."

For some reason, her acknowledgment of the "practical matters"—all the logistical nightmares that came with death —hit me harder than the more general condolences I'd been receiving. Tears welled up in my eyes, and I blinked rapidly, trying to maintain my composure.

"Abby is the strongest person I know," Foster said, his arm slipping around my waist. "But even the strongest people need support sometimes."

Maggie nodded. "Exactly. And you have more support than you might realize." She glanced over at the hockey players, who had spread throughout the room, helping serve food, move chairs, and generally making themselves useful. "They're a good bunch."

I followed her gaze, noticing how Gordy was now sitting with Mason, apparently showing him something on his phone that had caught my brother's interest. Sam hovered nearby also keeping an eye on the interaction. "They really are."

After Coach Maxwell and his wife moved on, another well-wisher approached—Mrs. Schmidt from the community center board, who launched into a tearful recollection of how Gram had reorganized their entire volunteer program.

I could feel my carefully constructed facade beginning to crack. The weight of the day, of maintaining strength for Mason, of accepting condolences with grace—it was becoming too much. My chest tightened, and I knew I needed air before I completely fell apart in front of everyone.

"Excuse me, I-I need to go check on something," I said, but instead I snuck out a side door and leaned against the exterior wall, breathing in the crisp mountain air. It was unseasonably warm for November in Montana, but there was still a chill to the air that made me wish I'd thought to grab my coat.

I was about to turn around and go back inside—even though I desperately didn't want to have to keep a smile on my face for another person to tell me how much they loved Gram when I was already missing her with every fiber of my being—when Foster came out.

I caught sight of the jacket in his hand first—my jacket—and when my gaze met his again, the dam broke.

My tears fell as he wrapped his arms around me, offering the warm comfort I'd grown so used to.

"What do you need?" he asked, his voice soft against my hair.

"A break," I said shakily. I wasn't just talking about a break from the people inside.

I wanted a break from loss. I wanted a break from worry, especially after my most recent meeting with Gram's lawyer.

I took a deep, shuddering breath. "I met with Mr. Holloway yesterday. He's the lawyer who handled Gram's will."

Foster's brow furrowed. "You didn't mention that."

I leaned back against the wall, suddenly exhausted. "Gram left everything to Mason and me—the house, her savings. But there's a problem."

"What kind of problem?"

"Mason's still a minor. He's only seventeen." I closed my eyes, remembering the conversation with the lawyer. "Gram didn't specify a guardian for him in her will. She probably thought she had more time, since his birthday is in seven months, or maybe she just assumed I would take care of him. But legally..." My voice trailed off.

"Legally, you need to be appointed his guardian," Foster finished for me.

I nodded. "Mr. Holloway says I need to petition the court. There will be hearings, home visits to make sure I'm providing a suitable environment. And I'll need to prove I can financially support him."

The enormity of it all washed over me again. I was barely keeping my own head above water with school, work, and my internship. How was I supposed to become the legal guardian of a teenager?

"I can't lose him, Foster," I said, my voice breaking. "He's all I have left. But I don't know how I'm going to manage all of this. The legal fees alone—"

"Hey," Foster interrupted, taking my face in his hands. "Listen to me. You're not alone in this. I'm here. Sam's here. The guys. We've all got your back. We'll figure it out. Isn't that what you're always telling me?"

"But—"

"No buts. We're a team. You're not doing this alone." His thumbs gently wiped away the tears on my cheeks. "When do you need to meet with the lawyer again?"

"Next week. He's going to start the paperwork, but there's so much to consider. Where we'll live, how I'll support us both, my school schedule..." I shook my head, overwhelmed. It was all so incredibly daunting. "And Mason—he's so withdrawn. I'm worried about him, but I don't know how to break through to him."

Foster pulled me close again. "One step at a time, okay? We'll make a plan. Maybe Gordy, Drew, and Liam can spend more time with Mason—they seem to be connecting with him. As for the rest, we'll figure it out. I promise."

I wanted desperately to believe him, to trust that somehow everything would work out. But the reality of my situation felt crushing—a college student with no parents, no grandparents, and now responsible for a grieving teenage brother.

"I'm scared," I admitted, the words barely audible.

Foster pressed a kiss to my forehead. "I know. But you're also incredibly strong and capable. And you don't have to be strong all the time. That's what I'm here for."

I hugged him tighter. "I love you so much."

"I love you too."

We stood there for a few more minutes, the sounds of

the reception muffled by the closed door. Eventually, I knew we had to go back inside. People would be wondering where I was, and I needed to check on Mason.

"Ready?" Foster asked, sensing my thoughts.

I took a deep breath and nodded. "As I'll ever be."

FIFTY-FOUR

Between my tutoring job, my internship, my classes, and dealing with Gram's estate, I felt like I'd barely had any time to breathe or grieve.

I'd been moving nonstop, and I felt myself breaking.

Something had to give.

The constant juggling left me exhausted, both physically and emotionally. Last night, I'd fallen asleep at the dining room table with my head on top of probate documents. I woke up at 3 a.m. with a crick in my neck and tears streaming down my face from a dream where Gram was still alive, making her famous huckleberry pie in the kitchen.

Foster had been gone at away games for a few days and I missed him immensely. He was coming home tonight and I couldn't wait to see him.

I had been living at Gram's house since she passed in order to keep things stable for Mason while we sorted everything out, but I wasn't sure how sustainable this was going to be long-term. The commute was killing me with all the other activities I had going on.

Foster showed up early, and I practically collapsed into his arms when I opened the door.

The familiar scent of his cologne—woodsy and masculine—wrapped around me as his strong arms pulled me close. I buried my face in his chest, feeling the steady rhythm of his heartbeat against my cheek. For the first time in days, I felt like I could breathe.

"Miss me?" he said, and I could hear the smile in his voice.

My arms tightened around his waist. "More than you could possibly imagine."

I hadn't realized how much tension I'd been carrying until this moment, when it melted away at his touch. Foster had become my safe harbor in the storm of grief and responsibility that had engulfed my life.

"I'm not so sure about that," he said, "because I've missed you like crazy. The last three days without you were rough."

He kissed the top of my head, his lips lingering there as his hands rubbed soothing circles on my back. When we finally pulled apart, I could see the concern in his eyes as he studied my face.

Before he could say anything, I said, "Come on in. Mason is over at a friend's."

Foster followed me into the kitchen where the table was set. "I just made spaghetti. I hope you don't mind that it's simple."

The kitchen still felt like Gram's domain. Her collection of ceramic roosters watched from the windowsill, and the recipe box she'd filled over decades sat on the counter. I'd been afraid to move anything, as if keeping her things in place might somehow preserve a piece of her.

"Not at all. You know I offered to bring dinner, so you wouldn't have to cook."

Foster pulled off his jacket and hung it on the back of a chair, rolling up the sleeves of his flannel shirt. Even in my exhausted state, I couldn't help but notice how the fabric stretched across his broad shoulders.

"I know," I said. "I just...I feel like I need to keep moving, or I'll..." My words faded.

The truth was too raw, too vulnerable to voice aloud. If I stopped moving, stopped doing, stopped being busy every second of the day, the grief might swallow me whole. It lurked at the edges, waiting for a quiet moment to strike.

He came up behind me and wrapped his arms around my waist, resting his chin on my shoulder. "Or you'll what?" he asked softly.

I spun in his arms, so I could face him. "I feel like if I don't keep moving, I'll fall apart."

My voice cracked on the last word, betraying the fragility beneath my carefully constructed facade of competence. Foster tucked a strand of hair behind my ear, his touch gentle.

"You know I'm here for you, right? You can call me anytime, day or night when I'm away for games."

"I know you are." He'd already proved his words. Hell, he was practically living here at Gram's house with me. Whenever he wasn't in classes or playing hockey, he was here for me and Mason.

"I just...I don't know what I'm doing. I finally got ahold of the lawyer, and I need to go to court to get official guardianship of my brother. They want me to show that I can offer him stable housing. Why am I even being questioned about this? I'm his family. Who else can take care of him and love him more than I can?"

The words tumbled out in a rush, my frustration building with each word. The legal system seemed determined to make an already painful situation even more difficult.

"I'm sure it's just procedure," he said.

Foster's thumb stroked my cheek, and his eyes never left mine. The steadiness of his gaze anchored me when everything else felt like it was spinning out of control.

I knew he was right, but that didn't make me feel better. I felt like I had to prove that I was worthy enough to take care of my own brother.

The weight of responsibility pressed down on me, threatening to crush me beneath its burden. I was only twenty-one—too young to have buried both parents and a grandmother, too young to be solely responsible for a grieving teenager, too young to navigate the complexities of estate planning and guardianship hearings.

"I feel like I'm failing at everything right now. I made a mistake on one of Holt's projects, which thankfully Parker caught, but it's made me feel awful ever since. I also didn't do so hot on a test for my Advanced Structural Analysis class, and I'm just... I'm—" My voice cracked, and the tears started spilling before I even realized they were there.

Foster wiped them away, his face calm, although concern was clear in his blue eyes. "You're allowed to fall apart, Abby. You're allowed to grieve and miss her. You don't need to beat yourself up for feeling sad or making mistakes."

His words were like permission—permission to be human, to be imperfect, to struggle under the weight of everything I was carrying. I leaned into him, letting my tears soak into his shirt as he held me, one hand cradling the back of my head while the other rubbed my back.

"I'm angry at her," I whispered. The guilt of that statement was eating away at my insides. "I'm so angry that she didn't tell us sooner, so we had more time to process this. So I could have asked her questions, and we could have gotten all of our ducks in a row before anything happened. She said she had it all covered, but she didn't. I'm so mad at her, and at the same time, I miss her so much."

The confession felt like a betrayal, but also a release. I hadn't allowed myself to acknowledge the anger that simmered beneath my grief.

He held me tighter. "I know you do, and I know you're overwhelmed. None of this is fair. It's okay to be mad at her."

Foster's acceptance of my complicated emotions, without judgment or platitudes, was exactly what I needed. He didn't try to fix it or make it better—he simply acknowledged the messy, contradictory feelings that came with my grief.

"*How* can I be mad at her? She's gone."

And maybe that was the root of why I was really mad. I was mad that she was gone. I was mad that once again someone I loved had been taken from me.

The pattern of loss felt cruel, as if the universe had singled me out for more than my fair share of grief. The unfairness of it all burned in my chest, a smoldering anger that had nowhere to go.

And then there was the fear that bubbled up closer and closer to the surface every day.

"What if they don't give me guardianship? What if they decide I'm too busy and have too much going on to look after Mason? What if they put him in a foster home or something? He's been through enough. I don't want him to deal with that—to have to live with strangers."

My voice rose with each question, the fear I'd been carrying finally spilling out. Mason had already withdrawn so much since Mom died; I couldn't bear the thought of him being placed with strangers, forced to adapt to yet another loss.

"Let's cross that bridge when we come to it. First, we need to show the courts that you can provide a stable enough home for him for the next seven months until he turns eighteen. But you also have to take care of yourself, Abby. Come on, why don't you take a seat? I'll finish up dinner and get it plated, okay? You just get off your feet. Take a break."

"Okay," I said reluctantly.

My body felt heavy with exhaustion as I surrendered control, allowing Foster to take over this small task. It was difficult to let go, to admit I needed help, but the relief that came with it was undeniable.

Before I could walk away, he cupped my cheek and kissed me gently. "It's gonna be okay. I've got you."

It was those three words that finally let me breathe again. The weight didn't fully disappear and it didn't magically solve any of my problems, but knowing that Foster meant every word gave me strength. Foster had my back and he'd proven he wasn't going anywhere.

Abby was working herself into the ground, and I wanted to help ease some of her stress. Every time I saw her, the dark circles under her eyes seemed to deepen. She was constantly checking her watch, rushing between classes, her internship, tutoring, and now dealing with her grandmother's estate and getting everything in order for Mason's guardianship hearing. It was too much for one person to handle.

Her biggest concern was about the guardianship case and having a stable house for Mason. The courts would be looking at her living situation, her income, and her ability to provide a suitable home environment for a teenage boy. But I knew the commute from Gram's house to campus for her classes and her internship was too long. The thirty-plus minute drive each way was eating into her already limited time, not to mention the gas money she was burning through.

When I went home the next day after spending the night with Abby, I decided to talk to Gordy about it. He was sitting at our kitchen table, reading through a sports psychology textbook and taking meticulous notes. Unlike Drew and Liam who were more likely to shoot from the hip, Gordy always thought things through carefully.

"Hey," I said, sliding into the chair across from him. "Got a minute?"

He looked up. "Sure, what's up?"

"It's about Abby. I'm worried about her."

Gordy closed his textbook. "Yeah, she's got a lot on her plate. How's she holding up?"

"Not great," I admitted. "She's trying to be strong for Mason, but she's exhausted all the time. And this commute situation isn't helping."

"Why can't she live at her apartment?" he asked, tapping his pen against the table.

"Because it's only a two-bedroom apartment and Sam has the other room."

I'd had an idea bouncing around in my head for the past couple of days, but I was worried Abby might think it was moving too fast, too soon. We'd only been officially dating for a few months, though it felt like so much longer given everything we'd been through together, and the fact we'd known each other for nearly a year as our online personas.

But Gordy was usually able to look at things objectively, so I ran it by him. "What if Sam and I swapped places? She could take my room here with the en suite bath so she wouldn't have to share with you guys. You all know each other and get along."

Gordy leaned back in his chair, considering the idea. His expression remained neutral, which I took as a good sign. If he thought it was a terrible plan, he would have said so immediately.

"Have you talked to Sam about this?" he asked after a moment.

"Not yet. I didn't want to bring it up if you guys weren't comfortable with it. But if you are, then I could move in with Abby into her apartment. Abby and I can share a room and Mason can have Sam's room." I leaned forward, warming to the idea as I laid it out. "That way, no one has to break their lease, and Abby's commute goes from over thirty minutes to five."

"You've really thought this through," Gordy said, a small smile playing at the corner of his mouth.

I grabbed the back of my neck, suddenly feeling self-conscious. "Is it crazy? I can't stand to see Abby working herself to the bone and stressing so much. If she's closer to campus, we can all pitch in to help."

Gordy studied me for a long moment, his gray eyes thoughtful. "You're in love with her, aren't you?"

I gave him a smile. "As if I stood a chance."

He chuckled. "I'm cool with it," he said finally. "You'd need to check with Drew and Liam, but I don't see why they'd have a problem with it. And I agree about her being closer so we can all help. Abby and Mason are part of our family now."

That last part hit me right in the chest. After everything that had happened with my own family, hearing Gordy say that Abby was part of our chosen family meant more than he probably realized.

"Thanks, man. I appreciate it."

After talking to Drew and Liam and getting their approval for the potential plan—Drew had immediately said, "Hell, yeah, Sam's cool," while Liam had shrugged and said, "As long as she doesn't mind our mess"—I texted Sam.

ME

Hey, can you meet me at The Grindhouse this afternoon? I was hoping we could talk about an idea I have to make things easier for Abby.

SAM

100% What time?

ME

My afternoon's wide open. What time works for you?

SAM

Meet me at 3.

ME

See you then.

I arrived at the coffee shop fifteen minutes early, ordering a black coffee with two sugars and grabbing a table in the corner where we could talk privately. My knee bounced nervously under the table as I waited. I knew my plan made logical sense, but I was still asking a lot of everyone involved.

At exactly three o'clock, Sam walked through the door and scanned the room. When she spotted me, she waved and headed to the counter to order before joining me.

"Hey, hockey boy," Sam said as she sat at my table, setting down her drink.

"Hey, thanks for meeting me."

"Of course. I hate seeing how stressed Abby is. It's not healthy." She stirred her drink, concern evident in her expression. "So what's this idea you had?"

I leaned forward, resting my elbows on the table. "It's kind of wild."

She mirrored my pose, her brow arched. "I'm all ears."

I took a deep breath and laid out my plan, watching her face carefully for any signs of reluctance or discomfort. To my relief, she nodded thoughtfully as I explained.

"It definitely makes the most sense without her having to find a new apartment, and yeah, I don't mind living with the guys for the rest of the year," she said when I finished. "I can find my own place once the lease is up, and they can have another hockey player take that room again, so it firmly remains the hockey house."

"That would be phenomenal, and like I said, you'd have your own bathroom and—"

She cut me off with a wave of her hand. "I'm not worried about that. Abby's my best friend, and she's always looking out for other people. She deserves a break, and I'm glad she has you looking out for her."

Her approval meant more to me than I expected. Sam had been there for Abby during her darkest days over the past couple of years, and I knew how protective she was of her friend.

"You really care about her, don't you?" Sam asked, studying me with a thoughtful expression.

"I love her," I said simply. There was no point in dancing around it.

A slow smile spread across Sam's face. "Good. Because if you hurt her, I'll have to destroy you, and I'd rather not. I'm starting to like you, Kane."

I laughed, though I didn't doubt for a second that she meant it. "Noted."

"So when are you going to tell Abby about this master plan of yours?" she asked, sipping her latte.

"Tonight, if possible. I want to give her some good news for once."

"Are the guys free tonight?"

"I think so. Why?"

She set her coffee down. "Because if I know Abby at all, she's going to think she's putting people out with this move. It might be better to run the idea by her with us all there to reassure her that it's not an imposition."

I wasn't so sure about that. "What if she feels ganged up on?"

Sam was already shaking her head. "Trust me. Abby can say no—and totally will if she doesn't want to do this. She doesn't have issues setting boundaries. But I definitely think this might go over better and she might be more receptive to considering the idea if she talks to everyone who will be impacted by it."

She made a good point. "I'll text the guys now and call a house meeting. Think you can get Abby there before her tutoring session?"

She smiled. "Yep. She's at our apartment now between classes and tutoring, so I'll head home and pick her up. We'll meet you at the hockey house in half an hour."

"That would be great," I said, feeling a surge of nervous anticipation. "Thanks, Sam."

"Don't thank me yet." She stood up, gathering her things. "She might think you're crazy for suggesting this."

I grimaced. "That's what I'm afraid of."

"For what it's worth," Sam said, pausing before she left, "I think it's a good plan. And I think she'll see that too, once she gets past the initial shock."

Now I just needed to get Abby on board with the plan. As I headed back to the hockey house, I rehearsed what I wanted to say, trying to find the right words to convince her that this wasn't just a rash decision but a practical solution to her current problems. But more than that, I wanted to live with her—to wake up and go to sleep with her and be there when she needed me. I only hoped she wouldn't think I was pushing too hard or moving too fast.

The truth was, I'd move mountains for Abby if I could. Moving apartments seemed like the least I could do.

FIFTY-SIX

Sam had been a little stingy with the details about why we had to go over to the hockey house, but I needed a mental break, so I went along with it.

"You'll see when we get there," was all Sam would say when I pressed her for the third time as we walked up the path to the guys' front door. The late fall air had a bite to it, and I pulled my coat tighter around me.

When we showed up, all the guys were already in the living room. They were arranged in a semi-circle—Drew and Liam sprawled on one couch, Gordy perched on the arm of the other, and Foster standing by the TV with his hands in his pockets looking uncharacteristically nervous.

I slowed my steps and glanced around the room, taking in their serious expressions. "Is this an intervention?" I asked, only half-joking. The setup certainly looked like those scenes from TV shows where friends confront someone about their problems.

Sam squeezed my arm reassuringly before she made her way to the couch and sat next to Gordy.

Foster closed the distance between us, his blue eyes soft

with concern as he reached for my hand. "Not quite, but I wanted to run something by you that might make things a little easier on you."

I was all for any suggestions he had because I felt like I was drowning and it had only been three weeks since Gram died.

Foster guided me to sit on the only other seat left in the room.

"We've all been talking," Foster began, gesturing to include everyone in the room, "and we've come up with a plan that might help with your commute situation and give you more support with Mason."

I glanced around at the faces watching me—Sam's encouraging smile, Gordy's steady gaze, Drew's uncharacteristically serious expression, and Liam's casual nod. Whatever this was, they all seemed to be in on it.

Foster laid out the plan methodically, the way he approached everything—thoughtful and thorough. Sam would move into his room at the hockey house. Foster would move into my apartment and share my room. Mason would take Sam's room. The arrangement would keep all our current leases intact while cutting my commute time dramatically.

As he spoke, I found myself mentally calculating the time savings. Thirty minutes each way, sometimes more with traffic. An hour of my life reclaimed each day. Time I could use for studying, for Mason, for sleep—the thought alone made my exhausted body ache with longing.

When Foster finished explaining, he watched me carefully, waiting for my reaction. The others remained quiet, giving me space to process.

"Yeah, this shortens my commute and makes things more manageable for me," I acknowledged slowly, turning the idea over in my mind. "But how will Mason get to school? The bus doesn't come out this far and he doesn't have his license." It was the first practical problem that came to mind, though I was already mentally listing others—Mason's adjustment, the logistics of moving, whether this was too much change too soon.

"I'll take him," Sam said immediately. "I have plenty of time before my first class in the morning."

"And we can rotate picking him up if there's ever days you can't," Drew said, pointing to Liam, Gordy, and Foster.

"We're happy to help pitch in," Liam added. "Mason's a good kid. We want to see him thrive, but he can't do that if he knows you're pulling yourself apart at the seams to take care of him."

Foster watched me carefully for a reaction, but I was so shocked and overwhelmed by what they were offering that I was worried my face was frozen in a stupefied expression. These guys—who'd barely known me a few months ago—were offering to rearrange their lives to help me and my brother get through this impossible time.

I knew I couldn't do this myself—not if I was going to convince the courts that Mason had a solid support system—but the generosity of it all made my chest tight with emotion.

"I appreciate you all so much," I said finally, my voice slightly hoarse, "but I don't want to put anyone else out." The last thing I wanted was to be a burden on these people who had already done so much for me.

"You're not putting us out," Gordy said firmly, leaning forward. His usually quiet demeanor made his words carry more weight. "You're part of our tribe now. We're here to help."

The word "tribe" hit me hard. Since Mom died, it had

just been Mason, Gram, and me against the world—although I couldn't deny how Sam had become an integral part of my support system during that time, which made me all the more grateful that she was here now. The idea that our family had somehow expanded to include these people was beyond comforting.

I glanced at Sam, searching her expression for any hint of reluctance. "And you're sure you're okay with moving in here and living with the guys?" Sam loved our apartment, and I couldn't imagine she'd be thrilled about living with three hockey players, no matter how cool they were.

"One hundred percent positive," she said, her smile genuine.

"You guys are all on board with this?" I asked, looking around at Gordy, Liam, and Drew, still not quite believing they'd all agreed to this disruption.

"We'll tell you as many times as we need to," Liam said, his usual playboy persona set aside for a moment of sincerity. "But this is your family now," he said, gesturing around the room. "And we've got your back."

Tears of gratitude burned behind my eyes, but I'd cried enough over the last few weeks, and I really didn't want to break down now. I blinked rapidly, trying to keep the moisture at bay.

My gaze met Foster's. His eyes were full of hope and love.

"And you want to live with me?" I asked softly, almost afraid of the answer. We'd only been dating a few months, and moving in together was a big step under normal circumstances, let alone with my teenage brother in tow.

His smile was sweet and sure. "Hell, yeah," he said without a moment's hesitation.

His response brought a genuine smile to my face—the

first one I could remember in days. The answer seemed obvious when he put it that way.

"Okay," I said, feeling like I could breathe a little easier already. "But first I have to talk to Mason and make sure he's okay with this. If he's on board, then we'll do it. But if he wants to stay at Gram's house, then that's where we'll stay."

Everyone reluctantly nodded, understanding that Mason's needs had to come first. Foster squeezed my hand, silently communicating his support either way.

As the conversation shifted to logistics and timing, I felt a weight lift from my shoulders. I was grateful to be surrounded by people who cared enough to create solutions I couldn't have managed on my own.

I was nervous about talking to my brother about the plan because if he said no, it was dead in the water, and a part of me really wanted this plan to work. I was stretched too thin, and I knew if we stayed at Gram's house, I was going to have to give up my internship. The commute was just too long to maintain with everything else on my plate.

I'd made Mason's favorite meal—lasagna with extra garlic bread—hoping the comfort food might make him more receptive to change. As he shoveled pasta into his mouth with the boundless hunger of a teenage boy, I gathered my courage.

"So what do you want to talk about?" Mason asked between bites, a smear of tomato sauce at the corner of his mouth. He looked so young in that moment, despite being taller than me now.

"Well, I wanted to talk to you about a potential change in our living situation." I tried to keep my voice casual, not wanting to influence his response one way or another.

His chewing slowed, and he looked at me with cautious eyes. "'Kay." The single syllable was guarded, and I could see him bracing himself for bad news. We'd had too many difficult conversations over the past few years.

"How would you feel about moving back to my apartment with me and Foster?" I asked, watching his face carefully for any reaction.

He frowned slightly, his fork pausing midway to his mouth. "Where would Sam go?"

Of course that would be his first concern. Despite his typical teenage moodiness, Mason had always been thoughtful about others.

"Sam would move in with the hockey guys and take Foster's room there," I explained. "Before you ask, Sam has already offered to drive you to school and the rest of us will figure out a schedule for pickup." Hurriedly, I added, "It's just an option, or we can stay here if you don't want to move. I understand we've been through enough upheaval for a lifetime."

He took another bite, clearly thinking it over, his expression unreadable. The silence stretched between us as he chewed, and I resisted the urge to fill it with more explanations or persuasions. Finally, he set his fork down with deliberate care.

"I think it's a good idea." His voice was quiet but certain.

I was momentarily stunned, having prepared myself for resistance. "You do?" I'd really expected him to say he was opposed to the idea, to insist on staying at Gram's.

"Yeah." He looked down at the table, tracing a pattern

in the wood grain with his fingertip. "It feels weird to be here without her, and it was never really our house, ya know."

I nodded, a lump forming in my throat. I knew exactly what he meant. Gram's home had felt comforting, but only when she had been here. Since she died, that feeling of sanctuary had gone with her. Now it just felt like a structure that carried memories without the heart—like a museum of our past rather than a real *home*.

"So you're on board with moving into my apartment," I clarified, still slightly disbelieving.

He nodded and picked up his fork again, some of his usual teenage nonchalance returning. "It's better than you working yourself into the ground. You've got dark circles under your eyes," he said before taking another bite.

I let out a surprised laugh, picking up my own fork now that my anxiety over this conversation had dissipated. "Yeah, I suppose I do." I took a bite and then confirmed, "You're sure about this?"

I didn't want him to feel pressured or like he didn't have a say. Too many decisions had been made for us over the years—by death, circumstance, or necessity. I wanted him to know his voice mattered in this.

He rolled his eyes in a way only a teenager can. "Do I need to pay for a skywriter for you to believe me?" He reached out and covered my hand with his, staring straight into my eyes and looking so grown up all of a sudden that my heart hurt. "I'm sure. I think a fresh place would be good for me. And getting out of this house would be good for both of us."

His hand was bigger than mine now, his fingers calloused from football. When had that happened? When had my little brother started growing into a man while I wasn't looking?

"Alright, then we'll move over winter break," I said, squeezing his hand before he could pull it away and be embarrassed by the show of affection.

As we finished our dinner, I felt something I hadn't experienced in weeks—hope. Not just the desperate hope of survival, but actual optimism about what our future might hold.

For the first time since Gram died, I could see a path forward that didn't end in exhaustion and defeat. And that, more than anything, felt like the first real breath of spring after a long, brutal winter.

"Dude, how many pairs of shoes do you own?" Drew complained as he carried a box labeled *Footwear* up the stairs to Abby's apartment. "You're worse than my sister."

I laughed, following behind him with my hockey gear. "Says the guy who has an entire shelf dedicated to hair products."

"It takes work to look this good," he shot back, pausing at the landing to readjust his grip on the box. "Some of us weren't blessed with naturally perfect hair."

Moving had turned into a full-scale operation with all the guys pitching in. Mason's stuff filled Abby's living room while we moved the last of Sam's stuff out. Liam and Gordy were handling Sam's move into the hockey house while Drew helped me with my boxes.

When we reached Abby's apartment, the door was propped open. I could hear Sam and Abby inside, laughing about something as they sorted through kitchen items.

"Where do you want this?" Drew asked as we entered.

Abby looked up from where she was wrapping mugs in

newspaper. "Bedroom, please. I cleared out half the closet for you."

"Only half?" Drew teased. "Have you seen how many shoes this guy has?"

"I do not have that many shoes," I protested, setting my hockey gear down by the door.

Drew snorted. "Says the guy with three different pairs of running shoes."

"They're for different surfaces!" I defended myself, though I couldn't help but smile. The lighthearted bickering felt good after weeks of stress and grief.

Abby wiped her hands on her jeans and came over to press a quick kiss to my lips. "How's it going at the house?" she asked.

"Gordy's already planning dinner for tonight. He says we all need a proper meal after moving all day."

"That sounds amazing," she said, her eyes lighting up. Gordy was easily the best cook among us, and his meals were legendary. "What time should we head over?"

"He said seven, but knowing him, food won't be ready until eight." I wrapped an arm around her waist, pulling her close for a moment. "How are you holding up?"

She leaned into me, her body relaxing against mine. "Good, actually. Really good. This feels like a step in the right direction."

I nodded, understanding exactly what she meant. After my confrontation with my father, I'd felt the same way—like I was finally taking steps toward the life I wanted instead of the one that had been preordained for me.

Abby wasn't a victim of her circumstances. She was making the best life she could for herself and her brother, and I felt lucky to be a part of their family.

Drew cleared his throat dramatically. "Not to interrupt

this adorable moment, but we still have boxes in the truck that won't unload themselves."

I reluctantly let go of Abby. "Alright, I'm coming."

The rest of the afternoon passed in a blur of boxes, furniture rearrangement, and good-natured teasing. By six thirty, we had most of my essential stuff moved in, and Sam's room at the hockey house was set up. Mason's new room—formerly Sam's—was ready for him, complete with the hockey posters Liam had insisted on hanging to try to convince him that hockey was the superior sport.

When we arrived at the hockey house for dinner, the smell of Gordy's cooking hit us the moment we walked through the door. Something with garlic and herbs that made my stomach growl in anticipation.

"We're here!" I called out, ushering Abby and Mason inside.

Gordy poked his head out from the kitchen, a dishcloth thrown over his shoulder. "Perfect timing. Drew, set the table!"

Drew groaned from his spot on the couch where he had just sat down to play a video game. "Why is it always me?"

"Because you're the only one who never cooks," Liam said, coming down the stairs with Sam following behind him.

"I thought we agreed that me cooking meant risking burning the house down and it should be avoided at all costs," Drew said, pausing the game and getting up anyway.

Mason hovered uncertainly in the entryway, and I noticed how he seemed to shrink into himself a bit, his shoulders hunching forward as if trying to take up less space. I'd seen the same posture from him at the hospital and the funeral—like he was trying to make himself invisible.

"Hey, Mase," I said casually, "want to help me grab some sodas from the garage?"

He shrugged, which I'd come to recognize as teenage for yes, and followed me through the kitchen where Gordy was stirring something that smelled incredible.

"What is that?" I asked, pausing to peek into the pot.

Gordy swatted my hand away. "Chicken cacciatore. And if you touch anything, I will end you."

Mason's eyes widened slightly at Gordy's threat, but I just laughed. "He's all bark, no bite," I assured Mason as we continued to the garage. "Except on the ice. Then he's terrifying."

In the garage, I opened the extra refrigerator where we kept drinks and snacks. "What do you want? We've got soda, beer—which you can't have—and water."

Mason peered into the fridge. "Coke?"

"Good choice." I grabbed cans of Coke for all of us. "Here, take these."

As I handed him a few of the sodas, I decided to take a chance on some conversation. "So, how are you feeling about the move?"

He shrugged again, but then surprised me by adding, "It's cool. Better than staying at Gram's house."

I was relieved he felt that way. Everything had changed so quickly, and I didn't want him to feel uncomfortable with the new arrangements. We made our way back to the kitchen just as Gordy was announcing that dinner was ready.

The dining table in the hockey house was barely big

enough for all of us, but we crowded around it anyway, passing dishes and fighting over the bread. Gordy had outdone himself with chicken cacciatore, roasted vegetables, and garlic bread that was perfectly crispy on the outside and soft in the middle.

"Dude," Drew said through a mouthful of food, "you need to open a restaurant or something."

Gordy rolled his eyes, but I could tell he was pleased. "It's just chicken and tomatoes."

"It's amazing," Abby said sincerely. "Thank you for cooking for all of us."

Sam raised her beer. "To our new living arrangements. May we all survive without killing each other."

"Hear, hear!" Liam cheered, clinking his bottle against hers.

"So Mason," Drew said, turning to Abby's brother, "You've been holding out on us. We saw all your football stuff and Abby said you've been playing for years. What position?"

He looked up, a sheepish expression on his face. "I'm a wide receiver."

"That's awesome," Drew said, leaning forward with interest. "What's your team like?"

Something in Mason seemed to light up at the question. "We're pretty good. Made it to state semifinals last year. We got close again this year, but lost one game too many to make it to the playoffs."

"No shit?" Liam said, impressed. "That's legit."

"Language," Abby murmured automatically, but she was smiling as she watched her brother engage with the guys.

"You must be fast," I commented.

Mason nodded, his posture straightening a bit. "Yeah,

I'm not the biggest guy on the team, but I can outrun most of the defensive backs."

"Speed beats size any day," Drew said with authority. "That's why Kane here is so good on the ice. He's not the biggest forward, but he's fast as fuck."

"Language," Abby said again, but she was laughing now.

"Sorry, Mom," Drew teased, winking at her.

The conversation flowed easily after that, with Mason gradually becoming more animated as the guys asked him questions about football and whether he thought the LA Wolves—his favorite team—had any chance this year.

At one point, I glanced over at Abby and found her watching her brother with a tender expression. When she caught me looking, she mouthed "thank you," her eyes bright with emotion. I reached under the table to squeeze her hand, feeling a surge of protectiveness and love for both her and Mason.

By the time Gordy brought out dessert—homemade apple crisp with vanilla ice cream—Mason was in the middle of describing a game-winning touchdown he'd caught last season, using salt and pepper shakers to demonstrate the play.

"...and then I got the game ball from coach for getting the touchdown," he finished, grinning widely. "It was pretty awesome."

"I bet," Liam said, looking genuinely impressed. "You got the play on video?"

Mason nodded eagerly. "Yeah, I can show you guys sometime."

"Fuck, yeah," Drew said, high-fiving him. "We need to come to one of your games next season."

"Language," Abby said for the third time, but she was

beaming now, watching her brother come alive under the positive attention.

The hockey guys had become my family over the past few years, and now that family was expanding to include Abby and Mason. Here we were, crowded around a table that was too small, eating food that was insanely good, laughing and talking like we'd all known each other forever. Mason was actually smiling—a real smile that reached his eyes—and Abby looked more relaxed than I'd seen her in weeks.

"What are you thinking about?" Abby asked quietly, leaning into my side as the others argued about which Marvel movie was the best.

I wrapped my arm around her shoulders and pressed a kiss to her temple. "Just that this feels like how family should be."

She nodded, her eyes moving from her brother—who was now animatedly defending *Thor: Ragnarok* against Drew's insistence that *Winter Soldier* was superior—to the rest of our mismatched family.

"Yeah," she said softly. "It really does."

FIFTY-EIGHT

Abby

The fluorescent lights of the courthouse hallway buzzed overhead, making my already frayed nerves feel even more on edge. I smoothed the front of my navy blue blazer for the tenth time, checking that my blouse was still neatly tucked into my skirt.

"You look fine," Foster whispered, his hand finding mine and giving it a reassuring squeeze. "Better than fine. You look like a sexy librarian."

I let out a shaky breath. "I need to look like someone who has her life together and can raise a teenager."

Foster's thumb traced small circles on the back of my hand, but it didn't ease my anxiety.

My lawyer, Patricia Winters, approached us with a file folder tucked under her arm. She was a sturdy woman in her fifties with salt-and-pepper hair cut in a practical bob. Gram's estate lawyer had recommended her, and she'd been giving me guidance on what I needed to show the judge to get guardianship of my brother.

"We're up in fifteen minutes," Patricia said. "Judge Harrison is fair but thorough. She'll want to hear about your living arrangements, financial situation, and education plans for Mason." She glanced at Foster. "It's good you're here. Shows family support structure. Did you bring the letters of support from your professors, coach, and past bosses like I requested?"

Foster held up the folder that had letters of support for both of us. Patricia had explained that the court would be most concerned about providing stability and financial support for Mason, so the letters of support were useful in speaking for our character.

I nodded, swallowing hard. "Will Mason need to speak?"

"The judge will likely ask him a few questions, but nothing too intense. His statement about wanting to live with you is already in the file."

My brother sat across the hallway, looking uncomfortable in the button-up shirt and khakis I'd convinced him to wear. He kept pulling at his collar and checking his phone. When he caught me watching, he gave me a small nod that somehow contained both reassurance and teenage awkwardness.

The doors to the courthouse opened and my heart filled with warmth as Sam, Gordy, Drew, Liam, and Coach Maxwell all walked in.

"What are you guys doing here?"

"Moral support," Sam said. "No matter what happens today, we're here for you."

I was beyond touched, but didn't have much time to appreciate their presence.

"Case number 47329, Walker guardianship petition," the bailiff called from the courtroom doorway.

My stomach dropped as Patricia gathered her things.

"That's us. Remember, honest and straightforward. Judge Harrison appreciates direct answers."

Foster stood with me, giving me a quick kiss on the forehead. "I'll be right beside you."

As we filed into the courtroom, I tried to channel the confidence I felt in the tutoring center or when solving a complex engineering problem. This was just another challenge to overcome, another problem with a logical solution. Except it didn't feel logical—it felt like my entire world and Mason's future hung in the balance.

I didn't want to be separated from my brother.

Judge Harrison was a Black woman with elegant silver-streaked dark hair pulled back into a bun. She wore reading glasses perched on the end of her nose as she reviewed the file in front of her. When she looked up, her expression was neutral but not unkind.

"Ms. Walker, I see you're petitioning for guardianship of your brother, Mason Walker, following the death of your grandmother, Daniella Thomas, who was his legal guardian after your mother, Leila Walker's passing two years ago."

"Yes, Your Honor," I replied, my voice steadier than I expected.

"And you're twenty-one years old, currently enrolled at Clark Fork University?"

"Yes. I'm in my junior year, studying civil engineering."

The judge nodded, making a note. "And you're employed?"

"I work at the university tutoring center and have a paid internship at Holt & Associates Engineering firm in Missoula. My tuition is fully covered under my scholarship."

Patricia had coached me to be thorough but concise.

The judge didn't need my life story, just the relevant facts to make her decision.

"And your living situation? I see from the file you recently moved Mason from your grandmother's residence."

"Yes, Your Honor. Mason and I now live in my apartment closer to campus. I share the apartment with my boyfriend, Foster Kane, and Mason has his own bedroom. Mason also has reliable transportation to and from school, so he doesn't have to change schools."

I felt Foster shift in his seat beside me. We'd discussed whether mentioning our living arrangement might hurt my case, but Patricia had advised honesty. Hiding details would only damage my credibility if they came to light later.

"And Mr. Kane is present today?" Judge Harrison looked next to me.

"Yes, Your Honor," Foster replied.

"You're a student as well?"

"Yes, Your Honor. I'm a junior at CFU, studying business, and I'm captain of the hockey team."

The judge nodded and returned her attention to me. "Ms. Walker, raising a teenager is challenging under the best circumstances. You're young, in school full-time, working two jobs. How do you plan to provide adequate supervision and support for your brother?"

This was the question I'd prepared for most carefully. I took a deep breath.

"I've arranged my class and work schedule to be home when Mason returns from school most days. On days when I can't be there, Foster or one of our friends is available. Mason's football coach has also been incredibly supportive, and the team provides structure and mentorship for him. He's been invited to off-season workouts with some of his teammates if one of us needs to pick him up later. We also have a friend group that is more like family, and they've all offered to help support Mason."

I glanced at Mason, who was watching me intently.

"As for finances, I get a small monthly stipend from a trust from the sale of our childhood home after my mom passed away. My grandmother left us her house, which I'm planning to sell. The proceeds will go into a trust for Mason's college education and give us a financial cushion. I receive a full scholarship at CFU, and my internship at Holt & Associates has offered me a position with increased hours this summer."

Judge Harrison made more notes, then looked directly at Mason.

"Young man, you've had a lot of loss in your life based on the information in your file. Your father when you were very young, your mother two years ago, and now your grandmother. How are you coping with all of this?"

Mason sat up straighter, his voice cracking slightly as he spoke. "It's been hard, but Abby's always been there for me. Even when she was away at college, she called every day after Mom died."

My throat tightened at his words. I hadn't known those calls and texts had meant so much to him.

"And you want to live with your sister? You understand she'll be responsible for making decisions about your education, health care, and daily life until you turn eighteen?"

Mason nodded. "Yes, ma'am. Abby's been taking care of me since Mom died, really. Gram was there, but she was getting older. Abby made sure I did my homework and went to football practice even when I didn't want to."

A small smile crossed the judge's face. "And do you feel safe and supported in your new living arrangement?"

"Yeah," Mason said, then quickly corrected himself. "I

mean, yes, Your Honor. Foster and his friends help me with school stuff. It's like...having big brothers or something."

I blinked back tears, not wanting to get emotional in the courtroom, but Mason's words hit me hard. I was glad he felt supported because that had been my biggest fear with all this change.

Judge Harrison turned back to me. "Ms. Walker, I see from the home study report that your living conditions are suitable, and the social worker noted the positive relationship between you and your brother. However, I remain concerned about your ability to balance your own education and career development with the responsibility of raising a teenager—especially in light of the letter I received from Dennis Kane."

My heart sank. This was worse than I'd feared. I'd been worried that despite all our preparations, I still wouldn't be seen as capable enough.

I hadn't even considered that Foster's dad might find out about all this and try to sabotage us.

Judge Harrison continued, her tone measured. "Mr. Kane submitted statements questioning your financial independence and raised concerns about the legality of your current housing arrangement. According to the documents reviewed, the apartment lease is held jointly by you and Samantha Lowe, who no longer resides at the property. Instead, Foster Kane—who is not listed on the lease—has taken her place without formal approval from your landlord. He also suggested that your landlord doesn't know about Mason living at the residence as well."

I felt the heat rise in my face. It was such a small detail, but one I'd missed.

"While not a disqualifying factor on its own," Judge Harrison said, flipping the page, "housing stability is a key consideration in guardianship cases. An unapproved tenant —particularly one with a direct personal relationship to the petitioner—raises legal and ethical concerns the court is obligated to evaluate."

Of course. He was turning Foster's presence into a liability. He'd left us alone since Foster confronted him, and in all the craziness and grief, I'd let my guard down where Dennis Kane was concerned. Foster was tense beside me, and I had no doubt he was furious that his father was trying to set us up as irresponsible when that couldn't be further from the truth.

But Dennis Kane once again underestimated me.

I straightened. "Your Honor, I understand why that detail raises concerns. The lease is in my name and Samantha's, and when she moved out, Foster took her place. The landlord was informed verbally about the change and is fully aware that Mason is living there as well. I can get you her contact information so you can confirm this yourself if you need it. We've never missed a rent payment and she can confirm that as well. Our home may not be traditional, but it's safe. I would never put my brother in an unstable position. The very reason I'm fighting so hard for custody is because the only one who can provide him true stability is me—his family."

Judge Harrison regarded me silently for a beat before continuing. "I appreciate your transparency, Ms. Walker. The court is less concerned with perfection and more with honesty and intentions—and it's clear yours have always been centered around your brother's well-being."

"Your Honor," I said, quietly but clearly, "Mason and I are a family. We've already lost our parents and our grandmother. Staying together isn't just what we want—it's what we need."

I took a breath, grounding myself in every sleepless night, every tutoring shift, every minute I'd fought to hold our lives together. "When our mom died, I thought about taking time off from school to help Mason, but my grandmother and friends convinced me I could do both—be there for him and stay on track with my degree. I've maintained a 3.9 GPA while working two jobs. I show up for him every single day. It hasn't been easy, but we're doing it. Please don't separate us. I know I'm young, but no one will care about his safety and well-being more than me."

The courtroom was silent when I finished. I could feel Foster beside me, calm and steady, the way he always was when I needed him most.

Judge Harrison removed her glasses and studied me. "Ms. Walker, your dedication to your brother is evident. I've reviewed your academic records and employment history as well as the reference letters from your employers, and they reflect both maturity and responsibility. The number of people here today demonstrate that you have a meaningful support system."

She replaced her glasses, flipping back through the file. "The court's primary concern is Mason's welfare and long-term stability. Based on the evidence presented— including the home study, character references, and Mason's own statement—I find that granting you guardianship is in his best interest, contingent on a letter from your landlord stating that the tenant swap is approved."

My breath caught in my throat.

"Thank you, Your Honor," Patricia said, already gathering her papers.

"Court is adjourned," Judge Harrison announced, tapping her gavel lightly.

I stood frozen, unable to fully process what had just happened until Patricia touched my arm.

"Congratulations, Abby. You did it."

Foster's arms wrapped around me, and he pressed a kiss to my hair.

Mason approached, looking relieved and slightly embarrassed by the display of emotion. "So it's official? You're, like, my legal guardian now?"

I pulled away from Foster to hug my brother, who stiffly returned the embrace before stepping back. "Yes, it's official. I'm legally responsible for making sure you don't flunk math and eat something other than pizza occasionally."

A small smile tugged at his lips. "Cool."

"There will be some paperwork to finalize, and we need to get that letter from your landlord ASAP," Patricia explained as we gathered our things. "But essentially, yes, Abby is now your legal guardian, Mason."

As we left the courthouse, stepping into the spring sunshine, I felt a weight lift from my shoulders. There was still so much to figure out—selling Gram's house, managing our finances, balancing all my responsibilities—but for the first time since Gram was admitted to the hospital, I felt like we were on solid ground.

Foster took my hand as we walked to his car. "How does it feel?"

I looked at Mason walking ahead of us, already loosening his tie and texting someone on his phone. "Terrifying. Overwhelming." I squeezed Foster's hand. "But also so freaking good to have that stress behind me."

"You know what this calls for?" Foster said, a mischievous glint in his eye. "Celebration dinner at the hockey house. Gordy's been planning a menu since yesterday just in case."

I laughed, and it came easier than it had since before Gram died.

"Never doubted you for a second, Walker. But don't worry—we had contingencies in place if you lost," Drew said, coming up behind us.

"What contingencies?" Foster asked, already sounding worried.

"Kidnapping, obviously," Liam said with a casual shrug.

"Thank God it didn't come to that," Gordy added with a shake of his head like he couldn't believe he cared about these guys.

All of it made me feel so full of love, I thought I might burst. They were insane, but wasn't that how family was supposed to be?

Tears pricked my eyes again, but this time they were happy tears. When Mom died, I thought our family was broken beyond repair. I never imagined we'd find a new kind of family—one we chose and who chose us back.

I'd learned something valuable over the last few weeks. Home wasn't a place. It was a group of people—our found family.

Two days later, there was an unexpected knock on the door.

Mason and Abby were both sitting at the kitchen table working on homework while I was sitting on the couch reviewing notes for an exam I had coming up.

"I'll get it," I said quickly, already moving toward the door before Abby could get up.

I looked through the peephole and my stomach dropped. My father stood in the hallway, his expensive suit wrinkled and his usually perfect hair disheveled. Even through the distorted lens, I could see the fury radiating from him.

My hand hesitated on the deadbolt. I'd wondered after the stunt he'd pulled with the guardianship hearing if he'd try something else, but I hadn't expected him to be so brazen to show up at our front door.

"Who is it?" Abby asked.

"It's my dad."

I unlocked the door, opening it just wide enough to see his face clearly. His eyes were bloodshot, and I caught the faint smell of whiskey on his breath.

"Foster." His voice was tight with barely controlled rage. "We need to talk."

"There's nothing left to say," I replied, my voice steady despite the adrenaline coursing through my veins. I'd never seen my dad in this state, but he'd lost any chance of gaining sympathy from me when he tried to pay my girlfriend to break up with me. His actions since then had only solidified my resolve. "I made my position clear."

"You think you're so smart," he sneered, pushing against the door. "Think you can just walk away from everything I've built for you?"

"I can, and I did." I started to close the door, but he slammed his palm against it, pushing it all the way open.

His glazed eyes landed on Abby and his face contorted into an ugly snarl. "I'm not done trying to destroy you."

I stepped in front of him, blocking his view of her. "You need to leave," I said, my voice deadly calm. "Now."

Instead, he did something that shouldn't have surprised me, but did all the same. He shoved me. I was so taken aback, I stumbled before catching myself as rage lit like a fire through my veins.

"Get out of our home," Abby said, now standing in front of her brother, her voice sharp with authority despite the fear I could see in her posture.

My father's cold gaze swung to her. "You did this. You ruined everything, you little bitch—"

The words weren't even fully out of his mouth before he lunged toward her, his hands reaching out to grab her.

I moved faster than I'd ever moved in my life, intercepting him before he could touch her and shoving him back against the nearest wall. My forearm pressed against his windpipe, pinning him in place. His eyes went wide with shock and something that might have been fear.

Good.

He should be afraid.

There was *nothing* I wouldn't do to protect Abby and Mason—my family.

"Don't you ever try to lay a fucking hand on her again," I growled, my face inches from his. Every word dripped with the promise of violence if he dared to test me. "Better yet, don't come near us, or I'll go to every client you have and tell them all your dirty secrets."

He tried to scoff, but it came out as more of a wheeze with my arm pressed against his throat. "I have no secrets."

I leaned in closer, close enough that he couldn't mistake the deadly serious look in my eyes. "You sure about that? How do you think they'd feel if they found out about your propensity to cut corners when costs get too high and then pay off your favorite inspector to look the other way?"

The effect was immediate and dramatic. He went completely still, like a statue, his face draining of color before flushing a deep red with anger and panic. His eyes darted around frantically, as if looking for an escape route.

"Bet you didn't think I knew about that, huh?" I continued, my voice low and menacing. "I know a lot more than that, and if you come anywhere near us again, I'll end that business you love so much."

I'd always had questions about some of the things my dad had done with the business, but I hadn't cared enough to dive deeper. But I'd learned some very valuable information when I'd requested a character reference for the guardianship hearing from one of my construction employers. My dad's business wasn't on the up-and-up like he'd always made it out to be. That was the reason certain construction companies had stopped working with The

Kane Group, something my dad had said was his choice, not the other way around.

It was information I'd been holding on to since I'd found out, not sure what to do with it.

But him showing up on our doorstep and threatening us had made everything clearer.

If holding this information over his head got him off our backs, then so be it.

I was done letting him think he could mess with us.

"You don't know what you're talking about," he managed to rasp, but the panic in his voice betrayed him.

"Don't I?" I pressed harder against his throat, not enough to actually hurt him, but enough to make my point crystal clear. "Jenkins Construction ring a bell? The Fairmont project? What do you think your biggest competitor would pay for detailed information about your payment schedules with Inspector Morrison?"

His face went from red to white again. "You wouldn't."

"Try me." I stepped back, finally releasing him from my hold.

"You think you're protecting her," my father wheezed, his voice filled with disgust as his eyes flicked toward Abby. "But you're just delaying the inevitable. I will find a way to—"

"No." I cut him off, my voice like steel. "You won't. Because if you so much as speak her name again, if you contact her employer, if you even think about interfering in her life, I will bury you. I have enough evidence to bring criminal charges for fraud and bribery. Is your hatred of my choices really worth spending your golden years in prison?"

The fight went out of him all at once. His shoulders sagged, and for the first time in my life, Dennis Kane looked old and defeated.

"This isn't over," he said, but the words lacked conviction.

"Yes, it is." I moved to the door and held it open. "Because the next time I see you, I'm calling the police. Get out."

He straightened his suit jacket with shaking hands, trying to salvage some dignity. His eyes found mine one last time, and I saw something there I'd never seen before—genuine fear of what I might do.

Without another word, he walked out of our apartment, and I hoped he was out of our lives once and for all.

I closed the door behind him and turned the deadbolt, then slumped back against it, the adrenaline finally starting to wear off. My hands were shaking, and I felt like I might throw up.

"Foster?" Abby's voice was soft, concerned.

I looked up to find her standing a few feet away, her brown eyes wide with worry and something that looked like awe.

"Are you okay?" I asked, my voice hoarse.

"I should be asking you that. You're shaking."

I was shaking. The rush of protective fury was fading, leaving me feeling raw and exposed. "I'm sorry," I said, running a hand through my hair. "I'm sorry he came here. I'm sorry he tried to touch you. I'm sorry about everything he's tried to do to you."

"Hey." She reached up and cupped my face in her hands, her touch grounding me. "You have nothing to apologize for. You protected us."

Mason appeared beside her, his face pale but his expression fierce. "Dude, that was awesome," he said quietly. "The way you just...damn."

I couldn't help but smile a little at his reaction, though my heart was still racing. "Language," I said weakly.

Abby smiled as her thumbs stroked across my cheekbones, her touch soothing the last of my rage. "Do you really have evidence of all that stuff he did?"

I nodded. "He didn't revoke my access to his computer files, and when my old boss told me about what he'd found out, I did a little digging and made copies of emails, receipts, and other discrepancies I found in his records. I hope I'll never have to use it, but I will if he ever comes near you or Mase again. I'll burn his whole world down before I let him hurt you."

She stood on her tiptoes and kissed me fiercely. "I love you," she whispered when she pulled back.

I pulled her into my arms, holding her tight against my chest. Over her shoulder, I caught Mason's eye. He gave me a solemn nod of approval, and something settled in my chest.

We were safe. Dennis Kane would never have power over any of us again.

We were finally free.

I balanced a stack of textbooks in one arm while trying to unlock the front door with my free hand. My backpack felt like it weighed a ton, and I was exhausted after a long day of classes and a tutoring session. But despite my fatigue, I couldn't stop smiling.

Things were finally looking up.

When I pushed the door open, I was greeted by the aroma of something delicious cooking. Foster had been experimenting in the kitchen lately, determined to expand his culinary skills beyond our go-to meals of chicken and broccoli, spaghetti, pizza, or mac and cheese.

"I'm home," I called out, dropping my backpack by the door and setting my textbooks on the entryway table.

"In the kitchen," Foster called back, his voice carrying a note of excitement that made me curious.

I rounded the corner to find him standing at the stove, stirring something in a pot while consulting a recipe on his phone. He was wearing an apron that Liam had given him as a joke—it had "Kiss the Cook" emblazoned across the front with big red lips underneath. The sight of him in that apron never failed to make me smile.

"Hey, Gorgeous," he said, looking up from his phone with that smile that still made my heart skip a beat. His blue eyes were bright with excitement.

"You look like you're about to burst," I said, walking over to peek into the pot. "What is it? And what smells so good?"

"Chicken Alfredo," he said proudly. "But that's not why I'm excited." He turned down the heat on the stove and wiped his hands on a dish towel before turning to face me fully. "I got a call from Coach today."

The way he said it—with such contained joy—made me hold my breath. "And?"

Foster's face broke into the widest grin I'd ever seen. "I got it, Abs. I got the scholarship. Full ride for my senior year."

"Oh my God!" I threw my arms around his neck, nearly knocking him back into the stove. "Foster, that's amazing!"

He lifted me off my feet, spinning me around in our small kitchen. "I can hardly believe it."

Coach Maxwell had learned that there were three leadership scholarships available each year for every grade level. Students had to be nominated by at least three faculty members to be considered. The competition was fierce, but Foster's coach had been confident.

"I'm so proud of you and not at all surprised," I said, reaching up to cup his face in my hands. "You deserve this so much."

The scholarship meant everything. After Foster's father had cut him off financially, we'd been worried about how he would pay for his final year of school. I'd offered to help with my savings from selling Gram's house, but Foster had been determined to find another way. He'd applied for every scholarship he could find and had already talked to one of the construction companies he'd worked for in the summers for a job once school was out.

"I wouldn't have gotten it without you," he said, his voice softening. "My grades have never been better, and that's all because of you too."

I shook my head. "No, that's all you. You did all the hard work."

He leaned down to kiss me gently. "Team effort, then."

"Team effort," I agreed.

The timer on Foster's phone went off, breaking our moment. He reluctantly pulled away to check on the pasta.

"Where's Mason?" I asked, noticing the unusual quiet in the apartment.

"Drew and Liam reserved the rink. They're determined to convince him that hockey is the superior sport. They said they want to take him out for dinner after, so it's just us tonight." Foster drained the pasta in the sink, steam rising around him. "I thought maybe we could eat and then use that extra time for some private celebrating."

"Mm, I think I could be persuaded," I said, moving to the cupboard to grab plates.

Since we'd implemented our housing swap plan a couple of months ago, Mason had thrived. The hockey guys had taken him under their wing, and Drew especially had become something of a mentor to him. My brother was talking more, smiling more, and his grades had improved significantly.

As for Foster and me, living together had only strengthened our relationship. Seeing him every morning when I woke up and every night before I fell asleep was something I never got tired of.

We hadn't heard a peep from his dad since Foster had threatened to expose him, and we were grateful. Family wasn't about blood anyway. It was about who showed up— and stayed. Between the hockey team, Sam, Mason, and me, we'd built our own little family. Even Coach Maxwell and his wife, Maggie, had taken Foster under their wing, inviting us over for dinner like he was one of their own.

"Have you decided about grad school?" he asked.

I nodded, excitement bubbling up inside me. My advisor, Professor Sinclair, had pushed me again on considering where to apply since I'd need to start that process in the fall. "I'm applying to the master's program here at CFU. The engineering department has that new green building initiative, and Professor Sinclair thinks I'd be perfect for it." I took a bite of pasta and closed my eyes in bliss. "This is delicious."

"Thanks," he said, looking pleased. "So you want to stay here then?"

"That's the plan. The program is two years, and then..." I trailed off, suddenly unsure how to finish that sentence. Foster and I hadn't explicitly talked about our long-term future yet.

"And then?" he prompted, his blue eyes intent on mine.

I took a deep breath. "And then I'd like to work for one of the engineering firms here. Maybe even Holt and Associates. Montana is home. I don't really want to leave."

"I get it. I don't want to follow my dad's footsteps, but I've been thinking more about using my business degree for something else, maybe starting my own business or using that knowledge toward another career."

"I think that's a great idea."

We finished our dinner talking about lighter things—the upcoming party at the hockey house, Sam's latest dating disaster, and Mason's improved grades. It felt so normal, and at the same time felt like so much more than I'd ever thought I'd have—especially at twenty-one.

As I took our empty plates to the sink, Foster came up behind me, wrapping his arms around my waist and pressing a kiss to the side of my neck.

"Leave those," he murmured against my skin. "I'll do them later."

I turned in his arms, looping my hands behind his neck. "Is that so?"

His eyes darkened as he looked down at me. "Mm-hmm. I think we should move on to celebrating."

"And how exactly did you want to celebrate?" I asked, playing innocent despite the heat building between us.

Foster's answering smile was wicked as he lifted me up and set me on the edge of the table.

"Well," he said, stepping between my legs and tilting my chin up to meet his gaze, "I was thinking I could eat dessert."

His kiss was sweet and hot and full of promise. As I wrapped my legs around his waist and pulled him closer, I knew with absolute certainty that this was exactly where I was meant to be.

I couldn't wait to see what the future had in store for us.

The student center ballroom had been transformed with string lights, a makeshift stage, and rows of folding chairs filled with excited students—mostly female. A buzz of anticipation hung in the air as I squeezed into a seat near the front row, clutching a small purse filled with a wad of cash I'd brought to support Foster.

"I can't believe the guys agreed to do this," I muttered to Sam, who sat beside me practically vibrating with excitement.

"Are you kidding? This is going to be epic," she replied, scanning the crowd. "Every sorority on campus is here. The hockey guys are going to make a fortune."

I fidgeted nervously with the auction paddle I'd been given at the door.

"You have enough money, right?" Sam asked, eyeing my small purse.

I nodded. "I brought two hundred dollars. That should be enough, don't you think?"

Foster and I had been dating for nearly seven months now, and while we'd agreed I should bid on him—because as captain he had to participate, but didn't want to go on a date with anyone else—neither of us expected the bidding to go too high. After all, everyone knew we were together.

Sam's expression turned doubtful. "Mmm, maybe."

My stomach dropped. "Everyone knows we're a couple. Would another girl really bid on him?"

"Hopefully not, but some girls like chasing what they can't have," Sam said with an eye roll.

Before I could respond, the lights dimmed and music started pumping through the speakers. Ava Dumontier, Drew's twin sister, walked out on stage with a beaming smile. She seemed completely in her element.

"Welcome, everyone, to the first annual Clark Fork University Hockey Bachelor Auction," she announced, her voice booming through the microphone. "I'm Ava Dumontier, your emcee for the evening. All proceeds tonight go directly to supporting our hockey team's travel and equipment costs. Remember, you're bidding on a date with these fine gentlemen, nothing more. And now, for the moment you've all been waiting for. Let the bachelor bidding begin!

"Let's get this show on the road with bachelor number one—the man, the myth, the legend—Liam 'the Hot Irishman' Farrell!"

Liam strutted onto the stage to the tune of "I'm Too Sexy," wearing jeans and a tight black T-shirt that showcased his athletic build. He grinned and flexed dramatically, causing several girls in the front row to squeal.

Ava read from a card. "Liam is a sophomore defenseman from Montana who enjoys long walks to the refrigerator and has been known to quote poetry when drunk. Ladies, the starting bid is twenty dollars. Who wants to try their luck with the Hot Irishman?"

The bidding for Liam started immediately, with

paddles shooting up across the room. It quickly escalated, finally ending at $175 when a pretty blonde in the back won him. Liam winked at her as he left the stage.

Several more hockey players were auctioned off, each introduction more ridiculous than the last. The crowd was getting rowdier, and the bids were climbing higher than I'd anticipated. My palms began to sweat as I realized my $200 might not be enough after all.

"Next up," Ava announced, "we have the strong, silent type—Harrison 'Gordy' Gordon!"

Gordy walked out looking slightly uncomfortable but managed a small smile. Unlike some of the others, he'd kept it simple with jeans and a dark button-down shirt that brought out his gray eyes.

"Gordy is our star goalie who stops pucks with the same efficiency that he stops conversations with his dry wit. Starting bid is twenty dollars!"

The bidding for Gordy was competitive but not outrageous, ending at $120. He looked relieved when it was over, giving a polite nod to the girl who'd won him.

"And now," Ava said, building suspense, "our team captain, the man with the moves both on and off the ice— Foster 'Candy Kane' Kane!"

My heart jumped into my throat as Foster walked onto the stage. He was wearing dark jeans and a blue Henley that made his blue eyes pop. His hair was slightly tousled, and he had that easy smile that had first caught my attention years ago. He looked confident but not cocky, giving a small wave to the audience.

"Foster is a junior business major who can skate backward faster than most people can run forward. When he's not leading our team to victory, he enjoys hiking, reading, and making his girlfriend blush—which, as you can see, he's doing right now."

The spotlight suddenly found me in the crowd, and I felt my face flame as everyone turned to look. Foster grinned and winked at me, which only made me blush harder.

"Starting bid is twenty dollars, though I think we all know where this one's going to end up," Ava added with a knowing smile.

I raised my paddle immediately. "Twenty!"

"Twenty dollars from the girlfriend," Ava confirmed. "Do I hear twenty-five?"

"Fifty dollars!" called a voice from the back.

I turned to see Brittany Armstrong, looking perfectly polished in designer clothes, her paddle held high.

Sam nudged me. "Ugh, that girl annoys me."

"Seventy-five," I countered, trying to keep my voice steady.

"One hundred," Brittany shot back without hesitation.

My stomach churned. This was escalating faster than I'd expected. I raised my paddle again, hoping to end this. "One fifty."

"Two hundred," Brittany said, smirking in my direction.

I swallowed hard. That was all the money I'd brought. I looked up at Foster, who was watching the exchange with a furrowed brow.

"Two fifty," said a deep voice beside me. I turned to see Gordy sliding into the seat on my other side, pressing cash into my hand.

"What are you—"

"Just bid," he said quietly.

I raised my paddle. "Two hundred and fifty."

"Three hundred," Brittany called, looking less confident.

"Three fifty," came another voice as Liam appeared, stuffing more bills into my hand.

My eyes widened as I realized what was happening. The hockey guys were pooling their money to help me win. My smile grew as I watched Brittany's wither.

"Three sixty," Brittany countered, her voice taking on a whiny edge.

Drew materialized behind me, leaning down to whisper, "We got you," as he added more cash to my growing pile.

"Three seventy-five," I called, my voice stronger now.

"Four hundred," Brittany said, her jaw tight.

This girl could not take a hint.

Sam pulled out her wallet. "Those hockey boys saved my drunk ass more than once. Here," she said, adding her own money to my stack. "Make it five hundred."

I looked at my friends in disbelief before turning back to raise my paddle. "Five hundred dollars."

A collective "ooh" went through the crowd. Foster was trying to suppress a grin on stage with his hand rubbing over his mouth, but his eyes gave him away.

Brittany hesitated, then raised her paddle, but before she could say a word, Sam stood up and turned to face her, fixing her with the most intimidating glare I'd ever seen Sam give anyone.

The entire room went quiet as they stared each other down.

After what felt like an eternity, Brittany slowly lowered her paddle, her cheeks flushed with embarrassment.

"Damn, she's fierce," Gordy whispered with a hint of admiration in his voice.

"Going once...going twice...sold to Abby Walker for five hundred dollars!" Ava announced triumphantly.

The crowd erupted in applause as Foster jumped off the stage and made his way to me. He slid his hand through my hair and pulled my mouth to his, kissing me fiercely so there wasn't a single doubt who he belonged to.

"That's my girl," he murmured when he finally broke the kiss.

"I had help," I admitted, gesturing to the hockey guys and Sam.

Foster looked around at his teammates and nodded in appreciation. "I owe you guys."

"You'd do the same for us," Gordy said simply.

I laughed, still overwhelmed by what had just happened. It wasn't just about winning the auction—it was about the way everyone had rallied around me. For someone who had spent most of college feeling invisible, it meant more than they could know.

Foster kept his arm around me as we settled back to watch the rest of the auction. Drew was up next, and Ava took particular delight in introducing her twin brother who jumped up onto the stage from where he'd been sitting near me.

"Next up, we have my brother, Drew 'Monty' Dumontier. Despite being related to me, he's actually not terrible at hockey. He enjoys long walks on the beach and getting caught with his pants down in inappropriate places—wish I were kidding. Starting bid is twenty dollars—though personally, I wouldn't pay more than ten."

Drew flipped her off discreetly as he walked on stage in jeans and a tight-fitting white T-shirt. He had the same easy confidence as Foster but with an added edge of mischief in his smile.

And in a move that surprised absolutely no one, he wasn't on the stage for thirty seconds before he pulled his shirt off and showed off his six-pack abs.

The bidding began enthusiastically after that, with several girls competing. When it reached $200, most dropped out, leaving just two bidders—a blonde sorority girl I vaguely recognized and a pretty redhead.

"Oh, fuck, is that Harper Tinsley?" Foster whispered beside me.

I knew a little about the feud between Drew and Harper from what Foster had told me. Something about their families having been enemies for generations, and Drew's failed attempt to prank her by plastic-wrapping her car a few months back. I hadn't met Harper myself, but I'd seen her around campus.

"Two twenty," Harper called, her voice clear and confident.

"Two forty," the blonde countered.

"Three hundred," Harper said without hesitation.

The blonde hesitated, then shook her head and lowered her paddle.

"Sold to Harper Tinsley for three hundred dollars!" Ava announced, looking as surprised as everyone else.

Drew's expression was priceless—a mixture of shock, suspicion, and something that looked a bit like eagerness. He stepped off the stage and approached Harper, who was sitting with a small group of music students just two rows behind us.

Drew leaned down to speak to Harper, his usual cocky demeanor nowhere to be found. He was smiling at her, and there didn't seem to be any snark or malice in it like I expected for two people who were supposed to be rivals.

"I'm surprised you bid on me," he said to Harper.

"Where do you want to go for our date? Dinner? Movie? I know a great spot by the river."

Harper's laugh rang out, clear and musical. "Oh, Dumontier, I don't want to date you. I wouldn't date you if you were the last man alive."

Drew's smile faltered. "Then why—"

"I need an assistant for my recital next weekend," she explained, her eyes glinting with mischief. "Someone to fetch coffee, carry instruments, hold cue cards, and act as my personal hype man. You'll be perfect."

Drew's face fell. "You're shitting me."

"I even had a special shirt made," Harper continued, pulling a folded T-shirt from her bag and holding it up. It was black with "#TinsleyHypeCrew" printed across the chest in bold white letters.

The group around us erupted in laughter as Drew stared at the shirt in horror. Even Foster couldn't contain his amusement.

"That's cold," Liam commented, shaking his head.

"That's brilliant," Sam corrected.

I couldn't help but agree. There was something admirable about Harper's creativity—and the way she'd managed to turn the tables on Drew so effectively.

Foster laced his fingers through mine, and I let myself lean into him, laughter still bubbling in my chest. Around us, the ballroom was alive with music, voices, and joy. I was surrounded by people who'd become family, and was happier than I ever could've imagined, despite all the loss I'd experienced.

I watched Drew sit back down, still holding the T-shirt like it was radioactive. Across the aisle, Harper smiled to herself and casually tucked her curly hair behind one ear, completely unbothered.

I wasn't sure if Drew looked more confused or intrigued.

Probably both.

Something told me that Drew and Harper's story was just beginning.

ABBY

One Year Later

Soft, steady flakes drifted past the wide picture window like someone had shaken a snow globe over the mountains. Everything was hushed and blanketed in white—except the inside of the little rental cabin we'd found tucked away in the woods outside Whitefish.

It was the perfect weekend getaway—quiet and secluded. A few days off the grid, just the two of us and no distractions. No classes, no hockey games, no tutoring shifts, no stress. Just crackling firelight, the scent of pine and woodsmoke, and the constant hum of desire that had been building between us all day.

I'd watched him earlier, out on the back deck with his flannel sleeves rolled up, his breath fogging in the cold air as he chopped extra firewood with that annoyingly effortless strength of his. And now he was stretched out on the couch in nothing but a pair of gray sweats, his chest bare and his golden skin lit by the flicker of the fire.

He looked like sin.

And I was done pretending I wasn't starving for him.

I came out of the bedroom wearing nothing but a slinky silk robe and a matching black lace set underneath, and his eyes darkened instantly when he caught sight of me.

"Fuck, Baby," he muttered, sitting up straighter.

I let the light from the fire dance across my skin while he looked his fill. Foster always made me feel like the most desirable woman in the room.

"I thought you were cold," he said, voice rough.

"I was," I said, untying the robe and letting it slide down my shoulders. "Now I'm burning hot."

He exhaled like I'd punched the air from his lungs. "Abby..."

I walked toward him taking slow and deliberate steps, and feeling like a goddess the closer I got to him. My body thrummed with awareness. Every step closer turned the heat between us into something molten.

"You've been teasing me all day," I said softly, straddling his lap. "Now it's my turn."

His hands came to my hips on instinct, but I pressed one finger to his lips before he could speak and say something dirty like he usually did. "Uh-uh. You don't get to take control. Not tonight."

His eyes flared, and he leaned back, a smug little smile tugging at the corner of his mouth. "You want to take charge?"

"I *am* taking charge."

I was already soaked.

The lace pressed against my center was practically useless, especially when I felt the way his cock strained beneath his sweats and rubbed me in just the right spot. I rocked against him, letting the friction build.

His breath hitched. "Fuck, Baby—"

"Shh." I brushed my lips against his neck. "Just let me make you feel good."

He groaned as I pushed at the waistband of his sweats, and he lifted his hips so I could get them over his butt and pull them down his legs.

While I was standing again, I hooked my fingers into the sides of my panties and shimmied them off. My body already ached for him, and tonight I didn't want anything between us.

"You should grab the condoms from my bag," he said, his voice hoarse with desire.

I shook my head and straddled him again, my bare, wet pussy against his smooth, hard cock. He instantly groaned at the contact, his gaze going hazy.

"I got my birth control shot last week."

His eyes widened. "You did?"

I nodded. "I want to feel you," I said against his lips. "Just you. No barriers."

He stared at me like I'd just offered him every fantasy he'd ever had. His hands trembled as they slid back to my hips.

"You sure?"

"Completely."

He reached up, cupping my face in his hands. "I don't know how I got so lucky," he said, keeping his voice low before he claimed my lips in a kiss that had my toes curling.

I hummed in the back of my throat, not breaking our kiss as I reached between us and guided him to my entrance, before slowly lowering myself down, savoring every single inch of him.

Nothing had ever felt like this.

Thick and hot and *bare*, every glide ignited a fresh spark

of lust inside me. I gasped as he thrust up, filling me and stretching me in a way only he could. There was nothing else but him and me and the feeling of pure, exquisite bliss.

"Holy *shit*," Foster groaned, his head falling back against the couch. "You feel unreal."

I started to move a little faster, rolling my hips as I slid up and down his shaft. His hands slid up my thighs, gripping me tight but letting me set the pace.

"Oh, *God*," I gasped, as he hit a spot inside me that made my core clench.

His fingers dug into my hips, but he didn't move. "God-damn, you feel so good like this."

I trembled as the pleasure increased, my orgasm growing closer and closer.

"Ride me, Baby," he growled. "Show me how you like it."

I did.

I found a rhythm—grinding down, then rising just enough to feel the head of him drag along my inner walls before slamming back down. All the while, Foster's hands roamed my body—one sliding up my back, the other cupping my breast, fingers brushing the edge of lace. He looked at me like I was something holy. Like he was worshipping me with every breath.

I clenched around him, watching his jaw lock tight as his abs flexed beneath my palms. His control was fraying. I could feel it in the way his hips bucked up to meet mine, the way his moans got sharper, needier. But I knew he'd never come before me. He'd always made sure I was well taken care of before he found his release.

But even though I could tell he was fighting his release, he let me keep going at my own pace. Let me chase my plea-sure. I moved faster, angled just right to hit the spot that made me see stars, and I felt it building—the coil of pleasure winding tighter and tighter—until he moved his hand between us and started rubbing gentle circles on my clit. That was all it took to tip me over the edge.

"Foster," I cried, my voice breaking as the orgasm slammed into me like a wave. I shattered around him, my body convulsing, clenching, burning with the intense force of my release.

As I shook and trembled around him, he let go with a harsh groan, thrusting up into me and then shuddering as he came deep inside me.

I collapsed against his chest, panting while my heart hammered like I'd just run a mile. He held me there, one hand stroking up and down my spine while the other rested on my thigh.

"I don't know if we can ever use condoms again because fuck, that felt amazing."

I smiled against his neck. "I agree."

We lay there for a while, me draped over him, our naked bodies kept warm from the heat emitted from the fire. The low crackling of the logs served as a soothing soundtrack while we snuggled together. Eventually, I lifted my head just enough to look at him. His hair was damp at the temples, his skin flushed, his eyes half-lidded with satisfaction.

"You okay?" I asked softly, brushing a thumb across his cheekbone.

He huffed out a laugh. "Baby, anytime you wanna fuck me like that, I'll be okay."

I couldn't help but smile. I was also continually grateful for a partner who not only let me try new things but encouraged it, especially when it came to our sex life. "I'll remember that."

His fingers traced lazy patterns on my back. "I don't think I've ever come that hard in my life. You know that, right?"

I arched a brow. "Are you saying I'm the best sex you've ever had, Kane?"

He grinned, slow and crooked. "Abby Walker, I can say without a shadow of a doubt that you are far and away the best *everything* I've ever had."

I kissed him—soft and slow, the kind of kiss that warmed me from the inside out.

And *I* could say, without a shadow of a doubt, that Foster was my happily ever after.

AFTERWORD

Two years ago, my friend said, "Cadence! You have to write a hockey book!"

I was deep in my football series and had no room in my brain for more characters, but the curse of ADHD (or blessing?) is that my brain loves to spiral with ideas. But her timing was impeccable because I'd had the niggling of an idea only a few days before she mentioned it. And once that seed was planted, there was no way to stop its growth. The characters came to me fairly quickly, followed by the story. But I was nervous about the sport. I grew up around sports, but hockey was completely unknown to me. I spent the last few years watching college games on TV and A LOT of YouTube channels to better understand the game. I'm still terrified I didn't do it justice, but I absolutely fell head over heels for these characters and I hope you did too. I can't wait for you to get to know the rest.

I also need to thank my editors, Ann Suhs and Ann Riza at Happily Editing Anns. They always make my books shine so much better than I ever could on my own.

To my incredible cover designers, Lindsey at Lily Bear

Design and Kate Farlow at Y'all That Graphic. Kate designed another smokin' man chest cover and Lindsey took a leap of faith on my illustrated idea, but both covers turned out absolutely gorgeous!

To my beta readers, Alyse and Kelly for your incredibly helpful feedback. The first version of this book was all wrong and I wasn't trusting myself enough until I got your feedback and it confirmed everything I'd feared. So thank you for always being honest with me.

To my husband, J, who is the best hype man a girl could ever ask for. I couldn't do this crazy dream job if it wasn't for all your love and support. Thank you for loving me and lifting me up when I'm second guessing myself.

To my miracles babies (who aren't such babies anymore), I love you so much and hope that I'm teaching you that no dream is impossible to chase no matter how wild it seems.

And to my readers for supporting my books and loving my characters. I'm beyond words with gratitude for you. Seriously, thank you!!!

ALSO BY CADENCE KEYS

LA Wolves Football Series

In the Grasp

Across the Middle

Down by Contact

Taking the Handoff

Scorched Turf (author website exclusive novella)

Defending the Backfield

After the Snap

Closing the Distance

Protecting the Boundary

Rapturous Intent Rockstar Series

Noble Intent

Forbidden Intent

Devoted Intent

Promised Intent

Breaking the Rules Series

Only a Kiss

Just for Tonight

About Last Night

CFU Hockey

Campus Crush

Campus Rival

Standalones

One Weekend in Montana

ABOUT THE AUTHOR

Cadence Keys is a bestselling sports romance author. When she's not coming up with plots for her books, she's chasing her rambunctious kids around or cuddling with her husband. She loves writing heartfelt stories with relatable characters and a guaranteed happily ever after.

Learn more about her and her books on her website: www.cadencekeys.com

facebook.com/cadencekeysauthor

x.com/cadencewrites

instagram.com/cadencekeysauthor

bookbub.com/profile/cadence-keys

goodreads.com/cadencekeysauthor

patreon.com/CadenceKeys